GRIT AND GRACE

GRIT AND GRACE

by

S. Marie

Order this book online at www.trafford.com
or email orders@trafford.com

Most Trafford titles are also available at major online book retailers.

Printed in the United States of America.

ISBN: 978-1-4669-0332-6 (sc)
ISBN: 978-1-4669-0331-9 (hc)
ISBN: 978-1-4669-0330-2 (e)

Library of Congress Control Number: 2011960299

Trafford rev. 11/09/2011

www.trafford.com

North America & international
toll-free: 1 888 232 4444 (USA & Canada)
phone: 250 383 6864 • fax: 812 355 4082

Chapter One

"I don't remember anything like this being in my horoscope today." Lucy thought wryly as she ran across the arid terrain.

Thirty yards more and she'd be protected by the row of rocks. Adrenalin propelled her as she leapt to safety behind the nearest boulder.

"Oomph!" expelled from her lungs at hitting the hard ground.

Trying to catch her breath, she inhaled sandy dirt. It tasted awful. Unfortunately, she had no spit to spit out the grit.

Off to the side she thought she heard "Lucy stay down!"

Lucy had long since learned to listen to the angels around her. She flattened herself as close to the ground as possible. Suddenly a body slid in next to her kicking up a thick cloud of brownish yellow dust.

"Are you hurt?" A hushed male voice asked.

She managed a "no".

The male voice asked another question. "How many are there?"

"Three." She answered, then corrected herself. "Two now."

"Are Wedo and Dahms okay?" He continued gathering data from her.

"Yes, but Dahms was starting to look pale." She was concerned he might be having a heart attack.

"Rhino one this is Peacock one. One target is down. I have the priority package. She says there are two inside with the parcels." His voice sounded familiar as she listened to him report.

A few moments passed till he spoke again. "Roger that Rhino one."

Silence ensued for several minutes. Lucy shifted to peek around the rock they were behind. The military man moved with her keeping her body shielded. In this position, she could see the majority of the open area where the mobile unit had stopped. A group of men in desert camouflage descended as one into its rear shadow.

"Roger that Rhino one. I see you moving into place." He spoke in a low tone.

Lucy saw one of the soldiers stealthily stepping along the side of the vehicle. He stopped to the side of the door. A few hand signals were made to the rest of his team. They swung around to flanking positions to their leader. Lucy feared they were going to storm inside the vehicle. Would Wedo and Dahms duck out of the way or be used as human shields by their captors?

"Lucy breathe!" the man pressing into her commanded.

She'd been unknowingly holding her breath. The director must have yelled action. One of the two remaining captors opened the door to call in Arabic. The soldiers were statues. As soon as the captor stepped outside to see what had happened to Lucy and her guard, the assault ensued. Yelling and shots could be heard. Then all went quiet.

"Roger Rhino one I read you—all clear." The soldier stood.

Lucy saw the American soldiers step out of the unit with Jack and Willie.

"Ma'am?" His hand reached down to help her stand.

Finally facing her protector Lucy gasped "Jed!"

Jed immediately spoke into his headset. "This is Peacock one. How far out is the chopper?"

Lucy took hold of his offered hand while he waited for a response. "Roger that. Have the doctor on stand-by. Peacock one out."

She stood, or at least tried to. The desert floor pitched unexpectedly causing her to fall against the well muscled marine.

"Take your time. You probably have a concussion." Jed said compassionately.

After righting her, they walked from behind their natural shield. They met the group mid way, but Lucy didn't stop. She continued towards the mobile unit.

One of the soldiers blocked her path. "Ma'am it's safer here."

Lucy looked around to identify the commander.

"Rhino one?" She approached the man who had led the charge.

"Yes ma'am, I'm Lieutenant Brawn." Rhino one responded.

"I need to see how much damage has been done inside the unit." She told him the purpose.

The lieutenant declined her request. "No ma'am."

"Excuse me lieutenant?" Lucy asserted her authority. "I have to assess the damage."

"No ma'am." Lieutenant Brawn was not going to willingly yield to her.

Willie Wedo interjected. "Lieutenant, I'm afraid she is correct. The unit must be assessed and the computer system shut down."

The lieutenant spoke to Willie. "Sir, then you can do that, but Seeir is not going inside with that dead body."

Lucy held her venom tongue.

Willie rubbed his face as he spoke. "Well lieutenant there's a problem with that. I am one of the mechanical engineers on this project and don't know how to shut down this computer system securely."

"One moment please." The lieutenant said to step away from them.

He put his hand to the mouth piece of the headset. Lucy could only guess he called his commanding officer to find out what to do.

Lieutenant Brawn waved her and Willie over. "Ma'am I apologize. I was not informed of your rank. Sergeant Major Warloc escort Seeir to the Armadillo."

Her title as staff or project expert had never been put that way before. And she'd spent plenty of time with the military over her twenty year career. But then again this was the first time she'd ended up in combat.

Sergeant Major Jed Warloc escorted her to the vehicle.

On the short walk, she asked him about what had transpired. "What happened on the radio for Brawn to cave?"

A smirk crossed the marine's handsomely weathered face. "Well he was told your equivalent civilian ranking would be somewhere around a lieutenant colonel. And you were not to be, excuse the language, fucked with."

She shook her head in amazement.

He stopped momentarily at the door into the unit. "Are you okay with this?"

She answered him with a glib remark. "Not like the highest ranking officer here can chicken out now."

The burst of gun fire rat-a-tat-tatting against the metal sides of the mobile unit took them by surprise. Sergeant Major Warloc grabbed her by the arm to drag her to the rear of the vehicle. The soldiers in the opening returned fire as they hurried to the row of rocks. Willie and Jack were both shielded by the other soldiers.

"Rhino one, I can't see anything!" The sergeant major yelled into the headset.

It felt like an eternity crouched behind the mobile unit. Scanning the area behind them, Lucy thought she saw something in the sky. She tugged on the marine's jacket then pointed.

He spoke into the headset. "Rhino one, whirlybird sighted five clicks out."

The gun fire fray continued. Lucy started getting nervous. A shadow caught her attention from the right side of the vehicle. Jed must have seen it too. He quickly and quietly switched spots with her.

He whispered one word into her ear: "Stay."

Then he sprang around the corner to open fire with his rifle. After a minute of this, he swung back next to her to change clips.

"You ready?" He asked.

Before she could think about what he meant, he grabbed her. "Run!"

The sergeant major sent her in the direction of where the soldiers had entered earlier. As they bolted across the stretch of vulnerability, Jed fired non-stop. There was a steep four foot high wall of dirt in front of them. At 5'3" in comparison to the marine's 5' 11", Lucy didn't know how she was going to scale it. Reaching the wall, Lucy didn't have time to think anymore about it. Sergeant Major Warloc quite literally threw her over the top. She was shocked she didn't stay aloft very long. The drop on the other side was barely two feet. The marine soon landed next to her.

"You still with me?" he checked.

She found her breath to say "yes".

The helicopter flew directly over them.

Evidently the lieutenant radioed the sergeant major. "We see it Rhino one, but we can't make it. Load up the parcels. We'll try for the original landing spot. Over."

The helicopter sent a few small missiles in the direction of the enemy. This allowed time to safely land and load. Then it took off again. Jed and Lucy began the trek to their pick up point. Even though they suspected the enemy assumed they had left too, the marine remained on alert.

They hadn't gotten very far when Lucy's brain began fully functioning again. "Can you get your commander on the radio?"

"Yes, but why?" He asked skeptically.

"I have to talk to him before those people get any part of the Armadillo." The seriousness of what she had realized undeniable in her tone.

Jed recognized the urgency. "Yes ma'am."

"This is Peacock one, Priority package urgently requests the commander." The marine said across the radio.

While he waited he took off his helmet revealing his silver trimmed military cut. "Yes sir, hold for Priority package."

He tugged off the headset to put it in place on Lucy. "Go ahead talk."

"This is Lucy Seeir, with whom am I speaking?" She asked sternly.

"Ma'am, this is Commander Spiers on the Arlington. Do we have an issue?" Commander Spiers had been briefed on the exercise when Lucy and her co-workers had arrived.

"Commander Spiers, I am ordering you to destroy the Armadillo for the sake of national security." Lucy knew she had no choice and neither did the commander.

"Ma'am is it really that serious?" He asked concerned.

"Yes commander, there can't be anything more than a scorch mark left of it." Lucy didn't sugar coat the true seriousness of her request.

"I understand completely ma'am. I need to talk to the sergeant major." The commander knew what had to be done.

As they were switching the headset, Jed abruptly threw her to the ground and started shooting above her head. Shifting to see what was going on, she saw a figure coming in from the opposite direction. Using pure instinct—Lucy pulled the marine's pistol from its holster, wrapped her arms around him to put her hands together, aimed and fired till the figure fell. When she stopped firing, Jed didn't move.

For a moment, she thought he'd been shot, but then he whispered, "Any others?"

"I don't think so." She answered feeling her hands start to shake.

The marine cautiously rolled off of her to peer around. Appearing safe, he helped her sit. The shakes were beginning to move along her arms into her body. An odd intermittent buzzing noise came from nearby. Jed stood to fetch the head set which had gone flying.

Putting it on, his eyes squinted in pain at the loudness of the commander's yelling. "This is Peacock one. We are alright. I repeat. We are alright."

Sergeant Major Warloc listened to the commander. "Yes sir. An ambush, but they've been eliminated. Priority package is safe. Will radio again when we are out of range. Peacock one out."

"How far is out of range?" Lucy asked trying to refocus to stop the shakes.

"We need to be one mile away when the missile hits the Armadillo." The marine stood her up to start walking that mile.

She remained quiet. Her brain was doing the math involved to identify the type of missile that would be used. This completely alleviated the adrenalin overload from the attack.

Only a few minutes later, they found a jeep. It probably belonged to the two that had ambushed them. Sergeant Major Warloc checked it over quickly for any incendiary devices before climbing into the driver's seat. As soon as he had the engine running, he motioned for Lucy to take the passenger seat.

Getting a mile away from the Armadillo didn't take long.

The sergeant major radioed in. "Peacock one to Arlington, over."

The ship responded.

"Yes sir. We acquired a jeep. We should be at the pick-up site in ten minutes, over." He kept it short.

The commander spoke longer than she anticipated.

"Yes sir. We'll look for Rhino one at the new rendezvous point. Peacock one out." The marine acknowledged his orders without question.

"I gather we have a newer new plan?" She asked.

"Yes ma'am" was the only thing the marine shared.

"How long till we get to the next rendezvous point?" She tried a different tactic.

"Approximately six hours ma'am." Again he didn't elaborate.

Her patience had run out. "Okay marine, we are stuck with each other for the next six hours. I've been kidnapped, pistol whipped, tackled, thrown and shot at. I have the Sahara fucking desert in my mouth, hair, boots and bra. I need you to tell me with great detail where the hell we are going and how you plan on reaching that objective. And don't ma'am me one more fucking time until we are in the presence of other military personnel."

As if to emphasize her point, the explosion destroying the Armadillo echoed and quaked across the barren landscape.

When the noise dissipated, Sergeant Major Warloc merely asked one question. "Is that an order ma'am?"

"Yes!" She exclaimed in exasperation.

The sergeant major obeyed her order. For the next five minutes, he explained. They were heading to a small town called Hacki. The lieutenant would have a helicopter waiting. The helicopter would take them to the USS Arlington for medical treatment and debriefing.

When he finished talking, she thanked him graciously. Knowing things were under control, she went silent. An hour into the drive, she began feeling nauseated. It was probably due to the suffocating heat and extreme thirst. A town appeared on the horizon within the next half hour. She hoped they could stop to find water to keep the rising nausea down.

The marine spoke. "We'll be stopping in this town for fuel and water."

"Thank you." She hiccupped.

Jed looked in her direction. "Lucy, are you alright?"

No sooner had he asked than she demanded "stop!"

He hit the breaks hard enough to cause the vehicle to slide a good distance. She didn't wait for the jeep to come to a complete stop before she bolted out. A few steps she fell to her knees to vomit. The last time she'd eaten had been breakfast ten hours ago. The vomiting turned into painfully exhausting dry heaves. When those stopped, she had no energy to move.

He knelt next to her. "Lucy please, it's only a few hundred yards into town. Once there, I'll take a good look at your head injury and find something to help you feel better."

She complied. With his strong arms helping her, she made it into the jeep. When they drove into town, the sergeant major drove directly to what looked like a market of sorts. By the time he parked, she had regained her composure somewhat. They walked into the array of tents filled with people. Oddly enough, no one seemed to take special notice of the marine in combat gear and the woman next to him with a bloody face.

Not far in, Jed directed her to a doorway. There was a sign down one side of it, but it wasn't in any language Lucy could read.

As they entered, the proprietor approached them. The marine conversed fluently in the man's native tongue.

After which, he leaned close to her to whisper in her ear. "There's a flaw in my plan that I hope you can help with."

Turning her head to look in his face, she cocked her head curiously as to what he hadn't considered.

Still whispering so the proprietor couldn't hear him, he admitted his error. "We don't carry money on a mission. How much do you have?"

As awful as she felt, this brought a smile to her bruised face. The mighty marine made a mistake. And the woman he'd been sent to rescue was going to trump him. Not feeling at all guilty about how horrendous her breath must smell; she put her mouth against his ear to answer. The skeptical look he gave her after hearing what she said, had her wanting to rub his face in the vomit stain on what had been a crisp white cotton shirt.

She nodded her head while giving him her "yeah buddy, I'm not stupid" look.

He shrugged, then moved away with the proprietor to close whatever deal he'd made. Jed motioned for her to join them. Embarrassed by her appearance she stared at her feet. It didn't take long for a woman swathed in dark heavy cloth from head to toe to appear. She led the way to a room on the second floor. Once there, the native woman left them alone.

Jed explained what they were doing. "We have the room for two hours. You can wash up while I find a few things we need in the market and get the jeep refueled. I need the money to take care of all this."

For lack of anywhere else to sit, Lucy sat on the bed. She tried reaching down to unlace her boot, but she became dizzy almost falling onto the floor. Strong arms caught her before she had another hard landing.

"Dizzy?" He asked as he sat her back on the bed.

Not wanting to share her atrocious breath, she nodded instead of talking.

Still kneeling in front of her, he asked "the money?"

She lifted her left boot. He loosened the laces to yank it off her foot. He put his hand inside the shoe in search of her stash. All he found was sand. She nudged his arm with her sock clad foot. First, he had to loosen the ties on the hem of her pants so he could remove the sock. As he scrunched the sock, a thick wad of folded bills popped out. He counted it to verify the amount.

"Why are you carrying around this much cash?" He inquired.

"We had made arrangements to go for lunch and shopping, but we wouldn't be stopping at the hotel before going." She answered.

"And the sock?" He asked with curiosity.

"It would've been too easy to pickpocket pretty much anywhere else." She explained her hiding spot.

He started to stand, but she put her hand on his shoulder to stop him. "Would you please take the other one off too?"

While he obeyed her request, there was a light knock on the door. Not waiting for a response, the woman and a young boy entered. The woman carried a tray of food and tea. The boy had towels and a box with a red plus on it. While the woman placed the tray on the table by the bed, the boy took his items into the bathroom. Jed thanked them, or that's what Lucy deduced, as they left the room. He went into the bathroom.

From there he called. "Lucy, come in here so I can look at your face."

"Gee, a girl doesn't get that kind of request very often." She said sarcastically.

He had her stand as close to the light as possible. With capable and astonishingly gentle hands, the tough marine cleaned the injuries on her face, then butterfly bandaged what he could.

She didn't want to look in the mirror without being prepared. "Is it bad?"

One corner of his mouth turned upwards slightly. "You need stitches on the cuts around your eye. There's also a lot of swelling and bruising."

"No big deal." She shrugged.

He continued examining her face. "Lucy, did they do anything else to you?"

It took a minute to understand what he meant. "No."

His always seriously stern face softened. "Then why were you smacked around and the men left without a scratch?"

The events flashed in her brain. "When they attacked us, they killed Corporal Pico. I took his gun to shoot one of their men who I knew was going to shoot Corporal Barnes."

"You did that?" The marine asked with awe.

"I wasn't going to stand there doing nothing." She remarked. "Is Corporal Barnes alive?"

"He took a round in the shoulder, but he should be okay." He held eye contact with her so she knew he was telling the truth. "But you killed one of the others?"

"Yes, one of them tried to take the gun from me." She said flatly. "Total kills—two."

"Are you okay with that?" It sounded like a strange question from a man who chose a profession where he had to kill people.

"Lives were at stake; it had to be done." She felt no emotion in regards to it.

His face hardened to its normal state. "Yes. It did."

He grabbed a piece of fruit from the tray. "You wash up and eat. I shouldn't be long."

When he left, Lucy felt relieved. Where military men, particularly marines, were concerned, it was always about who's on top. As she stripped her clothing off, she shook out as much sand as possible. For the moment, she didn't want to think about having to dress in them still dirty and smelly. She went into the bathroom to wash. The clothing remained heaped in a pile on the floor. Music could be heard from the market below through the window she opened. It felt good to rinse away the grit and blood. She used one of the gauze pads wrapped around her finger to brush her teeth. Ten minutes later, she stepped from the bathroom feeling refreshed. Wanting to stay clean as long as possible, she moved about wearing a towel. A few cups of tea and a scone helped settle her stomach. It also relaxed her. She stretched under the sheets on the bed to ease her sore body.

Chapter Two

"Lucy . . ." She dreamt someone was calling her name. Rolling to get away from the sound, she burrowed her face into the pillow. However, that caused excruciating pain which forced her awake. Opening her eyes, she peered directly into Jed's eyes inches from hers. This startled her.

"Lucy?" His face full of concern as his eyes scanned hers.

Groaning as she remembered the events of the day. "It was real."

This remark evidently relieved his concern; he removed himself from the bed.

He poured a cup of tea as he filled her in on things. "The jeep is fueled and ready. We have plenty of water for the remainder of the trip. I also purchased a burka to keep you warm since it gets rather cold at night here."

Sitting on the bed next to her, he offered her the tea. Lucy wriggled into an upright sitting position holding the sheet against her chest. Tucking the sheet tightly under her upper arms, she accepted the cup. As she drank, he told her an amusing story about a monkey in the marketplace. He stood to refill the cup for her. It was then she noticed he no longer wore his flack jacket. After handing the cup back to her, Jed removed his t-shirt and pants leaving him clad only in tan boxers. Taking his clothes onto the veranda, he shook them till they were sand free. The motion caused the muscles in his back and shoulders to ripple. Draping his clothes from the corner of the bathroom door, he went in to wash. Lucy felt like she had a front row ticket to a male burlesque show as she watched him glide a wet cloth along his sinewy arms, hard chest and well defined stomach.

Career military men irritated her to no end, but "oh baby! He was yummy with a capital Y." Leaving the bathroom, he selected a pear-like fruit from the tray. Opening his pocket knife, he sliced a piece from it. Sitting on the bed again, he sliced another piece to offer to her. She opened her mouth to allow him to feed her. A piece for him, a piece for her—he continued in this manner till the fruit was gone. Unable to keep eye contact with him the whole time, she focused on his chest. Since he hadn't bothered drying, water glistened in the furry thatch of silver and white. Oddly, he seemed to have the same problem keeping eye contact with her. His eyes dropped, too. She figured he was watching her mouth—guys and their oral sex fixation.

"When do you want to get on the road again?" She asked.

"We have the room for another half hour." He stated wiping the knife clean prior to closing it.

"What?! I slept the whole time?" She exclaimed in disbelief.

Forgetting her head injury, Lucy jumped from the bed to fetch her clothing. Her horizon tilted drastically. He swept her into his arms. This motion caused the already loosened towel to fall to the floor. Her bare naked chest pressed against his naked chest. This was an all time number one most uncomfortable position for her. Surprisingly, a part of him stood at attention on the double. This scared her. She tried to back out of his hold. Her upper legs made contact with the bed causing her to lose her balance and fall backwards. The marine came with her. The full weight of his body pressed intimately. This triggered a fear in her which she had managed to keep buried for years. Forcing logic to the forefront, she attempted to rationalize that he was one of the good guys.

Unfortunately her emotions choked her ability to communicate sensibly; all she managed was "Jed . . ."

It was interpreted as an opening, not a rebuff. His tea sweetened mouth covered hers. Lucy started responding to the wonderment of his kiss. But his hands became forceful and urgent. She tried to push down the panic. He shifted; one of his powerful legs forced her legs apart. Similar images from the past flashed through her mind—each with the same face and the same horrific outcome. The reality of this being a different man no longer registered. This was a man who took by force no matter the cost.

"No!" Her panic burst forth in an adrenalin surge. "Never again!"

Using strength she didn't know she had, Lucy threw Jed off her and onto the floor, then ran for the bathroom. She slammed the door behind her, sliding along it till she sat on the floor. Her body shook as she struggled to contain her run amuck emotions.

From the other side of the door, he asked. "Lucy what's wrong?"

"Like you fucking care!" She screeched.

"Lucy, please tell me what I did?" He pleaded with her.

"Just get me my clothing and we are leaving." She demanded. "That's an order marine!"

A few moments later, he tapped on the door. "Your clothes ma'am."

She heard him drop them onto the floor and step away. Opening the door a crack, she saw him collecting his shirt and pants from where they had landed after taking flight. She pulled the folded pile of clothing through the narrow opening. Even though she dressed quickly, she noticed they were clean rather than grungy.

"Why would he do that if he was going to . . . ?" She shook her head at the thought.

Taking a few more minutes, Lucy splashed cool water on her face. It felt so good, she doused her whole head. It helped bring her into the present. Towel drying her dripping curls as she emerged from the bathroom enabled her to hide her face from him. When the sergeant major saw her, he stood at attention.

Lucy looked for her boots to no avail. "My boots?"

Jed began an immediate search and rescue. He finally retrieved them from the veranda. However, he didn't give them to her. He motioned for her to sit. Not happy about being on the bed again, she folded her arms across her chest. He slid the boots onto her feet, then deftly laced them to fit snugly. This time when she stood, she took her time. Collecting his camouflage jacket and a cloth sack, the marine led the way.

In the lobby, Jed sought the woman who had delivered the tray. Lucy guessed she had also been the one who washed her clothing. The woman handed him a bottle. As he took it, he passed in return a few bills folded tightly.

At the jeep, he gave it the once over before allowing her to sit in the passenger seat.

Climbing into the driver's seat, he handed the sack and bottle to her. "Biscuits for both of us and tea for your stomach."

Pointing to the jug at her feet "water."

Reaching into his jacket pocket, he retrieved lip balm. He used it, then passed it to her. She blissfully applied it to her chapped lips.

When she handed it back, she said a quiet "thank you."

He responded with "keep it."

The marine put the jeep in gear and they were on the road to Hacki. Lucy sipped the tea. It was a heavier, sweeter mixture than the tea they had in the room. As a preventive measure, she drank half the bottle. It worked sufficiently. Her stomach had gotten queasy, but nothing compared to earlier.

Shortly after sunset, Jed slowed the jeep. He took a sharp right turn off the road to park between some large rocks.

"Is something wrong?" She asked.

"No ma'am, time to walk." To make his point, the sergeant major climbed out of the jeep.

She didn't budge. "I don't understand."

Reaching behind her, he tossed her a pile of dark cloth. "Please put this on ma'am. I'll explain as we walk."

Lucy watched as he pulled a lighter colored robe on over his combat gear.

"The water ma'am?" She did as he requested.

Jed slung it across his shoulder. As she stepped from the jeep, her aching body protested causing her to groan involuntarily. Jed took a step towards her only to stop before taking another.

He spoke gruffly. "The walk will loosen those muscles ma'am."

She attempted to put on the burka, but couldn't determine how it worked. Jed took hold of it to help her slip her arms into the sleeves. Taking the long scarf like section, he wound it around her neck and head. Another section of the front of the robe was pulled across her shoulder to drape down her back. Jed tightened where it needed. She wondered why he was going to so much trouble. The garment did prevent the evening chill from making her cold. She retrieved her bottle of tea from the jeep. It fit snugly into one of the folds of the heavy cloth. He grabbed the sack of food. They walked along the road towards a glow on the horizon. It didn't take long for the darkness to enshroud them. As Lucy gazed up at the stars like diamonds in the sky, the Beatles tune of the same name played in her head.

Jed's voice interrupted her pleasant diversion. "We need to enter Hacki as inconspicuously as possible. That's why we had to ditch the jeep and dress like this. Lieutenant Brawn and two members of his team will be waiting for us dressed like this, too. When we make contact, he will radio for the helicopter standing by."

"But we didn't slink into the last town and a helicopter landing isn't exactly low key." She countered.

"That was a nomad village. People come and go constantly. Plus, your stash bought us anonymity there. It won't in Hacki. As for the helicopter, by the time it's noticed, it will be too late for any enemy operatives to react." He subtly increased their pace as they talked.

Why the Marines needed to make something as simple as getting her back to her hotel into a special forces' operation, confounded Lucy.

As they neared Hacki, she noticed his stride not as long and strong as it had been. It was a limp, but not from a foot or knee injury.

Seeing low lying rocks a few yards ahead, she stated "Sergeant major, I need to rest."

"Can you make it to those rocks ma'am?" He asked.

"Yes, that would be perfect, thank you." She didn't like being sneaky, but knew he wouldn't have stopped otherwise.

He didn't sit when she did. Instead, he raised his leg onto the rock as if he were a conqueror of a new world. They finished the food and water. She hoarded the tea for later.

Jed finally sat next to her in the darkness.

His voice was sincerely apologetic. "Ma'am . . . , Lucy, I'm sorry. I wouldn't have forced you to do anything you didn't want to. But I thought from the other night that you wanted to."

She could hear the contriteness in his tone.

Placing her hand on his arm, she responded with understanding. "Jed, I know you weren't . . . , wouldn't have . . . As for the other night, we were drunk and we didn't. Let's chalk it up to a simple misunderstanding."

He cleared his throat. "So we are okay?"

She didn't know why it bothered him so much. It wasn't like she'd report the incident. She considered it a personal faux pas.

For whatever reason, she leaned over and placed a light kiss on his rough cheek before standing. "We're okay. Time to move again or I'll get stiff."

"Yes ma'am." The marine stood only to stumble.

"Jed?" She was worried.

With his guard still down, he answered truthfully. "Pinched nerve from hitting the floor; it aggravated an old injury. It's why I have to retire from the service."

"It's not that far. I'll go alone and we'll come back for you." She didn't want him in pain.

"No ma'am!" The marine interjected vehemently as he came to full attention in front or her. "My mission is to get you safely on board the Arlington."

Knowing it was pointless to argue with him, she moved aside. "Lead the way sergeant major."

She respected his honor to duty, but this was absurd. He was obviously in severe pain with every step. Then again with every step, they were that much closer to the USS Arlington.

For the last mile, she entertained her thoughts with the party in Jed's honor a couple nights ago.

He'd sent word to her hotel to join them at one of the clubs for the festivities. The fact he even remembered her motivated her attendance.

When she asked how he knew she was in town, he answered with a smirk "I have my sources.

It had been his last night with his unit. They were flying out the next morning for Germany. As a matter of fact, he hadn't been scheduled to catch a transport until today. The soldiers had gotten quite drunk. She did fairly well to only drink a fraction of what they did. But even that much had been sufficiently beyond her limit. Into the evening, the jarheads decided she had to dance with them when "She's a Brick House" started playing. Lucy liked to dance so she joined them as long as they didn't do anything inappropriate. At midnight, Jed ordered his boys to their bunks.

Then he remarked to her "the kids are tucked in, now for adult time."

At which point, he pulled her onto the dance floor for the Elvis rendition of "Unchained Melody". From his unsteady steps, she knew adult time would be short. She calculated he'd downed—ten beers and numerous unidentified shots—all in a few hours. She was amazed he could walk. When the dance ended, he took her by the hand. Stopping with the bartender, he bought a bottle of bourbon. They flagged a taxi to take them to her hotel. Normally she wouldn't have allowed him into her room. However, after an evening of eight men paying attention to her, mixed with alcohol, she felt a happy muzzy. He opened the bottle to pour two glasses. Needing ice for their drinks, she grabbed the ice bucket to fill in the hall. By the time she returned, she found him clad in only regulation boxers passed out across the bed. Before joining him, she washed her face and changed into an oversized t-shirt. There was a wide expanse between them on the king size bed. When she woke in the morning, his strong arm held her close with his snores in her ear. She let him sleep while she got ready for work. Before she left, she turned on the coffee maker hoping the smell would rouse him pleasantly. And that was the last she had seen or heard from him, until today behind the rock.

Hacki was a much bigger town than she had pictured. She also found it extremely busy for the late hour. As they mingled with the crowd, Jed grasped her hand. To which she felt most grateful. He navigated them through the people to a side street. They started down it. Three men advanced on them.

She heard as they neared "Rhino one to Hummingbird, we are a go. I repeat. We are a go."

Lucy wanted to cry with relief, but something told her not yet. With no words spoken between the five of them, they merged with the crowd. Jed kept within a step of the lieutenant. The other two soldiers brought up the rear. It took some time till they left the crowd behind. In the distance, she could hear the whap-whap-whap of the helicopter's approach. She realized they were heading for open desert.

The small group stopped. The other three soldiers removed their robes to expose their uniforms.

"Hummingbird, we are at the landing site." Lieutenant Brawn hollered.

Instantly the helicopter's spotlight flooded them. Seconds later, gun fire kicked up the sand around them.

"Get down" one of the soldiers yelled as they all flattened to the ground.

The four soldiers fired in the direction of the shots. The lieutenant was giving orders to the pilot, but the gunfire muted the words. The helicopter fired a round of small missiles, then landed on top of them.

"Load up!" the lieutenant ordered.

They stood to climb into the open door. She couldn't see anything with the dust the blades sent whirling around them. It was only as they handed her up to the men in the helicopter that Jed released her hand. The four marines made short time of safely climbing into the helicopter's compartment for them to be airborne again. Jed yanked off his robe while scurrying across the space to her. He undid her sand covered robe, checking her for any gunshot wounds. Finding none, he released a sigh of relief. He did come across her bottle of tea. She took it to ease her dry mouth and throat.

"She's okay lieutenant." He said.

Brawn spoke into the radio. "Arlington this is Rhino one. Priority package on board, over."

The USS Arlington replied.

Brawn handed the headset to Jed. "Arlington this is Peacock one, over."

The commander had a few words for the sergeant major.

"Yes sir. Thank you, sir. Peacock one out." He returned the headset to the lieutenant.

Jed tried to ease her pensiveness. "We'll be on board the Arlington in a half hour. You are safe now."

In a solemn voice, she said "not until we're on the Arlington."

He nodded at the use of his own words. Hidden from the others by the folds of cloth, he grasped her hand. They encountered no further incident en route to the Arlington.

Commander Spiers met them on deck when they landed. The marines jumped out first. The lieutenant and sergeant major assisted Lucy.

The commander walked towards her extending his hand. "Ma'am, I'm Commander Spiers, welcome aboard the USS Arlington."

The words swam in Lucy's head as everything went black.

Chapter Three

Lucy woke in sick bay.

Seeing her conscious, the doctor spoke to her. "Ah, look who has finally decided to make an appearance. Ma'am, I'm Dr. Doven. Do you know where you are?"

"Aboard the USS Arlington" she answered.

He ran her through a list of simple questions to determine her coherency level.

His last question "How are you feeling?"

"Queasy, headache, bruised, thirsty and worn out." She tried to smile, but even that hurt. "What did you find?"

Dr. Doven smiled. "Concussion, bruises, hairline factures to your cheek bone, mild case of dehydration and exhaustion—pretty much the same as you described. We've had an IV running for the last few hours. Now that you are conscious, I'll alter the dosage."

"Any chance you can turn the lights down?" The bright antiseptic white of the room hurt her head making her cranky.

"Yes ma'am." The doctor complied by dimming the lights. "Anything else?"

"How long do I have to stay here?" She asked.

He thought she was joking till he saw her face. "Ma'am?"

"Is there a medical reason preventing me from returning to my hotel?" Nothing he described had to be monitored.

She put the doctor in an uncomfortable position. "No ma'am, but the commander's orders are that you stay here."

"Dr. Doven, please inform the commander I'd like to talk to him." She requested.

"Yes ma'am." The doctor exited.

Since it was the middle of the night, Lucy was rather shocked when Commander Spiers appeared an hour later. "Ma'am, you asked to see me?"

"When can I return to my hotel?" Her question was direct.

The commander avoided giving a simple answer. "We need to debrief you."

"So get someone in here to debrief me." She would use logic to undermine his control. "There's no privacy in here; I feel like I'm on display. I want a long hot soaking shower or bath followed by a comfortable bed. Neither of which you can provide on this ship. Also with my concussion, the boat makes my nausea far worse."

"Ma'am, we need to keep you under protective custody until our investigation is complete." The commander stated his reason.

"And you can't do that at my hotel room? What difference does it make if there are guards assigned to me here or there? If I'm at the hotel, it might flush out the enemy operatives." Again she used a rational argument.

To Lucy's delight the commander's expression wavered. "Let's hear your version of the events and we'll see."

The commander exited with less starch in his stride.

Lucy dozed on and off until 0600 hours. She couldn't handle lying on the stiff cot any longer. And she wanted to take a shower—even if it was a regulation shower. On her way to the head in sick bay to empty her bladder, a member of the crew rushed into the room.

"Ma'am, are you alright?" He asked nervously.

"Yes petty officer. I need to use the facilities." She explained.

"Oh good, I mean, yes ma'am." And he saluted her.

As she continued on her mission, she bit her tongue from saying something sarcastic.

When she stepped back out with her IV pole in tow, she was greeted by the commander and the doctor.

She remarked first "good morning gentleman."

"Good morning ma'am." They said in unison.

Commander Spiers motioned for her to sit. "We will be ready to debrief you in an hour."

"I'd be more comfortable if I could take a shower and put on some clothing. Would that be possible please?" she requested sweetly.

The commander had anticipated this. "I have assigned Petty Officer Covey to you. You met him earlier."

Dr. Doven began undoing her IV. "If you get dizzy or have any other problems, tell him and he will contact me immediately."

"The petty officer is a tadpole. I'd appreciate if you play within the rules for his sake." Commander Spiers tone indicated it was an order not a suggestion. "Am I clear?"

"Yes commander." She agreed. "I understand completely."

They both expected her to challenge an experienced officer. Messing with an enlisted man's head crossed a line she wouldn't do.

"Thank you." The commander saluted her on his exodus from sick bay.

The petty officer re-entered the room while the doctor recorded her vitals and covered her stitches with fresh bandages.

He stood at attention and saluted her, again. "Petty Officer Covey, ma'am."

She could see how young he was. "At ease."

"It's okay to get your bandages wet when you wash your face. Expect quite a bit of tenderness." The doctor stated. "She's all yours petty officer."

"Thank you sir" the petty officer saluted the doctor.

The doctor reciprocated with a more lax gesture.

"Ma'am" another salute to her as she stood.

"Please lead the way petty officer." She ordered.

The petty officer took her to temporary quarters. "Ma'am, your luggage was brought from the hotel."

She selected an outfit for after her shower. "Um, petty officer, I don't have a robe."

"Yes ma'am. One was donated for your use." The young sailor pointed to it hanging on the door.

Collecting that and her toiletries, they made their way to the showers. Showers on naval vessels bamboozled her. It was how Lucy first met Jed. The memory filled her mind as she stood under the stream.

Lorning, her employer, sent her to the carrier USS Endeavor to write a report on possible enhancements for the Tomahawk missile launch program. While there, she'd stumbled across an intermittent satellite feed issue. It was a problem she couldn't recreate properly from her desk in the states. Lorning agreed to allow her stay as long as necessary to investigate, diagnose and fix. The Navy had been eager to accommodate her extended time on-board. She'd been given VIP quarters.

Her first shower on board went awry. She thought she'd followed the instructions. However, she couldn't get the water on a second time to rinse the shampoo from her hair. While she was trying to figure it out, there was knock on her door. Grabbing a towel to wrap around her, she opened the door far enough to see who it was.

"Excuse me ma'am, I must have the wrong quarters." The marine said to her as he apologized for his mistake.

"Sir, um, sergeant, before you go would you please help me?" She asked with desperation in her voice.

"Ma'am?" He sounded suspicious.

"I can't get the water back on to rinse my hair." She pointed to her hair full of shampoo bubbles.

His voice sounded somewhat condescending as he pushed the door open fully to enter. "If you aren't used to these, they can be a bit tricky."

She would accept the tone if it meant she could rinse. "Thank you."

"Ma'am" he motioned for her to step into the shower.

He pointed to each of the knobs and how they were to be used. Then he pushed a reset button for the count of ten.

"Okay ma'am, the water should turn on for you now." He backed out of the tight compartment to leave.

"Thank you" she said.

"Yes ma'am." His words were purely obligatory on his exit.

She hung her towel on the provided hook, then turned the faucet. No water came out. She tried again.

"Sergeant?!" She yelled, hoping he hadn't shut the outer door yet.

A few moments later, he spoke from the other side of the shower curtain. "Ma'am?"

"I'm sorry, but I'm not getting any water?" She felt stupid.

He reached his hand in front of her to test the knobs himself—no water.

"What the fuck is wrong with this thing?" He swore in frustration. "Sorry for the language ma'am."

She snickered at his outburst. "It's quite alright sergeant."

He spoke as he went about the steps to reset the water flow from outside the curtain. "Actually ma'am it's sergeant major."

"I apologize sergeant major. Some rank insignias, like yours, throw me a curve." Her first day on board and she'd already made a serious faux pas.

"It's quite alright ma'am." He used her words to let her know he didn't take it as an insult.

He tried turning the water on again; still nothing. The sergeant major muttered something under his breath which she was glad he meant at the faucet, not her. Lucy was pressed as tight against the wall as possible. But it was a tiny stall and she couldn't very well suck in certain parts of her anatomy. As the sergeant major worked the contraption, his arm brushed against her voluptuous chest repeatedly. He didn't appear to notice while he continued fighting with the plumbing.

Finally, water spurt from the shower head.

In her exuberance, she did a few happy jumps as she stepped under the spray. "Thank you, thank you sergeant major!"

The marine naturally responded by turning his head at her chirpy gratitude.

"You're welc . . ." His words broke off at seeing her bountiful boobs bounce.

It was then Lucy remembered she was still naked.

She exclaimed with embarrassed horror "oohh!" crossing her arms across her chest.

But the sergeant major did not remove himself from the shower.

"Now that it's turned on, do you want me to stay and work those?" He quipped suggestively.

"Kindly get out!" Lucy demanded.

As the sergeant major removed his head from the shower stall, his face tightened. "Yes ma'am. If there's anything else you need servicing, don't hesitate to ask for Sergeant Major Warloc."

Not wanting to have to ask for further assistance, Lucy quickly rinsed the shampoo from her hair. The water turned off with no difficulty. As she towel dried her long tresses, Lucy thought she heard the door into the gangway shut.

Lucy kept resetting her water limit to take a longer shower than allowed. The grit of sand needed to be gone. She put the roomy threadbare robe on for the trip to her quarters.

Petty Officer Covey stood at attention to salute her "ma'am".

"Petty Officer Covey let's make a deal. When it is just you and me—no saluting or ma'aming—okay?" She proposed to the young sailor.

The petty officer relaxed. "Really?"

"Yes really. But remember, if anyone else is around, you have to do all of that stuff." She couldn't let him get into trouble.

"Thank you ma'am. The commander said I was to get you breakfast. Do you want me to go now?" With his anxiety gone, his enthusiasm showed.

"Yes please. Fill the tray." She made it easy for him to succeed.

"Yes ma'am." He hurried away while she entered her assigned quarters.

This gave her time to dress in peace. As she slathered lotion onto her parched skin, she found more bruises than expected. Thanks to the sand in her bra, her breasts were chafed in spots. Even with lotion, it made wearing an underwire bra incredibly painful. She chose to skip the bra. Thankfully she had packed a camisole with a bra built into it. For the average size breasts it sufficed as a bra. For her 36DDs, it merely kept them to a jaunty jiggle. Without the structure of the usual minimizer bra, her button down shirt had to remain partially unbuttoned.

By the time she finished dressing, the petty officer had returned. The tray of food he served was perfect—toast, sliced fruit, scrambled eggs and bacon with cranberry juice on the side; almost perfect—no coffee.

"Thank you petty officer, this is wonderful." She couldn't fault him for her own omission.

They arrived for her debriefing on time. The petty officer was ordered to remain in the hallway. Those in the room were the commander and two other officers.

The commander began the debriefing. "Please run down the events of yesterday starting with when you left your hotel room."

"We all met for breakfast. While we ate, we discussed our plans for after the demo. It was no different than any other morning." She stated. "When we arrived at the Armadillo, we began reviewing procedures."

"And the attack?" One of the officers prompted.

She elaborated as much as possible. "We heard a commotion outside, then five armed men entered in a rush and were yelling in, what I can only guess, Arabic. Corporal Pico shot and killed one, then they killed him."

The other officer asked "why didn't Corporal Barnes use his gun?"

"It was setting out of reach. He removed it when we were working under the console because it kept getting in the way." She answered.

"So it was Corporal Barnes' gun that you used." They wanted clarification. "How did you know how to use it?"

"No, it wasn't Corporal Barnes' gun; it was Corporal Pico's. When they took Barnes outside, they herded us away from the door over by Pico's body. I knew they were going to execute him for everyone to see what they'd do to us. So I grabbed Corporal Pico's gun to shoot at the terrorists. My dad taught me how to use a shotgun: the principal is the same. Take off the safety, hold the gun securely with both hands, aim and pull the trigger. Luckily, I hit the one with Barnes giving him a chance to get away. Then one of them came at me, so I shot him directly in the chest. He fell forward landing on me causing me to drop the gun. As I reached for it, another one smacked me across the face with his. By the time I regained consciousness, the first one I'd shot in the arm had been bandaged and the second one lay dead next to Pico." She relayed the pertinent facts.

"The men you were with didn't do anything to provoke the terrorists?" It was the commander's turn to ask a question.

"They both have families and neither would do anything as rash as what I did." She remarked.

The next question was obviously read from the paper in front of them. "The doctor's report indicated you were not raped. Is that true?"

"Yes, but the man who took me outside had every intention. Thankfully Sergeant Major Warloc killed him." Her answer sounded crass.

There was a moment of quiet discussion before they continued. "What caused the Armadillo to send a signal to the satellite every ten minutes? And why did the Armadillo go dead?"

This required her to expound in detail. "We'd identified a possible issue that would cause a drain on the power to the whole vehicle. Since it couldn't be fully tested in the lab, I'd written a test script to force the condition during field testing. It executes shut down on the computer after running for eight minutes—this was to repeat for 40 cycles. One of the start-up programs locates and identifies itself with the closest satellite in its defined constellation."

"Basically, it was dumb luck you were running that program at the time of the attack." The second officer commented.

"No, the other two contractors were able to block the view of our captors long enough for me to bring up the operating system window to type in the command. My thought was strictly to send the signal to the satellite at regular intervals to allow us to be tracked. The Armadillo stalling was the dumb luck."

They wanted her version of the recapture of the Armadillo, and then losing it again. They were merely confirming what the rescue team had reported.

And yet another question asked. "What occurred on the trip to Hacki and the subsequent airlift?"

This she kept at a summary level. "It was hot, nauseating and exhausting."

Another officer entered the room. "Ma'am, why did you order the decimation of the Armadillo?"

"National security." She answered confidently.

Her answer didn't satisfy him. "Would you please be more specific?"

"Not without proper verification that everyone here has the sufficient security clearances." She would not be pushed into compromising her integrity.

"And the items you shared with us aren't classified?" He challenged.

"My debriefing due to the unfortunate events that transpired is required by the United States Navy. It was done by three officers in that branch of the service. They would not be here if they did not have DOD clearances. As for you or anyone else listening or watching who might not have DOD credentials, then that breach of security would fall on those three naval officers for allowing it to happen." Her patience with the questioning wore thin.

A voice in her head told her this man was a member of CIA, DIA or NSA. Since she'd worked programs for each of those agencies, the imposter in the uniform didn't intimidate her. It also made sense because the reason the Armadillo had to be destroyed was the common code used in interfacing with the satellite and its messaging algorithm. If an enemy operative could have salvaged parts of program code, it could be used to discover how to communicate with any DOD satellite and eventually spy satellites. The reason she'd been given this project was because of her previous experience on these programs. She had the unique ability to picture complete systems in her mind including obscure details. The system for use on the Armadillo was a streamlined version of the one used by COMSAT. By default, she had intimate knowledge of COMSAT because each of the satellite programs she'd worked were a periphery system with which it shared data. Those peripheries were of any level of classification dependent upon the customer and its specific use. She had worked a majority of these programs with clearances in the black operations realm.

"Why do you think the Armadillo was a target? And how do you think the information was leaked?" The imposter dug for information she lacked.

"I am strictly a technical expert employed by the number one data systems contractor to the U.S. government. It is not my job to ask those questions, let alone hypothesize on an answer. That's for an intelligence agency to tackle." It was time for her to turn the table. "So which one of those agencies are you from?"

The man did not flinch. However, the two lower ranked officers looked immediately at the commander. Both Lucy and the imposter saw it—end game.

The man reached across the table offering his hand. "Pleased to meet you Lucy Seeir. I am Benjamin McCallister, a field agent with the CIA."

She shook his hand. "Who else is watching?"

"We have Second Lieutenant Adam Bryans from JAG and Sergeant Major Warloc representing NCIS." The agent answered without subterfuge.

Lucy didn't like the fact Jed had been listening. Nor did she understand his connection to NCIS. But the list of attendees concerned her.

Not liking subterfuge, she put everything on the table. "Why do I get the impression I'm on trial for something?"

The agent addressed her concern. "Ma'am, think of it as a fact finding team."

"That doesn't wash agent McCallister. You are a hands-on investigator and there's a lawyer in the other room." She had no doubt there was more to it than a simple debriefing.

Before the agent could answer, the JAG officer and Jed entered the room. The second lieutenant shook her hand. Jed merely nodded.

JAG took the floor. "Ma'am, when a judge is recommended for the Supreme Court there are investigations followed by a congressional hearing to approve their appointment."

Not following, she asked "what does that have to do with me?"

"Think of us as your hearing." The second lieutenant answered cryptically.

"What the hell am I being charged with?" screamed in her head.

Lucy could keep the fear from showing, but not the confusion.

Jed jumped in to clarify. "You are not in trouble. It's a board review of your abilities for advancement within one of the agencies you've already worked for indirectly."

"But what does it have to do with yesterday?" the agitation in her voice apparent.

It was the agent's turn to explain. "Yesterday's events are under high priority investigation. Your involvement merely highlighted the importance of your abilities and the urgency to put you under protection."

"Are you sure you guys haven't been reading someone else's file? I'm just a staff software engineer." She downplayed her significance.

It was the commander's turn. "Ma'am, we may have met in person for the first time yesterday on deck, but I've heard your name from colleagues over the last couple years on how impressed they were with you. As a civilian, and a woman at that, it's an incredibly high compliment."

"You're unassuming personality belies what that brain of yours contains. This is a trait we are grateful you typify." Agent McCallister concluded. "Plus, your actions under extreme duress are to be commended."

All of the men in the room stood at attention to salute her. Lucy sat there dumbfounded.

Jed spoke. "Gentleman, the lady is looking a bit pale. Are we done here?"

The rest of the men confirmed they were.

Addressing her directly, Jed said, "Ma'am your petty officer has been ordered to escort you directly back to your quarters."

He led her into the gangway. The petty officer stood down the hall a few feet. He made no move towards her. Instead, he watched the sergeant major.

Jed spoke quietly for only her to hear. "I'm going to come by your quarters later. First, I have to finish this and then wrap up a few other things. Try to get some sleep."

He gave her hand a squeezed. She felt something; as he pulled his hand away she closed hers into a fist.

He motioned to the petty officer prior to re-entering the conference room.

Petty Officer Covey saluted when he was within a couple of feet of her. "Ma'am, please follow me."

She opened her mouth to chastise the petty officer when two sailors came by them from behind her. Rolling her eyes, she nodded to him.

At her quarters, the petty officer stepped inside long enough to verify no one else was there.

Exiting he said "I will be right out here if you need anything."

She sat on her bunk. Unclenching her hand, she looked at the tightly folded paper. She opened it carefully. Inside she found a small tie pin that resembled a peacock.

The note read: "Pack easy to carry bag. Passport & Security ID. Trust Me."

Opening her luggage, she pulled the overnight bag which was her carry-on bag when she flew. Sorting through her clothing, she selected two easy to wear outfits to pack. Her outfit from yesterday wasn't worth keeping. The suit and dress along with their accessories were hardly her favorites; no loss there. A suitcase could be replaced. And she always carried her minimal toiletries in the carry-on bag. Thankfully the only souvenirs—a pair of earrings and a unique tin of incense—could fit in the small bag. She kicked off her sneakers to pack. Bending to pick them up, she got extremely dizzy causing her to sink to the floor on her knees. Waiting for the associated wave of nausea to pass, she looked at her boots setting perfectly side by side under the bunk in military fashion. At work she was a neat freak; at home a borderline slob. These quarters constituted her personal space. She had set her boots under the bunk, but she distinctly remembered one of them on its side. Someone had been in her room. The boots were not going with her. She inspected her bag and everything she put into it thoroughly for any irregularities. Her bra and powder were thrown in the suitcase with the other discarded items. Her lotion would join them after she had slathered her skin one more time. She rolled the clothing as tight as possible to ensure it all fit in the overnight bag. To keep the bag within easy reach, she placed it on the only chair in the room. Her identification cards fit snugly in the breast pocket of the shirt she draped across the bag. The peacock pin prominently displayed on the pocket. She slid her suitcase under the bunk. Ready for whatever Jed had planned, she stretched on the hard mattress.

Chapter Four

A KNOCK ON the door disturbed her rest.

"Ma'am, Captain McCallister would like a word with you." Petty Officer Covey announced.

"Captain McCallister?" She tried to remember who, when agent McCallister brought his face into her line of sight. "Oh yes, Captain McCallister please come in. Thank you petty officer."

After she shut the door, the agent asked solicitously "How are you feeling?"

"My head is better, but not my stomach" she answered.

"I bet getting off the ship would help that." He commented oddly.

She turned to pour water into a small basin. "Funny, that's what I told the commander."

Splashing water on her face she asked. "What brings you by?"

"I'm on my way to board a helicopter and wanted to say it's been a pleasure to meet you." The agent stated.

Gently patting dry her bruised and swollen face, she smiled the best she could. "Thank you. I hope you have a safe flight."

"Hopefully, all will go off without a hitch." He commented.

As he opened the door, he stated "The sergeant major said he would be by shortly to take you for a tour of the ship. Marines don't like to wait so I recommend you be ready."

After the door shut behind Agent McCallister, Lucy made herself ready. When she put on her shirt, she saw her bag was missing. Okay, she had heard him correctly. But she couldn't determine how they were going to get her on the helicopter without being noticed. Jed's note said "Trust Me", so she would. No sooner had she finished the thought than another knock on the door. Opening it revealed not only Jed, but Commander Spiers.

"Hello Ma'am" in stereo didn't make it sound any better.

"Hello gentleman. Is there something I can do for you?" She asked.

The commander answered first. "I thought you would like a tour of the ship."

"Sounds wonderful, I'm going buggy in this tiny space. Thank you." She responded cheerily.

"I was going to be your tour guide, but they found room for one more on the outgoing helicopter." Jed hoisted his duffel bag in support of his words.

The commander made a suggestion. "If the lady is ready to go, we can walk with you to the deck."

Lucy announced "I'm ready."

"The doctor sent these." The commander handed her two pills and a bottle of water. "We don't want you puking."

"Thank you, commander." Lucy took the medication with one swallow.

The commander addressed the petty officer. "You are relieved Petty Officer Covey. The lady is in my charge and will contact you when she returns to her quarters."

"Aye-aye sir" the petty officer saluted everyone.

The trio made their way along the corridor. The two military men chatted about things which were of no consequence to Lucy. Up on deck, Jed handed his gear for loading to salute before climbing into the helicopter. Lucy feared his plan to get her off the ship had been scrubbed. The commander saluted back prior to escorting Lucy into a stairwell to continue the tour.

When the door to the deck closed, the commander did an about face.

Unzipping his jacket, he reached into it for a set of blue coveralls. "Hurry, put these on!"

Lucy didn't hesitate. The commander gave her the cap he had tucked in his back pocket and a naval identification placard.

"Ma'am, when I open the door, run for the helicopter. Keep your hand on the top of the cap. We can't risk anyone seeing your face." He ordered. "Good luck and may God keep you safe."

"Thank you, commander." She said in appreciation as she pulled the hat tight.

He re-opened the door to the deck, slamming it into the bulkhead.

He yelled from the open doorway. "Lieutenant! You have one more passenger."

Turning to her, he hollered loud enough for everyone to hear. "Petty officer when you are told 1420 hours, it doesn't mean 1422 hours. Move your ass and get on that helicopter!"

Lucy ran across the small stretch of open space to the helicopter. The sailors on deck flagged for the pilot to wait. She flashed the naval id for them to acknowledge, then tried to climb into the helicopter. Thankfully, Jed had unbuckled from his seat when he saw her coming. He grabbed her hand and arm to hoist her into the vibrating machine. Once aboard, she glanced around for an open seat. Jed re-took his.

"How convenient" she thought when she saw the only open seat between Jed and McCallister.

Luckily she didn't need help with strapping herself in for safety. It would have been quite odd to the other passengers if Jed had assisted her with that. Lucy kept her head down for the entire 40 minute flight. The helicopter landed on an airfield. The men grabbed their gear. McCallister handed a flight bag to Lucy. She accepted it knowing it concealed her obviously feminine brocade carry-on inside it. On the tarmac, McCallister and Jed kept Lucy between them as they jogged to the Air Force transport waiting for them. She balked at entering the cargo plane.

"What's wrong?" Jed said from behind her.

"Um, nothing." She swallowed hard, then stepped onto the winged freighter.

An airman checked their military ids. They were the only passengers. Yanking the jump seats down, they stowed their gear underneath. Before Jed stowed his, he opened it to retrieve two sweatshirts. He tossed a white one with "NCIS" on it at her. Removing his desert camouflage jacket, he donned a red sweatshirt with the U.S. Marine logo in gold.

Re-buttoning his jacket, he explained "You'll want to put that on under the jumpsuit to stay warm."

Glancing around, she looked questioningly at her liberators. "But I'm wearing civilian clothes under this."

McCallister responded. "Don't worry Lucy. They are too busy prepping for take off, which is in a few minutes. You better hurry up."

She did as she was told. To her pleasant surprise, the sweatshirt fit comfortably with plenty of room. However, when she tried to re-zip the coveralls she encountered a problem. It had been difficult on the ship, but with the extra layer it wouldn't close. Jed noticed her dilemma.

He commented "I told the commander to get you a pair with at least a 36 inch chest."

She replied. "You should've asked for bigger."

Grabbing either side of the opening, he forced the sides to meet to allow the zipper to go up. Doing this caused his strong hands to slide across her nipples through the material. Not used to being touched, they poked out in curiosity from the sensation. Closing the zipper pinched them beneath the layers of material. Lucy had never experienced the pain at having her ample breasts bound until this moment. It felt worse than squeezing swollen feet into dress shoes a size too small. Keeping this extreme discomfort to herself, Lucy strapped herself into the jump seat as the plane began rolling. The airman gave the thumbs up. Jed returned the gesture to indicate they were ready, too. At take off, Lucy clutched Jed's thigh, digging her nails into it. It took until the plane leveled for him to pry her fingers free. The pills the commander had given her for a queasy stomach were working. They had a side-effect which caused Lucy to become increasingly sleepy. She dozed for the next several hours.

McCallister woke her prior to the approach for landing. "Lucy, I need to explain the next step."

Focusing on his face, she nodded. "I'm listening."

"From here on out, we need to act like lovers who snuck away on a long weekend together." He took her hand. "It's the only way to get you off the base without drawing attention."

"No offense McCallister, but do you really think anyone will buy it since I'm 15 years older than you?" She identified a flaw in his plan.

"You look younger. Those bruises on your face help too. Just use a girlie tone, not the one we heard in the debriefing, and we have it made." He stated.

"How do we explain the sergeant major?" She asked in her low business voice.

Jed answered. "I was scheduled on a flight similar to this one two days ago. My being on it today wasn't all that unexpected. And since both of you are in Navy wear, it makes it more believable that you two are a couple."

"The rest we'll review in the hotel room." The agent didn't want to share too much with other ears nearby.

In a giggly voice, Lucy commented. "Oh Benny-bear, our first night together."

The CIA agent chuckled at her getting into character. The marine's face appeared to tighten. The plane landed smoother than Lucy had expected.

Exiting the plane, Lucy paused to speak to Jed. "Thank you for everything."

"Just doing my duty ma'am." his tone gruff.

Agent McCallister interrupted by taking her hand. "Come along darling. We have a jeep waiting for us."

During the drive, Lucy determined they were in Germany. Twenty minutes later, Ben checked them into a high end hotel. In their room, Lucy could hardly wait to take off the coveralls. As feared, the zipper refused to budge.

"Ben?" She called to the agent.

He emerged from the bathroom wearing jeans and a sweater. "Yes Lucy."

"The zipper is stuck." She said in irritation.

Ben's hands actually shook as he grasped the zipper. Lucy helped take the tension off the material as much as possible. It took a couple of forceful tugs for Ben to unzip it beyond her chest. In doing this, the teeth jumped off track along the way jamming the zipper. It didn't really matter. Once her chest had been released, the coveralls fell to the floor.

Lucy gasped a sigh of relief. Oblivious to Ben standing in front of her, she rubbed her boobs under the sweatshirt to ease the pain from being squashed for that long. The agent turned away with difficulty from the enjoyable, yet unconscious, display.

"How about a walk to the pub?" He suggested.

"I am starving." She exclaimed with enthusiasm.

Looking at the sweatshirt she remarked, "Is it okay to go out with this on? I don't have anything else warm to wear."

"You won't look the least bit obvious here. However, I would recommend not wearing the hat identifying the USS Arlington." He suggested.

"Okay, give me a few minutes to freshen up and we can go." She said as she closed the bathroom door.

Up to that point, Lucy had avoided using a mirror. She didn't have a choice as she gently washed her face. The dark bruising covered one whole side of her face. Her partially swollen shut eye explained why she had found it difficult to see. She applied Jed's lip balm to her lips, easing the soreness on that side too. Done, she emerged ready to see the town.

Ben held her hand again as they left the room to keep up their story. After a hardy stew and a few beers, they walked around town. Lucy window shopped for a warmer outfit, but only saw house frau clothing. At a bakery within a block of the hotel, she located pastries that would suffice for snacking on later. After paying, Ben sent her to the hotel alone while he went to handle a few things. Lucy figured he had spook business. Watching American television reruns in German proved to be amusing. Hours later the agent returned.

He handed her an envelope with a train ticket, cash and some kind of international cash card. "Early tomorrow morning we'll catch a train to Paris. Once in Paris, arrangements will be made for a commercial flight to the states. Avoid using anything with your name on it until you return home."

She nodded.

"I'm meeting some military buddies at the pub for dinner and drinks in an hour. Do you want to join us?" Ben asked.

"It probably wouldn't do much for your reputation to be seen with this face." She said glibly.

"Nonsense, we can tell them you were in a car accident." He seemed to want her to go along with him.

She was not up to play acting all night. "Ben, my head and body ache from the last two days. You go enjoy yourself."

"If you change your mind, you know where I'll be." He said. "What about dinner?"

"I'm not that hungry. Just send some coffee up when you go and I'll be good for the night." The less of a bother she was to him, the better.

Ben left within the half hour. When the coffee arrived, it included a basket with a bottle of honey milk bubble bath and lotion.

The note with it read:

"Darling,

A long, hot soak should put you in the mood.

Your Benny"

Lucy laughed. If only the agent weren't so young, he could have serious potential. Ben was a lot less stiff than Jed. Jed was serious enough for two people. Lucy had too serious a life as it was. And one person in a relationship should be the comic relief—based on the yin and yang principal.

She filled the tub for her long, hot soak. Sliding into the water amongst the heavenly smelling bubbles felt too good to be true after the last 36 hours. Luxuriating in the serenity of it, Lucy didn't hear the phone ring in the bedroom. A half hour later, with pruney fingers and toes, Lucy drained the tub. After drying, she began spreading lotion on her naked body. The large mirror over the vanity enabled her to identify all of the bruises she'd sustained.

Suddenly the bathroom door burst open.

A marine entered with his handgun fully brandished. "No one move!"

Lucy screamed, but stayed put.

The marine dropped his gun to his side after realizing there was no one else in the room.

Seeing it was Jed, Lucy moved to grab for the robe she'd gotten on the ship. "Jed! What the fuck are you doing?"

The marine spoke through gritted teeth. "Why the fuck didn't you answer the damn phone?"

"I was taking a relaxing bubble bath. But that's been shot to hell." She groused as she stepped around him into the bedroom.

Holstering the weapon, Jed continued his cross-examination. "Where the fuck is McCallister?"

"He said he was going down to the pub with some buddies from the base." She answered in irritation. "I stayed here because I ache all over and wasn't in the mood to play the lovey-dovey girlfriend. Does that end the interrogation sergeant major?"

The marine reigned in his anger before touching her arm. "So you are alright?"

"With the exception of the emergence of a new set of bruises every hour, yes." She answered glibly.

His next words—the articulation and sentiment—came quite unexpectedly. "It's a crime for a body as beautifully soft as yours to have such ghastly bruises inflicted upon it."

Lucy rebuffed his compliment. "You're just saying that to ease my embarrassment from you seeing me naked, yet again."

Jed stepped closer to gently rub her upper arms. "Do you remember when we first met on the Endeavor four years ago?"

She nodded.

"The memory of you thanking me so wonderfully for helping you, always provides immense joy." His voice had dropped to a seductive rasp.

Lucy's face flamed at her inability to handle the admiring comment.

Jed moved his arms around her back to pull her into a kiss. His lips tasted hers. She couldn't help herself from responding to him. Her lips parted to permit his deepening the kiss. It remained gentle yet exploratory. His hands began a similar discovery of her curves through the thin cloth. Cognizant of her bruises, the tough marine's touch stayed light.

However, when his hands cupped her breasts to tease her nipples, she yelped. "Ouch!"

He immediately ceased all motions and released her lips to discover why. "How?"

"They hurt from being pinched in those coveralls." She answered breathlessly.

"Mmm, it was a shame we had to do that." He muttered as he opened the robe to inspect her soreness.

It was as if she had been hypnotized. She was unable to stop him because she didn't want to stop him. Her eyes were fixed on his face. When he saw her pink feminine nubbin chaffed and discolored, he grimaced. Jed leaned down kissing it ever so delicately causing Lucy to gasp. His sure hands slid inside the robe to caress the skin at her midriff. Then he made a trail of similar feathery kisses from that nipple to its twin. Lucy's fingers found their way into his hair urging him along his path. At his destination, he paused to revel at its exquisiteness. Lucy felt it perk up from his undivided attention. Again, his hands gently cupped her bountiful breasts fully exposed to him. His mouth covered hers with more force than intended.

Lucy pulled away from the pain it inflicted, "ow".

Jed removed himself from her with a grunt. "This isn't going to work with as bruised and battered as you are. I can't control myself enough."

Before Lucy could say anything, Jed was gone. She stood with robe and mouth agape. How could she want this man? Moreover, how could he want her? He was the picture perfect marine. So he had a little snow on the roof, the man was in incredible shape. Lucy was a woman who spent a great deal of time at a desk on a computer or in meetings. She was attractive, but not the kind who turned heads when she walked by. With her current disfigurement people would definitely turn to look—in horror. Even with the disfiguring, this man wanted her. It boggled her mind. For a decade, no one had wanted her. Until this white haired Adonis . . . Aha, she thought. He must be feeling old. Add his age to the condition of his back, no wonder he had chosen her. To him, she was a safe choice. Standing there half naked wasn't going to resolve it. Lucy retied the robe securely. Going to her bag to get pajamas, she found she'd forgotten to pack anything in which to sleep. The robe would have to suffice. Crawling under the covers, Lucy pictured herself walking through a field of wildflowers. An image she had fallen asleep to many times when she wanted to shut down her brain.

In the morning, Lucy woke to the alarm she'd set. A quick shower washed away the sleep. She dressed hurriedly, unsure of when Ben wanted to leave for the station. Stepping back into the room, she noticed Ben had not returned last night. Nonetheless, she packed for departure. Lucy placed her bag in the flight bag with the sweatshirt. The way to the station would be chilly, but she didn't want to risk being identified. She checked the time on the ticket. Ben knew where she was going; it was up to him to make the train. The phone rang. It was the front desk notifying their taxi had arrived. Lucy said she'd be right down. She also took the complimentary pen and paper with the hotel moniker.

The driver stopped at a café for her to get a large coffee. At the train station, Lucy found her way to the correct train. A porter greeted her as she boarded. He took her bag to lead her to an empty compartment. It was a good thing she'd gotten the coffee to break a large deutschmark. Tipping the porter generously, he flipped the sign on the door to indicate occupied. She peered through the window, watching the platform for Ben. When the train began moving quite some time later, Lucy felt the trepidation of having to do this alone. Thankfully, no one else had joined her in the compartment. She opened the flight bag to retrieve her uneaten pastries from the previous evening. The passing countryside made for a lovely view as she ate breakfast. Taking inventory of the contents of the envelope, Lucy found the train schedule. At the halfway point, they would stop for an hour to drop off and pick up passengers. In the meantime, Lucy made a list of the steps she had to accomplish to get home from Paris.

When the train stopped, Lucy disembarked to stretch her legs. Her desert clothing in the mountains of Europe was not adequate. The shops in the small town had plenty from which to choose. She used the cash card. Donning the stylish cardigan she bought did the trick to make her warm. At an open market, she bought bread, cheese and beer for a late night meal on the train to avoid the dining car. Sitting in a café, she observed passersby till it was time to re-board.

Back in her compartment, Lucy discovered she still had it to herself. When the train began moving this time, she curled into the corner of the bench seat for some sleep. It had gone dark outside by the time she stirred. She had the feeling she wasn't alone in the black of the train compartment. Reaching slowly above her head, Lucy turned on a light. Asleep in a cramped position on the bench across from her was a man that was not Ben. At first, he was difficult to recognize in jeans and a battered suede jacket, but it was Jed. The light had woken him.

Squinting as he sat up, he commented dryly, "surprise."

"You're not Ben." Lucy stated the obvious.

"Agent McCallister got a lead on another case he's working. We couldn't let you travel unescorted. And since I was heading back to the states, we rearranged my plans to coincide with yours. A helicopter and truck ride got me to town in time to join you for the rest of this trip." He explained without being asked to elaborate.

"So what are our plans? All I know is that when I arrive in Paris I'm supposed to get a room anywhere and then the next flight to the US." She asked followed by a yawn.

Jed had to wait to respond until his answering yawn ended. "I have a room reservation in Paris. The earliest flight we could see from there to the US is four days away. I looked into other possibilities, but none without alerting to you moving around in Europe."

She followed his logic with one exception. "Won't I show up in Paris as soon as we buy the ticket?"

"I have your ticket under a different name." He hesitated as if there was more information he had to share.

"How will I get on the plane?-unless you have a fake passport for me." This made her nervous.

"Your passport will work fine." Jed stood to stretch. "McCallister didn't fill you in on this part of the plan at all?"

With aggravation in her tone, she replied "Apparently not!"

"You two were passing as a couple." Jed clued her in. "The best way to get you on a plane was under an assumed name. Forging a passport for one of us is no big deal. For you it would be too risky if you were caught. There's only one acceptable way to have an assumed name and have it still be legal."

The realization dawned rather unpleasantly on Lucy. "We have to get married?!"

"Yes and no." To show her, he withdrew an envelope illustrated with non-secular imagery from his inside jacket pocket. "The form and priest's signature are real. It just needs our signatures for it to pass at the airport."

She cocked her head in thought. "But if we both sign, it becomes legal doesn't it?"

Jed eased her concern. "It won't be registered anywhere to make it legal."

Lucy reached for the pen in her bag to sign the document. Taking the pen from her, Jed did the same. He folded the marriage certificate to tuck in his pocket.

"Mrs. Warloc would you like to take a walk to the dining car?" He suggested.

Not amused, she merely nodded.

When they arrived at the dining car, they discovered it was closed. They hadn't realized the train was only a couple hours from Paris. Lucy told Jed about her fare from the market. For which he was thankful, since he hadn't eaten all day. Back in the compartment, they enjoyed a feast of sorts. Lucy asked Jed what his plans were after retirement. He talked about the numerous offers he had, but not yet made a final decision. They discussed the pros and cons of each. He had already taken those not based in or around DC out of the running. By the time they pulled into the Paris station, the food and beer were gone. They grabbed their bags.

"Where's your big duffel?" Lucy asked noting he had a flight bag like she'd been given.

"I wanted to travel light so I shipped it home." He answered. "But I see you acquired more clothing to need the use of both of bags."

Giving him a dirty look, she stated. "I needed warmer clothing."

"If the rest is like this sweater, you'll look good while staying warm." He stated.

"That was the idea. But I didn't expect to be here more than a day. I only bought pajamas and the sweater." She said with chagrin.

"We're in Paris. I think you'll be able to find something to wear." A smile formed on his face as he teased.

Stepping off the train onto the platform, Jed led the way to the taxi stand. Lucy was impressed when they arrived at the hotel Jed had reservations. Between Jed's spotty French and the concierge's broken English, Lucy gathered their reservation had been changed. Instead of a standard room, they were upgraded to a suite to spend their honeymoon. It must have been McCallister for appearances. A bellhop carried their bags to the room. At the door of the suite, the bell hop held the door open. Without warning, Jed swept her up in his arms to carry into the room.

Still holding her, Jed said "tip in shirt pocket."

Lucy reached into his pocket to get the bills for the bell hop. With a knowing smile, the Frenchman pulled the door shut as he exited the suite. Jed took the extra few steps to the bed, then dropped her unceremoniously. He opened his bag in search of a prescription bottle.

"Jed?" She asked concerned.

After swallowing a few pills he replied. "Not your fault. It was already aggravated, but they'd have found it odd if I hadn't carried you over the threshold."

"Would a massage help?" The offer popped out of her mouth before she thought.

"Let's see how the medication works first." The tone of his answer sounded flat.

"Now what?" She asked.

"I don't know about you, but it's late and I'm going to crash." He said kicking his chukkas off. "What side of the bed do you prefer?"

"Doesn't matter" she stammered watching him begin to undress.

Forcing herself to look away, Lucy busied herself with unpacking her bags. Going into the bathroom, she changed into the pajama style night shirt she'd bought that afternoon.

When Lucy slid under the covers, she found two pillows forming a barrier between them. The bed was a lot more comfortable than the bench on the train. It didn't take her long to fall asleep to the soothing sound of Jed's snoring.

They woke to the sun shining through the open drapes. Jed told her to shower first while he stayed in bed a little longer. Lucy stepped from the steamy room wearing her robe. Jed was sitting up with stack of pillows supporting him. There was a knock on the door. It was a member of the hotel staff with breakfast. He wheeled the food cart into the room while Lucy located Jed's pants for francs.

Handing the tip to the uniformed employee, Lucy said her only French word. "Merci."

After the man left, Lucy spoke to Jed still in bed. "Are you joining me?"

"Would you mind wheeling the cart here so we can eat together?" He asked.

She moved the cart to his side of the bed as she spoke. "Jed, should I be worried?"

His face mirrored his discomfort at having to admit his weakness. "My back is giving me problems after the last few days. As a result, my legs are tingly and it's best if I take it easy for a day or two."

"Is there anything I can do?" She asked while she handed him a cup of coffee.

A grin transformed his face making him look decades younger. "Just keep doing what you're doing. I've never been served breakfast in bed."

"Yeah? That's one of those things I've never experienced either." She commented.

They talked about the weather and Lucy's game plan for the day. After breakfast, Lucy dressed then headed out shopping. On her way, she stopped at the concierge's to exchange her remaining deutschmarks for francs. Before she knew it, it was time to go back to the hotel. Upon her return to the room, Lucy found Jed sitting in a chair.

He greeted her a little too cheery. "Babe! I took a shower and got dressed so we can go to dinner, then dancing."

"Is that wise with you back?" She eyed him warily.

"I feel great!" He stood to emphasize his point.

However, when Jed took a step towards Lucy, his legs didn't exactly cooperate. She immediately moved to his side to stabilize him. And then she saw the glass of amber liquid on the table next to the chair.

Her irritation flew at him with her words. "What possessed you to mix alcohol with pain killers?!"

"I'm a big boy. I can handle it" was his response.

"Reeeeeally . . ." dripped with sarcasm as she let go of him.

As expected, Jed dropped to the floor in slow motion. He made an unsuccessful attempt to stand. Lucy picked her shopping bags up off the floor to move them to her side of the bed. Going into the bathroom she washed her face. Jed had moved far enough to reach for his drink. Not talking, Lucy put her new clothing on hangers to place in the armoire. When she completed this task, she left the room.

Twenty minutes passed till she returned carrying a small bag. While she was gone, Jed had managed to crawl to the bed.

"Any chance you can make it onto the balcony?" She broke the silence.

"Why? Are you going to throw me over the railing?" his response cranky.

"No, but it might be worth considering. After all, I would be a widow to a 25-year marine. There must be a nice death benefit that comes with that." Her dry wit caused him to smile.

"It would be the perfect crime." He agreed.

"Alas, if only I were bitter and vindictive." She sighed.

Their banter was interrupted with the arrival of room service. Lucy had the man set up their food on the terrace.

When he left, Lucy addressed Jed again. "Are you joining me for dinner?"

"You ordered dinner for me too?" He asked in disbelief.

"Yes. I even got you an incentive. It is yours on the condition no more alcohol, except a glass of wine or two, while you're taking those pills." Lucy handed the bag to Jed.

When Jed pulled the bottle out, he whistled. "Oh Babe, this isn't just any bottle of scotch. How did you manage this?"

"I have my ways." She said coyly. "Now get your butt out here so we can enjoy the view of the Eiffel Tower together."

Lucy wasn't going to tell him she'd spoken to the concierge that morning about what she wanted to find. It was supposed to be a thank you gift for him when they landed in the states. If it served as a means of bribery, she could play that game. While Jed hobbled slowly to the terrace, Lucy grabbed a pillow from the bed. When he sat, she slid the pillow behind his back for soft support. The view of the Eiffel Tower as it lit for the night was breathtaking. They listened to the sounds of Paris. The cool air bothered Jed's back preventing him from lingering outside. Lucy changed into pajamas. Donning the Parisian wrap she'd bought that day, she returned to the terrace. Since this trip was a once in a lifetime experience, she wanted to imprint as much of Paris as she could onto her memory.

The next day began like the day before. When Lucy went out for the day, she requested a massage appointment for Jed. The concierge would call Jed with the time the masseuse would arrive at their room. Lucy had plans to spend the day in the Louvre. She found the museum so enthralling that when closing time came, they had to ask her to leave. Walking in Paris at night didn't hold the same appeal as viewing it from the safety of a balcony. Thankfully, it didn't take long to flag down a taxi. After spending all day walking through the museum, it felt good to sit. Climbing out of the taxi at the hotel, Lucy's body reminded her of the injuries that had been inflicted upon it. She just wanted a hot shower topped with a pain killer, then to crawl into that comfortable bed. However, she expected to be yelled at for coming in so late. When Lucy found Jed sound asleep in the middle of the bed, she could hardly believe it. She took her analgesic and hot shower. Emerging from the steamy bathroom, she noticed an empty wine bottle on the floor. It didn't matter; it allowed her to evade the consequences of male fury. The haze of the pain killer was rolling in for her to confuse Jed with Trevor. Reminding herself the man lying there had saved her life, Lucy slid under the covers. Her movements disturbed Jed.

He rolled towards her muttering. "Did you have fun?"

His arm wrapped around her mid section to pull her against him.

"I'm glad you're back safe." Then he kissed her cheek before falling asleep again.

Lucy drifted off thinking it felt nice to be held like that without feeling threatened.

Chapter Five

Stretching reminded Lucy she'd overdone it yesterday. She burrowed under the blankets.

"Mm . . . you okay?" Jed's voice close to her ear was scratchy from sleep.

"I don't want to get out of bed." She murmured.

He nuzzled the back of her neck. "Who said we had to?"

She stiffened. "That's not what I meant!"

"Mm hmm." He acknowledged by snuggling his face into her neck.

His recent action made it possible for her to relax and fall back to sleep.

The ringing of the phone woke them.

Jed draped his body partially onto hers to answer it. "Ouie?"

He chuckled as he listened. "Ouie, ouie. Merci Rene'."

After replacing the receiver, he looked down at Lucy with a big grin.

"What was that about?" She asked not minding his weight on her.

"Rene' hadn't seen you this morning and we hadn't ordered breakfast. He said he hoped it meant we were finally able to enjoy our honeymoon properly." Jed relayed the conversation.

Lucy smiled too. "He is a very sweet man. I've never had a concierge that conscientious anywhere else I've stayed. You will give him a good tip when we check out tomorrow?"

"Yes Babe, whatever makes you happy." He gave her a soft kiss on the lips. "What do you want to do today?"

"I don't really know. Seeing the Eiffel Tower at night and spending a whole day in the Louvre are the only two things that ever interested me about Paris." She commented.

"I know I've been a lousy tour guide, but I might have one place you'd enjoy going." He still hadn't removed himself from on top of her. "Do you trust me?"

Lucy's eyelashes fluttered as she looked away shyly. "Yes."

"Okay then soldier, get that cute ass of yours moving." He exclaimed rolling off her and the bed.

"Yes sergeant major." Her response included extending her hands for him to help her stand.

Jed naturally obliged by pulling her up and into his arms. Their lips met for an inquisitive kiss. His hands released hers to gently skim along her curves. Lucy felt his manhood growing against her stomach.

Jed broke away from her. "You better get into that shower so we can get on the road. Or I'm going to take advantage of being honeymooners."

Even though his suggestion tempted Lucy, she hurried into the bathroom. While she showered, she heard Jed enter. Peaking around the edge of the shower curtain, she saw him hang the robe on the hook. How thoughtful since the towels didn't quite make it all the way around her chest. As soon as she opened the bathroom door, Jed went directly into the shower. Realizing it wouldn't take him long; Lucy dressed quickly in one of the outfits she'd bought the first day. Jed emerged from the bathroom with a towel tied around his waist. Lucy dodged past him to blow dry her hair. The mirror provided a provocative reflection of him dressing. Applying lipstick, she wondered why she bothered. With half her face in shades of purple, that simple touch of makeup hardly seemed noticeable. Already wearing his worn suede coat, Jed held her wrap. She picked up her purse—another item acquired in a French shop.

At the concierges, Jed spoke to Rene'. The Frenchman looked her direction with a delighted twinkle in his eyes. Returning his focus to Jed, he ran his middle finger along a map before handing it to Jed.

Outside, a valet held the passenger door on a jaguar for Lucy. They drove out of the city into the countryside of France. Jed maneuvered the twisty roads with the purring jaguar like an expert. Lucy wondered if he could handle her curves with the same ease. She turned to look through the window to hide the heat creeping into her face at the vision conjured.

It didn't take long for them to pull into an estate. It was a winery open to tourists. It had warmed enough they could leave their coats in the car. They took the tour and spent time in the wine tasting room. Jed bought a couple bottles before they left. They drove through the hills for a few minutes till Jed pulled over. Getting out, Jed grabbed a bottle of wine from his bag. Lucy followed him to the back of the vehicle. From the trunk, he retrieved a blanket which he tossed to her and a covered basket. They walked a short way to the crest of the hill.

"Oh Jed, it's breathtaking!" Lucy exclaimed at the view of the valley below.

Taking the blanket from her, he spread it across the grass. "You'll have to thank Rene'. He recommended it."

While Jed opened the bottle of wine, Lucy removed the croissants, cheese and pair of wineglasses from the basket. As they ate, they watched the frolicking calves in the herd of cows grazing on the hillside. Out of habit, Lucy put the remnants of their picnic into the basket when they were done snacking. Jed stretched on the blanket gazing at the passing clouds. The sun had gone behind those clouds for an extended period. The chill caused Lucy to shiver. Jed pulled her next to him. She cuddled into him seeking warmth. As they relaxed together, her mind wandered to what it might be like to have sex with him. Tonight would be their last night together. Why not? They were adults. Both knew there would be no strings. After they landed at LaGuardia, she would be returning to Denver and him to Washington, DC. But Lucy didn't know how to be a sultry vixen.

Thankfully Jed took care of that for her when he shifted to face her. Whether he read her mind or had his own plans didn't matter. What mattered was how wonderful his lips felt on hers. Their tongues tasted and teased each other. Jed's hand found its way under her shirt to bare skin. While his fingers caressed her back, his mouth released hers to nuzzle a path down her throat to her exposed cleavage. She giggled with delight as he buried his face in her ample bosom. Her response must have pleased him since she could feel his chuckle reverberate against her chest. All of a sudden, the burgeoning clouds that had been forming overhead burst. The couple jumped up. Lucy grabbed the basket; Jed, the blanket to hold over their heads. Even with only a short run to the car, the deluge drenched them. In the car, they laughed together.

Turning the engine, Jed made a suggestion. "Let's get back to the hotel to change into something dry."

"Sounds like a plan." She agreed.

At the hotel, Jed handed the keys to the valet. On the way passed the front desk, the concierge on duty called to Jed. When Jed walked over, he was given an envelope and box. Rejoining her, he had a cat that ate the canary smile on his face. In the room, Lucy went to the bathroom to undress. Before closing the door, she tossed a towel to Jed. She'd stripped to her new French bra and panty set. Towel drying her hair she noticed these too were damp. Being slightly chilled caused her nipples to perk up. This gave her an idea. Summoning all of her courage, she sauntered out to the bedroom. Jed stood there completely naked drying his wet skin. Upon seeing her, he froze. Lucy continued till she was directly in front of him.

Gazing into his dark blue eyes, she placed her hand on his fur covered chest. Her fingers toyed with the steel gray hair.

"Jed, it's been a very long time. But if you're interested . . ." she couldn't finish stating what she wanted for fear of rejection.

Jed tossed the towel aside exposing the measure of his interest. Which one closed the space between them didn't register with Lucy. Their searching lips and hands had her drowning in an eddy of wondrous new sensations. He yanked the comforter aside to lay her on the bed. When he removed her bra lavishing his attention on her breasts, she writhed and moaned at the exquisite pleasure. She arched her body against his wanting more. His hands glided from her breasts to her buttocks.

He shifted to speak into her ear with a voice deep with passion. "May I?"

"Please" she gasped lifting her hips to accommodate the removal of the final strip of lace which prevented them from merging.

Jed didn't need to ask for permission to go farther. Lucy spread her legs in welcome invitation to him. He made eye contact with her as he entered. Lucy could tell it felt as fabulous to him as it did to her when his eyes partially closed from the pleasure of it. She shifted her pelvis to take in more of him.

But he seemed to be holding back. Even the look on his face showed he was trying to keep control of his passion. Lucy tried everything—nibbling at his neck and nipples, tantalizing his skin with her long fingernails, rubbing her chest against his. She didn't know how to get him to totally let loose. Jed began to slowly and gently move in and out of her. She followed his lead, but she couldn't get enough of him.

"Jed, oh Jed, more please" she moaned aloud her need.

She could hear his restraint as he spoke. "I can't. We don't have a condom."

She stopped moving. "You have something I can get?"

"Only pregnant." He answered backing out of her at the broken moment.

"That's not a problem." She stated feeling empty and unwanted at his withdrawal.

His tone filled with frustration as he donned a dry pair of boxers. "Lucy, I know from Dr. Covey's report that you aren't on any kind of birth control."

She sat pulling her legs up to cover her nudity. "As I said before, I haven't done this in a very long time. But as far as the doctors can determine, I can't get pregnant due to scar tissue."

"What happened?" He asked as he sat next to her draping the robe around her shoulders.

"I was seven months pregnant when I fell down a set of stairs." She answered. "The results were a miscarriage, loss of an ovary, heavily scarred uterus, and soon thereafter, divorce."

Jed kissed the side of her head. He said nothing, but she thought she felt him shudder. Letting go of her, he went in search of the bottle of scotch she'd promised him. Lucy slipped the robe on correctly. He cracked open the seal to pour the amber liquid into a glass. After downing that, he filled two glasses. Returning to the bed, he handed her one.

He took a long swallow, then spoke. "Eight years ago my wife died from a ruptured ectopic pregnancy."

Lucy immediately grasped his free hand. Tears formed in her eyes at the thought of how awful that must've been for him.

"I was on a mission when it happened. They notified me after we'd returned to base. Michelle hadn't even told me she was pregnant. No one knew. She missed lunch with her girlfriend Anne. Anne went by the house that evening to schedule a rain check. When she found Michelle lying on the floor, it was too late. The doctors determined it had most likely ruptured the night before." He emptied his glass, then went for a refill.

From across the room, he completed his story. "If I hadn't gotten her pregnant and I'd have been home, she wouldn't have died."

Lucy went to him.

Wrapping her arms around his midsection, she rested her head on his chest. "You can't blame yourself. You didn't know."

He slammed the glass down sending liquid splashing onto the counter. "But I did know. It was her second pregnancy. The first one had to be aborted two years earlier because an ultrasound showed it was ectopic too. The doctors told us to prevent getting pregnant again since it was highly likely it would develop the same way."

"So why is that your fault?" She asked trying to understand.

"Michelle stopped taking her birth control pills without telling me." Jed jerked away from Lucy.

When he lifted the glass to his lips again, Lucy placed her hand gently on his free one. "Obviously she wanted a baby badly enough to be willing to risk the consequences. And she chose not to share that information."

Jed filled the glass yet again. "If she had told me, I'd have insisted using a condom or kept it in my pants."

"That tells me it wasn't your fault." Lucy stated quietly.

"But if it wasn't my fault . . . I won't blame her!" He sent the glass flying across the room.

His anger frightened Lucy, but she faced it head on. "Why do you have to blame anyone?"

Evidently no one had asked him that before. He filled her glass to take onto the terrace to be alone. Lucy figured there was no chance of an affair now. As she crossed the room, she retrieved the empty glass. While Lucy dressed, voices from the past began playing in her head. Unable to shut off the internal noise, Lucy grabbed her wrap to go for a walk. Heading outside, the doorman stopped her.

From behind her, the concierge spoke. "Madame Warloc, I called your name several times. Is everything alright?"

Turning Lucy spoke to Rene'. "My apologies Rene'. Did you need something?"

"Actually Madame, it is you who needs something—an umbrella." The kindly Frenchman handed her an umbrella.

Taking the item, Lucy said sincerely "Merci beaucoup."

Lucy walked without acknowledging anything around her. She concentrated on reminding herself the past couldn't hurt her anymore. Before she knew it, she was at the Arch d'Triumph. Well that was a smack in the face if there ever was one. Her head cleared. Turning around to go back to the hotel, Lucy realized she didn't know the way. Taking a taxi would solve that problem, if she had put money in her pocket when she'd left the room. Standing there trying to come up with ideas, she didn't see the form taking long strong strides in her direction.

It wasn't till Jed stood directly in front of her pulling her into his tight embrace that Lucy saw him.

"Don't ever do that again!" His deep voice said brusquely into her ear.

Glad to see him, she held onto him. "How did you find me?"

"When I discovered you'd left the room, I called the front desk hoping they'd seen you." He explained easing his grip on her.

"Thank goodness for Rene'!" She sighed in relief.

"He is definitely getting a big tip." Jed stated.

Taking her by the hand, Jed started walking. "I'm sorry I lost my temper. I've never had anyone with whom I've felt comfortable enough to really talk about what happened to Michelle, until today."

"I shouldn't have asked such personal questions." Lucy said contritely.

Still on Champs-Elysees, Jed stopped to look at her incredulously. "And you don't consider me inside you as personal?"

Lucy blurted out what she was thinking. "I do! I haven't been with a man since, well for a long time. But you are the kind of man who doesn't lack opportunity. Then when you didn't seem to really want to, . . . and got angry . . ."

"Lucy calm down." He tenderly placed his rough hands on her face. "You are right, there is no lack of opportunity. But I rarely do because it is incredibly personal to me. After the last few days, my feelings for you took me by surprise when I should have been prepared."

"I thought the marine motto was Semper Fi not Semper Preparato." She teased to lighten the mood.

It did the opposite. Jed went with the marine motto by saying a low "hoorah", to lean in for a kiss with gusto.

Passing Parisians cheered "Bravo".

Their joint laughter broke the kiss. They resumed walking and holding hands. Jed didn't rush them to the hotel. They went into a café for coffees. When they entered the hotel much later, Jed's happy relaxed demeanor disappeared in an instant.

He pulled her behind a marble column in the lobby. "Babe I'm sorry, but you're going to have to go up without me."

His serious tone concerned Lucy. "Jed, you're scaring me. What's going on?"

"An old associate is sitting in the lobby. I can't risk him seeing you with me. Depending on his purpose here, he could disrupt our plans to get you home safely." He explained.

"What do you want me to do?" She asked.

"Just head to the room, order us dinner and I should be there soon." He gave her a quick kiss, then shooed her on her way.

Once in the room, Lucy did as directed. The room service tray came with a complimentary bottle of champagne for the honeymooners' last night. She drank more than she ate wondering what happened to Jed. It was beginning to feel like her night in Germany. She packed while the bath tub filled. Her two bags pressed at their seams. Her outfit for traveling hung in the closet. Reviewing her paperwork for the airport, she realized Jed had the marriage license. She's the one who needed it, not him. Not relishing having to do it, she went through his things looking for his passport. As suspected, the envelope with the marriage certificate stuck out of it. Reading his passport, she saw to her surprise he was only a year older than her. Taking the document, she stuck it in her passport where it would be needed.

The bath filled with steamy water and honey milk bubbles beckoned. Her body cried its thanks as the therapeutic heat soaked into her sore muscles. About 15 minutes into her bath, Jed finally appeared.

He stuck his head into the bathroom, "I'm sorry. He insisted on a cognac and cigar."

"Whatever, just glad you came back in one piece." She said keeping bubbles gathered at her chest.

"Are you going to be in there much longer?" He asked.

"As long as I have bubbles and warm water" she answered.

He scrunched up one side of his face. "I smell like the smoking room. Do you mind if I use the shower?"

She smiled coyly. "I don't mind, if you don't mind."

"Great thanks." But he ducked his head out and closed the door.

Lucy closed her eyes again to continue enjoying the relaxation. Another ten minutes ticked by till Jed came into the bathroom. Opening one eye, Lucy watched as he stripped off his boxers prior to stepping into the shower stall. This time when she closed her eyes, she imagined the water sluicing over his chiseled body. Her eyes flew open with an idea. She climbed out of the tub. Letting the bubbles drip down her, she made her way to the shower curtain. Without making a noise, she stepped in behind Jed. He didn't startle when she slid her hands along his soapy back around to his chest, then down his torso. However, he did groan with pleasure as her hands worked their magic. He soon turned to clamp his lips over hers, his tongue velvety sweet from cognac. His hands explored every nook, cranny and curve of her body. Her hands reciprocated.

Jed paused ravaging her to turn the water off. She stepped out with him. He grabbed a towel to quickly dry her, then himself. Done, he resumed discovering her. Lucy couldn't take anymore; she tugged him over to the bed. Jed got her meaning. He scooped her up off the floor to drop her in the middle of the mattress. As Lucy parted her legs for him, Jed didn't hesitate to enter. He was hard and sure inside her. This time he didn't hold back. There wasn't an inch of him she didn't feel taking her to dizzying heights she'd never known. They rocked, moaned and called out as they came in a burst of blazing bliss.

Jed shifted his weight off Lucy, but kept his arms firmly around her. They fell asleep together. Numerous times throughout the night one of them would wake; who would enticingly rouse the other for another round of ecstasy.

At daybreak the alarm blared. Jed had to roll away from her to mute it. Lucy's body tingled with an afterglow she'd only read about. When he shifted back, he handed her a small square velvet box. Opening it exposed a silver band with rubies.

Lucy spoke with awe. "It's beautiful Jed."

He took it from the box to slide onto her finger. "Your wedding ring Mrs. Warloc."

He flourished her with kisses. One more romp climaxed just in time for the call that the taxi would be arriving in 15 minutes. They hurried to shower and dress.

When Rene' saw them in the elevator, he held up their bill. He had it ready for Jed's signature. Lucy blew the kindly clerk a kiss as she headed outside to meet the cab.

Jed climbed into the taxi a few minutes later. He and the driver discussed the destination.

"Did you remember to give Rene' the envelope with his tip?" She asked.

Kissing her on the cheek, he answered. "Yes Babe. He will be pleasantly surprised when he opens it."

The sunlight hit the stones on the wedding band making them sparkle. Lucy wiggled her fingers watching the prisms play.

Jed took hold of her hand. "So you like it?"

Gazing into his eyes, she smiled. "Definitely, but you could barely walk. When did you go shopping?"

"You weren't the only one to fully utilize Rene'." Jed explained. "He arranged for different jewelers to bring a selection of rings fitting my description in your size to choose from."

"How did you know what I'd like? Or my ring size? Heck, I don't even know that!" She questioned.

"The jewelry I've seen you wear is silver. I took a chance with the rubies; they seemed you. As for the size, Rene' helped me figure that out between when you used my gun and how our hands fit together." He described the lengths to which he went.

She didn't understand why he'd gone to that much bother. Instead of wondering about it, she turned her attention to viewing the last of Paris. Security check-in at the airport went without a hitch. Jed carried her flight bag and his; Lucy, her usual carry-on doubling as an oversized purse. At their gate, Jed left her with the bags while he went in search of coffee. When he returned, they waited in companionable silence for boarding. Lucy didn't realize they were in first class until called for boarding. When she questioned him about the expense, he explained he needed it for his back and it would look strange if newlyweds didn't sit together. Prior to take off, Jed held his hand open for her. Lucy grasped it with relief.

"You caused a cramp the last flight." He teased kissing her cheek.

In the cocoon-like seat with Jed holding her hand, Lucy felt a serene security. The hum of the engines lulled her to sleep. Jed woke her hours later as they prepared for landing. It was still morning in New York. He held her hand as they walked through the airport. After they got the rental, Jed stopped for a bag of bagels and coffees.

Lucy loved coffee, but she'd had enough. "Do you always drink this much coffee?"

"Yep, is that a problem?" He answered.

"No, I just don't know how you don't have an ulcer." She commented after she ordered a latte.

They took their hot drinks and fresh bagels to eat in the car. Jed merged onto the interstate which struck Lucy as strange.

"Where are we headed?" She asked.

"DC." He answered. "There's a flight to Denver that leaves Dulles at 9am tomorrow morning. If we can't get you on that, we can get you on a military transport in the afternoon."

She merely said "Okay."

Chapter Six

Two more coffees and six hours later, Jed drove the rental into an older residential neighborhood with a distant view of the capital building. He pulled into the drive of a brick cape cod.

Turning off the engine, he stated "We're home."

"This is your place?" Lucy asked dumbfounded.

"Yep, I'll get our bags." He said as he went to retrieve them from the trunk.

Lucy followed the walkway to the front door. Reaching around her, Jed put the key in the door to unlock it. The house felt surprisingly warm for having been closed since Christmas. Jed hung his coat, then removed her wrap to hang next to it. A familiar smell wafted in the air. Lucy moved to the partially opened pocket doors off the foyer to seek its origin. A fire burned in the corner of the sitting room.

Remarking suspiciously "How can there be a fire burning when you said you've been gone for the last two months?"

"One of the guys from the base keeps an eye on the place when I go away. I called him earlier to have him warm it for us." He explained carrying their bags back the hall.

She followed. The room on the other side of the sitting room wall was the master bedroom with a bathroom directly across the hall. He placed their bags on the bed. Then he gave her a tour of the rest of the house. The large eat-in kitchen filled the back of the house. The stairs led to a dormer with two small bedrooms with a shared bathroom. Back in Jed's bedroom, Lucy unpacked only what was necessary.

He poked his head in the doorway. "The only food in the house is the bagels we didn't eat, a few beers and a can of baked beans. Do you want to run to the grocery store with me?"

"Sure." She pulled her purse from the one bag.

Waiting by the door, Jed held her wrap. Instead of going outside to the rental, they went through the laundry room into the oversized garage which contained a work shop and ten year old Range Rover. Jed assisted her into the passenger side. The leather seats were cold. Reversing out of the garage, Jed maneuvered easily around the rental. At the grocery store, Jed filled his cart to the top with no assistance from Lucy. Other customers stared at her as they walked by. In Europe, no one treated her any differently because of the bruises on her face. Even in New York, no one took any notice. Here in the nation's capital, they were staring.

Lucy tugged on Jed's coat sleeve. "Why are they so fascinated with my face?"

"Yeah, I noticed it too." He steered the cart into a check-out lane.

As they were ringing out, the lady cashier chattered to them. "Hello Jed. Did you just get back? Looks like you'll be home for awhile. Stocking up for the storm they say is coming? Did you hear about those folks from Denver being kidnapped by terrorists over in one of those Arab countries last week?"

The woman took a breath for Jed to fit in a non-committal response. "Hello Jane. Got home about an hour ago to stay for a while."

Jane looked up at seeing Lucy shadowing Jed. "Now Jed, who's your lady friend?"

Jed introduced them. "Lucy this is Jane; Jane, Lucy."

Lucy greeted the cashier. "Nice to meet you Jane."

"Well hello there. We've never seen Jed here with a lady before. Goodness that wrap is lovely. Is it cashmere? Jed, you really do have a lady here." Jane noted Lucy's clothing as she continued scanning the groceries.

Embarrassed at the attention, Lucy put her left hand to her chest. "Thank you, y-yes it is."

Lucy noticed Jane eyeing the wedding ring. She quickly put her hand down hoping the cashier wouldn't comment on that too.

Instead, the woman began studying her face. "Where are you from Lucy?"

"A little farm town near Amish country in Pennsylvania." Lucy evaded naming her current state of residency by mentioning where she was born.

Jed gave her an odd look, but before he could say anything the cashier interrupted. "Did you know you look an awful lot like that woman from Denver who was kidnapped by those terrorists? What happened to your face?"

Jed answered for Lucy. "She was in an accident and I'm her emergency contact."

He pursued the other topic. "What kidnapping?"

"Jed, I thought they let you boys watch CNN." Jane remarked.

"Well, you know, for special missions they keep us sequestered." He winked at the cashier.

"Some special defense contractor demo was attacked by a group of terrorists. The civilians were held at gun point until they were saved by a squad of Navy seals. What was the name of the ship involved? The Arlington!" Jane unknowingly clued them in that the story had leaked to the media.

Jed quickly paid for the groceries, then ushered Lucy to the range rover.

On the drive home, Lucy voiced what they were both thinking. "How did the story get out?"

Jed gripped the steering wheel fiercely. "I don't know, but when we get home I have a few phone calls to make."

"Oh my God! My Dad and LuLu must be frantic. Can I call them?" The repercussions of it began dawning on Lucy.

"Yes, yes. I hope Lorning contacted them after we got you safely to Germany." The tires squealed from him taking turns too quickly.

After they carried the bags into the kitchen, Jed got his cell phone from his study.

"Call whoever you need to. I'm going to use the phone in my study." He kissed her lightly on the lips. "Don't worry if you hear a lot of cussing."

Once he was in his study with the door closed, Lucy called her dad.

"Hello?" Her dad answered after the second ring.

"In her brightest voice she said. "Hi Dad, it's me Lucy."

"Lucy-Q you had us so worried! Are you alright?" The tears could be heard in her dad's voice.

"Yes Dad, I'm okay. A bit exhausted from keeping up with the marine who got me out, but otherwise fine." She answered keeping it light to stop his worrying.

"They said seals rescued you." He needed clarification.

"It was, but they had a marine specialist available who joined the team. I'm with him now." She could still hear he was unsettled. "I just arrived back in the states. We had no idea the story had leaked to the press. Is the media leaving you alone?"

"I've had a few calls. When I told them Lorning had called to notify me you were safe, they stopped." Her dad told her enough to know things were back to normal.

"I'm sorry to have worried you. Love you Dad." Lucy said holding in the tears.

"Love you too Lucy-Q". He hung up.

Lucy began putting groceries away to contain her emotions before calling LuLu.

Crumbling the last plastic bag, she could hear Jed through the wall. "And you didn't think we needed to know that?!"

Apparently her phone calls were far more pleasant than his. She dialed LuLu.

Danny answered. "Hello?"

"Hi Danny. It's Lucy. Is LuLu home?" She greeted LuLu's husband.

"Lucy! It's good to hear your voice. She should be back soon. She ran into town for a few things before this blizzard hits." Danny stated.

"Would you please have her call me when she gets in?" She asked.

"Sure thing" he read the number on the caller id to verify it. "Glad you're safe."

"Thanks Danny. Bye." She clicked off the phone as Jed emerged from his study.

His stern face told her before his words did. "Things are a mess. Even though both Lorning and the Department of Defense tried to contain the story, it became human interest. And because Dahms and Wedo returned without you; you were an unanswered question."

"I can only guess the media is camped on my front lawn. Now what?" She asked concerned.

Jed rubbed the razor cut back of his head. "A member of the state department will be here in a half hour to talk with you."

Holding his hand up, he continued. "Before you ask, I don't know what they are going to propose. We just have to wait and see."

Lucy chewed at her bottom lip as she nodded. Jed put his arms around her, then rest his head on hers. They stood like that for quite a while until his cell phone rang from the kitchen.

Lucy jumped. "That must be LuLu."

As she fetched the phone, Jed followed. His hand slid down her arm to hold hers.

Lucy flipped open the phone with her free hand. "Hello?"

"Lucy is that you?" LuLu's voice cracked.

"Yes, it's me LuLu. You can stop worrying, I'm in good hands." She literally meant that as she squeezed Jed's hand.

Jed let her lean into him as Lucy listened to LuLu cry tears of relief.

Cried out LuLu finally spoke again. "Where are you sweetie?"

"I'm in DC. We just flew to the states this morning." Lucy stated.

"The other two men stated you didn't return to the ship with them; that you were still in the desert. What happened? Where have you been all of this time?" LuLu questioned.

"It's a long story that I will tell you the next time I visit. Suffice it to say, I am safe now." She would tell LuLu as much as she could after the dust settled.

LuLu's voice held concern, but she also understood Lucy worked in an industry where secrets were a necessary evil. "Okay, but make that visit soon! We love you!"

"Love you, too." Lucy said before disconnecting.

Jed nuzzled her neck. It felt good, but Lucy's guilt at making those closest to her worry was too overwhelming. When Jed moved to kiss her lips, he encountered the tears running down her face.

He ceased the seduction. "Lucy, you had no idea they even knew you were in danger."

Her tears increased. "But they did, and for it to be a headline story on CNN makes it that much worse. I've done everything in my power to prevent them knowing where I'm going, not only for national security, but for their peace of mind."

Gently wiping away her tears, Jed asked. "What did you tell them when you were on the Monroe during Desert Storm?"

Lucy's tears stopped streaming. "How did you know I was on the Monroe?"

"It's in your file." Jed's eye contact didn't waver. "What did you tell them? For that matter, what did you tell your husband?"

"They all thought I came to a two week defense conference here in DC." She answered.

"That doesn't wash. It was an emergency trip." He pushed her explanation.

She filled in the holes easily. "The story was the program director's secretary had a family emergency and I was chosen in her stead. I was living in Philadelphia at the time making it a reasonable drive to DC. From there, they put me on a military transport."

"But you've always been technical not admin. How did that make sense?" He shot another hole.

"My ex bought it because he convinced himself and everyone he knew that I was nothing more than a glorified secretary. That the only reason they kept me around was because they liked looking at my chest." Bitterness crept into Lucy's voice. "My dad was happy I'd been chosen to go to the conference. LuLu knew my title was real and figured it was a trip about the Gulf war, but didn't know it took me into it."

Jed made a face that showed it made sense no matter how bizarre it sounded. The door bell rang. His marine mask slid into place as he answered the door. Two men and a woman entered Jed's house. All five of them went into the sitting room. As if it were her own home, Lucy asked if they wanted tea or coffee. They declined. They reviewed the released media story and how it affected Lucy. Now that she was in the states, they wanted her to do a news conference to show everyone she was alive and well. As expected, Lucy was highly resistant to this. When the trio exited Jed's home an hour later, they had managed to convince her to do it. On the condition it is done Lucy's way. Her way—she would write the statement she'd read; it would be taped, not live, from the steps of the Lincoln memorial, with only two highly reputable reporters—who would be subject to final approval by the Directors of the State Department and Department of Defense. Arrangements were made for a follow-up appointment the next morning. If at all possible, they wanted to bring an end to the whole mess by the next evening. Lucy was agreeable to the sooner the better.

Jed escorted them out. After closing and locking the door, he returned to the sitting room to kneel in front of her.

"Are you okay?" He asked taking both her hands in his.

Staring into the flames, she answered with the obvious. "A little overwhelmed; especially since it could've been avoided if the right people would've kept their mouths shut."

He slid his hands from hers to around her back. "Lean on me and I'll get you through it."

She shifted forward to rest against his strong chest. "You have to decide a new path in your life. You don't need me throwing a wrench into it before it starts."

"You let me worry about that." He gave her a quick kiss on the cheek. "Ready for something to eat?"

"Actually, if you don't mind, I'd rather lay down." She said trying not to sound contrary.

He led her into his bedroom. While she took off her shoes, he pulled the pillows out. After she lay down, he tucked a blanket around her form. Prior to leaving the room, Jed kissed her gently on the lips. Lying there in the dark quiet, Lucy wondered why all of this was happening. What she wouldn't give to spend a few weeks at Danny and LuLu's till the incident became old news. She worked a plan in her head to do exactly that. Her bills were withdrawn directly from her checking account, so not like she had to return to Denver for that. Work owed her a few weeks of vacation. Lorning could survive without her for a while. Plus, it was time other people stepped up to the challenge. Months ago, Lucy had applied for several transfers to move back East. She'd done numerous phone interviews and signed follow-up releases without anything solid materializing. There was that odd comment on the Arlington in regards to an appointed position. Her brain couldn't begin to conceive to which they were referring. Dwelling on these things was not allowing her to relax. She imagined herself in a field of wildflowers. Some time later calves appeared frolicking among the flowers. She was on the hillside with Jed. But his kisses turned hard, his hands hurtful and ripping at her clothing. It wasn't Jed's face.

Lucy woke screaming "no Trevor, stop!"

Jed rushed into the room. "Lucy?"

Sitting up, Lucy tried to clear her head.

When Jed tried to put his arms around her, she growled. "Don't."

Needing to do something, he switched on the lamp by the bed. The light helped Lucy distinguish from the nightmare. Seeing it was, in fact, Jed sitting next to her, she leaned against him.

Lucy realized she had obviously confused him. "I'm awake now. When you came in I was still clearing the nightmare."

"Do you want to tell me about it?" He asked placing his arm around her.

"At the moment soldier, you don't have a need to know." She tried to kid with him.

"Let me know when the moment comes. I don't want to miss it." He stated seriously.

"I promise." She meant it as she kissed him on the cheek.

"Okay then, how about a snack while you work on your statement for tomorrow?" He suggested.

Lucy nodded.

Jed sat her at the kitchen table with pen, paper and a glass of chocolate milk. While she wrote, he prepared a late dinner for them. Lucy found it strange that he kept going outside. She tuned him out to get her thoughts on paper. It formed exactly how she wanted—short and to the point:

I am only here to dispute anyone questioning the truth of the Navy's previous report that I am alive and well. My return to the states was delayed due to a concussion and dehydration which required a few days rest. I'd like to thank the crew of the USS Arlington for their hospitality and the special force sent to rescue us. With special thanks to my marine escort to the states.

Lucy knew the last sentence may get removed. Since she would be meeting the Director of the Department of Defense, she would impress upon him what a terrific job Jed did.

Jed came inside with what looked like a plate of burgers. They smelled delicious. She tucked her final draft into her pocket. Soon he brought two plates to the table. Each contained a burger on a bun with all of the trimmings on the side. He placed mayonnaise and ketchup on the table before making Lucy another glass of chocolate milk. Lucy was sufficiently stuffed after her first burger while Jed ate a second. He shooed her from the kitchen when she tried to help him clear. Taking the pen and paper, she returned it to his study. It was a sparse room like the others. But she did find a stack of picture frames on a book shelf. Most of them were letters of commendations with a couple of medals. Lucy was impressed. She knew he was good, she hadn't realized how good. There were a few pictures. One was of him and a woman with blonde hair. They looked to be in their early twenties. He was wearing his dress uniform and she was in a white dress. Lucy felt an odd pang of envy. It was probably because they looked so much in love. And the way he spoke about her yesterday, in all likelihood still was.

"If only someone could love me with even a portion of that" she sighed to herself.

Restacking the frames, Lucy headed to the fire in the sitting room. She tossed her rough drafts into the flames. Curling in the corner of the sofa, Lucy became mesmerized staring into the dancing colors. She heard the phone ringing in the study and Jed answer it. Unable to discern actual words, Lucy drifted away again. Quite a bit later, Jed came into the sitting room after locking the house for the night. He stoked the fire, then took her hand to lead her to bed. He let her use the bathroom first. Washing her face, she examined her stitches. They were healing nicely. Brushing her teeth on that side had to be done slowly to not aggravate the sore inside of her cheek. On the outside, face moisturizer and lip balm soothed the tender skin. Lucy was surprised at how tired she was when she slid between the sheets. When Jed came to bed, he patted his chest for her to snuggle. Much to her surprise, he didn't make any moves that he wanted sex. Lucy couldn't decide if this was good or bad. Good meant he respected her; bad, he didn't want her anymore. Her mind didn't go any farther since she fell into a deep sleep.

During the night Jed stirred to feed the fire. Lucy heard him prowl around the house checking doors and windows. When he didn't return to bed as expected, she went in search of him. She found him in the kitchen standing with the refrigerator door open drinking a beer. Since his back was towards her, he didn't see her.

She spoke softly to him. "Jed?"

He turned his body full profile. Silhouetted by the light, she could see quite undeniably Jed still wanted her. But he didn't move towards her. Instead, he took another long swallow of the cold beer forcing himself to look away. Lucy didn't know how many more nights they'd have together. She decided to take a chance he wasn't ready for their affair to end yet either, but was the model of constraint in deference to her.

She called to him again. "Jed."

This time when he looked in her direction, she began unbuttoning her nightshirt. At the middle button, she slid the cloth slowly off her shoulders to cascade around her chest. As she began to fully expose her 36DDs, Jed startled her by slamming the refrigerator door closed. Two long strides had him pulling her roughly into his arms. His mouth ravaged hers. Lucy couldn't believe how the growing pleasure numbed the pain. Her nightshirt fell in a pile on the vinyl floor as her hands let go of it to eagerly stroke him. As their ardor grew, Lucy shivered in anticipation. Jed took it as a chill from the coolness of the kitchen. He moved them into the bedroom. Laying her on the bed, he slipped off her panties to caress and coax her. Dipping his fingers into her moistness had Lucy calling to Jed with intense desire. This pushed him beyond control, he tore off his boxers. Instead of ramming into her, he threw himself onto the bed pulling her on top of him. She wasn't exactly sure what to do, so she let his hands guide her. The feel of him inside her this way had her climaxing quickly and stronger than before. When she stopped to catch her breath, Jed waited patiently. He continued caressing her wherever it made her tingle. Still inside her, it didn't take much to entice her for another ride. During each build up, Jed voiced his definite delight with the feel of being inside her. The third time around, Jed came with Lucy in shudders of pure pleasure. They kissed tenderly as they drifted back down. Jed rolled onto his side pulling Lucy along with him. He tugged the blankets over them to stay warm while they slept.

The aroma of fresh brewed coffee drew Lucy out of her dreams. Opening her eyes, she looked around the room. Yes, she was in Jed's bed naked—the overnight romp had been reality not a dream. A steaming cup had been set on the nightstand. Lucy inhaled deeply. Checking the clock on the other nightstand, she saw she had plenty of time to get ready for their morning appointment. Lucy sat, putting a pillow behind her for support. Sipping at the coffee, she reviewed her clothing choices.

Jed entered the room wearing her robe.

"Good morning Lucy" he boomed cheerily.

Feeling shy, she responded quietly. "Good morning Jed."

Removing the almost empty cup from her hands, Jed leaned in to kiss her—a long, deliberate, assuring kiss.

Straightening slowly, he asked: "Eggs or bagel for breakfast?"

"Toasted bagel with cream cheese please", she requested. "After my shower?"

"Okay, I'll give you some privacy." He smiled accommodatingly as he left the room.

Not comfortable parading around naked, Lucy donned her nightshirt. Jed must've laid it across the bottom of the bed when he'd brought the coffee. As Lucy soaped in the shower, her body tingled at the memory of Jed's hands. She even thought for a moment Jed had entered the bathroom with the intention of joining her. When the shower curtain wasn't pushed aside,

Lucy experienced an unusual disappointment. Drying she noticed her robe hanging from the hook on the wall. She happily put it on. Not bothering to put anything else on, Lucy headed into the kitchen. Jed finished smearing the cream cheese on her bagel. He set it on the table along with a fresh cup of coffee.

"Thank you" she chirped.

"You're welcome" he replied. "Will you be ready to go in a half hour?"

"Yes, why so early? Our appointment isn't for another two hours." She asked.

He explained. "They called while you were showering to see if you could come earlier."

"Okay then, I won't dawdle." She bit into the bagel.

Jed left her alone in the kitchen. After she finished eating, she went into the bedroom to dress into a pair of pressed trousers, mock turtleneck and feminine sweater. It didn't take more than few minutes in the bathroom. A little lotion on her face smoothed the lingering dry patches. Dabbing ointment on the stitches, Lucy wondered if Jed could take her to the base to have them removed later today. A quick swath of lipstick gave a little feminine color. Curls softly framed her face. Collecting her purse, Lucy headed for the foyer with a minute to spare. Jed stood there waiting in full marine regalia. Lucy barely kept her mouth from falling open in astonishment at how formidable he looked. It was hard to imagine this as the same man who'd made passionate giving love to her the last two nights. As usual, he helped her with her wrap; placing a light kiss on her bruised cheek. They took his range rover since the rental company was fetching the other car sometime that morning. The sun shined bright. In the distance, gray snow clouds could be seen.

At the capitol building things went smoothly. They had a doctor waiting to remove Lucy's stitches. It made her not look as injured. The trio they'd met the day before seemed almost as anxious as Lucy to get this done. As soon as things were cleared, the reporters selected were phoned. Both eagerly agreed to meeting at the Lincoln Memorial immediately. The small group traveled to the well-known building. Jed stayed within arms distance of Lucy at all times. His demeanor was that of the protective marine bull dog. Both news crews arrived within minutes of each other. A representative for the Department of Defense stood on the side lines. He motioned to Jed. The two men spoke a few words, then Jed returned to Lucy. With the guidelines reviewed they were ready to tape.

The State Department introduced her. She read her short statement.

One of the reporters asked "Ms. Seeir, we understand you ordered the destruction of the Armadillo. Would you tell us why?"

The gentleman from the Department of Defense took a step towards the camera, but stopped as Lucy answered deftly. "I'm sorry. To answer that would be a breech of security."

The reporter followed up still trying to ascertain the reason. "Is that why the terrorists wanted the Armadillo?"

"You would have to ask them that, not me." She averted a revealing answer.

The other reporter spoke. "Ms. Seeir, we can see the bruising on your face. Would you please tell us what provoked your captors to brutalize you when the two men were left relatively untouched?"

Before Lucy could answer, a familiar male voice spoke from behind her. "She shot one of the terrorists to prevent them from getting a kill shot on me."

Lucy turned around to see the young soldier with his arm in a sling.

"Corporal Barnes!" She exclaimed.

Ignoring military protocol, she gave the young man a hug. "I'm so glad you are alright."

The corporal returned the embrace the best he could with his free arm. "Yes ma'am, thanks to you. It's good to see you're safe, too."

"If you were both taken back to the USS Arlington, why is this a surprise?" The reporter's question reminded Lucy of the situation.

Tears of relief ran uninhibited down her face as she broke free of the corporal. He immediately stood at attention next to the sergeant major.

"Yes, we were." Corporal Barnes replied. "I was flown out as soon as they stabilized my wound."

The reporters played off each others questions. "Ms. Seeir, a source stated your departure from the USS Arlington was unexpected and unexplained. Could you clarify please?"

Lucy kept the sarcasm from her voice. "I had a concussion; being on the ship made it impossible to avoid the resulting motion sickness. My departure was planned by the pertinent parties. One might suspect the reliability of your source."

The man from the Department of Defense cracked a momentary smile at her answer.

"Where did you go and why did it take so long for you to return to the states?" One of them shot another question.

Lucy glanced at Jed for help. He nodded to the man from the Department of Defense. The gentleman intentionally walked between the reporters and their camera crew. He stopped directly in front of Lucy to obviously block further contact. Both Jed and Corporal Barnes flanked the man in the suit to prevent the cameras from capturing any more of Lucy.

The man turned to face the reporters and their cameras. "Ms. Seeir has been through enough of an ordeal. And with her injuries, we didn't want her traveling alone. We had her escorted to the states by a highly competent and experienced marine. Now that Ms. Seeir is safely home, we hope this ends any further intrusion to allow her to return to a normal life. Thank you."

The three men and Lucy didn't move until the news crews had been ushered to their vehicles by the group who coordinated the news conference.

When the man in the suit turned to face her again, Lucy sighed in relief. "Thank you."

"You're welcome ma'am. If you need anything, please give me a call." He handed her a business card prior to walking away.

Lucy and Corporal Barnes talked about his injury. Jed handled the three from the state department.

Jed returned to Lucy's side. "We need to get going for another appointment."

Lucy wasn't sure what he meant, but she played along. She and the corporal hugged good-bye. Jed shook the young soldier's hand.

In the range rover, Lucy asked, "What appointment?"

"You are having lunch with the Director of the Department of Defense." Jed explained.

When they arrived at the federal building, Jed escorted Lucy to a conference room.

At the door, he took Lucy's hand. "Here's my cell number. Have one of the secretaries call me when you are ready to leave."

"What? You're not coming?" She asked in a panic.

"This meeting is strictly for you." He glanced around them to verify the immediate perimeter was safe before kissing her. "Don't worry, you'll do fine."

Jed strode away. Placing her hand on the door, Lucy took a deep breath. Entering the room, she received a welcome greeting from the director. He set the security level so Lucy knew she could talk freely. It seemed unusual that lunch was a buffet. Lucy soon discovered why. Throughout lunch, other directors and the like came in to talk to her while they grabbed lunch, too. With the level of attendees, Lucy understood why Jed had not been invited. An hour later, a curtain opened to reveal a plasma screen covering the entire wall. Her news conference listed as next on CNN. Everyone in the room quieted to listen.

The clip began with a shot of Lucy walking along the front of the Lincoln Memorial with Jed. Luckily, they hadn't held hands or kissed. Then it cut to her on the steps making her statement. The close up displayed her bruised face, but with the way the heavy gray clouds had moved in the natural lighting hid the depth of the discoloration. Lucy noticed when they panned back that she was filmed off center. The camera frame included her marine protector behind and to the side of her. The rest of the interview played uncut, including the director's assistant stepping in at the end.

The individuals in the room congratulated her on the statement and how she handled the questions. The luncheon continued for another two hours. The buffet had been removed. The coffee urn remained. A cup of coffee kept her hands busy. Plus, the constant caffeine kept her alert. As the meet-n-greet wound down so did Lucy. The director shook her hand, then excused himself. One of his assistants phoned Jed. When the assistant left her alone in the lobby, Lucy located a ladies room. Out of habit, she refreshed her lipstick. It was then she noticed dark circles had formed under her eyes since the interview. Hoping fresh air would improve her color, she waited outside. The sidewalk had a thick white coating and flakes continued falling. By the time Jed pulled to the curb, Lucy had to shake the snow off prior to climbing inside.

Jed gave her a big smile. "How'd it go?"

"Okay" she said with a yawn.

She noticed he was still in his uniform. "What did you do while I was schmoozing with the higher ups?"

"Had some of my own schmoozing to do and figured might as well take care of it today." He stated.

She could tell their discussion of his post military career had helped. "Aha! You narrowed your job choices."

"Yep, down to two, but they need to work it out. They'll let me know in a few weeks which one." His voice was full of pride with his decision.

Traffic and the weather made the drive take quite a bit longer. Lucy dozed.

Jed roused her with a kiss. "Sleeping beauty, we're home."

Opening her eyes, she saw they were in his garage. He was standing next to her on the passenger side with the door open. She took his offered hand to help her from the vehicle. He didn't let go of her hand until they were in the house. He went into the sitting room to stack wood on the glowing embers. Lucy followed feeling lost. And her yawning wouldn't stop.

Jed caught her yawning again. "Looks like jet lag has caught up with you; go lay down. We have no plans tonight."

She willingly complied with his suggestion. Unable to locate her nightshirt, she searched his dresser till she found a soft t-shirt. She stripped to her panties, then pulled on the t-shirt. Jed had a well muscled chest where her chest fit comfortably in his t-shirt. The chill in the room quickly chased her under the blankets. Laying there drifting, she heard him enter the room. Opening one eye slightly, she watched as he removed his uniform. Unexpectedly, he slid under the sheets with her. He snuggled into her, his hands coming to a rest on her butt. For as tired as she was, she wanted to stay awake to revel in their coziness. If only she could have a relationship like this permanently, not just for a few days. This wasn't good letting her heart get involved. She allowed herself to enjoy the closeness, but she forced her mind to review the luncheon.

Several minutes later, Jed sighed. "I thought you were going to sleep."

"That was the idea." She remarked.

"Is it because I joined you?" He asked.

"What? It's not that or maybe it is. Never mind, it doesn't matter." Lucy rambled.

Jed shifted to look into her face. "Lucy?"

Being overtired made her reckless. "I like this too much."

He chuckled. "That should be a good thing."

"How is that good?" She climbed out of bed in a huff.

"You're not making any sense." Jed sat causing the blankets to fall to his waist exposing his bare chest.

"Whatever!" She stormed from the room.

Her mind warred within itself. She wanted to go home to what she was used to. This would all become nothing more than an excerpt from a really good book. But she also wanted to stay to experience as much of Jed as possible. Was the Jed she got to know this week the real Jed? Or was he merely accommodating her because it was his duty and to get a little on the side? What was reality and what was delusion? As usual, she overanalyzed everything. She yanked open the refrigerator door. Not finding what she wanted, she slammed it shut.

"Are you going to tell me what's going on?" Jed leaned against the door jam watching.

"No!" She exclaimed in irritation.

He didn't budge. He merely waited.

This infuriated Lucy even more. "What are you standing there for?"

"Just waiting for you to either calm down or talk to me." He stated peacefully.

"Ooh!" She threw her arms up and banged out the back door.

As she stood in her panties and his t-shirt getting covered in snow, Lucy came to her senses. Going back inside, she discovered Jed drinking a beer with the refrigerator door open.

He closed the refrigerator door. "Have you cooled off sufficiently?"

Her teeth chattered as she answered. "Y-y-yes-sss."

"Is it safe to warm you?" He asked seriously.

"J-jed-d I'm s-sorry-y-y th-this is a-a-a-ll n-n-ew-w to me-e." She shivered from the snow melting down her neck.

"Don't worry about it." He said sincerely. "And as much as I enjoy you wearing my t-shirt with strategically placed wet spots, I don't want you catching pneumonia."

Taking hold of the hem of the t-shirt he tugged it off over her head leaving her in only her bottoms like Jed. He led her into the bathroom where he tossed the wet shirt into the tub. Grabbing the hand towel, Jed dried her hair.

"Come on, we are going to bed so you can sleep, not fool around." He commanded.

Once again between the sheets, they curled into each other. Lucy's cold perked up nipples rested against his warm hairy chest. This sensual contact perked up Jed's boxers. However, he kept to his word. Amazingly, it took only a few minutes for Lucy to fall asleep. Several hours later she woke alone again. She was beginning to wonder if Jed ever slept. A light shone from the study. Remembering she only wore panties, she donned her robe. When she knocked lightly on the door frame, Jed looked up with a smile.

"Well hello sleepy head. Do you feel better?" He extended his arm inviting her to sit on his lap.

She obliged. "I do and I'm sorry for earlier. I went a little berserk."

He kissed her. "With all that happened over the last week you were entitled to 'a little berserk.'"

"How do you know I'm not that way all the time?" She asked.

"I think I could deal with it." He stated.

Not sure if he was kidding, Lucy changed the subject. "Whatcha doin'?"

"Sorting through pictures looking for a particular one." He answered.

Lucy looked at the pictures, too. There were team shots of missions he'd been on. There was one that seemed familiar to her. It was a group of eight men in black gear standing in front of a ship insignia—the USS Monroe.

"Aha" she thought. "I've been in that war room."

But the next picture tweaked at her memory too. It was a candid shot of only four of the men climbing out of a helicopter. She'd seen this picture before. Only it wasn't a picture; it was a memory as she was being ushered onto another helicopter.

"Oh my God Jed!" She could hardly believe what she was about to say. "You were on the black ops team that . . ."

". . . that you saved by locating and deciphering our transmissions." He finished her sentence.

She looked incredulously at him. "You knew it was me?"

"At the time, I didn't know who you were. I caught a glimpse of you as you were loaded onto the other helicopter. You were crying." Melancholy laced his words

"Yes, I was. I stalled until I knew your team had made it safely on board." Her eyes got misty reliving that feeling.

Unable to hold the bottled emotions that day had created, Lucy gave him the big bear hug she'd wanted to give them all. He held onto her with equal emotion. Three of his crew had been killed and the remaining five had no idea if they'd get out alive. One didn't because of the extent of his injuries. If only they'd been retrieved a few days earlier. Lucy replayed her time on the Monroe.

The call had come in for two experts on satellite communications. Lucy had been selected because of her software knowledge on the type of satellite. Jim Hughes was the hardware expert on the radio devices used for sending and receiving. They had exactly six hours to get to an Air Force Base near of DC. They had been briefed on transport that communication with a certain satellite had gone down and were unable to re-establish protocol with it. They needed to know if it was being controlled by another party or if it had been damaged. Then get it operational as soon as possible. Both experts were irritated that they were not given the specific satellite and radio device prior to their departure. They could've reviewed the technical documentation on the flight to the Gulf. Error read outs would've been useful, too. They would soon discover that what the military felt they needed to know about the actual situation versus what they needed to know to do their jobs effectively varied greatly. For two days, Lucy and Jim worked the problem around the clock. They determined it was a sending malfunction due to damage. The receiver and satellite were functioning properly. There was nothing left for them to do. They believed the few hours of data they'd been given from the satellite download indicated that whatever the radio was attached to had been destroyed beyond salvaging. The officer in charge of the mission chose to release the entire download from when the team had lost initial contact. However, Jim and Lucy still did not know people were in grave danger on the other end. She kept seeing the same pattern repeated every four hours; she felt it was significant. Based on the information they had been given, it could be considered static or device feedback from trying to uplink to the satellite. Meeting again with the officer in charge, they had uncovered nothing useful. On the way out of the room, Jim overheard the officer's assistant make reference to notifying families. A heated exchange ensued between the marine in charge and the civilian experts. The commander of the ship had been called to deal with the tension. In the best interest of the team they needed to extract from in country, the commander briefed the civilians fully on the situation. Keeping her ire in check, she determined what information she needed to decipher the static if it was what she thought it was. With the help of the ship's commander, she got the specifics from the marine on their communication protocol down to the exact phrasing and code names used. Jim had to be excused prior to the marine divulging such sensitive details. Plus, she had to sign yet another non-disclosure agreement. Armed with the script the special operation team would use, she set to work deciphering the encrypted binary code into words. A few hours later she had it. She gave the coordinates and conditions to both the marine officer in charge of the mission and the ship's commander together. At first they weren't confident. She pushed for any pictures from satellite reconnaissance which might include those coordinates since the team had gone missing. Consecutive night shots from the infrared satellite confirmed hot spots at her coordinates. It would be another few hours till extraction could occur. The marine officer wanted her and Jim off the ship. The ship's commander felt he needed all of his resources to be on alert for saving the lost marines. For safety reasons, Lucy and Jim were restricted to quarters. They were also told that as soon as the marines landed, the civilians would leave. The few hours they waited frayed her nerves. There would be no other way to know for sure those men were safe unless she saw them herself. When they were ushered from their quarters, she mutinied. She could see the approaching rescue helicopter. The departing bird waited for the civilians on the smaller helipad a few hundred yards from the main helipad. She intentionally dumped the contents of her bag. A gust of wind helped her by sending a pieces tumbling along the deck. Sailors chased after her clothing. By the time they retrieved all of it, the other helicopter had landed. Her escorts were perturbed by her obvious actions. As the four haggard looking soldiers climbed from the rescue helicopter, Jim and Lucy were loaded onto theirs. She stopped to watch with tears running down her face as her heart reached out to them. Her heart squeezed when one of the marines looked in her direction.

"If that pig-headed colonel had given us all of the information at the start, there would be five in that picture." She could finally vent her anger about that situation.

"Wow! I bet that felt good after all this time." Jed used comic relief to ease their strong emotions related to the incident.

Lucy agreed. "It does actually."

"I'll let you in on a little secret." He whispered. "The colonel was asked to resign his commission after his failure in judgment on that mission."

"Really?" She hoped he wasn't pulling her chain.

"Yep." He tried to hide the smile of joy he felt, too.

She kissed him. Jed took full advantage of her lips. The robe gaped open giving his hands easy access to her bare skin. Her chest his prime target. As his hands slid lower, his mouth took extreme pleasure suckling.

Lucy called out his name at the dual delight. "Jed, oh Jed . . ."

He maneuvered around his boxers and her lace panties so they could merge.

"Lucy, you are so incredible." Jed grunted and groaned to his climax.

Lucy rode the breathtaking wave with him.

Sated she nuzzled his neck; he caressed her back. They relaxed in their afterglow. A gust of wind rattled the old windows of the study.

Jed said quietly. "According to the weather channel, the storm has churned into a full blown Nor'easter. It looks like you'll be stuck here for another day or two."

Pressing her torso against his, she replied. "Can you put up with me for a bit longer?"

"I think I can manage." He chuckled while sliding his hand to fondle one of her bountiful breasts.

Lucy gasped as the tips of his fingers tenderly teased the nipple. Since they hadn't disentangled, she felt him grow inside her. This stoked their passion. Lucy began rocking her hips to urge him along. Jed gripped her buttocks to stand. She clung to him unsure of his intentions. It was only a few steps from the study into the bedroom. Jed laid her on the bed, lying on top of her to stay together. They made love slowly—touching and discovering each other at an intensely intimate level. It gave Lucy a wonderful new experience of what a man and woman could share.

Chapter Seven

In the morning, Lucy woke to Jed's body tucked into hers.

"He does sleep without the aid of strong muscle relaxants." She thought as she carefully slipped out of his embrace.

There was a substantial chill in the bedroom. Donning her robe, she went to check on the fire. As suspected, it had burned down to glowing embers. She stirred them to add logs from the nearby rack. Taking the hall to the kitchen, she prepared a pot of coffee. As she waited for it to brew, she recalled seeing wood stacked yesterday afternoon. Slipping her size sevens into Jed's boots, Lucy stepped outside. Wind blew the snow every which way. Wearing only the robe, the chill crept in everywhere. It immediately chased her back inside. She shivered uncontrollably at that stupid stunt. There were two ways to warm up—curling into Jed or taking a hot shower. Since she didn't want to shock him awake, Lucy chose the shower. Steam escaped from the small room when she opened the door. Padding quietly to the bedroom, she opened the flight bag for her khakis and his sweatshirt. She closed the bedroom door when she exited to keep any noise she might make from disturbing him. Her wrap wouldn't be substantial enough to fend a raging blizzard. One of Jed's coats hung on a peg by the back door. Even though her feet would get soaked in her canvas tennies, they could dry in front of the fire. If she wore his boots, the snow would go inside making the insulation wet and difficult to dry. Outside, she found the huge stack of wood. The tarp covering it was weighed down from the snow. She managed to free one side to pull out a pile of the split logs. A few trips later, she had the rack by the fireplace stacked precariously full. On the last trip, she secured the tarp to prevent the wind and snow from getting underneath. Retracing her steps in the house, she wiped the floors dry. She poured herself a cup of coffee prior to perusing the groceries Jed bought the first day home. The man certainly liked beans. She located a large crock pot in a box on the top shelf in the pantry. The pork roast Jed selected was in the refrigerator, not the freezer with the other meats. Pork and beans for dinner should be satisfactory to the man of the house.

"Lucy?" It sounded like Jed had called her name.

Opening the door to the bedroom, she asked quietly. "Are you calling me?"

"Yes." He sounded relieved as he patted the bed.

Per his behest, she moved into the room to sit next to him. Peering up into her face, he put his hand on hers.

"Jed, what's wrong?" She asked because he was acting strangely.

"While you slept yesterday afternoon, I chopped enough wood to last the storm." He paused.

Lucy teased. "Were you expecting it to last a month?"

Ignoring her interruption he continued. "I kind of over did it and I, um well, my back is giving me problems today. I'm sorry."

"Why are you apologizing? We over did it." She corrected kissing him. "What do you need other than your medication?"

"That's a start." He replied hesitantly.

She fetched the bottle of medication from the medicine cabinet and a cup of coffee to wash down the dose. She left to make eggs and toast for breakfast. Hearing he was up, she moved to view the hallway. He was wearing her robe making his way slowly into the bathroom. It didn't take long for the shower to be heard running. She kept their breakfast warm in the oven. Going into the bedroom, she fetched his empty cup. From the bathroom, she heard a bang followed by explicit vulgarities.

Opening the door slightly, Lucy called into Jed. "Is everything okay?"

A few more vulgarities elicited under his breath before he answered her directly. "Would you please help me?"

She poked her head around the shower curtain to see him leaning against the wall with a grimace of pain on his face. She shucked her shirt and pants. Pulling the shower nozzle from its hook, she rinsed the heavy lather from his skin. To rinse his hair, she had to join him. He kept his face down evading any eye contact. With him suds free, she shut off the water.

"I need you to help me or we're both going to end up falling." She stated the obvious.

Standing him up straight was easy. Getting him over the edge of the tub was a challenge. With that managed, Lucy quickly dried him. In the hallway, they had a disagreement.

Jed demanded. "I want to go to the sitting room."

"You're not dressed." Lucy tried to dissuade him.

"You can bring me something to wear." His disposition was surly at best.

Merely to keep the peace, she got him to the sofa. However, she didn't stay to help him get comfortable. Instead, she went to fetch him something to wear. Back in the sitting room, Lucy helped him dress. The whole time his face was made of granite. When Lucy went for their breakfast, she checked the medication bottle. It wasn't the same as what he'd taken in Paris. She located his bag. It had been unpacked. Checking the trash in the bathroom, she found the empty bottle. Dr. Doven had evidently only given him enough of this kind to get him home. She could understand why his regular prescription was different. It wasn't addictive like the ones Dr. Doven had doled out. Plus, it dealt with decreasing the inflammation to relieve the pain, not mask it. With a marine it made sense. Unfortunately, it would take a couple doses till Jed felt relief. It also meant in the meantime, he'd wear his face of stone. Rolling her eyes heavenward, Lucy sighed. With the good came the bad. This bad would be a walk in the park compared to the past. She got their food from the oven to dish onto plates for both of them. By the time she re-entered the sitting room, Jed had propped himself in the corner of the sofa with the television remote in hand. He took the offered plate. She placed his coffee on the side table within easy reach. They ate in silence. Before taking their empty plates to the kitchen, she fueled the fire.

As she left the room, she asked "Is it okay if I use your cell phone to make a some calls?"

"Yeah, whatever you want." He grumbled inhospitably.

In the kitchen, she placed the dirty dishes into the dishwasher. The cell phone had been on the desk last night. She closed the door of the study to talk privately. First, she phoned her boss, the division manager who happened to be Jim Hughes. He'd made a name for himself on their USS Monroe mission, which hastened his climb up the corporate ladder. Jim was thrilled she was okay, but needed to call her back. Playing with the phone, she saw LuLu had called yesterday afternoon. The 12 minute length of the call indicated Jed had spoken to her. On the list of calls made, there was also one to her dad for 18 minutes yesterday. Lucy had called him the day before. Pressing dial, she figured she might as well hear from the other end. Her dad explained Jed had called to tell him CNN would be airing a short interview with Lucy. He thanked Jed for informing him and for watching over his little girl. Of course, this led to the usual conversation with her father voicing his opinion that she needed a man to take care of her. And Jed sounded like a good man she should consider. Lucy made light of it to quickly end the connection. Her father failed to understand it wasn't because Lucy turned men away. It was that none approached her for anything other than business. Prior to phoning LuLu, Lucy took a fresh cup of coffee to Jed along with his bottle of medication. She placed the items on the side table without his noticing. Or if he did, he didn't acknowledge it.

Back in the study, the cell phone buzzed across the desk. Lucy answered it. It was Jim. They talked about what happened. He understood her sketchy answers. When she broached the subject of what project she would be placed on next, he danced around the topic. This caused her to ask directly if her employment with the company had been put in jeopardy.

Jim's answer couldn't have been any more cryptic if he tried. "The only way your employment with us would be terminated would be by your choosing."

They discussed the weather postponing her return to Denver. Jim told her to take as long as she needed. She needn't worry; he and his wife would continue to keep an eye the house. The company had allotted a month's recovery from the trauma for those involved. As her boss, he would not allow her access into the building until the end of those 30 days starting today. Plus, she had five weeks of vacation she could tap into at any time. As her friend, he expected her to call if she needed anything.

"Huh", her mind in awe, "I do have a couple of weeks to spend with LuLu."

The phone began beeping it needed charging. She ended the call with Jim. Digging in the desk drawers for the charger, Lucy learned more about Jed. First, all but one of the drawers was organized efficiently. Bills and important documents were in marked file folders. Office supplies: pens, pencils, stapler, paper clips, scissors, tape—were neatly arranged. The charger was in its labeled box in a drawer with other similar devices. Even with having plugged in the phone, Lucy continued opening drawers. She found his gun, or rather one of his guns. Its loaded clip located in a different drawer. One drawer had a box with a lid. Removing the lid exposed pictures of his wife, letters she wrote him, their marriage and her death certificates. Lucy replaced the lid knowing that would be an unforgivable intrusion of privacy. She opened the messy drawer. It was where he kept his mission pictures. They were not boxed nor clipped together, merely in a loose pile. She pulled them out to put them in some semblance of order to place in one of the empty file folders she'd seen.

Lucy came across a picture of him in uniform with a team in black operations gear on the USS Endeavor. The date on the picture indicated a week after she'd been on board the Endeavor. But she was interested in why he wasn't in gear. Something prevented him from joining the mission. She went to a previous drawer to pull his medical records file. It ordered by date, making it easy to find what she expected. Jed had experienced a serious injury to his lower back on another mission five months prior to the Endeavor picture. He'd required a second operation a month after the initial surgery. The prognosis from both had not been optimistic. Three months of intensive physical therapy enabled Jed to pass the physical permitting him to stay in the marines. Reading the letter from his physician and his commanding officer, Lucy surmised he'd been relegated to the sidelines because of his back. Unable to be on the front line, he was made the officer in charge coordinating from base, which happened to be the Endeavor. The mission must have gone successfully since she found a picture with the same team at an air force base with a date two months later. Her mind created a timeline of events. From the information Jed had told her earlier, his wife had been dead for a few years before the Monroe. Lucy felt oddly relieved that he was a widower by the time they'd met. It crossed her mind he might have realized while they were on the Endeavor that she was the one from the Monroe. Recognizing him had been impossible. Their operations gear and face paint intentionally made them look nondescript. Hearing a noise, she replaced everything to check. Jed was slowly making his way across the sitting room to the hall. Lucy removed the empty coffee cup from his hand to take into the kitchen. But first, she fed the fire. On her way to the kitchen, she passed him going into the bathroom. She prepared a glass of ice water for him, then carried it to the sitting room.

The weather channel reviewed the latest on the storm. Current readings indicated 15 inches in DC. They were predicting it would cease snowing late evening. Some nearby rural areas had reported loss of power from the wind gusts knocking down trees and power lines. The Nor'easter stretched far inland. The states north of them were being pummeled as well. Central Pennsylvania, where her father lived, showed ten inches. LuLu and Danny were located on the fringe of the storm in western New York. Nonetheless, a foot had fallen there because of the generating lake effect snows.

At Jed's return, he spoke in a subdued tone. "Lucy, would you please get me a glass of water?"

She smiled. "Already done, anything else?"

He reached his hand to rub the length of her arm. "Thank you, no."

"If you do, just holler" she responded in a bubbly tone on her way from the room.

In the study, she called LuLu. First topic was naturally the weather. Lucy brought up her conversation with Jim. LuLu was ecstatic. Danny would be leaving on a business trip in three days. He'd be gone for ten so the timing would be perfect. The subject of Jed was broached. However, Lucy side stepped it safely for the moment. There would be no avoiding the topic upon her arrival at the farm. She had to make sure it was after Danny's departure. The weather discounted the next two days. It would take a day of travel to drive there. Then again it might not be a smart move with a concussion. She asked LuLu to see if there were any flights. LuLu teased Lucy that she didn't know how Lucy was surviving without her laptop. Normally, Lucy had it with her whenever she traveled. However, staying in a hotel in a different country was not the same as being on a U.S. military base or ship. Lucy remained silent while LuLu searched on the computer. There was a flight arriving at the Buffalo airport the same day Danny was scheduled to fly out. The flight would leave Dulles first thing in the morning with a connecting flight in Pittsburgh after a four hour layover. LuLu began booking it while Lucy went into the bedroom to get the only credit card she had taken overseas. Lucy returned to the study to write down the flight information and confirmation number. Knowing they would see each other in three days, the best friends ended their call.

Not knowing what to do now, Lucy sat at Jed's desk playing with her credit card. It flipped onto the edge of the desk causing Lucy to grab for it. In stopping her card from falling, she knocked a ledger book onto the floor. When Lucy picked it up, a manila envelope slipped out dumping its contents. As she retrieved the scattered papers, Lucy saw a picture of her. It was her standing in the helicopter with tears streaming down her face staring at the returning team members. It must've been taken by the same person who snapped the pictures of the special operations team. This prompted her to see what the rest of the papers were. There were a couple pictures of him from those moments.

Also a note stating: "Her name is Lucy Seeir. She's a tech expert from Lorning."

Lucy looked at the post mark on the worn envelope. It had been stamped a few weeks after his initial back injury. When she tried sliding the photographs and letter into the envelope, they caught on something. Intentionally dumping the envelope, two more pictures floated out. They were both of Lucy from on the Monroe. One was taken in the mess hall where she drank lots of coffee while she worked on her company laptop. The other was her smiling at a sailor. She had gone on deck to get fresh air. The sailor responsible for her not falling overboard had been telling her an amusing story. The papers went into the envelope without a problem this time.

Lucy thought "if he has a picture of me . . ." as she pilfered one of the pictures of him.

She put it in her purse with her credit card and flight information. In the sitting room, Lucy found Jed clicking impatiently through the television channels.

"I can't believe the crap they have on tv." He complained.

"I take it your medication hasn't made a dent yet?" She wasn't going to act like he wasn't cranky.

His answer was truthful. "No, it hasn't so I took another dose."

She raised her eyebrows. "Is that wise?"

"You should be happy I didn't take the whole damn bottle." He said bitterly.

Lucy didn't reply. She merely left the room. With Jed's foul mood and the storm outside Lucy felt trapped. If she'd had her laptop, she'd have a distraction. Dinner didn't need her to do anything. Making cookies would keep her busy for at least an hour. When the cookies were done, Lucy carried a few on a plate along with a glass of milk to Jed. He gave her the strangest look.

She couldn't help herself. "I figured I'd help you along by baking cookies laced with arsenic."

Okay, now they were both cranky. Not liking her deteriorating disposition, Lucy decided to lay down in the bedroom. A half hour had passed when Jed disturbed her mental walk in the wildflowers. No words were spoken. He stretched next to her, resting his hand on hers. The music on the radio flowed around them. As they shared the serenity, she recorded every detail in her memory as an alternative to the field of wildflowers. After a while, his snoring indicated the overlapping doses had taken affect. She gently removed herself from the bed to leave him sleeping in peace. He may have thought there was only crap on television, but she came across a Doris Day-Rock Hudson movie. Since she couldn't spend all day making love with Jed, Lucy fell to tried and true habits. She curled under the blanket he had used earlier. It smelled like him making her smile.

He remained in the bedroom the rest of the day. She checked on him once on her way to the bathroom. He appeared to be asleep. Whether he was sleeping or staying away because of his surliness, she let him be.

Late evening, the bear emerged grumpy from his cave in search of food. Lucy prepared a plate for him. While Jed ate, she put the leftovers into the refrigerator and cleaned the kitchen. When he finished eating, he kissed her on the cheek prior to retiring to the bedroom. At least his gait seemed less cumbersome. She wanted to follow him. If he wanted her to join him, he'd have indicated as much. Her ability to understand this man rather amazed her. Brushing it off, she went to watch another movie.

The snow had tapered to intermittent flurries leaving twenty inches of snow by the time Lucy needed to refill the log rack. The back light popped when Lucy flipped the light switch. There was no way she was going to attempt replacing it until daylight. Instead, she went about the task of fetching wood in the dark. However, she misjudged where the edge of the patio was resulting in her tumbling into the thick white layer. At least it was softer than her recent landings. Scoops of the white cold flakes made it inside Jed's coat. She shook them out the best she could without removing the coat. After she completed her task, she removed her cold wet khakis and sweatshirt. Wearing only her underwear, Lucy warmed her skin in front of the fire prior to curling under the blanket on the sofa. While watching television she dozed.

The next morning, Lucy was disturbed by a scraping noise. After throwing on her stiff dry clothes, she poked her head out the front door. A young man in camouflage was shoveling the walk.

Lucy called to him. "Good morning."

"Ma'am" the soldier snapped to attention.

"At ease soldier, would you like to come inside for a hot cup of coffee when you finish?" She offered.

The young marine looked uncomfortable. "I don't know if I should ma'am."

Lucy played him. "I'll be insulted if you don't."

"Yes ma'am." He answered.

"Just let yourself in. The kitchen is straight back the hall." She closed the door.

Lucy pulled the bedroom door shut to prevent the young marine from hearing Jed's snoring. By the time the marine walked into the kitchen, Lucy had made breakfast. She motioned for him to sit. A plate full of food was placed in front of the young man along with the promised cup of coffee.

"Thank you ma'am, but you needn't go to all this trouble." His twang accentuated by nervousness.

Before Lucy could say anything, Jed's voice boomed from the doorway. "I didn't know we were entertaining enlisted men this morning."

The soldier snapped to attention knocking the chair to the floor. "Sergeant major!"

Jed made the young marine sweat for the extended time it took him to cross the kitchen to sit at the table. "You're food is getting cold grunt."

"Sir?" the young marine queried.

"Sit down and eat Grainley." Jed ordered.

"Yes sir" the marine obeyed.

Lucy placed a plate and cup in front of Jed.

As he was filling his fork, Jed gave a gentler order to the soldier. "Grainley savor it; it's not mess hall food."

Grainley noticeably slowed the emptying of his plate. Jed began conversing with the young gun. The two marines chatted through breakfast. Lucy enjoyed listening while making sure their coffee cups never reached bottom.

When Grainley completed his meal, he stood. "Thank you Mrs. Sergeant Major Warloc, you cook just like my mama."

"That explains the extra weight you put on over the holidays." Jed pointed out as he stood, too.

The young marine acknowledged. "Yes sergeant major, that's why I'm doing errand duty."

Lucy felt guilty. "I'm sorry. I didn't know feeding you was a bad thing. I was trying to . . ."

Jed kissed her. "It's okay Babe. He needs the protein. It's the sweets he has to avoid."

The young marine headed for the door. Jed leaned on Lucy as they followed.

"Sergeant major, I couldn't help notice your back is giving you problems. Is there anything else you or the missus needs?" Grainley asked.

Jed looked at Lucy. "You need a few things don't you?"

Amazed he'd read her mind, she merely nodded.

"I'll call your C.O. to let him know I need you back at 1100 hours for use the rest of the day." He arranged.

"Yes sir. Ma'am." Grainley saluted prior to exiting.

Lucy hugged Jed. "How did you know?"

"Being cooped up with me in this condition can't be fun." He answered holding onto her.

She didn't want him feeling guilty. "I don't mind that. But I don't know what to do to help."

"You are doing great. I'm just not used to having anyone around." Jed admitted.

"I hope you still think so after I share my plans." She remarked, then filled him in on her flight to visit with LuLu.

He seemed truly glad she arranged to spend time with her best friend. But it did make Lucy wonder if he'd be relieved to be rid of her. For the time being, Lucy would take advantage of her day out of the house.

The first errand they had to take care of would be filling Jed's medication. Jed also gave her his cell phone to keep with her for the day. Driving around the nation's capital blanketed with snow made Lucy wished she could've seen it decorated for Christmas. After the girl behind the counter at the pharmacy stared strangely at her, Lucy kept her cap tipped down in front. Of course, the military escort didn't help. She had no problem getting the young marine to not "ma'am" her. But she couldn't persuade him to use Lucy instead of Mrs. Sergeant Major Warloc. As the day progressed, she discovered why. The young man worshipped the ground on which Jed walked. It got weird when he saw her buy the suitcase. Explaining the fake marriage would be too hard. Plus, it would sound better coming from Jed. Instead, she told him the truth of having lost hers and needing a new one to visit a friend for a couple weeks. When she got to the lingerie department, Grainley politely excused himself. They agreed to meet in front of the Dunkin' Donuts in an hour. Lucy had planned on getting a few essentials, but seeing an adorable baby doll, she added it to her selections. The regular women's wear was on the same floor giving her the opportunity to find jeans. At the coffee shop, Grainley waited at a table with her cappuccino.

"It's 1500 hours. Were there any other stores you wanted to go into Mrs. Warloc?" He asked.

"You know Jed is retiring right?" Lucy prompted.

"Yes ma'-missus." The young man responded.

She stated. "Well I need your help picking a few shirts for him in his new job."

"I don't understand." He replied while following her.

"You have the same upper build as Jed. I want the shirts to be comfortable, not binding." She explained by squeezing the young man's bicep.

"Oh" the marine mouthed his comprehension.

Grainley tried on every shirt and sweater Lucy loaded into his arms. Of which, half fit comfortably. From those, only four met the approval of her discerning eye. There was one more shop she wanted to try. Here she looked for a sport coat. It had to be classic while reflecting Jed's rough edge. Lucy laughed at the diametric opposition of this notion. One of the five sport coats she initially picked fit the bill rather nicely. She also found two more shirts for him to wear with it. Pants she had to leave to Jed. With his manly parts and lower back issue, he would have to try them on for the proper cut and size.

At 1705 hours Jed called the cell wondering when she'd be home. She told him they were walking across the parking lot as they were speaking. He suggested pizza for dinner. Since she was agreeable, she told Grainley that was their final stop on the way home. Plus, he had an invite to stay for the meal which he willingly accepted. Once home, it took the young marine two trips to carry all of Lucy's shopping bags into the bedroom. Jed stood in the hallway watching.

"Babe, did you buy out the whole mall?" He asked when she kissed him.

She giggled. "Not quite. You know, I usually hate shopping. Since Paris, I kind of enjoy it."

Wrapping his arms around her, he moved them the few steps into the kitchen.

"I'm glad you had a good time. Guess Paris was good for you." He hugged her.

"In more ways than one", she remarked playfully.

Molding her body into his, Lucy kissed Jed—a long kiss full of promise and passion. Jed made a noise of pleasure in his throat as he deepened the kiss.

"E-excuse me" Grainley said in embarrassment.

Breaking apart only their lips, Lucy called after the retreating young marine. "It's okay, come back."

Grainley's voice echoed back the hallway. "Are you sure?"

Jed's marine in-charge tone reverberated from his chest into hers. "Grainley return to the kitchen."

"Jed must you yell at him?" She whispered.

"He's a marine Lucy." Jed responded quietly showing he wasn't angry.

"I like him, he's a good kid." She said still keeping her voice low.

The young man stepped into the kitchen. "Sir, missus."

"There's a blown light on the back porch soldier." Jed ordered.

The marine obeyed by picking up the fresh bulb from the counter on his way out the door.

Looking down at Lucy, he finished. "I like him too. But we need to make him a man who can handle anything."

"Hard like you?" Her voice held sympathy, not sarcasm, as she caressed his face.

Kissing the palm of her hand, he said, "Only on the outside."

Not giving her a chance to comment further, he opened the back door. "Let's eat soldier."

Jed grabbed cold beers from the refrigerator by the time the young marine re-entered the kitchen. After one slice, Lucy left the two marines alone.

She went into the bedroom to take care of her purchases. With all of the tags removed, Lucy carried it to the laundry room to wash on light cycle. Jed's sport coat she left the tags on in case he didn't like it. However, she did hang it in his closet next to his dress uniform. The shirts she'd bought him would be placed there as well after they were done being laundered. She unpacked her other two travel bags into the large suitcase. There was plenty of room for her new purchases. Recalling Jed's dresser drawers stuffed with t-shirts and sweatshirts, she purloined a couple of each. By the time she had finished the laundry, Grainley was leaving. When she checked the fire, she noticed the log rack had been filled.

Jed came up behind her putting his arms around the front of her. "You didn't have to leave us."

Lucy rubbed his arms. "After spending the day with the 'missus', I figured he'd be more at ease with just you."

He nodded. "You're probably right. We had a good talk."

He kissed her neck gently causing her to relax into him. They stood like that for a while watching the flames dance in the fireplace.

Lucy yawned. "I'm tired. I think I'll go to bed."

"Do you mind if I join you?" He asked.

"It's your bed." She replied.

"Lucy? Is something wrong?" Jed asked turning her to face him.

Gazing up at him she smiled. "No Jed. Really, I'm just sleepy."

"Sleep it is." He said leading the way.

They were woken by the phone ringing. Jed answered it. Lucy got up to make coffee. She and Jed met at the bathroom door.

Jed spoke first. "I have to be on base in an hour."

"Okay let me pee, then you can have the bathroom while I make you breakfast." She stated.

"Hurry up woman!" He swatted her butt.

Forty minutes later, he kissed her good bye at the door. "Call the cell if you need anything."

Lucy puttered around the house doing little domestic things. There was a knock at the door. A FedEx driver had a package for her. Jim had shipped her cell phone and laptop express mail as promised. She called to thank him. He didn't answer; she left a message. It took a while to handle the numerous emails and phone messages on both devices. There was one message she saved. It was dated yesterday from the Assistant Director of the Department of Defense. She called the number he'd left. It went to his secretary. She needed an address to send paperwork for Lucy. Lucy explained to the secretary she'd be staying with a friend in New York for a couple weeks. The secretary took that address and told Lucy to expect a packet. The assistant director would call her as soon as he had an opportunity. Lucy called Jed to let him know she had her phone. It was late afternoon till he called to tell her he was on his way home.

When Jed arrived, she greeted him at the door wearing the baby doll nightie. The look of surprised delight on his face dissipated her personal embarrassment at doing this. He pulled her into his arms for a passionate kiss. His hands roved her curves. Tugging out of his hands, she moved backwards towards the bedroom unbuttoning his uniform as she went. Jed's reach enabled him to continue stroking her soft body parts. In the room, Jed assisted Lucy with removing his clothing. When Jed was completely naked, Lucy pushed him backwards onto the mattress.

Jed rasped. "Climb on."

She slipped off her panties, but kept on the enticing lace shortie which accentuated her breasts. As she straddled him, they both moaned at the incredibly pleasurable sensations.

He groaned. "Lucy, you are so hot."

Hearing him say this rocketed her to climax. As she came down from her high, he hugged her close.

Rubbing her face in his neck, she spoke. "Wow! To think, I almost didn't have the courage to wear this."

He chuckled. "I'm glad you did. The medication usually dampens things. Your greeting gave me quite a jump start."

Not knowing what to say, she giggled.

Heolled her over smothering her with kisses. "You are one hell of a woman."

"Gee and you haven't even seen what I made for dinner." She teased.

"Lucy, I'm serious." He touched her cheek with his fingers.

The intensity in his eyes caused her to look away. The rest of her couldn't move. Whether or not Jed felt her stiffen, he only commented about his stomach grumbling. "I'm starving."

The rest of their last night together was full of enjoyable companionship. He stuffed himself at dinner. He raved at how good it tasted. She made enough to freeze a couple of meals for him. They cuddled in front of the fire watching television.

The next morning Jed didn't speak much. He touched: her hand, her arm, her butt—at every opportunity. Her luggage was setting by the door awaiting Grainley's arrival. He would be driving her to the airport since Jed had to report to the base by 0700 hours. Lucy discreetly snapped a few pictures of him with her cell phone as he dressed. He caught her taking one while he filled his travel mug so he hammed it up. They laughed at his silliness. The sound of Grainley at the front door reminded them they both had to go. After opening the door for Grainley to get her bags, Jed held Lucy's wrap for her. He grasped her hand for the short walk to the military insignia jeep.

Jed and Lucy shared a long, slow, warm kiss.

Giving an extra squeeze to his hug, Jed whispered in her ear. "Please let me know when you land safely."

"I will." She answered unsure of why it would matter to him.

Jed spoke to the young marine as he shut her door. "Keep her safe Grainley."

In military fashion, they saluted each other. "Yes sir."

Looking in the side mirror, Lucy saw Jed watching as they drove away. At the airport, Grainley didn't drop her at departures. He parked, then carried her bag for her. He insisted he had orders to stay with her until final security check. Lucy explained to him it would only make people notice her that much more. She needed to blend into the crowd. He walked her to the security point.

She hugged him to make it look natural. "Take care of Jed."

"Yes missus." He did an about face to walk away.

Lucy released a sigh of relief when she made it through security without anyone recognizing her. After locating her departure gate, she perused the nearby shops. Boring of that easily she took a seat at the gate to people watch for the few minutes prior to boarding. Once at the Pittsburgh airport, Lucy pulled out her laptop to surf the web. She ordered a few things from LLBean to be delivered to LuLu's. Checking new emails, she had none of any pertinence. She sent an email to Jim's wife, Melinda, asking how things were. It filled in the layover hours effectively.

Chapter Eight

When the flight touched down in Buffalo, Lucy allowed the excitement of seeing LuLu bubble up. As promised, she sent a short text message to Jed. It didn't take long to get to baggage claim. At seeing each other, both women squealed with delight as they hurried together. The best friends hugged.

"Did Danny get off okay?" Lucy asked.

"Yes, but what a goings on till we got here." LuLu replied. "He's so afraid you and I are going to drink ourselves silly for the next ten days."

"Well we are." Lucy said soberly.

"Stop! We aren't that bad!" LuLu feigned innocence.

Lucy merely looked at her friend with raised eyebrows.

"Okay so we are!" LuLu gave Lucy a good squeeze and giggled.

LuLu acted 17 years younger than Lucy rather than her actual age of 17 years older. When the luggage began popping onto the conveyor belt, Lucy joined the crowd. LuLu chattered about how Danny didn't pack until an hour before they were supposed to leave for the airport. It took a few times around for Lucy to recognize her new suitcase. The brisk wind whipped the loose snow off the plow piles as they walked across the parking lot to the van. Lucy stowed her suitcase and carry-on bag behind the passenger seat next to a bunch of department store bags.

Peering over the backseat, she made comment. "What? No dogs?"

Climbing into the driver's seat LuLu answered. "I thought about it. But with the mood Danny was in, I had second thoughts."

"How many times did he get the tractor stuck in the snow clearing the driveway yesterday?" She asked the obvious reason for his crankiness.

LuLu merged onto the interstate before answering. "At least three times. And that was after he'd done a pass with the front end loader."

The best friends conversed continually on the 90 minute drive to the farm. Surprisingly, LuLu didn't mention Jed or the ordeal in the Mid East once during the drive. The mile long driveway was clearer than Lucy had expected. Danny probably did that to prevent LuLu from needing to use the tractor. The man truly loved his wife. LuLu led the way into the house via the front door rather than across the all-season room to the side door. Going through the front door was a direct route for the stairs. When Lucy put her bags in the guest room, she was shocked to see it had been re-decorated. Stepping into the bathroom to wash her face, she saw it had been completely redone—new vanity and mirror, tub unit replaced with shower stall, a cabinet built into the extra space created. On the landing, Lucy realized that had been freshened.

"LuLu, you two have been quite busy." She commented as she walked into the master suite.

This too had been completely remodeled.

LuLu asked eagerly. "Do you love it?"

How could she not? "It's wonderful! When you said you were redecorating, I had no idea you'd convinced Danny to do major renovations."

LuLu explained. "It hadn't been the original plan. But when we started discussing specifics, Danny suggested we do it all the right way."

"Danny was willing to spend this kind of money?" Lucy could hardly believe it.

"It surprised me too. We took it one room at a time. Wait till you see what we did on the main floor." LuLu said leading the way down the stairs.

"I wondered why we came in through the front door instead of the garage." Her curiosity peaked.

"I wanted to show it to you all at once." The owner of the house giggled.

The downstairs had been opened up from the living room into the kitchen and dining room. The corner that had once held the desk and computer now had an overstuffed chair with matching ottoman. That must be where LuLu sat to read or knit. Danny had even modernized the fireplace for easy maintenance.

"With all of this, are the dogs allowed inside anymore?" Lucy asked moving her arm in a wide arc.

"Danny thought of everything." LuLu opened the bottom half of the pantry door.

It fit perfectly between the wall and the counter. This partitioned the living room from the rest of the house. The living room had been freshly painted, but the furniture had remained the same as the last eight years. However, there had been one major addition. A full size plasma screen television hung the wall that had contained the entertainment center.

"Wow-life size!" Lucy exclaimed.

"It has its draw backs." LuLu stated.

Lucy quipped. "The dust?"

LuLu's face became serious. "No, seeing my best friend on CNN with cuts and bruises covering her face was a bit disconcerting."

Lucy felt embarrassed. "If there had been a way I could've gotten out of it gracefully, I would have. The press wasn't going to leave me alone until I'd given them something. It was the cleanest way to handle it."

"I know Luce. You've always been able to handle things like that with grace." LuLu stated. "Are we going to talk about it while you're here?"

"I told you on the phone we would. Let's wait until we've had a margarita." Lucy clarified.

"And you will tell me about that wonderfully hunky marine I spoke to and saw standing by your side?" LuLu's impish grin and twinkling eyes removed decades from her face.

"That will take a pitcher of margaritas." She teased.

The laughed together as they went outside. Three large northern breed dogs howled enthusiastically at seeing their Aunt Lucy. LuLu released them in succession from their kennels. Grandma Daisy danced in the background while her daughter Luna and grandson Brando greeted Lucy. When the younger dogs ran off to play in the snow, the two women took the older dog indoors. Lucy sat on the sofa so Daisy could snuggle with her.

LuLu spoke from the kitchen, "the older she gets, the more she looks like Venus."

"Yes Daisy, you do look like your momma." Lucy talked to the dog like a person.

Daisy accepted the compliment by gently licking Lucy's chin.

"Do you miss not having a dog?" LuLu asked while she put the ingredients for their first round of margaritas in the blender.

"Terribly." Lucy stated.

Before they could talk any further on the subject, the doorbell rang. It was FedEx. Lucy had to sign for it. LuLu watched as Lucy pulled the tab on the outside envelope. Inside, Lucy found five separate packets. Each bore an insignia—Department of Defense (DOD), Defense Intelligence Agency (DIA), Central Intelligence Agency (CIA), National Security Agency (NSA), National Reconnaissance Organization (NRO). LuLu continued preparing their drinks and started dinner. When the drinks were ready, she slid one across the counter to where Lucy sat reading. Engrossed in the offers, Lucy didn't realize she'd downed the potent drink in short order. LuLu refilled it without Lucy having to ask. When dinner was ready, LuLu put a plate of spaghetti squash in front of her. Lucy had cleared her plate by the time she finished the fifth packet. She cleaned the kitchen from dinner while LuLu fed the dogs. The two younger dogs were kenneled; Daisy remained indoors. Coming in from outside, LuLu stood in front of the fire to get rid of the chill.

Finally, the older woman gave up waiting. "You're on your fourth drink; it's time to spill everything—the Mid East, the marine, and that dossier you've been reading for the last hour!"

"Okay, okay. I'll tell you about the first two, but the last we'll save for tomorrow after I've had a chance to fully understand it." Lucy replied.

They emptied a second pitcher of margaritas while Lucy relayed the events of the last nine days to LuLu.

"When are you seeing him again?" was LuLu's response to all of it.

"What makes you think I'll see him again?" Lucy knew she meant well.

"The fact that you are still wearing the ring he gave you." LuLu pointed out.

Her tone was aghast as she spied it still sparkling on her finger. "Oh my God! I forgot to give it back to him."

"He obviously wasn't that anxious to get it back if he didn't ask for it." LuLu remarked with a sly smile.

"Knock it off Lu. It was a fling; nothing more." Lucy's tone edged with irritation.

In a patient, motherly tone LuLu stated. "Lucy, you don't do flings. Plus after speaking to the gentleman in question, you are more than a fling to him as well."

"But that doesn't make sense. Jed could have any woman he wanted. Why would he want me?" Lucy finally said her fear aloud.

LuLu shook her head. "Why wouldn't he want you?"

"I'm not anything like you—fun, perky, beautiful." LuLu was the one person Lucy knew with whom she could be totally honest.

The feeling went both ways. "Not every man wants someone like me. Remember 'beauty is in the eye of the beholder'. And that man has been a holdin' you."

The phone interrupted their laughter. It was Danny. Giving them privacy, Lucy went to unpack. Daisy followed her to climb on the bed. Lucy didn't have the heart to chase her off. Instead, she stretched next to her for a few minutes.

A few minutes turned into the whole night. Daisy nudged her awake. Lucy immediately got off the bed to follow. As expected, Daisy led her to the back door. Since it was still dark, Lucy turned on the outside light. This caused the other two dogs to stir in their kennels. However, being part of the daily routine, they remained quiet. The clock chimed six times. Lucy pushed the button on the coffee maker. It didn't take long for Daisy to scratch at the door. Letting the old dog inside, Lucy stepped out momentarily to release the other two for exercise. Over the last three years away, she had forgotten how cold it could get here. She ran upstairs to take a hot shower. By the time she finished showering, the dogs would want their breakfast.

After taking care of the dogs, Lucy curled in the big chair with a cup of coffee. She reread the papers she'd received late yesterday. The offers were incredible. Now the entirety of the debriefing on the Arlington made sense.

It also explained why so many people spoke with her at the lunch with the Director of Defense. The job descriptions from the NRO and NSA interested her to a greater extent than the others. It was too early to call Daniel Duquette, the Deputy Director of Defense. A hand written note on letter head had been included in the packet from him. They'd hit it off remarkably well at the luncheon. Working for different agencies would give both of them a comfortable contact. Lucy had to wait even longer to call Jim in Denver. She wanted to know how much he'd been told. Something they had in common was the ability to read people's inflections quite well for a deeper meaning to their words. If he had gotten a certain impression while speaking with any of them, she wanted to hear about it. The thought crossed her mind to call Jed. Until she had more information, it would be premature. She wondered from which agency he'd chosen to accept a job. He'd been leaning heavily towards NCIS. He felt an allegiance to stay within an attachment of a branch of the military. Plus, spooks spooked him. Too many thoughts crowded into her brain at once causing an overwhelming feeling of panic. The best way to deal with it was to list all of the issues and tasks needed to reach completion. Each item would have a resolution or plan of attack to be handled; thus breaking down the big scary change into small benign pieces. On her way to get her laptop, she took a cup of coffee upstairs for LuLu. Entering the master suite, Lucy heard the shower running. She placed the steaming cup of caffeine on the dresser where LuLu would find it easily. Lucy grabbed her cell phone along with the laptop. She checked to see if she had any messages. There were none. Disappointment nagged at her that Jed had already dismissed her from his life. But then again, wouldn't he be in for a surprise when he bumped into her in DC. They'd both be working for an intelligence agency. Their paths would inevitably cross. Well, that answered the first item on her list—if she was going to take one of the jobs offered. She worked on her list. LuLu came down the stairs ready to go. Where they were going, Lucy had no idea since it was only 8am. However, she played along.

First, they had breakfast at a diner in town. Next they went grocery shopping. The weather channel predicted wind gusts beginning late in the day. This meant the road to the farm would be blown shut. LuLu was obviously taking precautionary measures. Lucy called Jim while she pushed the shopping cart. He was thrilled they could talk about what was going on with job offers. Granted, they had to use code names. It was better than not talking at all. Lorning had basically been informed that they were to comply with any timeline Lucy gave for leaving. Unfortunately, with everyone he'd talked to since even before the Armadillo incident, Jim could not pin down specifics about any of them. One thing had been clear—they wanted her within easy reach. Months earlier, when she'd applied for positions with Lorning on the east coast, it brought her name to the attention of a few interested parties. They'd begun investigating her weeks prior to the Armadillo. Plus, Jim knew she'd been chosen for the Armadillo trip as a way to keep her from becoming a key player in any upcoming projects. They just had no idea it would make her a highly coveted asset to the family of intelligence agencies. He promised he would call her if he heard anything she'd want to know. Also, he'd have Melinda work on putting Lucy's house on the market. It didn't take long for Melinda to call Lucy after Jim told her Lucy was moving to DC. Since Lucy didn't have much in the way of furniture, Melinda recommended a 6x12 storage pod. Melinda and Jim could pack it for her. It could be put in storage till Lucy found a place in DC. Lucy agreed to the pod but wanted to pack it herself with the couple's help. Melinda understood it would be closure for Lucy. As soon as Lucy had her flight back to Denver, she'd let Melinda know to make the necessary arrangements. In the meantime, Melinda would list the house for sale for in-house showings exclusively through her. She recommended a sale price far higher than Lucy had imagined. Melinda would never try to sell a house for a listed price if she didn't feel confident she could.

In the van again, LuLu spoke. "I take it you are accepting the offer that was mailed to you?"

"Actually Lu, it was five. I've narrowed it down to two, but I need a bit more information. In the meantime, I'm trying to get my ducks in a row for a quick and easy move." Lucy explained.

LuLu's happiness was apparent. "DC is a whole lot closer than Denver. Wait until your dad finds out!"

Lucy rolled her eyes at the latter comment."I will do that in person once I have final dates. When we get back to the house, would you coordinate my flight back to Denver for the same day Danny returns?"

"What about seeing your dad?" LuLu pushed the parental issue.

"Okay, see if there's a flight into Harrisburg that day with a flight out to Denver two days later; no longer." She caved knowing her dad wanted to see her after recent events.

LuLu smiled smugly. "Thank you."

Back at the farm, they took care of any necessary house tasks prior to tackling Lucy's travel and move. Lucy went to her room to call Daniel.

The secretary put her on hold.

When the line connected it was Daniel's deep baritone."Ms. Seeir how's the weather in western New York?"

"Starting to get a little blustery Mr. Duquette." Lucy quipped.

"When you move here the only difference will be hot air instead of a chill factor." He volleyed.

"Well that was an interesting segues to the topic of interest." She pointed out.

"So what have you decided?" The assistant director stopped playing too.

"I've narrowed it down to Nancy and Norman." She used code in case it wasn't to be common knowledge.

"After meeting you and reviewing the job descriptions, I suspected that's the way you'd go. Do you have specific questions regarding either one?" The tone in his voice let her know she was choosing the best fits.

"They are not management, right?" She asked.

He explained. "Correct. Technical advisor, special projects, trouble shooting teams, loaned out in joint efforts to other agencies."

"Oh good. But how do I choose between them?" She wanted his opinion.

"During lunch you met both. Nancy was the one who said they should have had someone hide or at least lighten your bruises. Norman was the man wearing the road runner tie." He refreshed her memory.

"Oh! Wile E. Coyote, Genius", she mimicked the cartoon character.

Assistant Director Duquette chuckled. "Yes, Ms. Seeir you are quite correct. I will give Norman the good news. With your permission, I'll have our secretary type the thank you letters for the others. She will email them to you at your personal email address for final approval."

Surprised by his handling it all, Lucy asked for clarification. "Is that standard protocol?"

"When it's all in the family like this—yes. It's similar to Sergeant Major Warloc staying within the military family." His voice hinted he knew a secret.

She didn't take the bait. "When will I be expected to start?"

"We will coordinate that based on your trauma leave and remaining vacation time with Lorning. A letter with those kind of specifics will be sent in an over night package before you leave New York. It will include the name of your move coordinator. Also, we will notify Lorning. I do apologize for not allowing Jim Hughes to share any information with you until we had completed our investigation and recommendations." The assistant director's sincerity was not merely a formality.

"Do you need anything else from me?" her last question.

"We understand you need to make certain arrangements, but please keep this as quiet as possible. Ask your friends and family not to share this information with anyone. Your name is still news we need to fade away. Also Ms. Seeir, please do not tell Sergeant Major Warloc as of yet. His final decision won't be approved until after his surgery." Again the assistant director alluded to information with good intentions.

"Not a problem Deputy Director Duquette." She noted, but did not react to his comment regarding Jed.

"We'll be in contact a lot from now on—please call me Daniel." His voice relaxed.

"Okay Daniel, as long as you call me Lucy." She responded in like manner.

"Talk to you soon Lucy." They disconnected.

It would be eight and a half a weeks till she had to report to work. They provided company housing for up to six months. That should give her plenty of time to find a place of her own.

Lucy went to the kitchen to fill LuLu in on dates. LuLu had Lucy's flights confirmed. She also had a margarita waiting for Lucy along with a grilled ham-n-cheese. The clock chimed 12 noon.

"I can't be slurring my speech if the Deputy Director of Defense calls back." She stated.

"Oh my, I'd have never even guessed you were applying for a job within a government agency." LuLu's voice filled with awe.

"Actually, I'll be working for the National Reconnaissance Organization or NRO. But LuLu, you can not tell anyone. When Danny gets back you can tell him in person and in private. Definitely not while he's overseas." Lucy made it perfectly clear. "From now on, we refer to it as Norman."

"I think Norman would understand you needing a little stress relief after all you've been through." LuLu stated.

Thinking of Jed, Lucy raised her glass. "To stress relief."

They clinked glasses. Lucy turned off her cell phone to resist temptation to answer it. LuLu had a stack of chick flicks for them to watch. By the time the credits of the third movie displayed, both women had passed out. It took Daisy's incessant whining and pacing to rouse Lucy. She let the old girl outside to relieve herself, then went to do the same. Seeing it was dark, Lucy dished the dogs' evening meal. There was an iffy moment when all three dogs came into the house to be fed. She'd forgotten Luna and Brando had been running the yard. Grabbing food dishes the two younger dogs eagerly followed her outside. The adrenalin rush saved her from noticing the bitter cold. When Lucy went back inside, Daisy was standing in the middle of the living room howling as loud as her old, scratchy throat would allow. LuLu stirred long enough to open her eyes, see Lucy, then fall contentedly back to sleep. Daisy followed Lucy into the laundry room where the dish had already been placed in a raised feeder. It made Lucy smile seeing the old girl dive into her food. The lack of food in her own stomach after all of the alcohol had it gurgling in protest.

"Another grilled ham-n-cheese should do the trick", she thought.

No sooner had she finished making it than LuLu stumbled out of her chair. "That smells good."

When LuLu emerged from the powder room, Lucy had the sandwich cut in quarters on a plate for them to share; and in the process of preparing a second one. They watched the weather channel while they ate. The next few days were going to be cold and windy. That suited Lucy fine.

One day before Lucy's flight to see her dad, Melinda called. She had a buyer for the house already—full asking price. One problem, they wanted to close and move by the last day of the month. The only hitch would be Lucy not agreeing to it. Today is the 16th. She would be in Denver on the 20th. Melinda would schedule the pod to arrive at the house on the 22nd with pick up on the 28th. They could schedule closing for the 29th. The realtor would also handle transferring or canceling all utilities and services for the last day of the month. Lucy would wait to transfer her cell phone service till she had a DC address.

LuLu and Lucy had run the tractor down the dirt road everyday to keep it clear of snow drifts. The morning of Lucy's flight was no different. The flight into Harrisburg was uneventful.

There were tears in her dad's eyes when he saw Lucy. Thankfully, her bruises had completely faded. A dab of make-up on the dark pink scars made those barely noticeable. They hugged. Her step-mother Mae laughed and cried at seeing father and daughter together again. It was only a half hour drive to their home. As soon as they got there, Mae disappeared into the kitchen to prepare a big meal at having Lucy with them. Lucy and her dad went into the living room to talk about flying on military transports. They avoided the topic that would upset him. When she told him she would be moving to DC, he couldn't have been happier. She allowed him to think it was a transfer within Lorning. It was easier and safer.

He hopped up from his chair to go into the kitchen. "Mae! Lucy is moving to DC! She'll only be a few hours away."

Mae chirped with glee. "That's wonderful! You will have to come for Christmas. Your marine friend is invited, too."

Lucy didn't want to make a promise she couldn't keep. "I'll have to wait and see how this division handles the holidays. But I will visit again before the end of the year."

That appeased the older couple. For the next 48 hours, Lucy ate more food than she usually ate in a week. Mae insisted on sending cookies along with her. Her step-mother was fabulous in the kitchen, but Lucy's metabolism was not up for the challenge. Nonetheless, the cookies were a good idea since Lucy didn't recall having anything in her cupboards.

Only Melinda greeted Lucy at the Denver airport. Melinda filled her in on every detail on the sale of the house. She even had the paperwork for Lucy to sign while they drove. Turning the corner at Lucy's block, she got a call for a showing. Melinda dropped Lucy at the house with a promise she would call later. It felt good to step foot into her own house again. However, it had become a short-term living space. Out of habit, Lucy took her suitcase to the bedroom to unpack. On her way, she checked the empty bedrooms and guest room. Melinda had been busy. A stack of empty boxes were in the spare bedroom along with rolls of packing tape and paper. After unpacking, Lucy took the cookies to the kitchen. Her stomach had the nerve to rumble. A loaf of bread and packages of disposable plastic plates, cups and utensils were setting on the counter. Opening the refrigerator, she sighed at Melinda's efficiency. A to-do list with dates had been stuck to the outside of door with magnets. Inside on the main shelf, Lucy found a half gallon of milk, a dozen eggs, lunchmeat and sliced cheese. She poured herself a glass of milk to go with the cookies. Standing in the kitchen looking into the living room, it struck Lucy how very little she'd invested making the house a home. It contained the bare minimum—television on a non-descript stand, love seat sofa, end table, high back chair, small bookcase, and a buffet table against the far wall with a Van Gogh print above it. In the kitchen, there were four barstools around the large breakfast counter; no kitchen table. Strolling upstairs with her snack, she mentally inventoried those rooms too. The guest bedroom contained a queen size bed on simple metal frame and a nightstand. A dresser hadn't been necessary since the closet had an organizer which included drawers. Her bedroom contained the most furniture—wrought iron queen size bed, refinished antique three-drawer dresser with mirror, corner stand, small television, blanket chest and a print on each wall. Putting her empty plastic cup on the dresser, Lucy opened the walk-in closet. As usual, it echoed. Everything in here would be needed.

Three soft-sided under bed storage containers would hold it all; another two for the clothing from the dresser. They would fit nicely in the back of the Land Rover. Lucy had found it interesting that Jed owned a Range Rover. Taking into account the differences in models and years, she'd decided it wasn't that significant.

There was no point in not getting started. Lucy grabbed supplies from the spare room for packing the contents of the kitchen cupboards. With the television on for company, Lucy began her move. All cabinets were emptied. Anything she would need over the next week, she placed on the wide eating counter. She set an empty box on the floor in the corner as the last box to be loaded into the pod. Unaware of time, Lucy continued from room to room. She also worked on how the furniture was to be loaded into the pod for maximum capacity.

Before Lucy realized it, morning had dawned. With it, the realization her insomnia had kicked into effect. It had been inevitable with such a huge change. Checking the prescription bottle in the medicine cabinet, it contained almost the full three months. She placed the bottle on the sink top to remember to take one to sleep the next night. Taking a shower, Lucy wanted to complete the errands she'd listed. While she was out, she called Jim to see if she could come into the office to empty her desk. He let her know he'd taken care of it. He'd bring the box by on Saturday when they helped her load the pod. It made Lucy run the timeline in her head. While she waited in line at the credit union, she phoned LuLu.

"How's the packing going?" LuLu asked immediately.

Lucy answered. "That's the thing. I did it all last night."

"Ugh. Insomnia?" LuLu really did know her too well.

"Yeah. But the reason I'm calling is I may be able to leave here a week early if Melinda can get the settlement papers drawn up." Lucy explained.

LuLu interrupted before Lucy could finish. "If you need to come a week early, there's no problem. Matter of fact Danny has been thinking of booking a week in Jamaica while you're with us."

This made Lucy happy. "That would be great. I'd feel less of an imposition if I'm there to dog sit."

"You are never an imposition! Have you scheduled a few days with your DC realtor yet?" LuLu asked.

"Was going to check in with her later today to see how many houses she's found for me to view." Lucy answered.

"Let us know. See you next week." LuLu hung up.

On her way home from WalMart, Lucy got take-out Mexican. That would be one thing she'd miss—authentic Mexican food.

Melinda drove into the driveway behind Lucy.

She rushed into the garage. "Lucy! We have a problem."

Lucy stayed calm. "Continue."

Melinda helped Lucy carry her purchases into the house. "The family buying the house needs to close by Tuesday or they have to re-apply for their loan."

"Works for me as long as you call to have the pod picked up Monday." Lucy solved the problem.

Melinda hugged her ferociously. "Thank you, thank you, thank you!"

Standing still till Melinda stopped bouncing, Lucy commented. "Jim and Rob better eat their Wheaties Saturday morning. I want the pod packed and ready to go by the time they leave."

"But Lucy, I have a client who can only view houses Saturday morning." Melinda pouted.

Lucy had too much experience dealing with high maintenance women. "I'm disappointed you can't be here, but I understand you have to work. If the boys get here early, we should have all of the heavy lifting done by the time you can join us."

"Are you sure you can deal with the two of them?" Jim's high strung wife asked with the utmost seriousness.

Lucy choked back her laughter. The three of them had worked many projects together. They would actually have fun packing the pod without Melinda directing every movement they made.

Keeping her face sober, Lucy finally answered. "I think I can manage."

Melinda patted Lucy's arm. "If you start stressing, you call me and I'll yell at those boys for you."

Lucy smiled her thanks.

"Have to go. I'll call the pod place today to confirm drop off tomorrow and pick up Monday." She blew kisses on her way through the door.

When the door shut behind her, Lucy burst out laughing. Lucy wouldn't want Melinda's job for anything. She truly was a godsend for Lucy to coordinate everything. If Melinda hadn't been in charge, things would have been a constant battle. The woman got her total control fix along with a hefty commission. This allowed Lucy to avoid the frustration of trying to accomplish the necessary details of a long distance move.

Packing the pod with Jim and Rob went smoothly Saturday morning. The guys also helped her load her vehicle for the cross country drive. By the time Melinda arrived with two pizzas, the trio was sitting on the floor drinking beer reminiscing. After eating, they shared hugs and good-byes. Lucy signed proxy papers for Melinda to sign the closing papers for her on Tuesday. The check along with the finalized sale papers would be sent via FedEx to her in New York.

The sun went down. Lucy spread a blanket on the floor for sleeping. With both televisions in the pod, there was nothing for Lucy to do. Since she'd planned on starting the long drive at 3am, going to bed at 6 o'clock made sense. In the morning, Lucy made a final sweep through the house after she'd loaded the last of her personal necessities into the Land Rover.

Even though it was winter, Lucy chose to drive east via Nebraska rather than Kansas. Nebraska may have been as long as Kansas, but it had more landmarks to feel like she was making progress. Driving the interstate across Kansas was like being stuck in a time loop. Every 50 miles the view—the same billboard, same farm house, same tiny truck stop—never changed. Lucy drove for16 hours; stopping only when she needed gas. At which time, she would use the restroom and buy a soda or coffee. She didn't need to purchase food since she'd been able to make more than enough sandwiches for the trip. The ice in the cooler would last till she could get ice at whatever hotel she stayed that night.

She forced herself to make the trip in two days. It was a lonely trip, unlike the one west years ago. Venus had kept her company. This trip her ashes were in their cedar box in one of the cardboard boxes on the backseat. When she was an hour from the farm in New York, Lucy called to let LuLu and Danny know she'd be there soon. The greeting was full of hugs like the last time. Danny assisted carrying a few things up to the spare bedroom for her. They discussed schedules over the next four weeks. The couple had chosen the middle two weeks to take a ten day cruise. Lucy would be taking a trip to DC to view houses a few days prior and again when they returned.

While the couple was at work, Lucy took care of the dogs. For each of the first three days, she bathed and groomed one to perfection. With Lucy at the house, the dogs were able to run the acre of fenced in yard all day. When the couple would return home at the end of work, dinner was waiting for them.

Lucy's trip to go house hunting in DC was cancelled. The realtor sent her internet video tours of everything in the price range Lucy had indicated. None were close to what Lucy wanted. Even though she received a hefty sum from the sale of her house in Denver, Lucy didn't want to be a slave to a mortgage payment. The Deputy Director of Defense, Daniel Duquette, called to see how the move was progressing.

"Overall smoothly. A little disappointed with the house hunting. It will just take a bit of time to find one that fits me." She remarked.

"Don't rush into anything. We want you to find exactly what you want so you stick around for a long time." Daniel responded.

"Yes, but I have limited temporary housing." Lucy reminded him.

"Remember, everything is negotiable." He countered.

She stated. "I didn't think of that soon enough where salary was concerned. I should've checked housing costs before accepting any of the offers."

Daniel sounded perplexed. "Unless you are looking for a mansion, I can't imagine there's too much you can't afford."

It was her turn to be confused. "With the price of homes in DC, my salary is barely making a dent."

"Um Lucy, did you get a packet from Norman?" He asked.

"No, I've only received a few emails from Wily E. Coyote's secretary with dates of employment and answers to a few move package questions I had." She answered.

"Hold on a minute." Daniel said to put her on hold.

Lucy walked circles around the butcher block table in the kitchen while she waited. Every fourth lap she'd open the fridge to peruse its contents. Till Daniel clicked open the line again, Lucy had given up on lunch.

"I'm sorry Lucy. There was an oversight. The package was sent to your Denver address. It had to be signed for only by you. When the new owner's told them you had moved, it was returned to Norman. But for some reason, no one realized it." Daniel clued her in on what he found out. "It is being re-sent to you in New York. You should have it in your hands tomorrow afternoon."

"Okay, then I won't go anywhere till it gets here." She didn't know what to think.

"I have a lunch date. Give a call if you need anything else." Daniel brought their call to a close.

"Thanks." Lucy replied before disconnecting.

She went about her daily routine—relishing the total relaxation of watching television all afternoon and evening while cuddling with one of the dogs.

By noon the following day, the Fed Ex truck arrived at the farmhouse. It was the packet from Norman. It included all of the pertinent facts—official start date, briefing date, report location, report manager—about which Lucy had been wondering. It also included a welcome to Norman letter from her new boss Wile E. Coyote, whose actual name was Director William Edison. The fact she'd be reporting to someone that high in the organization filled her with anxiety. There was also a page listing her yearly salary, bonus structure, and bi-monthly pay with deductions. Lucy had to read it twice for the large dollar amount to register. She couldn't think of what she knew or could do that warranted all of this. As a plus, it allowed her to substantially increase her house buying budget. Lucy shot an email to her realtor informing her of the new range. Later in the day, a return email directed Lucy to a link with new listings. A few peaked her interest. None were a must have. If any were still available when she got to DC, she'd ask for a showing; otherwise, no great loss. Her time with LuLu and Danny would have a few days cut off the end. Not surprising to Lucy; it matched the amount of days she'd added unexpectedly at the beginning of her move east. Karma had a way of balancing things.

When the couple returned, they were blissfully relaxed with a healthy tan. Unfortunately, Danny hadn't been back a full 24 hours, when he had to make an emergency trip to Houston for work. The two women didn't mind. It would give them girl time before Lucy had to head south.

One night after a pitcher of margaritas, LuLu asked. "Have you told your marine you're moving to DC?"

"No. He hasn't called and I'm under orders not to tell him." Lucy answered.

"Why on earth not?" This made no sense to LuLu.

Lucy sighed. "It's one of those things you just have to accept."

"That's ridiculous" her tone indignant. "It's unrealistic to believe he won't find out once you are there."

"Exactly LuLu, but for the time being I cannot tell him." Lucy used her stern work tone as a deterrent to further questions on the matter.

LuLu noted it and took a different approach. "Will you be glad when you do bump into him?"

"I know where you are going with this. Yes, I will be. But no point in thinking anything more of what happened." She shrugged. "Aren't you the one who bought me the book 'He's Just Not That into You'?"

"Didn't you say he was having more back surgery? Maybe he wants to be healed from that before he shows up on your doorstep with a bouquet of daisies professing his intentions." The older woman wanted the best for her single friend.

Lucy rolled her eyes. "Okay Lu, when that happens I will call you so you can tell me 'I told you so.'"

It was LuLu's turn to sigh in exasperation.

To lighten the mood, Lucy sought a new subject. "Any word from Kayla if Ruby had her puppies?"

"Not yet. I hate to call her if she got nothing again." LuLu stated.

"That's true. She hasn't had much luck lately with breedings." Lucy nodded.

"Were you thinking of taking one?" LuLu asked.

Lucy remained non-committal. "It crossed my mind. According to the letter I received from my new boss, I won't be traveling. It would also mean I need to be moved into a house in the next eight weeks."

"But you want one, don't you?" LuLu didn't need to ask.

Since LuLu already knew the answer, Lucy didn't bother answering. Lucy missed having warm fuzzy faces of her own.

Chapter Nine

A couple days later, Lucy checked into the Marriott per instructions. The following morning she had her security briefing. When she arrived at reception, a young man escorted her through two security checkpoints to a conference room.

"Ma'am, please wait here." The young man spoke before exiting the room.

The door re-opened a few minutes later. It was Director William Edison.

As he extended his hand, he spoke. "Lucy, I am so glad to see you again."

She returned his firm handshake. "And you sir."

"Shall we get started?" He asked.

"That is why I'm here." She answered logically.

He picked up a remote. Pointing it at the front wall, it opened to reveal a plasma screen. Simultaneously, the lights dimmed. A presentation began to play. It explained the pieces she had always felt were missing. At intervals, he paused the video to explain specifics relevant to her position.

When it ended, Edison stood. "Let's take a walk."

She followed. They entered a large room filled with cubicles. He led her to a quad.

Clearing his throat, he announced their presence. "Gentlemen, this is Lucy Seeir from Lorning."

The two men in their forties swiveled in their chairs to greet her. Neither seemed very interested in meeting her. At recognizing Director William Edison, they quickly stood, straightening their rumpled shirts.

"Gentlemen, Ms. Seeir is a consultant here to gather intel on some of our projects. She has been fully cleared for any and all data." The director intentionally veiled her true purpose.

The two men nodded.

"Good. She'll be here at 0700 tomorrow. Be prepared." He walked away giving them no chance to voice the protest showing on their faces at the early hour.

As they walked along the corridor, Lucy decided to see how open her new boss would be with her. "Care to explain what that was all about?"

"I'll let you figure it out. Till then, I'll be waiting." The director smiled as he answered.

"Sir, I don't understand." Lucy was mystified.

"You will or I misjudged your capabilities." His face sobered. "We're done for today. Go take care of any errands and plenty of sleep. Tomorrow will be a long day."

The young man who had escorted her earlier appeared. He handed a box to the director who opened it to verify the contents. Then the director waved the young man on his way.

The director removed one of the items to slip into his pocket before handing the box to Lucy. "You're credentials. I don't think I need to remind you not to let them laying around at home or here for that matter. However, I am going to request you wear them at chest level. This is not a sexual harassment comment, but a security suggestion. You have plenty to distract anyone from examining them too closely."

This bothered her. "Why wouldn't I want anyone looking at them too closely?"

"You've been given special accesses that I don't want anyone to recognize prior to you completing your first project." He explained in a quieter tone.

"Why not just issue me a lower grade id?" She asked the obvious.

"Because I need you to be able to go anywhere and see anything. A laptop will be given to you tomorrow when you arrive. Have a nice day." Her boss made it clear he was done with her for the day.

Lucy hung her clearance placard around her neck for the walk to the lobby. Once there, she put it in her purse with another identification card she found in the box. The box also contained a cell phone and accessories. She drove back to the hotel to start charging the phone.

The note in the box read: For work & personal. Will E.

Lucy's other cell rang. The realtor wanted to know if they could reschedule their appointment that evening. When she heard Lucy's day had become available, they agreed to meet right after lunch. It would give them a couple hours to view homes.

By the time she and the realtor parted ways, Lucy felt defeated. None of the homes fit what she wanted. On the drive to the hotel, she stopped at a grocery store to get a few things for in the hotel room.

At the register, the woman spoke to her. "Well hello. It's been a while. I almost didn't recognize you now that those awful bruises are gone."

It took a few moments for Lucy to respond. "Hello Jane. I was traveling and got back into town only yesterday."

"That explains why Jed has been so sullen lately. I bet he was happy to see you." Jane chattered.

Glad it didn't take long to be rung out, Lucy merely smiled. "You have a nice evening Jane."

As Lucy walked to her vehicle, she tried to determine how she'd ended up in Jed's neighborhood without noticing. How odd the realtor directed her to the hotel this way. She debated whether or not to drop in on Jed. She reminded herself he hadn't bothered getting in touch with her. On her drive, she pressed the search button on the radio every time a love song began to play. The food she bought went directly into the mini-fridge where it remained untouched the rest of the evening. Lying across the bed, she went for a walk in a field of wild flowers that kept leading to a field of cows on a French hillside. She didn't find any answers, but at least found sleep.

She woke feeling well rested. The time on the clock indicated her alarm wouldn't blare for another 40 minutes. Nonetheless, her eagerness to dive into her new job rolled her willingly out of bed. Even though the two analysts were dressed on the casual side, Lucy chose to wear one of her suits. Looking outside via the window confirmed the weather channel's prediction of rain for the next few days. She put on her two inch heel dress boots. Her hair had grown to where it could be pulled into a clip for a sleek look. She replaced her purse with her briefcase. Her new laptop would fit in the main pocket.

Arriving a half hour earlier than scheduled, Lucy had no problems passing through any of the security doors with her identification card. An armed marine guard blocked her progress as she passed through the third checkpoint.

One hand was poised on the handle of his still holstered gun while the other held a cell phone on speaker. "Sorry to wake you sir, but an entrant red flagged the system at level three. The only contact name on her file is you sir."

The voice on the other end was Will's. "Is it Lucy Seeir?"

Reading the I.D. in her outstretched hand, he responded. "Yes sir, it is."

"Let her pass. She's the new charge I told you about last week. The strip in her badge must not have been activated properly yesterday." The soldier's firing hand relaxed at the director's recognition. "Also there should be a package for her in the cabinet under the desk. Would you please give it to her?"

"Yes director, thank you sir." The soldier stood at attention.

"See you later." Will hung up.

Speaking to Lucy as he moved to fetch the package for her, "My apologies, ma'am."

"You were doing your job that's what's important." She smiled as he handed over the cardboard box containing her laptop. "Thank you."

"There's fresh coffee in the break room if you'd care to join me." He remarked.

"That would be wonderful." She walked with him.

As she prepared her cup, she noticed the man staring at her. "Is there a problem soldier?"

With a look of getting caught, he queried. "Do we know each other? You look incredibly familiar."

It was her turn to be embarrassed. "CNN—I was one of the Lorning contractors on the Armadillo when it was hijacked."

He shook his head. "No, it's not that. I mean, I did see that and the director had already briefed me on it. But no, it's without the bruises, from years ago."

Looking more closely at him, she realized he was right. "What's your name?"

He chuckled. "That would help wouldn't it? Major Jack Wentz at your service ma'am."

"Major, I don't think the director would have a problem with you calling me Lucy." She suggested.

Jack agreed. "Will did mention you dislike being ma'amed. You can call me Jack."

They shook hands. "Well Jack, we'll have to chat again. Right now, I have to meet with two analysts and I want to be waiting for them."

He stood. "I understand. See you later."

They parted ways. A few wrong turns later Lucy made it to the cubicle farm she'd been in yesterday. As she waited, she set her laptop on the worktable in their quad.

Another note from the boss: Locker 15 at checkpoint 3. Look forward to your report. Will E.

The next three days, she listened, watched, took notes and asked technical questions.

Friday morning had her up earlier than the days prior. Substantial winds were drying the rain soaked city. The wind also tugged Lucy's curls free from the hair clip as she trekked across the parking lot. At the front door, she heard a male voice call her name. Turning, she saw Jack waving to her. Standing there waiting for him, her curls whipped about her face. A few feet from her, Jack stopped for a moment. As quickly as he halted, he hurried his gait to reach her.

Once inside, he stammered "Were you on the USS Monroe about five years ago?"

It hit Lucy too. "Oh my God Jack! You were on the same mission that went awry as Jed Warloc!"

"Yes ma'am." Emotion caused his voice to crack.

Jack hugged her lifting her off the ground. Lucy's eyes filled with tears. She couldn't believe after all these years, she'd now met two of the four men she helped save.

After a few minutes, Lucy stated. "Jack . . . It's time to put me down."

"Yes ma'am." He wiped the moisture from his face with his big hands. "I'll meet you for coffee in a bit."

"I'll have it ready Jack." She agreed as they went their different directions.

Ten minutes later, Jack joined Lucy in the break room. Lucy busily typed on her computer and Jack read the paper while they drank their coffee. A bond had been quickly and quietly formed.

When Jack's cup hit bottom, he stood to leave. "Have a good day Lucy."

"You too, Jack." She responded.

A couple hours later, Lucy's new cell rang. It was the director requesting her presence in his office. When she arrived, his secretary informed Lucy he was running late and she should go on in to wait for him. Lucy settled into one of the leather wing back chairs positioned in front of the presidential style mahogany desk. She looked around the room taking in the framed commendations and photographs with important people. A family portrait—wife and two boys—set on the corner of his desk.

Will's voice boomed from behind her as he entered awhile later. "So what do you think Lucy?"

Rotating easily on the leather, she watched him stride across the room to his desk chair. "How candid do you want me to be?"

In Jack Nicholson style, Will smiled and raised his eyebrows. "Let it rip."

"Where do these two guys rate in comparison to the other analysts?" She needed to set the stage.

"Mid to expert according to their bosses" he responded looking at her intently.

"How were most of the analysts hired? By educational credentials or ex-military favors?" Again she led him to what he wanted to know with a question.

"Uh huh. Have you documented the failings you found?" He needed proof to clean house.

"Yes, I have. And not just on the two you gave me. There were others I had casual conversations with on technical details they lacked. Also there are a few kids not far out of college who are quite knowledgeable, but the good ole' boys block them. They are smart enough to feel threatened, yet too comfortable to step up their own game." Lucy summarized her findings.

The director's face had gone stony as he processed what she'd confirmed for him. "Please copy it to a thumb drive for me to copy onto my computer. I'll copy the list of the projects I need you to review. From those, you will put together a list of people and requirements to create teams for long term projects versus names of those who can adapt to handle emergency assignments. We will not send emails regarding this or it will leak before the restructure is ready to be put into place."

Lucy tilted her head to one side. "If you already knew, why bring me in?"

Will's eyes opened wide in astonishment. "Because you are what I need to distinguish between those who can do this job and those who are merely getting by. Plus, you are the kind of person who will set an example of what we need."

She fidgeted at the compliment.

He noticed her reaction. "Lucy, we investigated a lot of candidates before choosing you. We have a plan, but it will take time to unfold. This all seems strange compared to what you are used to. It's only been a week; you need time to adjust. Please hang in there with me."

She nodded. Opening her laptop, she copied off the file the director wanted. He copied it onto his computer prior to pulling the list of projects. Lucy accepted her thumb drive back.

"You've put in a lot of hours this week; head out. Don't forget to lock up your laptop." The director ordered.

"Thank you sir" she exited his office.

The lockers were actually small safes installed in the wall like post office mailboxes. Setting the lock combination went easily thanks to the directions she found in the box. The only things she needed from her briefcase were the cell phone, wallet, ids and keys. Her suit coat pockets bulged as she left the building. A purse would be needed for coming and going. The weekend yawned in front of her. The realtor hadn't called with any new homes to view.

Early Saturday morning, Lucy ran to Dunkin' Donuts for coffee and donuts. No sooner had she propped herself on the bed with her treat than there was a knock on the door. The view through the peephole revealed Grainley.

Lucy flung open the door. "Grainley how did you . . . ?"

Standing next to Grainley was Jed slightly hunched over leaning on a four-footed cane.

Grainley greeted her with a "ma'am".

Jed's face appeared drawn as he looked at her. "Hello Lucy, may we come in? It's important."

"Yes, yes come in." She motioned.

Grainley assisted Jed to the only arm chair.

"Thank you, I'll call when we're done." Jed dismissed the young soldier.

On his way through the door, Grainley directed his words to Lucy. "Please take it easy on him. He's only been out of the hospital a couple of days, but insisted coming here."

Lucy sat on the corner of the bed closest to Jed. "What's wrong? How did you know I was here? How'd surgery go?"

Jed reached for her hand to quiet her. "I tried to get in contact with you."

He pulled a certified letter from his coat pocket to show her it had been returned as undeliverable. "My cell phone went through the laundry so I couldn't get your number until the bill came. When I tried to call, it said it had been disconnected. Last night Jack Wentz stopped by and told me he met you. I deduced you had started your new job."

Lucy had a sinking sensation in her stomach. "What do you need to tell me?"

Jed leaned on his cane pulling himself forward in the chair. The chintz upholstery allowed for easy sliding, sliding him onto his knees with a jolt and a groan.

Lucy reached down joining him on the floor. "Are you okay?"

"I'll survive." He made eye contact with her. "Lucy we have a problem."

"Just spit it out Jed!" She exclaimed.

"When we were in Paris, I asked Rene' to make a copy of the marriage certificate. He must've noticed it hadn't been registered. So he registered it." He told her the basics.

Lucy blinked a few times letting the information process. "Our big problem is that we are legally married?"

He grimaced. "Yes."

She exhaled her breath in a rush of relief. "Oh thank goodness. I thought you were going to say they found a communicable disease when they did the blood tests for your surgery."

"You aren't angry?" He looked at her in amazement.

"Are you?" She asked sensibly.

"No I wasn't, I'm not. I thought you would be upset." He relaxed some.

"How did you find out?" She doubted they mailed a follow up marriage registration.

"When they were doing an updated background investigation for my NCIS employment file, they wanted to know why I hadn't mentioned my wife and why she wasn't living with me." He explained.

"Oh Jed, you took the job with NCIS!" Both still on the floor she hugged him.

"If I can't produce my wife and explain where she's been, they will find me a questionable candidate. My job is in jeopardy." He added.

"Why not just tell them the truth? That it was a cover to get me home." She didn't understand.

He tried to stand. Lucy helped him. He paced a few steps leaning heavily on the cane.

"Edison stopped by to see me in the hospital right before my surgery. He said when they were finalizing your paperwork there was an inconsistency he hoped I could explain. I told him the truth. He said we might be able to make use of it so I wasn't to tell anyone else." He continued filling her in.

"But didn't you think I needed to know? What if an investigator had come to me and I told them the truth?" The pitch of her voice rose with concern.

"That's why the letter. Then surgery had a few complications causing my stay to be longer than anticipated. And with the drugs I'm taking, I forgot all about the certified letter coming back until Jack showed up last night. It's not that I didn't want to see you, but I wanted to be less broken." He finished.

"So what do we need to do to fix your file?" She had an inkling of where this was going.

He sat in the chair again. "Up until you got to DC on Sunday, we can explain it as you taking care of your move. It's the last week I don't know how to answer."

"We could say with the complications and the medication you were miserable to me so I stayed away until you came by to apologize." She tested how much he'd take. "Grainley would even be able to back up part of the story by telling the truth."

"That'll work." He flipped open his cell phone. "We need your help loading Lucy's car."

"Wait a minute Jed. Are you okay with me moving in with you?" The anxiety in her voice went unnoticed by him.

Jed gave her a blank look. "It is the logical step."

Grainley knocked on the door before entering.

Lucy spoke to him. "Please take my husband home. He is in no condition to be gallivanting about. I can manage here and will follow shortly."

When the young marine looked in Jed's direction, Lucy interjected. "That's an order soldier!"

"Yes ma'am." He saluted her before helping Jed stand.

As Jed passed her, he said "Thank you."

She dismissed the two men with a shooing hand motion. As soon as the door closed behind them, Lucy hurried to re-pack her things. She was glad she'd packed the storage containers with outfits she'd be wearing, not pants and shirts separated. Three of the containers had remained in the land rover. Her toiletries didn't re-pack as easily. Luckily, she had kept the plastic grocery bags for carrying the contents of the refrigerator. An hour later, she pulled into Jed's driveway. She felt a moment of indecision when she got to the front door—knock or open? They were legally married.

Taking a deep breath, she stepped inside. "Hi honey. I'm home."

Grainley emerged from the sitting room to give her a hug. "Missus, I am so glad you are here!"

She dropped the bag of food to pat the big marine's back. "Have you eaten?"

"No. He didn't give me a chance to make the two of us breakfast before coming to see you." The young marine sounded defeated.

"Let's go to the kitchen to talk while I make you something to eat." She pushed him along the hall.

Hearing Jed's snores as they walked by the bedroom answered the question she hadn't asked yet. The lack of groceries in the refrigerator made Lucy cringe. There were eggs. Her bag contained ham, cheese and bread. It would do.

Grainley gave her the facts she needed. The scar tissue they removed had done much more damage to the nerves than had been anticipated. Thus surgery took far longer than scheduled. Because of that and the amount of blood lost, Jed's heart had to be kick started. After surgery, it was worse with passing clots followed by infection. They released him only to rush him back from an extreme adverse reaction to the antibiotics. Grainley shoved food in his mouth between sentences.

"Missus, he gave me strict orders not to call you no matter how bad he got." Tears formed in the young man's eyes.

Putting her arms around him in a motherly hug, Lucy kissed him on the head. "I'm here now. But I will need your help."

"Whatever you need missus, as long as I don't have to hear him say he wants to kill himself again." Grainley's admission stabbed at Lucy's heart for both men.

"Don't worry. It was the fever and the pain killers talking." She handed him her keys. "C'mon marine, my vehicle needs to be emptied. Put it all in the study and I'll unpack from there."

"Yes missus." He went to do her bidding.

Lucy tiptoed into the bedroom to check on Jed. He was mumbling incoherently in his sleep. Sitting gently on the bed, she tenderly touched his face to feel for a fever.

Jed startled. "Wha . . . ?"

At seeing Lucy's face, he calmed. Her fingers continued brushing through his silver streaked hair in a soothing manner.

She spoke in a sweet hushed tone. "Hi. Grainley briefed me on recent events. Anything you'd care to add or dispute?"

Even though he cleared his throat, his voice remained froggy. "No. His account would be factual. I've been a self centered fucking rat-bastard."

Leaning down to kiss his cheek, she stated. "I'll stay if you promise not to scare him anymore."

His hand wiggled out from under the blanket to touch hers. "Now that Beauty is here, the Beast will be subdued."

Standing she brushed off his compliment. "Sounds like the pain killers are taking over again—you rest."

When Grainley finished, he went into the sitting room to watch television. Lucy started a crock pot meal for dinner before unpacking. It didn't take long for her to become frustrated. Jed had only furnished his house with what he needed. Even though she didn't have many clothes, she couldn't decide where to go with them without re-organizing his. She did manage to fit her suits into the bedroom closet amidst his uniforms and the new clothing she'd bought him. Depending how long this arrangement would last, she would be getting a few pieces of furniture from her storage pod.

At dinner, the young soldier roused the retired soldier to join them at the kitchen table. Lucy told them how quickly the house sold, the trip cross country, and dog sitting stories. Grainley asked questions and laughed at the appropriate times. Jed ate his dinner with what appeared to be no interest in the conversation. After the meal, he indicated he wanted to join them in the sitting room. Lucy grabbed extra pillows to help prop him comfortably in the corner of the sofa. When Jed was situated, she went to clean up from dinner. As she left the room, the two marines began chatting. An hour later, she joined them. The only place to sit was on the sofa next to Jed. She carefully perched on the other end with her legs curled underneath. Much to her surprise, Jed slid his hand across the upoholstery to rest on her sock covered foot. Grainley excused himself around 10pm. The steps creaked on his way upstairs. It was at that moment she realized she would be sleeping in Jed's bed. Not that it bothered her since she liked sleeping with him. She wasn't exactly sure how he felt on the subject. He didn't make her wonder much longer.

"Bedtime Babe?" as he struggled to stand.

She gave him her arm as a hoist. He limped into the bathroom first, giving her time to change into an over sized t-shirt. Then they swapped rooms. When she re-entered the bedroom, he was already snoring. At least she didn't have to worry about jostling him as she crawled into bed. She released a long sigh—a breath she felt like she'd been holding from the time she saw him at the hotel.

Chapter Ten

First thing Monday morning, Lucy went in search of Director Will Edison. It took till mid-afternoon for him to free up to see her.

By the time she walked into his office, Lucy had hit her boiling point. "Exactly when were you going to tell me I was legally married to Jed Warloc? And that you had a plan related to it?"

There was that smirk of his again. "So our marine finally found you here in DC."

Lucy jumped on his glib comment. "What do you expect having Jack Wentz as your personal attaché guised as a guard? You knew he would figure out who I was."

The sudden awareness that it had all been maneuvered struck her silent. The smirk left the director's face.

He paced in agitation as he spoke. "Lucy, please listen. The re-organization we—fully endorsed by the director of the defense department—are planning will cause quite an uproar. We may have modern technology, but we are using it as a crutch. Our staff sticks to old scenarios; no one seems to be stretching their minds to think outside the box. We need new blood, but who still believe in loyalty. We need you. Oh hell! I need you!"

His last words astounded Lucy.

Director Edison responded to her expression. "Don't look so shocked. You were a strong candidate when we were putting things in place. The incident with the Armadillo went in both our favors. You exemplify everything we want. Jed's decision to assist in extricating you and your co-workers was again everything we are looking for in our sister agencies. Your marriage is a symbol of how the agencies can work together instead of against each other."

"Now that's reaching for straws!" She disputed his last statement.

"Lucy, you know it's all about perception and interpretation." his voice cajoling.

She took a few minutes to digest what all he'd said. Even if it was a ploy to gain her acceptance, it made sense.

Lucy kept her tone flat. "Listen carefully Wile E. Coyote, my husband and I are not mere pawns in your game anymore. If you want to use us in a power play, be direct."

"Trust me Lucy. You are the queen in this chess match." Will remarked.

"Wiley" she said sternly.

He held his hands up in surrender. "I promise I will talk with you prior to any maneuvering that involves you or your husband."

"Thank you director." She stood to leave. "By the way, I'll be leaving by noon tomorrow to join my husband for his doctor's appointment."

"How is marital bliss?" Will asked.

Her answer was the click of her heels across the marble tiles as she walked out of his office. On her way to lock up her laptop for the evening, her cell phone rang. Seeing it was Will she debated whether or not to answer.

Her sense of responsibility forced her to answer it. "Yes director?"

"Don't be second guessing anything you said in my office. I enjoy your moxie." His chuckle echoed in her ear.

"Good afternoon Wiley." Then she snapped the phone shut.

The following afternoon, Jed seemed surprised seeing Lucy home early.

He asked "Another candid chat with the director?"

"No, I came home to go along to your doctor's appointment." She answered.

The strange look on his face bothered her. "Is it a problem I want to go?"

He shook his head. "No, but I don't understand why you would want to."

"Because I'm your wife and would like to hear what the doctor has to say." She explained.

"Mm hmm" was his final response on the subject.

At least Grainley was glad she was joining them. The drive and wait at the office were done in silence. A male nurse put Jed in a wheelchair for a trip to x-ray. On his return, he remained in the wheel chair. When the nurse called him into the exam room, Jed didn't stop Lucy from pushing him. The doctor was pleased to meet her. He removed Jed's bandage to expose the stapled incision. Since Lucy didn't avert her gaze, the doctor demonstrated how to clean it. As he talked, the doctor reviewed what the surgery had entailed, including the complications. He also stated erectile dysfunction as one of the side effects from which Jed would suffer during the healing process and possibly long term. Jed's annoyance displayed on his face at this disclosure. There were questions Lucy wanted to ask, but didn't want to aggravate Jed any further. Her understanding was the pain he had been suffering from would be completely gone. However, due to the irreparable nerve damage, they were unsure of what exactly would be a permanent problem. On the upside, with the staphylococcus infection gone, Jed's body was healing rapidly from surgery. Physical therapy could start by the end of the week. This news didn't improve his mood. Lucy filled Grainley in on the basics during the drive home. Once home, Jed went into the garage to his workshop. At dinner, Lucy left Grainley setting the table to fetch Jed.

"Jed?" Lucy called for him as she opened the door connecting into the garage.

He didn't answer. She walked across the garage to him. He was working on a wood shelf.

She placed her hand on his back as she spoke. "Hey you, dinner is ready."

"I'll be there in a minute." He stated flatly.

Her hand still on his back rubbed across his shoulders. "When you want to talk, I'll listen."

She waited a couple of minutes for an acknowledgement. Not getting any, she went inside the house. Jed eventually joined them in the kitchen. After dinner, he escaped to the garage again. Lucy left him alone. Working with his hands would be a good way for him to spend his time. Plus, it would allow him the solitude to deal with whatever was bothering him. The rest of the week's evenings continued in the same sullen manner.

Saturday morning Lucy tried to reach him. Since his first physical therapy session had been a bit rough, she made him breakfast in bed. When she heard him rouse, she hurried to prepare the tray.

"Good morning" Lucy said cheerily as she carried breakfast into him.

He struggled to sit. "Um, good morning. What's the special occasion?"

Placing the tray across his lap, she answered. "Because you're my husband."

He grunted "Mm hmm".

Lucy left him to eat his breakfast.

About fifteen minutes later, Jed bellowed for her. "Lucy!"

She rushed into the bedroom to find a rather amusing view. He had apparently stretched over to her nightstand. He had slid off his pillows sideways. The tray teetered precariously upright on his lap. First, Lucy removed the tray. Then she leaned over to pull him up. His position caused her to lose her balance. She sprawled across him. It made her laugh. Thankfully, the humor of what happened hadn't been lost on him. He too chuckled. They both tried to wriggle free at the same time. This only caused them to end up in a rather intimate face to face position. Their laughter ceased immediately. Jed lifted his head to join their lips. She opened her lips slightly to indicate her willingness. He deepened the kiss. His hands slid under her sweatshirt to discover no bra. He broke their kiss to take a peek. She giggled at the playfully leering look he gave her. She sat up straddling him to pull off the sweatshirt to give him full access. He couldn't get enough of touching her exposed bare skin. She moaned in enjoyment. Then to their surprise, a noticeable bulge formed pressing between her legs. Both of them checked it out.

When her hand met with his attentive manhood, Jed groaned loudly. "yeesss."

Jed pulled her down to him for a passionate hungry kiss. As their lips played, Lucy thought she heard a voice in the distance.

"Do you hear that?" She interrupted their kiss to ask.

"Hear what?" He nuzzled her neck. "Where's Grainley?"

"He had to run to the base. Must be the tv." She answered against his skin as she nibbled her way down his fur covered chest.

He tugged at her flannel lounge pants. They came off easily. He shifted so she could ease his off too. Then they positioned to consummate their activities. But his erection hadn't gotten to full hardness. Lucy didn't force the issue. Instead, she kissed and stroked him. However, he was on a mission.

He took hold of her hips to put her back into place. "I want to be inside you."

Using one of his hands and a thrust of his hips, he got just that.

She moaned her pleasure at the feel of him. "Mmm Jed."

"I agree Babe." He rasped.

Lucy slowly moved her hips to coax his enjoyment along with hers. Jed's manhood grew inside her. So did his confidence. He began to move eagerly with her. Suddenly his grunts of passion changed to those of frustration. She felt him go limp.

"Jed?" She asked not sure what happened.

"I can't feel it anymore." He couldn't look at her.

Cursing angrily, he rolled out from under her, dumping her to the side. She reached to put a comforting hand on his arm. He flinched in shame as if she'd burned him.

She wanted to reassure him. "It could be too soon. We should have taken it easier."

He fumed as he extricated himself from the bed. "Don't patronize me! We both heard the doctor the other day."

When he stood, it was apparent that his leg had been affected too. He grabbed for his cane to stay vertical. Naked, he banged his way to the bathroom. She waited until she heard the shower to burst into tears. Her cry didn't last long. The Looney Tunes melody play. She scrambled for her cell phone. It wasn't on the nightstand. It played again. It was on the floor flipped open.

Picking it up, she answered sniffling back her tears. "Yes director?"

In a worried tone the director asked "are you okay?"

"That can't be why you are calling." She responded on guard.

"Not originally no. Jed answered the first time I called. I take it he forgot when you entered the room. So I got an earful of your activities including the anti-climax." The director explained.

Lucy didn't know whether to be angry he heard or grateful he cared. "A true gentleman would have hung up rather than listen."

Will actually sounded ashamed. "True, but in my own way I wanted to know my strategy hadn't been detrimental. Watching the way you and Jed interacted, I thought for sure you two would be happy."

"Will this has nothing to do with you. It's a minor setback." She answered graciously. "What prompted the initial call?"

Director Edison explained. "Tomorrow when you come in, I need you to go to Mark Whitney's group. We had a telemetry hiccup last week in his area I need you to double check his findings. I'll email the copy of the report he sent."

"Yes director. Any contradictions I discover will be brought to you directly." She agreed.

Jed returned to the bedroom as Lucy ended the call. He averted his gaze from her still naked body. Finding her pants on the floor by his feet, he hooked them with his cane. Accentuating the fact he didn't want to see her without clothing, he tossed them at her. Purposefully flaunting her nudity, she dressed in front of him. If she were a different kind of woman, she'd have had the audacity to pleasure herself in front of him. But Lucy didn't have the heart to be cruel.

"Do you have to go into work?" Jed asked after she was fully clothed.

"Nope, Wiley needed to re-direct my priority for next week." She answered.

"Wiley? Pet name for the boss?" Jealousy drenched Jed's jibe.

Lucy didn't appreciate the inference. "Knock it off Jed. You're upset about what happened. Don't re-direct your anger at how I interact with the director. We discussed this the other night. You know I wouldn't be here if I didn't care about you."

Judging from Jed's response, her interpretation was a direct hit.

"Don't psychoanalyze me!" He raged. "How do I know you being here isn't part of your director's plan? Damn spooks!"

"Okay, now you are just being paranoid." She remarked.

Jed stormed out to the garage. His lashing out, Lucy could handle. His paranoia worried her. She went into the bathroom to double check his pain killers. The doctor had merely dropped the dosage. However, she found something she hadn't expected—a bottle of anti-depressants. They were the ones the hospital had dispensed to him. Grainley had told her about them, but Jed refused to take any. Evidently Jed had found the forgotten bottle in his toiletry bag. From the pill count, he'd started taking them the morning after the appointment with the specialist. Lucy went to her computer to read the side effects. This brought up bigger questions. Was she the reason he started taking the anti-depressants? Were his mood swings from the anti-depressants, the pain killers, or not wanting her there? If it were her, then why did she wake every morning with his arms wrapped around her? Lucy shook her head to chase away the past which fueled her insecurities. She never fantasized she'd come into Jed's house to be happy newlyweds. However, she did expect their respect for each other would give them the ability to talk. One thing Lucy was sure of was they did like each other. For the time being, she'd leave it unmentioned.

The week at work didn't give Lucy time to dwell on Jed. She didn't see daylight all week. Mark's group had bungled their explanation of the telemetry problem. His group had also already managed to submit program changes to fix it. The programs had been submitted into the build process that morning. It would take another six weeks until the changes became fully operational. This allowed Lucy to review and test the programs without anyone being aware she was doing it; unless they were watching. Lucy had met in person with the director to inform him of her findings. The frown on his face told her they both had the same suspicions. She worked the weekend testing all threads of the new programming. The only unusual thing she noticed was that she couldn't recreate the original problem in its entirety. When she went to update Will on Monday she asked for help. She needed a database expert. A database build had gone through the week prior to the incident. It had been written as necessary due to a product upgrade and benign to any programs. What she found odd was that it had been treated like an emergency build, not a planned product upgrade. Also, the sign offs for the upgrade included the same signatures as Mark's program fixes. The director gave Lucy two new hires. They both fit the bill and were from two different universities. Lucy also requested an outside agency verification on the members of Mark's group. Because of the incorrect evaluation of the original problem, the director had Mark Whitney suspended pending further investigation.

Lucy and her boys were given an office in the basement. Whiteboards were lined up on two walls. The third wall had two plasma screens linked into the computers. Only the director, Jack Wentz and her had the combination to the door. Her MIS guys, Jacob and Tyson, had to be escorted beyond first checkpoint. They were under strict orders not to talk to anyone about what they were doing. They came in at 5am and departed at 9pm with Lucy by their side. Every day, Jack fetched their lunch to deliver directly to them. They made great progress. Both Jacob and Tyson, using different approaches, found what she suspected. Jacob learned the design quickly. He even began assisting Lucy in trying to recreate the original issue to determine what the fix would eventually cause. Will wanted to pull the programs in the build process. Lucy dissuaded him. Based on whoever had been clever enough to create this, would also have put a trigger in place should the fix programs be pulled. She had Tyson searching for programs which would embed data or code into unchanged programs should certain conditions be met. This embedded information would then be triggered by either a program or database change—something as simple as the date or version stamp on a program.

Friday evening, Lucy released the boys early—6pm. Lucy decided it was futile to continue working without them. She exited the building shortly before 7pm. Not thinking anything of it, she headed across the parking lot alone. All week they had arrived at the same time. Lucy always parked on the far side of the lot so she got a good walk in twice a day. She hoofed it across the lot to her land rover. Getting there, she found she had a flat. Rolling her eyes she called Jack. He didn't answer so she left a message. She called home. Jed didn't hesitate saying they were on their way. She called the guard's station. They would send someone as soon as they finished switching shifts. The skin on the back of her neck began to crawl. After stowing her purse in the vehicle, Lucy chose to walk to the guardhouse to wait for assistance. On the walk, she called Wiley to make sure Jed and Grainley would be allowed admittance. When she told him she'd gotten the creeps, he teased her.

Suddenly someone grabbed her from behind. The phone flew out of her hand. The assailant swung her around so they were face to black ski mask. In the darkness, Lucy didn't see the fist coming at her nose. It dropped her to the ground. Fighting the stars dancing in front of her eyes, she fumbled for the phone. All she found were broken pieces.

The assailant ineffectually kicked her while yelling "yankee bitch!"

Lucy grabbed his stationary foot, making him fall on his ass. This gave her time to run. Her dress shoes lacked any kind of traction allowing the assailant to tackle her. It knocked the breath out of her. She heard yelling and military boots approaching. The man in the ski mask got off of her to run into the darkness.

She recognized Jed's voice giving orders. "After him! Is there perimeter lighting we can turn on?"

Jack Wentz kneeled next to her. "Lucy, can you sit up?"

Taking his offered arm, she pulled herself into a sitting position. Jack flashed a light on her face to assess her injuries. He fished out a handkerchief for her bloody nose.

Again she heard Jed's man-in-charge voice. "Edison, call your people inside the buildings. Let's make sure this wasn't a diversion."

A woman knelt beside Jack. She introduced herself as NCIS special agent Myra Westin, then asked Lucy to tell her what happened. Lucy described what had transpired. Jed's cane clomped across the few feet to her. Myra and Jack helped her stand. Jed immediately put his free arm around her, pulling her against his broad chest for a tight embrace.

He kissed the side of her head. "Babe."

Myra did a quick recap for him.

Clearing his throat, he stated. "Special agent Westin will go with you to the hospital. Myra make sure to get x-rays and snapshots of any bruises. Jack, would you help while we canvas the area?"

Jack nodded. A pair of footsteps came jogging across the parking lot.

Jed's voice dripped with sarcasm as he addressed the newcomer. "Nice of you to join us Naples. Next time you better be here before I am."

Jed walked with Lucy to Myra's car.

Opening her door, he said earnestly, "I have to stay to coordinate the investigation."

"Jed, did you start your job early?" She asked nasally.

"You requested an outside agency handle an investigation." He stated.

"Naturally Wiley requested NCIS, and you specifically." She filled in the rest.

"Did you expect anything less?" He asked rhetorically.

He kissed her on the cheek, then let her get settled in the passenger seat.

"Westin keep my wife safe." He ordered closing the passenger door.

On the drive to the hospital, Myra reviewed Lucy's testimony. It helped Lucy remember more specifics including the "yankee bitch" reference. The x-rays confirmed a broken nose. Two hours later, they wrapped at the hospital. Myra phoned Jed to let him know she was taking Lucy home. Her orders were to stay with Lucy until someone came to relieve her. Lucy made the agent a pot of coffee while she secured the house. Then Myra let Lucy take a much wanted shower. Lucy was careful not to get her nose bandage too wet. Donning her flannel robe, she went in search of the agent before crawling into bed.

"Good night special agent Westin." Lucy said cordially.

"Good night Mrs. Warloc. Your husband said he'd call the land line in a few minutes to talk to you." Special agent Westin relayed.

Lucy lay in bed with the portable phone resting in her hand.

She answered it as soon as it rang. "Jed?"

"Yes Babe, it's me. Are you doing okay?" He sounded like a husband in love.

The forming tears could be heard in her voice. "I wish you were here."

"Babe, please don't cry. I should be home within the hour." He ended the call without saying anything else.

The pain killers the emergency room doctor had given her finally carried her away. When her sleep entered dream stage, she replayed the attack.

Jed's voice lured her from dreamland into reality. "Babe, wake up. I'm here. You're safe."

Opening her eyes revealed a wet naked Jed sitting on the edge of the bed shaking her. She sat up throwing herself into his arms. Jed held her tightly.

Eventually she spoke. "Did you find him?"

"No. So you won't be going anywhere without one of my people, Jack or Grainley." He loosened his hold on her.

She didn't argue. He kissed her gently on the lips, then stood to put on his flannel pants. Climbing into bed, he patted his chest for her to rest her head.

When Lucy woke again, it was morning and she was alone. Adjusting the robe, she headed for the bathroom. The reflection in the mirror brought back last night's events. Raccoon eyes accentuated with a bright white wad of bandaging. In the kitchen, she found a fresh pot of coffee. Going into the study, she selected clothing and dressed. In the sitting room, she found an empty coffee cup. Jed wasn't in the garage either. Had she dreamt Jed had come home last night? Through the panel windows, Lucy noticed a figure outside the front door. Peering outside, she saw it was Jed. He was on his cell phone. Lucy backed away at seeing him flip the phone shut.

He walked into the house. "You're up?"

"Yes. Any news?" She asked.

"I can't discuss it." He sounded cranky.

"Excuse me?" She had higher clearances than he did.

"Explain to me why you didn't just wait in your vehicle for us?" He inquired for her reasoning.

"I got the creeps and I figured it'd be safer at the guardhouse." She answered.

"But walking across the dark parking lot alone didn't 'creep' you out?" He continued his line of interrogation.

"I didn't think much about it. Plus, I called Will to let him know we'd closed up early." It was the same information she'd shared with special agent Westin.

"You made yourself a target." Jed stated harshly.

"I was still on secure grounds. And it's not like I invited that man to assault me." She didn't understand.

"Like you haven't done that before." His sarcasm bit into her.

Lucy didn't appreciate Jed's verbal attack. "Thank you for having such compassionate understanding. I walked away from that a decade ago."

'Yeah and it took you a decade to leave!" Jed wouldn't let it drop.

"So you don't think I paid enough with each beating and . . . ?" Her patience with his attitude was not without limit.

His face changed from interrogator to confused caring husband. "And what?"

"The next time you put anyone on trial make sure you've done all of your homework special agent Warloc." Lucy grabbed her coat and purse to storm outside.

Jed called to her. "Lucy stop!"

She ignored him slamming the door behind her. She saw no sign of her land rover. This made her madder.

Stomping back inside, she yelled at Jed. "Where the fuck is my rover?"

Jed answered evenly. "It's in the NCIS garage being swept for evidence."

"Then give me your keys!" She demanded.

"No." He responded.

Lucy hollered up the stairs. "Grainley!"

"He stayed at the crime scene", Jed stated.

"You should have stayed with him." She sniped.

His tone was level. "I was worried about my wife."

"Really! You're attitude as of late has me feeling like an uninvited guest. Hell, it's been almost a month and my clothing is still in storage containers on the floor in your study." Tears of defeat dripped onto her cheeks.

Jed moved to her. He took hold of her purse. She let him take it from her to hang on a coat rack hook. He eased her coat off to hang it up, too.

Resting his cane against the wall, Jed wrapped his arms around her tenderly yet firmly.

In an emotional voice, Jed spoke directly into her ear. "I'm sorry. I haven't been handling things well. I promise I will do better."

It's exactly what Lucy needed to hear. She also believed he meant it. The emotions she had kept bottled discharged in sobs. Having a packed broken nose, it soon became painful. The pressure build up of mucus instigated a sneeze. Lucy yelped in pain. A snot ball, blood clot and part of the wadding hung from the front of her nose. Jed led her into the bathroom. As carefully as he could, he removed the loosened goopy gauze from her nose. Blood gushed from the cleared nostril. Jed held a cold wet cloth to it.

"Where do you have your feminine supplies?" He asked politely.

"In the rectangular floral bag." Her voice sounded incredibly nasal to her own ears.

Jed went to fetch the supplies he needed. He returned tearing apart a tampon. Taking out his knife, he cut it in half lengthwise. He removed the washcloth.

"This is going to hurt." He warned her before shoving it up her nose.

Lucy gritted her teeth against the pain. After the new packing was in place, Jed wiped Lucy's bloody face.

Cocking his head completely sideways, Jed gave Lucy a light peck on the lips. "That should work."

She put her hand on his bicep to delay his exit from the tiny room. "Jed? Are we okay?"

He made eye contact with her. "If you are willing to continue putting up with me, then yes."

She batted her eyelashes at him. "I think it's a two way street."

He grinned. "You want breakfast?"

"That would be good." Lucy answered glad they were back on even footing.

Chapter Eleven

Around noon director Will 'Wiley' Edison stopped by the house. Jed showed him into the sitting room.

Lucy stood at hearing his voice. "Director?"

Will grimaced at seeing her face. "Ouch! That looks worse than the last set of bruises."

"It only hurts when I laugh." She made light of it.

He handed her a new cell phone. "They found your chip undamaged last night. We put it into a new phone."

"Thanks. Did you call Jake and Ty?" She asked.

"Yes, the boys will be waiting for you to say when you are ready for work again." He answered.

Concern filled her voice, "Are they safe?"

"The situation has been explained to them. Jed coordinated to have an agent assigned to each of them." Will explained.

"Thank goodness." She felt relieved.

The director got serious. "I don't want to rush you, but you've evidently stirred a hive. If you find the answer on our end, it may help Jed's team identify who all is involved."

"Or if they identify who did this, it might help us narrow our search on the computer." Lucy countered.

Will chuckled. "Take it easy. Now I must talk to your husband."

"Thanks Wiley" she responded appreciatively.

Jed and Will went outside to hold their conversation. When Jed re-entered the house he had someone different with him. It was a fit young man in his early thirties. The way his hair waved around the edges of his crew cut indicated he was overdue for a trim. His sunglasses prevented her from seeing his eyes.

Jed introduced them. "Babe, this is special agent Leo Naples. He'll be staying with you this afternoon while I run to the office."

Special agent Naples smiled brightly as he extended his hand. "Ma'am, call me Leo."

Lucy gripped his hand. "Leo. We'll get along fine if you don't ever call me ma'am again."

"Yes ma' . . . er, missus." Leo flexed his hand after Lucy released it.

Leo looked at Jed. "You said there's coffee?"

"Kitchen is back the hall." Jed pointed.

When the agent left the room, Jed stepped in to give Lucy a hug and kiss.

"Feel free to be hard on Naples. He needs refining." Jed commented. "Call if you need anything."

Lucy flipped on the television in search of an old movie. TMC was having Alfred Hitchcock day. When Naples saw her watching 'Suspicion', he plunked down on the sofa next to her. By mid-afternoon, Lucy and Leo were the best of friends. They sat on either end of the sofa sharing the same blanket with their feet stretched towards the other. Leo had a foot on either side of Lucy's hips; Lucy had her feet in Leo's lap. The current movie playing was 'North by Northwest'.

Leo's cell phone rang. "What's up boss?"

Jed said a few words.

"As long as you need; everything is secure here." Leo responded.

Jed said something else. Leo handed his cell phone to Lucy.

Lucy spoke into it. "Hi Jed."

"How are you?" He asked concerned.

"Other than a headache, okay. I take it you are going to be gone longer?" She said.

He answered contritely. "'Fraid so Babe. Is that a problem?"

"Nope special agent Naples and I are doing fine. I've only had to smack him around a few times." She teased.

"Careful he might like that kind of thing." Jed played back. "See you later."

Lucy returned the phone to Naples. "Anything else sir?"

Jed replied, then Leo flipped the phone shut.

"So missus what do you say I make you pasta ala Naples for dinner?" Leo asked with flare.

She giggled at his silliness. "Sounds yummy, but do we have all of the necessary ingredients?"

He stood from the sofa. "I'll make us some popcorn while I check."

He returned in ten minutes with a bowl of popcorn and two sodas. Later during 'Rear Window', he disappeared into the kitchen to make dinner.

He came back stating "dinner will be served in an hour" as he hopped over the back of the sofa.

The only time Lucy had to move was when nature called. Otherwise, Leo waited on her. She enjoyed the special treatment. Lucy went to bed around ten o'clock with no further word from Jed. Sometime overnight she roused long enough to register he'd climbed into bed. Around dawn Lucy woke to Jed calling her name. Opening her eyes she saw him facing the other direction sleeping. It must have been a dream. Relieved that he was fine, she tried falling back to sleep. Again Lucy heard him say her name.

Putting her hand on his back she spoke. "Jed?"

He rolled to face her, snuffling at being disturbed. "Is something wrong?"

"No, I thought you said my name." She replied.

"Mmm" he mumbled rubbing his face in his pillow. "Coffee?"

"I'll get up and make it." She offered climbing out of bed.

With the coffee on brew, Lucy thought about what to make Jed for breakfast. Hearing feet shuffling across the floor, Lucy turned.

Special agent Naples clad in boxers and t-shirt stood in the doorway yawning and stretching. "Good morning missus, how . . . ?"

Lucy interrupted him agitatedly when his hand dipped below his waist band. "Special agent Naples, I realize that is a reflex action. However, it is not acceptable behavior in front of any woman except the one you are dating or married to!"

Naples had the courtesy to be embarrassed."Sorry missus."

"You'd be really sorry if Jed caught you doing that in front of me." She stated in a softer tone.

Leo brushed it off. "Aa, nothing to worry about. The old man didn't come home till oh two twenty. He won't be up for hours."

With no tap of the cane as warning, Jed's voice growling from directly behind the young agent came as a shock."Is that so Naples?"

Rolling his eyes at getting caught, the younger man tried appeasing his boss."Now Warloc you are just cranky because you've only gotten five hours of sleep in the last forty-eight hours."

Jed used his marine in charge tone in Leo's face."No, I'm pissed that one of my subordinates is disrespecting my wife by standing in front of her in his underwear."

"Sorry again missus" Leo said before hightailing it to get dressed.

Lucy waited for the young man to be out of earshot to release the giggles. For a moment, Jed gave her a hard look. Then he grinned wide as he closed the distance between them.

"I should yell at you too for not wearing robe. It's chilly in here." He accentuated his point by cupping her breast to tease a perked nipple.

"Jed" she sighed at his touch.

His hands wandered as he nuzzled her neck. When she pressed her body against his with responsiveness, she felt he'd perked up too.

Sliding her hand down to encourage him, she whispered."No cane? Are we going try again sometime soon?"

He stopped his caresses to hold her in his arms."We need to wait for both of us to be in better shape."

She glanced at him."So you're done obsessing on what happened the last time?"

"About that . . ." he rubbed the freshly razored part of his haircut as he explained. "I reacted poorly all the way around. Hiding in the garage. Shutting you out. I even took anti-anxiety meds without discussing it with the doctor. And blaming you yesterday morning."

"You were reacting in a totally understandable way. But it means a lot that you shared it with me." She appreciated his admission.

Her head rested on his chest; his chin, on top of her head. They stood in each others' arms like that for some time. Even when Leo re-entered the kitchen to pour a cup of coffee into a travel mug; they stayed that way, ignoring him.

Before Leo left the kitchen, he spoke. "Looks like we are good here for now. I'm going to run home for a shower. Any orders boss man?"

Jed told him "I'll meet you at the office at 0900 hours. That gives you 90 minutes. Myra will be on duty here."

"See you then." And Naples was gone.

A few more minutes passed before either of them moved.

Jed sighed. "Babe, are you up for making breakfast while I shower?"

"Not a problem." She dropped her arms to her sides.

Forty minutes later, Lucy put a steaming plate of cream dried beef over fried potatoes on the table. Lucy left him alone to eat in peace to prepare his game plan for the day. By the time she showered and dressed, Myra had arrived. Jed dropped a kiss on Lucy's cheek on his way out the door. Yesterday with Leo had been great relaxation. Today, Lucy was going stir crazy. She called Jake, Ty and Jack to meet her at the office. Then Myra drove her there. The special agent could only enter as far as the lobby. If she didn't have to stay, she could spend those hours assisting Jed and Leo tracking leads. Jack agreed to be Lucy's bodyguard until one of the NCIS agents could rendezvous with them. Ty and Jake's babysitters remained in the lobby. At the end of the day, all three of them felt frustrated at their lack of progress. Knowing that they had become targets made them anxiously determined. Plus, they knew whatever they were looking for must have serious repercussions if someone was willing to assault the team lead. They agreed on their usual 5am start time the next day. Grainley and Jed met Jack at the turn into the facility. Lucy exited Jack's truck to climb into the range rover.

At the house, Jed went into the kitchen to "rustle up a dinner".

Lucy washed her face, then went to talk to him.

"Don't worry about me for dinner. I'm going to bed." She stated.

He stopped what he was doing to ask with concern "Is something wrong?"

Putting her hand to her head, she answered. "Nothing that can be fixed tonight."

"No progress?" He asked.

Frowning and shaking her head, "Not really, we're doing it the hard way—by process of elimination."

Kissing her cheek, he said "We'll keep the volume down. Sleep well."

Lucy fell asleep almost immediately. Nightmares—current threats and cruelties from the past—plagued her all night. At one point she must've cried out. Jed woke her to pull her into the safety of his embrace. When the alarm blared, he got up with her. He planned on going into work after handing her off to Jack at the NRO facility.

Special agent Westin took her to her follow-up appointment for her nose. At seven o'clock that evening, special agent Naples fetched her. Again, she skipped dinner to crawl into bed. And another night filled with nightmares. Jed comforted her like the previous night. The next couple days were the same. After the fourth night of bad dreams, Lucy's subconscious took control. When her mind started to go into dream stage, she'd wake. Worse yet, she couldn't fall back to sleep. This lack of sleep pattern continued.

Her team worked straight into the following weekend. They documented every scenario they tested. They had lists of any possible set of sequences that would run specific sections of code. Not only did they list actual data parameters, but instances of parameters that would never occur unless they were forced into the system. Saturday night they found an anomaly with a data field in conjunction with a nested if statement calling a rarely accessed subroutine. None of them wanted to leave. They all wanted to follow it to conclusion. To test their data processing sequences end to end could take anywhere from four to twenty hours. Lucy called Jed to inform him they would be staying indefinitely. Jack coordinated with the two agents in the lobby to fetch dinner and a Dunkin Donuts carton of coffee. By 2am, they had traced everything with no definitive resolution. Lucy couldn't determine if the bug in the program was intentional or just a programming error. However, they were able to identify the data base change for the field had been so subtle in the upgrade, it took all this time to identify it as significant. When Lucy reviewed the description of the exact modification, this particular variable did not require a change. She had Ty and Jake read the build versus upgrade information independently to see whether or not they caught it too. They were both sufficiently indignant that the field had been altered unnecessarily. Finally, they could narrow their search to the programs which used that data field. Interestingly, they identified subroutines where the field was a passed parameter as opposed to being read directly from the data base. This gave them the adrenalin surge they needed. Lucy wasn't going to call the director until they had all of the evidence. Jack coordinated another coffee run at 5am. Shortly before 8am, the team regrouped to review and validate their individual findings. While Lucy wrote her report, the boys organized the files on the computers. From past experience, giving them a menial task would allow their brains time to reset. Lucy knew the Edison family would be in church. She sent Wiley a text message so his phone would only beep once.

The text message read: "Found it."

He replied with: "Need briefing."

She typed in: "1 hr".

Since the director didn't respond to the last message, Lucy deduced that suited him. She handed her report to Jake and Ty to read and pull the screen snapshots of code she had indicated. While they did that, she went into the hall to call Jed. Jack followed keeping a respectable distance to give her privacy.

Jed answered right away. "Hey Babe! Just got off the phone with Edison."

"Oh that rat took away my moment." She pouted.

"It's okay. He needed to give us time to get our group together for this." He stated.

"Uh huh" she indicated she understood.

Her phone beeped she had another call. "I'm sorry Jed, it's Will."

"We'll talk later." Jed ended their call.

Lucy connected to the incoming call. "Yes director?"

"The earliest I could get everyone together is in two hours. Don't worry about the security level. I'm declaring it 'Eyes Only'. Jack has already coordinated with the main gate and called in personnel to escort the attendees to my conference room. My assistant will be there momentarily for any administrative support you need." Her boss explained.

"Thank you. We'll be ready." She reassured.

"See you then." He disconnected.

She called Jed again. "Is there any chance you could please bring me fresh clothing and my toothbrush? Nothing dressy, just clean and comfortable."

"Um yeah sure." Jed's reply lacked confidence.

Back in the lab, the boys had completed their current task. While she incorporated their suggestions, they put together their presentation slides and her script. Because Lucy was unsure of whom all the director had coming, she would do the presentation. If questions were asked, she would directly address either Ty or Jake when she wanted them to answer. They moved to the conference room. Ty prepared the laptop connection for use with the plasma screen. Everything was ready except Lucy's appearance. To fill in the wait time, they added details to their outlined resolution plan. Thirty minutes before the presentation, the attendees began arriving. Twenty minutes prior, Leo came rushing up to her with her brocade bag.

"Lucy! I am so sorry. We didn't get back into DC until a little while ago." The special agent stated.

"Um, not a problem." Lucy took the bag to make a beeline for the ladies room.

Opening it, she was pleasantly surprised with the outfit. Jed had chosen the sweater from Europe. He'd even remembered to include a change of underwear.

Special agent Westin joined Lucy in the restroom a few minutes later.

Seeing Lucy, she began to chat. "I didn't think we'd make it in time for the briefing. We were doing fine until they put us in a holding pattern. Your husband had to pull rank to get them to move our slot. Then we ran to the house to get your clothing. You should have seen the way the two of them carried on about what to pack in your bag."

"Really?" Lucy asked surprised they'd put much thought into it.

The female special agent laughed. "It was funny watching them run across the hall between rooms bickering over outfits."

Lucy smiled at the image in her head.

Then she followed with another question. "Where were you guys that you needed to take a plane?"

"We found on a credit card statement that Mark Whitney had bought tickets for yesterday afternoon's Georgia Tech playoff game. We were in mid-flight when the BOLO we put out on him came back with a sighting. His car had been identified at a rest stop off the interstate not far from the university. When we got there, we found his body in the nearby woods. Because it was a high traffic area, Jed had us bag everything and walk through probable scenarios before he would release the site." As Myra filled her in on the details, Lucy wondered why Jed hadn't mentioned any of it.

At the moment, she had to finish making herself presentable. The white racing stripes taped across her nose explained away the dark shadows around her eyes.

Turning to the special agent, she queried. "How do I look?"

Myra's eyes went wide. "How did you do that? I still look like I spent the night hiking in the woods."

"Thanks." Lucy responded.

The two women walked to the conference room together. The room was fuller than Lucy had anticipated. Director Edison began introductions immediately. Diving into it like that prevented her usual case of butterflies at giving a presentation. The briefing went without a hitch. The different agencies delineated themselves by their questions.

At the end, the director excused Lucy and her team from the conference room. The agencies wanted to discuss how they were going to handle apprehending the suspects. Will's assistant led Lucy and the boys into the director's office to wait. The small side table contained food and beverage for them. Ty and Jake helped themselves. Lucy couldn't eat; she needed feedback from both Will and Jed. While the boys ate, Lucy conversed candidly with them on how they liked doing a project of this nature. They agreed it had been an incredible learning experience. Neither wanted that to be their core responsibility. Ty wanted to dig into a project long term to learn every intricacy. Jake, on the other hand, was questioning overall if he'd made the right decision accepting the job with the agency. Neither response had been a revelation to her. Both had done an awesome job. This she would include in her letters of commendation. But she also wanted to discuss with the director where she felt they would thrive based on their interests and abilities.

Will entered the office with two agents in tow. He released Ty and Jake to go home to sleep. But he expected them back regular time tomorrow to begin working the code to correct what they'd discovered. Their watchdogs were required until all suspects had been brought into custody. In the meantime, they were to act like they were still searching for a bug in the system. If anyone asked them about the visitors to the building, they were to respond they hadn't noticed. After all, they did their work in the dungeon. Will walked Lucy back into the conference room. Each head honcho representing an agency shook her hand prior to taking their leave. Jed, Leo and Myra remained in the background.

After the room emptied, Lucy addressed Will. "I would like time to discuss Ty and Jake."

"I'll have my assistant schedule a time for us. Right now, you need to get some sleep." The director stated.

Feeling like he'd given her the brush off, she became adamant. "Wiley they deserve special consideration as recognition for the work they've done."

"Lucy, I promise we will meet this week with that specifically in mind." Will assured her.

"Special agent Warloc!" The director called across the room. "Take our girl home and put her to bed."

Jed and his team encircled Lucy. "Let's go Babe. We all need showers and sleep too."

Lucy complied with their wishes. Jed gathered her bag. On the way out, she had to lock up her laptop. Leo and Myra continued to the car. Jed stayed with Lucy. As they walked, Jed took her hand in his free one.

"By the way, you were wrong this morning on the phone." He squeezed her hand as he expounded. "Your moment was the receiving line there at the end."

She shrugged. "That was just a formality."

"Yes it was, but not in the way you think. That was their way of formally accepting you as one of us." He stated with pride.

Leo parked the sedan at the curb as they exited the building.

"Now how about you fill me in on what's going on?" Lucy requested after they climbed into the backseat.

The three agents took turns telling the story. Mark Whitney had been her attacker in the parking lot. However, he hadn't flattened her tire; someone else had. They had studied the surveillance cameras to locate dead zones. No extra prints were found on her land rover. This included not finding Whitney's. Lucy's description of her attacker had included he hadn't been wearing gloves. This had been corroborated by extra epithelial cells found on Jack's handkerchief. Myra had bagged it at the emergency room. Those epithelial cells were matched to Mark's DNA. The DNA sample had been obtained from a hair brush on a search at his house. Since Mark was the prime suspect, they had no problems getting a warrant for the search. However, the discovery of Mark's dead body meant they didn't have direct access or proof of who had assisted him. Or in this case, set him up as the patsy. Whitney didn't have the brains for a complex plan such as the one they were trying to unravel. The names Lucy's team had given them still left doubt as to who the real mastermind is. With this in mind, all of the agencies agreed to work on ferreting them out. Thus, the reason why Lucy's team had to act as if nothing significant had happened.

Exhaustion didn't hit Lucy until she stood under the hot shower. She didn't bother waiting for Jed to finish his before sliding under the covers. Snuggling her face gently into his pillow, she fell sound asleep.

She startled awake. Listening to Jed's snoring, she tried to fall back to sleep. When her empty stomach rumbled louder than his snores, she headed for the kitchen. Opening the refrigerator was a disappointment. There were no leftovers, or much of anything else for that matter. Everything in the freezer would take too long to prepare. There was a mini mart a few miles away. But it didn't seem reasonable to wake Jed. Inevitably, if she went, he'd wake up to find her missing. Unable to eat or sleep, she decided to drink a beer and write a grocery list. It worked. After a little bit, Lucy began feeling sleepy; she went back to bed.

Jed stirred. "Everything okay Babe?"

"For now." She answered.

Chapter Twelve

Lucy's team continued working a minimum of 12 hour days Monday and Tuesday to keep appearances. Each day, Lucy would sit in one of the leather chairs in the director's office. He briefed her on what had been coordinated with the other agencies. Jed and his team were busy with closing any remaining unanswered questions with help from NSA. The FBI would make arrests mid-week. Hopefully by the end of the week, they'd have any others who were involved in custody as well. The department of Homeland Security would hold a news conference. The CIA stayed out of everyone's way. Lucy and her team were to come to work Wednesday for a couple hours. Then leave by noon. Thursday and Friday, he didn't want them in the building. However, none of them were to leave town in case he needed to call them in.

The director did hear her opinion of Ty and Jake. It was difficult for him to understand why they didn't want to be permanent members of Lucy's team after doing such a stupendous job. As for her recommendation about Jake, he seemed completely unreceptive. This bothered Lucy, but it wasn't a point she would push. At the end of the day, Grainley picked her up at the main gate. The only time she saw Jed was in the morning when her alarm went off. The first evening she had Grainley take her grocery shopping. The next, she did laundry and cooked. For Wednesday afternoon, Lucy made arrangements for her storage pod to be delivered. Making this decision, Lucy called the realtor to inform her that her services would no longer be required. She asked Grainley if he could get a couple guys from the base to help empty it. Payment would be homemade lasagna. Lucy could hardly wait to leave the office Wednesday. When they got home, the pod sat in the drive. Unexpectedly, special agent Naples was there too. He watched as two soldiers with dogs sniffed the large container.

He opened the passenger door for her. "Lucy, you got some 'xplainin' to do!"

"What did I do?" She asked with trepidation.

"You should have cleared this thing's arrival with us first." The agent stated in a terse voice.

"Why? It's my stuff from Denver." She remarked.

Leo explained. "Someone could have booby trapped it while it was in the storage lot or on its way here."

Lucy felt stupid she hadn't considered that possibility. "Oh dear."

"Yeah 'oh dear'. Be happy Grainley called me instead of your husband." The agent's voice dripped with sarcasm.

"He's going to be furious isn't he?" Saying the words aloud made it rhetorical.

The soldiers called the "all clear".

Lucy handed the key to Naples. He and one of the soldiers opened the container while everyone else stood across the street waiting. To be safe, Leo had the dogs sniff around a second time with the container open. The special agent remained to aid in the unloading. He was delighted when Lucy handed him a list of the contents. Every piece of furniture and box was examined and sniffed by the dogs prior to being taken into the house. It was a great exercise for the dogs. They proved they understood they were working. Both dogs reacted with tail wagging at a box of dog toys. Even when the box had been opened for the dogs, they both shoved their noses in to sniff. Their tails wagged in wild circles, but neither one took a toy. Lucy's eyes misted with sentiment. When the wood container had been completely emptied, there wasn't anything missing or extra. The agent called the pod company pretending to be Lucy's relocation contact. He informed them they had to retrieve the emptied pod immediately or the township would levy a fine. This would then be charged back to the pod company for failure to comply. Before they had time to respond with a negative answer, the agent hung up on them. In a matter of seconds, Lucy's cell phone rang. It was the pod company. Answering it, she acted like a crying child who had lost her favorite toy. There was a momentary silence on the other end. The coordinator verified her information, then told her a truck would be there in the hour. The soldiers with the dogs entered the empty wood crate for a final sniff. Lucy grabbed two stuffed toys from the dog supply box.

She held them up for the dog handlers to see. "May they have these?"

They nodded. She began walking towards them, but they halted her by holding up a hand palm out. Lucy stood like a statue waiting for the go ahead. The soldiers jogged the dogs to the humvee parked across the street.

After the dogs were loaded into their metal crates, one of the soldiers motioned to her: "ma'am".

She hurried to them. They opened the kennel doors one at a time for her to hand the toys into the dogs. A loud metal banging could be heard from the force of their tails wagging excitedly. Lucy could swear the dogs smiled at her.

The dog handlers saluted her. "Thank you ma'am."

"Thank you for your service and taking good care of these special soldiers." Her eyes misted again with the sincerity of her words.

Special agent Naples had followed her. Putting his arm around her shoulders, he guided her back to house. The two marines who Grainley recruited for the unloading task stood on watch by the pod.

Inside Lucy began to cry. "I'm sorry Leo. I didn't know this would create such a fuss."

"Oh God missus, don't cry." Leo said frantically putting his arms around her in a wide arc. "That monstrosity will be gone by the time hubby comes home."

Sniffling she looked at Leo with water filled doe eyes. "But he'll notice the stuff in the house; especially the pile of dog stuff."

"We will figure out where to go with it. Right now, let's get these boys and you fed so we can think clearly." He tenderly wiped away the tears on her cheeks.

In the kitchen, Grainley had already removed the heating lasagna from the oven. Big squares of the hearty meal were served onto plates with slices of garlic bread. Grainley carried the heavy laden plates and bottles of soda to the two men on guard duty.

Leo checked his watch. "I have to go. Do you have something unbreakable I can put three pieces into?"

Lucy went into the pantry to get a suitable Rubbermaid container. "You said 'we' would figure out where to put everything."

"Isn't there a shed in the backyard? The folding table and crate can go in there. As for the rest of your stuff, it should nicely offset the boss man's decorating taste of sparse functionality." Leo stated.

Lucy cocked her head sideways. "Are you sure you're not gay?"

"Ouch! That hurt! I can't help it I have a sense of style." He feigned having a knife stabbed into his chest.

Lucy finished packing the grocery bag with the NCIS team's lunch. "Thank you for coming to save the day special gay-gent Naples."

Naples teased back. "You better get this mess cleared before hubby gets home."

Lucy stuck her tongue out at the young man. Leo's chuckle echoed in the hall as he headed for the front door.

A few minutes later, one of the marines brought the dirty plates inside. "Missus sergeant major?"

"Yes private?" She poked her head into the hall from the kitchen.

The marine strode to her. "The truck is here. The driver needs you to sign something."

Grainley took the plates to put in the dishwasher. Lucy grabbed her coat while the other private held the door open for her. Outside, the marine escorted her to the driver. Lucy signed the release paperwork. The driver's hands shook as he handed her a copy. She couldn't really blame the driver for feeling intimidated at having two well muscled marines with side arms exposed watching his every move.

The private escorted her to the front door. "Missus sergeant major, thank you for the meal. We can't remember the last time we had food that delicious."

"You're welcome private." She responded graciously.

Inside the house, Grainley came from the kitchen. "Missus, where do you want to start?"

For a moment, Lucy felt overwhelmed glancing at her stuff commandeering every bit of floor space. However, she'd been visualizing where her pieces would go since Monday night.

It was her turn to act like the officer in charge. "The sofa, television stand, nightstand and Jed's bed can go upstairs as soon as the two privates free up. Also switch out Jed's old television for my bigger flat screen. That should give you your own space instead of always being stuck with us."

"Missus I don't need . . .", Grainley started.

But Lucy shut him down. "Don't argue with me marine."

"Yes missus." He responded with a cough to cover his chuckle.

"My bed has to be assembled before the dresser can go into the bedroom. Just toss the sheets and blankets in the laundry room. I'll use mine as soon as I find them." She pointed at stuff as she explained.

"If you guys handle that, I'll work on emptying boxes. After all of the furniture is in place, I'll decide where to go with the pictures." Lucy finished sharing her plan.

"Sounds like a good plan missus." Grainley was glad she trusted him to follow her directions.

The two other marines entered the house. After hanging their coats and gun belts, they went to work. Lucy went into the kitchen to deal with those few boxes. Thankfully, she'd thought to have the boxes put into rooms separate from the furniture. There was plenty of room in the cupboards and pantry to accommodate her kitchen supplies. Very few items were duplicates. With Jed's kitchen, it was good she had left the bar stools for the new owners of the house in Denver. There were boxes in the study with collectible glass items, pictures, books, DVDs and bedding. Until the strong men completed moving the big stuff upstairs, Lucy was stalled. She decided to check out the shed.

Lucy hadn't spent any time in the backyard. Mature shade trees at the corners accentuated what a good size it could be for a dog. A six foot wood fence on either side provided privacy from the neighbors. At the far end of the yard, Lucy peered through the antique metal gate at the corner of the stone fence. The yard on the other side was expansive, but unkempt. She wondered about the history of the house. It looked to be a period two-story colonial with stone fencing separating it from its neighbors. Lucy sighed at the thought of living in a house like that with such a huge yard. Returning to the task at hand, she went to the shed. Opening it took a little elbow grease. It had plenty of room for the dog crate and grooming table. The toys and grooming supplies could go on a shelf in the laundry room. Giving the guys extra time, she examined the wood fence. It needed repair in spots. Overall it could withstand a mischievous puppy. The patio stretched the width of the house and extended into the yard eight feet. The slate pieces were well established needing no apparent maintenance. Heading for the door, she noted the stack of wood had been diminished to scattered wood debris. They had only been using the fireplace to fend the dampness caused by April showers. Stepping inside, Lucy saw they had started carrying Jed's bed out of the bedroom. She steered clear by get the grooming table to put in the shed. Inside the shed, she propped the folded table against an empty section of wall. Grabbing the rake she went to clean the wood debris. By the time she finished, they had gotten her wrought iron bed assembled in Jed's room. While Lucy was making the bed, her antique dresser was carried into the room. Before they put it against the wall, she'd indicated the etched mirror had to be attached. Grainley fetched the tools needed. Lucy had to leave the room since she couldn't watch without telling them to be careful every 15 seconds.

The sitting room no longer contained extraneous furniture. One of the privates was in the process of connecting the television. After unwrapping all of the artwork, Lucy propped the pieces against the walls on which she wanted them hung. Carrying a print into the bedroom, she saw them positioning her dresser. She smiled with appreciative delight. The two marines nodded on their way upstairs to re-assemble the old bed. It felt good emptying the remaining storage bags into the dresser. Reappearing with the hammer, Grainley began hanging the pictures with Lucy's final approval of placement. After fussing a little bit longer in the bedroom, Lucy felt a sense of accomplishment. Going into the sitting room, she only made a couple more small additions for that room to be completed. Even though her clothing didn't clutter the floor anymore, her half empty boxes made the study messier. Hearing the guys still working upstairs, Lucy filled her bookcase in the study. Soon marine boots clomped on the wood stairs.

"Missus sergeant major?" One of them called.

Stepping out from the study, she responded. "Yes private?"

"Anything else you would like us to do before we leave?" He asked.

"Would you please break down all of the empty boxes? Grainley will show you where they can be stored in the garage. And a metal dog crate needs to go into the shed." She stated.

The young men said in unison. "Yes missus sergeant major."

When they finished their final tasks they said their good-byes. Lucy thanked them for their hard work. What she didn't tell them was she would send a thank-you letter to their commanding officer. She turned her attention to the last two boxes.

Grainley popped into the study behind her. "What next?"

"Just hammering nails for hanging photographs." She answered.

"You tell me where." He seemed to be enjoying himself.

As Grainley broke down the last box, Lucy sighed with relief. Looking at the study walls with both her and Jed's photographs and letters of award on display made her feel like she belonged. She went into the bathroom to wash. This room still frustrated her. There was nowhere for her feminine items except in her bag on the floor under the sink. She had placed her towels in an emptied storage bag under the bed. Her extra blankets were in the blanket chest which had been located in the sitting room. With a feeling of accomplishment, she stood in the entry way peering into the sitting room and study. Grainley emerged from the kitchen with two bottles of beer.

He handed her one. "When we started carrying everything into the house today, I couldn't for the life of me guess where we would put it all. But missus, it looks real nice; like it was all made to fill in those spots. And the sergeant major will be pleased to see his mission pictures on display."

"Thanks Grainley. I just hope he isn't upset because I didn't consult him before doing it." Lucy responded wondering when he'd be home.

The mantel clock chimed nine times.

She hadn't realized it had gotten that late. "I forgot to stick the sheets in the washer for your bed."

The young marine chuckled. "No problem missus. My sleeping bag will sleep a whole lot better on the bed as opposed to the cot."

"Very true." She laughed at her own silliness. "Did you get the cable working upstairs?"

Grainley answered. "Yeah, the box was configured for two tvs."

"Well that's good." Yawning Lucy stated. "I'm going to take a shower, then crawl into my bed. Thanks for your help today."

"My pleasure missus. Good night." The young marine patrolled the house one last time.

Even with a relaxing shower, Lucy couldn't fall asleep. She was too anxious about Jed's reaction to what she'd done to his house. But he didn't come home. Checking her phone she found no messages, nor missed calls. Around midnight she drifted off. Out of habit her body woke before dawn. Lucy pulled her flannel robe on over her pajamas. Wandering from room to room, she finally felt at home.

Missing Jed, she sent him a text message. "Good morning. Howz it going?"

Dropping the phone into her pocket, she went into the kitchen to make muffins. Still no response an hour later; she re-sent the message to Leo.

Leo responded right away. "Making progress. Hubby cranky."

Lucy typed, "Y cranky?"

Leo send. "missing link & U"

With the last text, Lucy decided to call Jed.

He answered right away. "Hey Babe, what's wrong?"

In a pouty voice she said. "I slept alone last night."

"We're kind of busy here interrogating suspects." He stated tersely.

"I understand. Just thought you'd like to hear I miss you." She took a risk saying it.

There was a pause before Jed commented. "I, er uh, I'll call you later."

He disconnected without waiting for a response. Lucy tried not to take his coolness personally. After all, he did have a lot on his mind. The phone beeped an incoming text message. Lucy's stomach did a flip thinking it was from Jed. It wasn't.

It was Leo. "Whatz 4 lunch 2day?"

She ignored him. But it gave her an idea. She got one of her baskets. After lining it with tea towels, she filled it with muffins. Retrieving her ten cup carafe from the pantry, she filled it with coffee. She made another partial pot for Grainley.

As he entered the kitchen, she commanded. "Good morning. I want to run muffins to NCIS. Have a cup of coffee and muffin while I shower."

"Yes missus." He stood at attention until she left the room.

As she completed her shower, she heard the young marine run up the stairs to take his. Without thinking, she went into the study to get clothes. She laughed at herself. Going into the bedroom, she smiled at how cozy it looked with his and hers dressers. Ten minutes later, they were on their way. When they got to the main gate, they were admitted without question.

"How was that possible?" She asked.

Grainley explained. "We are both on the list to be admitted."

"Okay, I get you on the list. But how am I?" She didn't understand.

"Missus, all spouses are allowed through the main gate. Getting beyond the front desk is another story. But judging by the rainbow on your badge, I'd have to guess that won't be a problem either." He explained.

The young marine had been correct. When she swiped her badge and entered her key code, the light went green. She'd have to thank Wiley for putting her in the NCIS system without provocation. Standard security protocol dictated the access into other facilities wouldn't be activated until requested for a specific purpose. Lucy wondered what other facilities Wiley had given her carte blanche. Grainley led the way to where Jed and his team were based. Special agent Myra Westin was the only one working at her desk. Lucy located her husband's desk, but no husband.

Myra saw Jed's wife. "Good morning Mrs. Warloc. What brings you here?"

Lucy said "good morning" while raising the basket and carafe.

Seeing no name plate on the fourth desk in their quad, Lucy set her bounty there.

Leo came around the corner. "Hey, whatcha doin' here missus boss man?"

Myra answered for Lucy as she helped herself to the fare. "The missus brought us muffins and coffee."

Leo gave Lucy such an enthusiastic hug, he lifted her feet off the ground. "I love Lucy!"

Jed bellowed from the far side of the room. "Naples put my wife down now!"

Leo obeyed. "Sorry boss man, had a caffeine and sugar rush fantasy."

It only took Jed seconds to enter the quad.

At a lower volume, but terse tone Jed remarked. "You can fantasize about coffee and muffins all you want. Just make sure my wife isn't included in that fantasy."

Leo winked at Lucy as he headed for his desk with food and drink. Jed took hold of his wife's hand to lead her away from the group.

In a gentler voice he asked. "What are you doing here?"

"I thought you and your team could use breakfast." She explained her purpose.

"Well, we're really busy." He sounded strange.

"I know. That's why I did this. We weren't planning on staying more than a couple minutes." She stated her intentions.

"So you aren't mad or upset?" He asked with an edge to his tone.

"Why would you think that?" She shot back.

"You complained about sleeping alone. And Naples had his hands all over you." Jed groused.

Lucy realized she had to make it crystal clear with her husband. "Wait a minute. I called this morning to tell you I missed you. When you asked what was wrong, I answered with an observation not a complaint. As for Leo's hands, it's Leo for goodness sakes. I'd much prefer your hands all over me."

"You're not mad at my attention being on my current case?" He asked again.

"Were you upset with the hours I was spending at work?" She turned the tables.

"No, I was concerned, but I understand." He replied.

Then his words must've made hers ring true, as he got it, "oh".

Her mouth ran ahead of her brain when she added, "As long as my only competition for your attention is your work, I won't be a shrewish wife."

Leo interrupted by saying really loud so she, and the whole room for that matter, could hear him. "Missus these are scrumptious."

Jed's face tightened.

Lucy wanted to defuse Jed's apparent irritation with Leo. "Scrumptious? Are you sure that boy isn't gay?"

It worked, Jed's face relaxed into a smile at her remark. They moved to his desk. He motioned for her to sit in his chair. He sat on the edge of his desk facing her after taking a muffin and refreshing his coffee. He must've been hungry with the way he inhaled the muffin, then went for another.

Jed whispered to Lucy. "I hate to admit it, but Naples is right. These are scrumptious. And so is my wife."

Lucy blushed at his compliment. Jed answered his ringing phone with his mouth full of muffin.

When he hung up, he announced. "The FBI harnessed Josiah Banes. They'll hold their questioning till we arrive."

"Sorry Babe, we have to go." He addressed Lucy.

She smiled "okay".

"We can all ride down in the elevator." He suggested taking her hand in his.

Jed didn't let go of Lucy's hand when they stepped off the elevator. She walked with them to the car.

He tossed the keys to Naples. "You can drive."

Lucy tried to say good bye. "I'll talk to you later."

He stopped directly in front of the car.

He leaned in to put a kiss on her cheek. "Thanks for coming by."

As Lucy walked away, Jed made a show of grabbing her butt. It meant a lot that he was trying to be playful. Doing it in front of Leo probably added to Jed's enjoyment.

Chapter Thirteen

Later that afternoon, Grainley drove Lucy to her doctor's appointment. When they came home, they noticed Jed's coat hanging on the coat rack. In the quiet of the house, they could hear his snores coming from the bedroom. Lucy went into the room to check on him. Watching him sleep tugged at Lucy's heart. The exposed upper portion of his naked torso made her want to gently glide her fingers across his skin to tangle in his chest hairs. Instead, she backed out of the room, closing the door quietly to not interrupt his peaceful slumber. Hours went by without Jed's emergence. Unable to stay awake any longer herself, Lucy decided to join her husband. While she was changing into her t-shirt, Jed grumbled unintelligibly, then got out of bed. He hobbled to the bathroom. Lucy didn't wait for his return to get comfortable in bed. When Jed climbed back into bed, he encountered Lucy's frame.

Shifting his position to face her, he asked. "Where did you come from?"

"I was standing there changing when you went to the bathroom." She stated.

Sliding his hand to rest on her butt, he muttered, "Sorry I missed the show."

"If you're still here in the morning, I might ask for a participant from the audience." She teased.

Drifting off Jed mumbled "that would be nice".

Morning dawned. By the pocket of warmth next to her, Lucy could tell Jed hadn't gotten called away. She quietly went to make coffee. Expecting the smell of coffee to wake him, Lucy began fixing a hearty breakfast. Grainley appeared first.

He grabbed a travel mug to fill. "Morning missus. Gotta go; called to the base."

On his way to the front door, the young man spoke again. "Morning Jed, surprise maneuvers."

"Semper fi", Jed said.

"Hoorah!" The young marine responded as he pulled the door shut behind him.

Lucy called cheerily to Jed. "Good morning."

Jed hobbled into the kitchen. "Morning."

Placing his coffee in front of him first, she gave him a kiss on the cheek. Jed sipped at his cup of caffeine. Lucy completed cooking his breakfast. Setting two plates on the table, she joined Jed for the meal.

"How did the rest of your day go?" She asked.

He spoke after swallowing his mouthful of food. "The interrogation at the FBI was fruitful. It got us the cell choreographing the whole thing."

"That's wonderful!" In excitement, she reached across the table to grab his hand. "No more babysitting details?"

His fingers fidgeted with her wedding ring. But he didn't say anything.

"Jed?" She prompted.

He pulled his hand away. "It led to an altercation. We are waiting for forensics to identify if we got everyone involved or not."

"The bruises you're sporting are from the altercation?" She mentioned what she'd noticed.

"It got a little rough." He shrugged.

Concern filled her face. "Is everyone okay? Myra? Leo?"

Jed briefed her on his team's condition. "Myra is okay. Leo took a gun butt to the face. He now has a set of raccoon eyes like yours."

Putting another forkful of food in his mouth was an indication for her to stop asking about the case. They finished eating in silence. She cleared the table. He turned in the chair as if he was going to stand. Instead, he remained seated watching her. Finally, he stood—white knuckling the table and chair to stay standing slightly hunched.

She stopped wiping the counter to rush to his side. "What's wrong?"

"I told you it got rough." He answered through gritted teeth.

Moving underneath his right arm, she supported his weight. "Bed or sofa?"

"Bathroom for a hot shower" he answered.

In the bathroom, he turned on the shower, then began undressing.

When she tried to leave, he spoke. "Babe, I don't want to impose, but I need you to stay with me."

"Jed, do you want me to take a shower with you?" She asked in an insinuating tone.

"Yes, but only to keep me steady." He replied tossing his pride aside.

She commented mockingly as she undressed. "Way to make a woman feel wanted soldier."

"That's not what I meant." He grumbled.

She had to press her naked body against his to step under the water spray. Feeling his involuntary physical reaction, adequately mended her ego. The hot water seemed to ease the soreness in his muscles. He began standing upright. However, as they soaped she noticed he kept his hands to himself. She slid her hand forward over his buttocks. He stopped her.

In a strained voice, Jed stated. "Don't, it won't."

"That doesn't mean you shouldn't enjoy touching." She tried to reassure him.

"Not if I can't make love to you the way you deserve." He said taking a step away from her in the confined space.

She didn't know how to feel from such a flattering remark. But his movement away from her felt like an insult. Ignoring Jed, she stepped full under the spray to rinse the suds from her hair and skin. Evidently while Jed stood there watching her hands skim across her own body, he realized his mistake. As she checked her curls for any lingering shampoo, he put his hands on her. He worked his way from her butt to her breasts. He seemed to have problems keeping his balance.

Lucy kissed him on the cheek. "Thank you. We're done here."

She turned the water off. Facing him, she put her arms around his torso for stepping over the edge of the tub.

Standing safely on the absorbent rug, Jed didn't let go of her. She stood with him. Her hands resting on his lower back; fingers touching his incision scar.

"Does that bother you?" He asked against her wet hair.

"No. It's no different than any of your other scars." She remarked as she grabbed a towel to dry. "As much as I enjoy naked and wet with you, I don't want your back tightening."

"Lucy I . . ." Jed started and stopped. "Lucy . . . I . . ."

"C'mon let's get you dressed." She interrupted leading him across the hall.

Not noticing her own nudity, she pulled clothes from the dresser for him. When she got a pair of boxers for him, she donned one of her bra and panty sets from the same drawer. He dressed as she tossed the pieces of clothing on the bed next to him. Done getting his clothes, she moved to the other side of the room to her dresser.

Becoming conscious of Jed watching, Lucy questioned him on it. "What? Is something wrong?"

A playfully cocky grin erased the lines from his face. "What would be wrong with enjoying my sexy wife prancing around in her underwear?"

A heated pink glow infused her skin from head to toe.

The lightness in her voice sounded forced as she deflected his admiring comment. "You just like the sexy lingerie."

Grunting at the effort, he rose from the bed. "Babe, it has to do with who is in the lingerie that makes it sexy."

Till he maneuvered around the bed to her, she had quickly yanked on a sweatshirt and jeans.

"Covering it all up doesn't matter. You are still sexy." He remarked reaching for her.

Saved by his cell phone ringing, she dodged his arms to fetch it for him. Leo's name displayed. She hoped Jed didn't have to go into the office. She exited the room to give him privacy for the conversation.

A few minutes later, he joined her in the sitting room. The sound of his cane as he walked eased her conscience over stranding him.

"Leo's apartment flooded so he'll be staying with us for a while." He stated sitting in her high back chair.

She looked at him incredulously. "How on earth did his apartment flood?"

He explained. "The girl in the room above his was preparing to take a bubble bath when she got an emergency call. She was so frantic, she rushed out without turning the water off. It overflowed the tub, saturating her floor and Leo's ceiling all night."

"Oh my, did the ceiling cave in?" She asked curiously.

"Not yet. They had to turn the water off for the whole building and evacuate." Jed relayed Leo's story.

"It's a good thing Grainley got called for maneuvers this weekend." She remarked.

He leaned forward in the chair. "Babe, it was Grainley's last weekend with us."

"I don't understand." She didn't know what he meant.

He explained. "Grainley was going back to the base Monday anyway. The agreement was he'd stay until I could work. Then with needing a guard for you round the clock, they extended his assignment with me, or rather, you."

"Why didn't he tell me?" She felt slightly hurt.

Switching from the chair to next to her on the sofa, he admitted, "I told him not to, that I would tell you when we had the all clear."

"Oh okay." She shrugged. "It makes sense."

"You're not upset?" He wanted to be sure.

She shook her head. "That would be a really silly thing to be upset about."

He didn't say anything, just gave her a genuinely happy smile.

Realizing she had stuff to do if it was three again, she stood. "You relax. Let that vicadin kick into affect. I have to change the bedding upstairs."

"Is that where my bed was moved to?" He asked slightly accusingly.

"Yes, it's a guest bed instead of a cot." She answered innocently fluttering her eyelashes. "And with my bed frame there's something to hold onto when you need it."

He nodded. "I did make use of it several times since I got home yesterday. I also noticed your mattress is more comfortable."

"I'd hoped it would be better for your back." She remarked. "You are okay with the more feminine style?"

"I do like the bed and the comforter." He commented. "It's amazing how your dresser fits perfectly on the side wall."

"I was amazed too. So you aren't mad with me moving my stuff in?" She asked with trepidation.

Taking her hand, Jed stated. "I am happy you finally felt like it was your home too. And am surprised it didn't make the house feel cramped."

"No, that would be the bathroom." Lucy teased on her way out of the sitting room to take care of things for their expected guest.

After stripping the bed, she checked around to see if anything else would be needed. No trace of Grainley remained. He'd even emptied the trash can. Lucy tossed the bedding down the stairs ahead of her. Carrying it to the laundry room, she began the regular laundry too. Finding blood on Jed's clothing reminded her that his new job would have its dangerous cases. If it didn't, Jed would be miserable. Her own revelation was how all of the key characteristics needed to do what he did and have a passion for, astoundingly, were the things she respected and loved about him. Her stomach did a flip. Before she had a chance to follow that train of thought any farther, the doorbell rang.

"I got it!" she hollered for Jed to hear.

Leo's matched set of black-n-blue eyes peered through the side window at her approach.

"Good morning Leo! Or should I call you Randy raccoon?" She greeted him cheerfully opening the door wide.

He responded with a boyish grin. "Hey Lucy, hope you are alright with this."

"Of course, carry your stuff to the guest bedroom. I'll be right up with fresh sheets." She pointed towards the stairs.

"Great, thanks" he said appreciatively. "It'll take a few trips. The firemen let me get my clothing and anything personal."

Lucy went into her and Jed's room to get the spare sheets from under the bed.

Jed's cane thumped across the floor.

"Naples, do you need help with anything?" He called with slightly slurred speech.

Leo winked at Lucy when he was in the house again. "I can handle it. Why don't you go sit down before the vicadin literally knocks you on your ass."

Jed responded to the rhetorical question. "If you don't watch your step, I'll knock you on your ass."

She went upstairs to avoid the two posturing males. He made his last trip by the time Lucy finished making the bed. Putting down the last box, Leo hoisted Lucy up without warning. She shrieked as he tossed her onto the bed. He threw himself down next to her.

"Leo! Jed's going to be furious!" She chastised.

"Your old man is on the sofa sawing wood like a lumberjack." He stated.

Since Leo merely lay next to her, Lucy didn't scurry away. "How bad is your apartment?"

He rolled onto his side to face her. "A dripping noise woke me. A puddle had formed on the sofa. The sagging ceiling didn't look like it would burst right away. After calling the fire company, I unplugged everything to prevent anyone getting electrocuted. As I went, I placed my bags in the hall. By the time the firemen got the water turned off in the building, it was raining in my apartment. That's when I was banned from entering it anymore."

"Will your renter's insurance replace your electronics and furniture?" She wanted to make sure he was covered.

"Yeah, kind of nice too, I wanted to upgrade my entertainment center. Now I won't have to foot the whole bill." He smirked at his good fortune.

Bouncing the bed intentionally as she climbed off, she teased. "Yeah, but we're stuck with you until the apartment is habitable again."

Leo tried grabbing her to pull her back onto the bed. Instinctively, she turned quickly to flee. In doing this, she bumped Leo's nose. He winced in pain.

"Oh my God Leo, I am so sorry!" She exclaimed.

Tears of pain ran down the macho man's face. "Ice."

She tore downstairs to get the cold pack from the freezer. Leo met her at the bottom of the steps. They went into the sitting room where Jed was stirring from the commotion. Leo sat in the cushiony low backed chair. Tilting his head back, he positioned the cold pack across his nose.

Jed spoke. "What happened?"

Lucy said upset. "I whacked him in the nose."

"Babe, don't fret. Naples has been due for a good woman to pop him." Jed assessed.

Leo's muffled voice unmistakably perturbed. "Hey, let's not add insult to injury."

"If you were expecting kid gloves, you chose the wrong place to stay." Jed harassed.

Leo grumbled under the cold pack. Not wanting to listen to them bicker, Lucy went into the kitchen. She poured a cup of coffee to take outside with her. Walking around the yard, she found herself at the back gate. As she approached it, a figure startled her.

The woman on the other side apologized. "I'm sorry I scared you."

Lucy laughed. "It's okay. It was my own fault for wanting another look at the house."

"Oh were you over while my mother-in-law was gone for the winter?" She asked curiously.

Lucy didn't want the woman getting the wrong impression. "No, I've only moved here in the last couple months and when I saw the house through the gate the other day it intrigued me."

"Were you interested in seeing inside?" The woman prompted.

Lucy answered eagerly. "I'd love to, but I don't want to impose."

"My husband will be taking his mother to church tomorrow morning at ten. I'll meet you here then." The woman stated.

"Are you sure?" Lucy couldn't believe the offer.

Pulling a business card from her pocket, the woman passed it to Lucy. "See you tomorrow morning."

"Thank you" Lucy said taking the card.

The woman walked to the gazebo where a man and elderly woman were sitting. Lucy read the card. The woman was a realtor from South Carolina. Meandering around the yard, Lucy found herself excited about seeing the neighboring house. Back inside the house, she went to take a peek at the men. After verifying there had been no blood shed, she went into the kitchen again to plan meals for the next few days. Sometime later, her cell phone played Looney Tunes.

Pulling it from her sweatshirt pocket, she clicked it on. "Hello director. What can I do for you?"

"I need you here as soon as possible to discuss some information I've just been briefed on." His tone clearly denoted it as an order.

"Okay, I'll be there right away." She responded.

The director disconnected the call without saying anything further. Since her two protectors were doped with pain killers, Lucy wrote a quick note. Grabbing her purse, she headed out the door. It felt good to drive her vehicle again. Arriving at the office, Jack met her at the front door of the building.

Lucy became very nervous. "Am I in trouble Jack?"

"No, the director needs to brief you on the results from the FBI and NCIS." Jack smiled to ease her tension.

"It couldn't have waited?" It seemed odd to her.

Jack laughed. "I'm surprised your husband didn't make it pillow talk."

"He was awake for a full 48 hours. Snoring face first into his pillow is the extent of last night's pillow talking." She made light of it.

Jack agreed. "Heard it got rough; how's he doing today?"

Lucy clued him in. "Jed and Leo are in pharmaceutically induced comas in our sitting room."

"Don't tell me you're adopting Naples with Grainley back on base!" Jed's marine buddy's voice laced with mock horror.

"Fate likes pulling practical jokes on me." Lucy laughed. "Leo's apartment flooded thanks to his upstairs neighbor."

They had reached the conference room. Will came in carrying a tray with a carafe of coffee, condiments and cups. He poured them each a cup, but let them handle the extras. He opened the "Eyes Only" hash marked folder to brief Lucy and Jack.

The cell originated from a disgruntled CIA agent. The agent had pitched an idea to their superiors to test NRO's capability of detecting an internal threat. However, the list of people recruited from NRO's own ranks had shocked the director. They also attracted real terrorists into their circle. It went so far as to vouch for these individuals for lower level jobs—secretaries, facilities, within the intelligence agencies. Anyone hired into any of the intelligence branches in the last two months had come under suspicion—including Lucy and Jed. That was until Lucy had become the cell's number one target. Because the director had given her carte blanche access and the questions she'd been asking, the leader of the cell knew it would only be a matter of time till they were revealed. Particularly with Lucy's new husband a highly decorated marine and recently hired within another branch of the intelligence agencies. Mark Whitney, the man who'd attacked her, had not been a member of the cell. His connection was members of the cell worked in his group. When he was suspended, they tried to make him the fall guy by instigating his attack on her and hopefully scare her to back off. They got him drunk and smuggled him into the facility. However, that's the difference between real terrorists and those playing at it. The real terrorists had already booby trapped her land rover the same night of Whitney's attack. NCIS impounded her vehicle to search for evidence. The forensics indicated Whitney had not flattened her tire. The closest he'd gotten to her vehicle was when he'd grabbed her. The land rover had been rigged such that the placement and use of the jack would cause the gas tank to blow. If she had survived the explosion, there would have been severe trauma. NCIS and the FBI both suspected Whitney too incompetent to set that type of bomb. The FBI headed the investigation on who planted the bomb while NCIS chased Whitney. This enabled them to find the answers quicker. Especially when their independent leads continually had the two agencies crossing into the other's case.

At the end of the briefing, Lucy sat silently stunned. She now understood fully why Jed had flown off the handle at her the day after the attack. Also, why the director had been short tempered after they'd developed the re-build of programs to eradicate the Trojan horse. Looking closer at the director's face, she could tell he had not relaxed even with the individuals responsible either dead or in custody. Because of the nature of what happened, the director had no one he could talk to in regards to the betrayal he felt. Administratively, there were plenty who he had to report on his organizational response. Scrutinizing the newly formed lines on director Edison's face, Lucy could tell he needed to talk.

Lucy decided to approach with caution. "Will is your re-organizational plan being accepted as a sufficient enough response?"

Will closed the folder with slow deliberation. "Some of the agencies understand it was a proactive plan. That if we hadn't begun instituting it, the problem would not have been found. However, there are a few individuals arguing I responded too late and are asking for my resignation."

"What about the CIA? Are they being reprimanded too?" She pointed out the catalyst to the issue with national security.

"The NSA is doing a deeper investigation into the individuals who approved the secret test scenario." Will stated, his voice cracked with the last words. "And on me."

"Will?" Lucy reached across the table, laying her hand palm down next to his.

Will cleared his throat. "Jack, would you mind waiting in the corridor for us?"

"No problem." The marine answered as he stood.

The director stood, too. He walked the long way around the conference table.

His controlled demeanor broke the second he heard the door shut. "I haven't slept all week. Every time my wife tries to help, I lose my temper. Worse yet, I can't share what's going on or how serious it is. This is all so different than the usual crisis."

Lucy turned in her chair to face him as he sat next to her. "Wiley I know it's difficult, but you need to re-orient it in your own head. It's the same as any other situation you've come under fire. Because it was in-house, you are taking it as a personal betrayal. Your emotions are clouding your perspective."

"Exactly! But I can't detach. I take pride in this organization." Will pounded on the table with his fist.

"What if this had happened at the NSA? Would you be berating or defending the director over there?" Lucy hoped this tactic would work with him. "Better yet, do you want the CIA director fired because his agent was corrupt?"

Will answered immediately. "Well no. He's fighting the same battle we all are. There will be cancerous cells that need to be excised from time to time."

Lucy batted her eyelashes at him. The director contemplated his own words. It took a few laps around the table for it to sink in completely. He nodded his understanding.

Collecting his folder, the director motioned to the door. "When this is behind us, Sara and I will have Jed and you join us for dinner."

In the hallway, the director headed for his office. Jack walked in companionable silence with Lucy.

At her land rover, he finally spoke. "I may be out of line, but I think you should know something about Jed."

She raised her eyebrows to indicate he should keep talking.

"When I heard you were Jed's wife it struck me as strange. Jed's first wife Michelle was a tall blonde who had no aspirations to be anything except a trophy wife and mother. You couldn't be more different. It made me wonder if he married you overseas from a sense of honor for you saving us years ago. Particularly when I discovered you weren't living together. I don't know what changed to bring you two back together, but what matters is you are. The night you were I attacked it was obvious how much he truly cares. I hadn't seen him that upset since Michelle's death. He was a man on a mission and no one dare get in his way or question his orders. If we'd have caught Whitney that night, I believe Jed would have beaten him to within an inch of his life." Jack finished his narration.

"Uh, thanks Jack." Lucy had difficulty finding words with the myriad of emotions swirling in her mind.

She climbed into the rover. The drive home was a blur. The possibility that Jed could be falling in love with her was incomprehensible. Walking to the front door, Lucy saw Jed open it. He stood there with a scowl on his face.

In the background, she heard Leo doing his Ricki Ricardo impersonation. "Lucy, you got some 'xplainin' to do."

Jed turned his head to growl at the younger man. "Go to your room!"

His obvious irritation with her dispelled her happily ever after daydreams. Nonetheless, she smiled as she neared. When she tried to kiss his cheek, he stepped back for her to enter the house.

He shut the door with force before speaking angrily. "You should have woken me to tell me where you were leaving."

Keeping her voice calm, she responded. "I wrote a note and put it where you could find it easily."

"You weren't here when I woke up and I didn't know what happened to you." Jed's tone hadn't eased any. "What was so damn important to Edison, it couldn't wait until Monday?"

"He briefed Jack and me on what you all had uncovered." She answered.

From the top of the stairs Leo hollered. "Did he tell you about the awesome tackle your husband made?"

"My next project is installing a door up there." The older man groused.

Lucy slid her hand up his arm to rest on his bicep. "I'd rather hear about that awesome tackle."

Jed had no response other than to intentionally bang his cane on the floor as he walked into the sitting room. Lucy followed. He sat on the sofa.

"I was worried." He stated taking hold of her hand.

Jed tried tugging her down next to him. Instead, Lucy straddled his lap. His face showed complete surprise.

She placed her hands on his shoulders as she kissed him gently on the lips. "Thank you for being my hero again."

Unexpectedly Jed emitted an odd growling kind of groan, then proceeded to ravage her. Their lips joined. Their tongues danced. Their hands roamed. Shirts were removed. He deftly unhooked her bra to get to her nipples. They poked out to meet his eager hands.

Breathlessly she said "We aren't alone."

Nuzzling her neck, he suggested. "Bedroom."

She helped him stand. Ignoring their discarded clothing, they hurried to the bedroom. Jed kicked the door shut for privacy. Lucy stripped down to her lace panties. Jed managed to get his jeans removed. On the bed, he caressed her skin with his rough hands and tantalizing lips. She kept her moans of pleasure low so Leo wouldn't hear them.

But when Jed's lips encircled her nipples, Lucy couldn't contain the groan of delicious pleasure. Then his hand went underneath the lace. Lucy's hips thrust upwards in response to the intimate motions.

"Jed I want you." She moaned shifting her body to reach for his boxers.

There was no bulge.

Jed's voice husky with passion, he whispered into her ear. "It won't work, but I want to do this for you."

He repositioned to suckle her breasts and dip his hand below the lace waistband.

Lucy called out. "More . . . please more."

Her own wanton behavior shocked her, but the sensations he was creating in her were undeniably fabulous. The way he stoked her passion had her crying out his name. She gripped the curved metal rungs of the head board as he took her to multiple climaxes. Spent, Lucy curled into Jed's arms.

He kissed her. "Mm, I had no idea it would be that good."

Lucy snuggled her face into the fur on his chest. "You have that affect on me."

"Feeling is mutual." He tightened his hold on her.

Chapter Fourteen

Lucy lay in bed. Her body ached. She slid her hands along it. Her breasts were oversensitive to touch causing her to wince with pain. Moving down to her hips, she found tenderness from bruising. There was a sticky substance on her upper thighs. Gazing at her upheld hand it was covered in blood. A male figure entered the bedroom. She tried to speak. No words would come out. She needed help; she needed Jed. As the figure came near she recognized the smile—it belonged to Trevor.

He leaned in close to her face, sneering at her as usual. "He won't want you when he finds out."

Lucy startled awake! Much to her relief, it had been a dream. Jed's arms were still holding her.

"Another nightmare?" Jed asked his voice husky from sleep. "It's okay Babe, I won't let anyone get you."

If only Lucy could tell him. The nightmares had been instigated by the attack. But the idea that Jed might actually love her . . . It frightened her a hundred times more than flying. She shivered. He pulled her closer and tucked the covers around them. She pushed everything else away in her mind to enjoy the safe cocoon she shared with her husband at this moment. It was a short moment. There was a knock on their bedroom door.

"Jed? Lucy?" Leo opened the door a crack.

"This better be damned important Naples." Jed growled at the young man.

"There's a Ben McCallister from the CIA here." He stated opening the door wider to stick his head in the room.

Jed threw the covers back climbing from the bed. "Tell him I'll be right out."

Leo nodded, but failed to move. He was too distracted by the view. Lucy grabbed at the blankets. Jed noticed too.

Banging the door hard into Leo's shoulder, Jed ordered. "Now Naples!"

"What could Ben want?" She asked slightly alarmed.

Pulling his pants on, he remarked. "He was following some tangents for me."

He yanked on a t-shirt on the way into the hall.

Naples reappeared a couple minutes later. "Lucy?"

"Shouldn't you be in that meeting?" She responded holding a blanket up to cover her bare chest.

From the door, Leo tossed their clothing from the sitting room. "I am; figured you didn't want agent McCallister examining your girlie holsters."

After the door closed, Lucy dressed. Not wanting to intrude on the meeting, she went into the kitchen.

Leo strode back the hall. "If you don't mind, hubby would like coffee brought to us."

"Sure, it will take a little time to brew." She stated.

While the coffee brewed she got the serving tray ready. Jed didn't have a serving set. Lucy used her creamer, sugar container and matching cups. The pocket doors into the sitting room had been closed tightly. Leo saw her through the small opening. He walked over to open the doors for her. She set the tray on the buffet table.

As she poured the coffee she asked. "Agent McCallister how do you take your coffee?"

"Lucy is that you?" He asked eagerly.

"Yes Ben." She held up the cup to indicate she was waiting for an answer.

"With sugar." He stated.

Leo spoke. "If anyone wants to know, I take my coffee . . ."

". . . with cream and sugar." Lucy handed Leo his cup.

As she handed Ben his, he spoke. "Wow, I can't believe it's you. You look great!"

"Yeah right, this time I'm sporting a broken nose and raccoon eyes." She remarked.

Not allowing Ben to pay her another compliment, Jed ordered. "Lucy, would you mind leaving us alone again to wrap this up?"

"Sure. Good seeing you again Ben." She said leaving the room.

"Definitely good to see you." Ben stated before Lucy had closed the doors completely.

She went back to the kitchen to prepare dinner. Agent McCallister left 45 minutes later without saying good bye.

Leo brought the coffee tray into the kitchen. "Mmm, that smells delicious. When do we eat?"

She began clearing the tray. "Ten minutes; would you please set the table?"

Leo carried out his chore.

"Where's Jed?" She asked stirring the pot.

Leo answered "He went into the study. Do you want him?"

Lucy giggled at the question.

"Didn't you get enough earlier?" Leo teased.

She volleyed. "Jealous?"

"I am", he said seriously.

His comment stunned her. "Excuse me?"

"What man wouldn't want the woman he loves calling out his name with the passion you did the old man's earlier?!" Leo remarked rhetorically.

Lucy's face flamed with self-consciousness she'd been that loud.

To deflect, she placed dinner on the table. "Please tell Jed dinner is ready."

"Lucy, I didn't mean to embarrass you." The young man explained to dispel her discomfort. "It was meant to be a compliment. I've only known the old man for a few years, but I've never seen him happier. Hell, I've never seen him happy till now."

He didn't let her respond before going to knock on the study door. Jed came at the beckon.

His cheery tone sounded forced when he spoke. "It smells delicious."

Lucy dished food onto plates. Leo dug into the meal. Sounds of enjoyment were made between mouthfuls. Jed on the other hand took his time. He stared intently at her while he chewed. When they were done eating, he insisted on helping her clean up from dinner.

Joining Leo in the sitting room, Jed gave a command. "Naples, run to the Turkey Hill and fetch us ice cream."

"Yes sir. Any flavor preferences?" He asked.

Lucy answered right away: "Mint chocolate chip or heath bar crunch."

Jed merely nodded. "Whatever my wife wants."

As soon as Leo shut the door, Jed asked far too serious. "Are you okay from earlier?"

"Yes" she wondered what was wrong. "Are you?"

He continued in the same vein. "Was what we did, what caused your nightmare?"

She felt trapped. The only way to keep it concealed was to lie. And she couldn't lie to him.

"Yes . . ." she hesitated trying to find the right words to explain.

He didn't wait for her to finish. "I'm sorry. The last thing I wanted was to hurt you or dredge up something to cause you nightmares."

She averted her eyes from his searching ones. "You didn't hurt me."

"Why don't I believe you?" He probed further.

Her eyes darted up to meet his. "It scares me how much I enjoy when we are, uh, intimate."

The astonishment on his face caused her to divert her gaze again.

The Looney Tunes theme song could be heard playing in the silence. She jumped up to get her phone. It was charging in the study.

"Yes director?" She answered.

In a slurred voice, Will talked. "Lurcy, don't want to worry Sarie!"

"Where are you?" She asked fearfully.

"The Moronic Bar." He stated.

"Don't go anywhere! We'll be right there!" Disconnecting, she rushed to the sitting room.

Seeing her frantic face, Jed stood immediately. "What's wrong?"

"It's Edison! He's drunk at the Moronic Bar." She voiced her concern. "We have to get him home. He's a sitting target if anyone is watching."

"I agree!" He hooked his holster onto his belt. "Get your shoes on. I don't want you here alone."

Lucy slid her feet into her fur-lined leather boot slippers. "I won't be. Leo will be back soon."

Talking on his cell phone, he corrected her. "Naples, meet me at the Moroccan."

Following him to the range rover, she said. "He said the Moronic."

"Put your seat belt on!" Jed ordered as he reversed from the garage too fast for her taste.

Lucy did eagerly and held onto the handle above the door as Jed negotiated turns.

As he drove he explained, "There is no bar called the Moronic. It's the Moroccan. He hasn't been there drinking since he read the full report after Donny died."

Who's Donny?" She asked.

"Leave it to Edison to conceal pertinent facts. Donny Edison, his younger brother. On the Monroe, he was the soldier we carried off the helicopter in a body bag."

"What?! Why didn't he tell me?" She was indignant.

"Maybe he thought I told you." Squealing the tires into a parking space, he stated. "Stay here!"

When Jed got out, he locked the door. Leo joined him on the walk into the bar's festively lit entrance. It only took a few minutes for them to emerge supporting the drunken director. They dumped him into the backseat of a Hummer. Leo climbed into the driver's seat. Jed hurried to the range rover.

He handed the keys to her. "Follow us to the director's home."

Then he climbed into the backseat of the Hummer. Leo waited for Lucy to pull out of the parking lot. On the drive, shortly after leaving the city limits, Leo slammed on the brakes causing her to do the same. Waiting and watching, Lucy could see by their silhouettes, an altercation was occurring in the back seat. It appeared as though Jed managed to subdue Wiley with a wrestling hold. They continued driving at a much higher rate of speed. At the director's address, they drove through a security gate at the end of a half mile long drive. A set of floodlights turned on as they pulled up to the front steps. Leo turned the engine off. Lucy did the same. The earlier scuffle re-started with the opening of the back door. A glint from metal in Wiley's hand erupted with a loud bang. Lucy flattened onto the driveway.

Jed cursed. "Damn it Edison!"

Tackling the director broke the gun free. It skittered across the macadam to stop by Lucy. She grabbed it, dropped the clip out and opened it to empty the chamber.

"Naples, take the director." Jed ordered standing with difficulty.

Flipping open his phone, he spoke. "Sara this is Jed again. Everything is okay. Your husband just felt the need to fire a gun."

Soon a woman, not much older than Lucy, emerged from the grandiose home. She ran to where special agent Naples held the director in an upright position.

"Oh Will!" She cried flinging her arms around his waist.

The director comforted his wife.

Tears could be seen shining in Will's eyes. "I'm sorry Sarie."

He leaned on her while they moved into the house. "Thank you Jed. Please, all of you come inside."

"We don't want to intrude." Jed stated as a way of declining her invitation.

Momentarily stopping their progress, Sara pleaded. "If you don't mind please, I don't think I can handle him alone."

Reaching for Lucy's hand, he replied to Sara. "Yes ma'am."

"You okay?" Jed addressed Lucy.

"Yeah, I'm getting used to hard surfaces." She remarked.

He flashed a relieved smile.

Holding his gun upside down with one finger in the trigger, she said. "And I'm guessing you want this back."

He took it from her, clicking it open to verify it was empty. She also handed him the round and clip from her pocket.

Kissing her on the head, they followed the others into the manor. "That's my girl."

The home was as elegant on the inside as outside. Sara ministered to her husband sitting haphazardly on the sofa. Lucy determined Sara had done the decorating herself. The director's wife wore one of Will's cardigans to cover the emerald green satin nightgown. Nonetheless, her beauty: spray of freckles, copper red hair, bright green eyes, full lips, perfectly proportioned curves accentuating her tiny waist—couldn't be hidden. Will played with the fine straight hairs that had strayed from her braid. The couple spoke in quiet tones to each other.

Finally Sara straightened. "Lucy, would you please help me in the kitchen?"

By complying, Lucy allowed Will's wife the facade of saving her husband's dignity in front of an employee.

As the director's wife made tea, she dropped any pretense. "So you are the infamous Lucy Seeir-Warloc."

Taken slightly aback, Lucy responded. "Well I wouldn't use that description."

Pausing her actions, Sara put her hand on Lucy's. "I didn't mean that the way it sounded. It's just I've heard so much about you between Will and Jack, I feel inadequate at times. And with Will's mood as of late, it did have me wondering about your relationship with my husband."

"I can assure you Mrs. Edison that would never happen!" Lucy had to dissuade this woman's misconception.

Sara Edison smiled softly. "I realize that now. Seeing the way you and Jed look at each other, I have no more doubts where you are concerned."

Lucy smiled back with relief. But her mind questioned what the other woman had seen that Lucy didn't.

She asked a different question. "How long have the director and Jed known each other?"

Sara reminisced. Will had been a captain in the Air Force and Jed a green marine when they first met. Their paths crossed from time to time even after Will had left the military. Donny, Will's younger brother had been assigned to Jed's unit. When Jed's first wife died, Jed spent many a night in bars brawling. Donny had called on Will to help bail the marine out on many occasions. Upon Jed's return to the states from the Monroe and that devastating mission, the two men had shared a bottle or two of scotch regularly. For a certain period of time, it hadn't been unusual for Sara to find

Jed and her husband passed out on furniture in the study. Two years later, it was Will who'd campaigned for Jed to command the special operation from Endeavor. Because of the sensitivity of that mission, he'd also pushed for a contractor expert to be on board to prevent a repeat of the mission where Donny had died. With the resounding success of that mission, Will had been promoted.

As Sara finished, the director burst into the kitchen wearing sweatpants and a t-shirt. His hair wet from the shower they'd coerced him into taking. If they'd thought it would sober him, it failed.

Will kissed his wife sloppily on the cheek. "Sarie is the tea ready?"

With her nod, Will staggered away with the two special agents in tow. Sara carried the tray into the living room. For a few minutes, they sat quietly while she poured the hot liquid into delicate china. Will carried his cup to the bar in the corner of the room.

Opening a bottle with amber liquid, he boomed. "Here Jed! This will sweeten that brew."

"I'm sure it will, but haven't you had enough." Jed spoke deliberately.

"Listen to you all high and mighty like you've never been this far into a bottle." Will smacked his open palm against the marble bar top.

Without his cane, Jed struggled to stand.

Will antagonized him. "A couple shots of this might loosen your strut Peacock one!"

Jed retorted. "Ask my wife, my strut is just fine."

In his current state, the director went on a tangent. "Have any of you heard how Jed's wife actually gave him his permanent code name?"

Not waiting for any responses, Edison dove into the story. "You all know he was my eyes and ears aboard the Endeavor for mission Donny Do Right. During that time a certain contractor, whose name won't be mentioned, had also been on board. One of the crew members overheard her saying on the phone, and I quote 'he struts around like a peacock in full color'. When the guys in his unit heard this, it stuck."

With eyes wide and hand on mouth, Lucy gazed remorsefully in Jed's direction. But he seemed unbothered by this disclosure.

"If you gentlemen would prefer brandy and cigars, then we women will take our tea into the kitchen again." Sara tossed Lucy a life line.

Lucy grabbed for it. The two wives went to the quiet of the kitchen. They busied themselves with washing and drying the tea set. Lucy clued Sara in on what she could about why Will had been so moody.

Leo entered the kitchen. "Mrs. Edison your husband has passed out on the sofa. Would you like him carried upstairs?"

"No, agent Naples. He can sleep it off down here." The lady stated.

"Yes ma'am, then we'll be going." He left to report to his boss.

They met in the foyer.

"Thank you for bringing my husband home." Sara said appreciatively.

"We're here to serve ma'am." Jed responded.

The two women smiled at each other with a new understanding.

The trio took a detour on the way home to get Leo's car. Back at home, Lucy got ready for bed. Jed waited for Leo. Lucy heard Leo arrive, but he didn't go up the stairs right away. The two men patrolled the house to secure it for the night. She fell asleep without hearing anything else. Like clockwork, Lucy jerked herself awake from a nightmare. Since Jed didn't stir, Lucy surmised he'd taken a full dose of vicadin. Lucy paced the house. Curling under a blanket on the sofa, she turned on the television. Finding a succession of movies to watch, Lucy eventually dozed.

Jed woke her after daybreak. "Babe, come back to bed."

"What time is it?" She asked.

"0600 hours" he stated.

"Are you coming too?" She wanted to snuggle into him.

He stated pensively. "If that's what you want."

She nodded. Their cuddling was short lived. Leo bounded down the steps. The door slammed shut behind him on his way for his morning jog.

Jed got out of bed in irritation at the loud disturbance. Lucy buried her face in Jed's pillow. Her nose barely bothered her anymore. Laying there contemplating what to do with her day, the phone rang. It didn't ring again indicating Jed picked it up from somewhere else in the house.

Ten minutes later Jed entered the bedroom. "Are you awake?"

Rolling to face him she answered. "Yes."

He was carrying a tray. Lucy quickly sat for him to place it in front of her.

She covered her awe with a big happy smile. "Thank you."

Jed sat on the bed with her. "That was Edison on the phone. He wanted to thank us for last night."

"How did he sound?" She nibbled on the sesame bagel.

"Like he has one hell of a hangover." He smiled knowingly.

"Been there a few times yourself?" She asked.

"Like you have to ask." He leaned in to kiss her.

She giggled. "Just checking, my way of getting to know you."

"Babe, you understand me better than anyone." He squeezed her hand. "When Leo returns, we're going into the office to review some of what McCallister uncovered."

She pouted. "For how long?"

He stated. "Just a few hours, not the whole day."

"Okay, but you are bringing Chinese take-out home with you." She blinked her eyes at him.

He chuckled. "Mark the take-out menu in the kitchen with what you want."

He gave her a noisy kiss on the lips, then went to take his shower.

When she finished her bagel, she carried the tray into the kitchen. She was pleasantly surprised to find he hadn't expected her to clean up after him. All she had to take care of was the tray's contents. Not only did Lucy circle what she wanted on the take-out menu, but she wrote extras on it: "Ice cream" and "YOU—xo".

She laid the menu with Jed's gun. When he stepped out of the bathroom, she went in for her shower. Under the spray, she recognized the sound of sneakers taking the stairs two at a time. Not relishing a blast of cold water, she quickly rinsed away the suds. In the bedroom, Jed still wore a towel draped across his hips.

Seeing her, he asked, "There was a bit of blood on my shirt. Would you please check my incision?"

"Lean against the bed frame so I can see it better." She agreed.

Inspecting it she saw what he meant. "Nothing serious. Looks like from the rough housing last night the scab tore away. A little ointment should do the trick."

Done taking care of it, they both went about dressing. Without asking, Jed handed Lucy her underwear from their shared drawer. By the reflections in the mirrors, she saw him watching her dress via his mirror. Catching his gaze in the mirror, she smiled shyly. He returned a similar smile at getting caught with his hand in the cookie jar.

When Jed was ready to go he hollered, "Naples, you take longer than a woman!"

Lucy laughed at the way Jed rolled his eyes at having to wait.

"Let me make your wait worthwhile." She said seductively, then kissed him.

His lips parted inviting her to play with her tongue. Neither of them noticed Leo's presence until his throat clearing evolved into actually coughing.

"You should get something for that cough." Jed harassed the younger man.

Leo nodded.

With the men gone, Lucy called LuLu to chat. Two hours later, the friends were saying good-bye as Lucy walked to the back gate. The woman from the day before unlocked it. The yard, three times larger than Jed's, was completely enclosed by the stone fencing. The original foundation of the house dated pre-Civil War. The expansive half moon flagstone patio had been laid in the roaring twenties. A fire had gutted the house during the winter of 1941. The house remained in disrepair until 1968 when the realtor's in-laws inherited and restored it. The French doors on the back took them into a summer porch which led to the eat-in kitchen. To one direction was a laundry room leading to a two car garage. Behind the garage was a workshop similar in shape and size to the summer porch. The living room in the front of the house had a gas burning fire place and multi-paned picture window. A set of stairs to the side led to two standard size rooms upstairs with a full bath between them. The rooms had a nice view of the backyard. On the first floor, the hall behind the stairs led to a master suite.

Lucy sighed at claw foot tub in the master bath. The realtor explained the house had been under renovation the last five months in preparation to put on the market. They'd maintained the colonial feel while modernizing for safety and efficiency. Out the front door were budding cherry and dogwood trees. The house sat on the end of a side street. Only two other homes with similar properties shared the street. It was odd how this and Jed's house abutted properties, but it would take numerous streets and turns to navigate from one front door to the other. When the woman stated the asking price, Lucy didn't flinch. It was within the range Lucy had been comfortable with spending. Lucy negotiated for a ten percent drop in price. Her argument, there was no other realtor to share fees and no time spent giving tours. Also, if they couldn't close the sale in four weeks, Lucy got another ten percent deducted from the price. The woman was ecstatic. They scheduled an appointment to meet late Tuesday afternoon to sign the initial agreement papers. It would take another week after that until all conditions were met.

The full impact of what Lucy had done didn't hit her till she stepped back into Jed's home. She and Jed hadn't discussed anything remotely close to moving separately or together. When she viewed the house, she'd envisioned him in it with her. In her mind's eye, she could even see where the furniture, his and hers, would be placed. She had to stop making decisions without talking to her husband. The hours till Jed and Leo came home, Lucy rehearsed different approaches. Plus, she had the table set in preparation. Hearing the garage door mechanism, she dashed into the bedroom to check her appearance. In a moment of desperation, she fluffed her curls, applied lipstick and misted body spray. Leo emptied the bag of Chinese take-out boxes onto the kitchen table. Jed put the ice cream into the freezer. The trio sat at the table. They opened containers to identify what was whose. When Leo reached into the Crabmeat Rangoons, Lucy smacked his hand with the wide end of her chopsticks. Apparently amused by this, Jed had a hard time swallowing the swig of beer in his mouth. While they ate Leo talked about growing up in Hartford, Connecticut and Chicago, Illinois. Jed interjected comments regarding his hometown. At which point Lucy chimed in they'd lived within a hundred miles of each other the first seventeen years of their lives. Leo rented a couple of movies for them to watch away the afternoon.

Jed pulled Lucy onto the sofa with him. They cuddled for the first movie, a romantic comedy.

A couple of instances she asked him "do I do that?"

There was even a scene where he asked, "that works?"

Leo finally had to say "Give it up, you two are no where close to normal!"

The couple smirked at each other.

The rest of the day went as pleasantly. Lucy chose not to talk to Jed about the other house yet. Sleeping that night had been like the night before. When her alarm blared, Jed found her on the sofa. No chance for extra sleep could be gotten with it a work day. At work, she verified the planned program builds had successfully completed. Not all departments had heard the rumors regarding last week's events. This enabled her to continue reviewing projects and people with relative anonymity. By next week, everyone would be cringing at her appearance for their department dissection. She definitely wouldn't get bored. Appointments for the home inspections were arranged with no interference to her work or home schedule. Dinner was ready for Jed and Leo every night when they arrived home. There were a few nights they were later than others.

Thursday evening Jed joined Lucy on the patio.

He asked. "Do you mind company?"

"Not as long as it's just you." She remarked.

He sat on the cast iron bench with his arm across her shoulders. A silent serenity surrounded them. Twenty minutes passed peacefully.

Facing her, he spoke. "Please tell me what chases you from sleep and out of our bed."

Lucy responded vaguely. "It just needs to work itself out."

He didn't buy that. "There must be something I can do to help. Unless it's me; is it?"

"My subconscious is resolving issues from the past with the present." She answered.

"Then why not wake me? After all, I am the present." He reasoned.

"You need your sleep." She stated.

"And you don't?" He countered.

"Jed please? It's all been so fast and at times too much." She gripped the hand in his lap as she pleaded for his patience.

Rubbing her cheek with his thumb, he stayed in pursuit. "Are you unhappy?"

"That's not it." Her answer did not help clarify anything.

"So you are unhappy." He tried finding a logical answer. "What can I do?"

She sighed with frustration at her fear of opening herself up completely to him. The answer her heart screamed was "Love me for me, no matter what".

It felt childish and from her experience unrealistic.

"I don't know how to do this!" She blurted.

Whether he understood or gave up trying to, he hugged her close. Then he gave her a slow gentle kiss. Afterwards, he repositioned them to watch the stars twinkle in the sky like diamonds. When she began to yawn, he led her inside for bedtime.

Friday afternoon, Jed called Lucy at work to tell her not to make dinner. He was picking up take-out on the way home. Jed entered the house carrying two big handled bags. He dropped one in the bedroom. The other one he carried into the kitchen had Salty's Seafood stamped on it. Leo went upstairs right away. Till Jed emptied the bag's contents onto the table, Leo joined them in the kitchen.

He spoke. "Lucy, please don't let the old man shoot me when I come in after midnight."

Lucy nodded with a laugh. "Enjoy your hot date!"

"You guys enjoy yours too." The young man said walking out.

A familiar popping noise got Lucy's attention. Jed handed her an empty wine glass which he filled. He poured a second partial glass for himself.

Raising his glass, Jed toasted "To the present."

Lucy raised hers in response. They both took a sip. She smiled at the flavor.

Arching his arm wide towards the table, he stated. "Dinner is served."

She could hardly believe the food—shrimp cocktail, oysters, and lobster tail. Even more astounding, he talked. Usually Leo and her chatted during dinner. Not that he was ever excluded, but he never said much. She relaxed and enjoyed the conversation with him while they ate. After the meal, they cleaned up the kitchen together. He touched, kissed and brushed against her at any chance. He kept it playful, never pressuring her. She felt secure enough taking his hand to lead him into their bedroom.

When she began removing clothing, he stopped her. "Babe, we don't have to rush."

She froze wearing only her bra and panties, unsure what she'd done wrong.

Reaching in the bag by the door, he said. "I bought us lavender massage oil. You like lavender, right?"

"Um yeah, just your back or full body?" She asked dutifully.

"Actually, I was planning on giving my wife a massage." He stated pulling her close to nuzzle her neck.

She giggled. "How do you want me?"

"Oh Babe, there are lots of ways I want you." He murmured into her ear.

"Tell me more soldier." She dropped her hand down to the front of his pants.

He groaned. "Sorry, I don't snap to attention like I used to."

Rubbing methodically, she said calmly repeating his words. "Babe, we don't have to rush."

Chuckling, he picked her up by the waist to toss her backwards onto the bed. He stripped down to a pair of non-regulation boxers. Reaching over she tugged at the hip seam. Modeling the red plaid cotton with teddy bears, he shifted from one foot to the other ending with a wiggle of his butt. They made eye contact while smiling in joyful camaraderie. In that instant, Lucy fell in love with Jed. Her breath caught in her throat. Thankfully he didn't notice a change in her demeanor. He poured oil on his hand. Expectantly she rolled onto her stomach. He straddled her thighs to begin with her lower back and buttocks. His strong sure hands kneaded her muscles sensually.

Working up her back, he unhooked her bra to slide the straps down her arms. As he rubbed her upper back and neck, she relaxed a bit too much.

He whispered in her ear. "This is supposed to turn you on not put you to sleep."

Through the happy muzzy she said, "But you are giving a wonderful massage."

Her bra finished coming off as she rolled to face him.

He gazed down at the view. "You are so beautiful."

Her blushing from head to toe must've turned him on since the teddy bear on his boxers came to full attention. She sat up to kiss him wantonly. He broke them apart long enough to help her wriggle out of her panties and yank down his boxers. She willingly parted her legs. He didn't hesitate. They groaned each others names as they joined. With him fully functional, their passion soared to a climatic conclusion. As they lay sated in each others' arms, she lightly traced patterns on his chest.

"Mm, I missed being with you that way." He murmured planting kisses on her skin.

They kissed, caressed and shared all evening. It all felt so natural. Much later they made love again. When he dozed, she walked to the kitchen naked to get a bottle of cold water. The coolness from the open refrigerator caused a chill to spread across her overheated skin. She heard the front door. Closing the refrigerator door, she waited to hear Leo on the stairs. But his footsteps came in her direction. Frantic, she dove into the pantry. He got something from the refrigerator and remained in the kitchen.

Jed's voice entered the kitchen. "Babe, I . . . Naples!"

"Hey Jed, lose you wife and your clothes?" The younger man remarked glibly.

"Where's Lucy?" Jed's tone turned stern.

Naples answered calmly. "I don't know. I just got . . ."

"I'm in here." She yelled unable to tolerate her predicament any longer.

"Why are you in there?" Jed asked approaching.

She said panicky. "Don't open the door!"

Leo began laughing.

The frustration in Jed's voice was clearly detectable. "What?"

Still laughing Leo said, "If you're naked, I can only imagine your wife is too."

"Get out!" Jed barked.

Leo's laughter could be heard echoing in the hall and up the stairs as he obeyed. Lucy sprang from the pantry into Jed's arms.

"Babe, you're freezing." He commented rubbing her back vigorously.

Pressing against him, she whispered. "Warm me up?"

He answered with a hot, wet devouring kiss.

Breathing heavily from building passion, he asked. "Here?"

"Yes!" she agreed without hesitation.

Jed's strong arms lifted her for them to fit together. For leverage, he propped her against the wall. This pushed him deeper inside her. She moaned uncontrollably loud at the sensation.

Jed stopped moving. "You okay?"

"Yes, keep going." She answered breathlessly.

This seasoned soldier knew how to follow an order with gusto. Their crescendo burst with success.

Chapter Fifteen

Strong hands caressed her skin. His mouth nuzzled from the sensitive spot behind her ear down to focus on a nipple. She moaned with pleasure. Lifting his head revealed his face. It was Trevor's. The sensual touch became harsh. She struck out at him.

"You whore!" Trevor grabbed and twisted sections of skin to inflict pain.

She yelled at him "we're not married anymore."

Trevor forced her legs apart. Ramming inside her, he tore sensitive skin.

Lucy screamed "No! Not again!"

"Lucy, wake up!" Another voice came from somewhere.

She scratched and kicked to get Trevor off of her.

But hands grabbed her wrists and shook her. "You're dreaming!"

Light flooded in. Lucy blinked.

"Lucy? Come back to me." Jed's voice could be heard from nearby.

Blinking repeatedly, the room came into focus. Jed peered intently into her face. Leo stood in the doorway in his boxers. Returning to Jed, she connected he was holding her wrists. She jerked her arms away. He let go.

He spoke again. "Do you know where you are?"

Not quite fully coherent, Lucy didn't answer. She looked around again trying to distinguish reality from nightmare. Leo's hand, holding his sidearm, hung down by his hip. Jed's face, chest and arms had fresh scratches. She tenderly touched one of the injuries she'd inflicted. As realization dawned, her emotions erupted into tears.

Between sobs, she apologized. "I'm so sorry Jed. I couldn't escape."

Jed cautiously placed his arms around her to comfort her. When she clung to him, he tightened his embrace.

"Ahem" Leo cleared his throat. "Since you don't need me, I'll be heading back to my room."

"Thanks Leo." Jed said.

The young man pulled the door closed with his exit.

Jed spoke softly. "Please tell me what's in your nightmares?"

She shook her head negatively.

"Babe, I can't protect you if I don't know." He pleaded.

Burrowing into his chest, she cried harder. He rocked her soothingly; giving her tissues as she needed them. Eventually the tears abated. He pulled them down under the covers. Every time she dozed, she'd jerk herself awake. By 5am she gave up.

"Where are you going?" He asked when she wiggled away from him.

"Bathroom" she answered.

Maybe if she wasn't there, he'd fall asleep. She turned on the shower to warm up the water. Climbing under the spray, she stood there letting it run down her.

His concerned voice broke in as he joined her. "I thought you were coming back to bed."

Startled she replied. "What was the point? I couldn't sleep anyway."

He poured liquid soap onto a cloth. After making it sudsy, he began washing her and himself. They didn't speak. When his manhood perked up, he did nothing to insinuate he wanted sex. She wouldn't look at him when they dried off. In the bedroom as they dressed, she could see him watching her intently in the mirror. He went into the kitchen with her. She made breakfast; he helped. After breakfast, Jed went outside to do yard work. Lucy did house work. Jed came in at noon for lunch. Leo joined him. Not hungry, she went to fold laundry. As she carried towels to put into the linen closet, she could hear them talking in low tones. She didn't want to know about what. By mid-afternoon, lack of sleep caught up with her. Lying across the bed, she fell into a restless sleep. Much later Jed came in to check on her. He sat on the bed next to her, lightly placing his callused hand on her cheek. She opened her eyes.

Speaking softly, he said. "I'm sorry. I didn't mean to wake you."

"I wasn't sleeping." She replied.

"Did you get any rest?" He asked.

She answered. "Not really."

He leaned down to give her a tender kiss. "What can I do to help?"

Wriggling over to put her head on his lap, she said "You're doing it."

The look on his face clearly showed it wasn't enough. However, he remained silent while gently playing with her curls.

Leo knocked on the door. "You two decent?"

Jed replied. "Come in."

Entering the room, he whispered. "How are we doing?"

This irked her. "I'm awake. What do you want?"

"Uh sorry Lucy. It's after six. Should I order us pizza for dinner?" He suggested.

"Is that okay with you Babe?" Jed rubbed her cheek with his thumb.

"Whatever, I'm not hungry." She groused.

"Yeah Naples, order a pizza. And check the fridge to make sure we have enough beer." He directed.

After the younger man went to make the call, Jed stated. "Not eating isn't going to solve anything."

She ignored his comment.

"I have something to show you, but you need to get up." He stood extending his hand.

She accepted it. He led her to the bathroom. Turning on the light, he motioned for her to go in. She did.

"So what am I supp . . . ?" She stopped in mid-bitch.

A good-sized wood cabinet had been hung in the corner by the sink. Opening the doors revealed three shelves.

"I know you've been frustrated with not having anywhere to put your feminine items." He said proudly. "I started making it after you moved in, but with everything that's been happening. It took longer than I wanted to get it finished."

Running her hand along the smooth wood, she commented. "Thank you, it's wonderful."

"Glad you like it." He kissed her cheek. "I'll leave you to fill it."

Much to her delight, it held everything in her bag. Plus, she finally found her sleeping pills. She popped one in her mouth not caring that her proper dosage was half a pill.

Jed stepped into the hall from the kitchen. "Did everything fit?"

Mustering up a smile, she answered. "Very nicely, thank you."

Seeing he had a bottle of beer, she took it from him for a swallow. They went into the sitting room to watch television. Leo had gone to buy more beer and the pizza. Lucy continued drinking from Jed's bottle. He didn't appear to mind. A half hour later when Leo returned, the sleeping pill began taking affect. Leaving the boys to their own devices, she went to bed.

Twelve hours later she woke to Jed shaking her frantically.

When she opened her eyes, he pulled her into his arms. "Why did you do that?"

Her voice hoarse from sleep, she answered. "I needed to sleep."

"Taking sleeping pills, and then drinking a bottle of beer—all on an empty stomach." His tone mirrored his obvious displeasure.

She didn't respond.

"How many did you take?" He demanded.

"One. Half is usually effective, but I didn't want to dream." No point in not telling the truth.

"You've been having problems sleeping before now. Why didn't you take any then?" He again demanded an answer.

She explained. "I couldn't find the damn bottle until yesterday when I was putting my stuff into the cabinet."

He stormed out of the room to make breakfast. She joined him to sit at the kitchen table sipping coffee.

Leo burst in after his jog. "Good morning Mr. and Mrs."

Jed replied "Morning Naples."

She kept her face averted. The young man filled a cup with coffee to head upstairs for a shower.

Jed put a plate of food in front of her. "Eat!"

She managed to eat a few bites, then merely pushed the rest around the plate. Thankfully, Leo reappeared. It gave her a chance to escape to the bathroom. Not in the mood for company, she didn't dawdle in the shower. It took a minute to remember her stuff was in the newly added corner cabinet. While she was bent over drying her hair, Jed entered the bathroom. He patted her butt as he stepped behind the vinyl curtain. She went to the bedroom to dress in jeans and a t-shirt. Back in the kitchen to fetch coffee, she encountered Leo.

"Hey Lucy." Leo said at her appearance.

Not looking at him, she murmured "Leo."

Taking her cup, she went outside to sit on the bench. Some time later, Jed joined her with the insulated carafe filled with coffee. After refreshing her cup, he put his arm around her. They sat watching the birds.

Leo interrupted for a moment. "Hey, don't worry about lunch for me. I'm running to my condemned apartment to meet the landlord and the insurance adjuster."

"It's Sunday?" Jed stated.

"They made special arrangements with everyone's insurance companies so it could be done in one day when everyone was available. This could take a few hours." The young man explained.

Jed nodded. Leo headed out. Lucy leaned forward to pour coffee for both of them. Another hour passed in contentment.

He kissed her on the side of the forehead. "I have some calls to make. You relax."

The morning turned into afternoon. Too much coffee with too little food drove her to raid the refrigerator. The men had eaten all of the pizza. A small bowl of fruit was leftover from Friday evening. The flavors made her think of what a wonderful time they had. Finishing the fruit, she went in search of her husband. She knocked lightly on the study door.

"Come on in Babe." He called.

She smiled seductively as she entered. He raised his eyebrows questioningly as she approached. Pushing his chair away from the table, she straddled his lap. The kiss she gave him left no doubt what she wanted. He eagerly responded.

Her hands began pulling his t-shirt out of his jeans, "I need you."

"Babe, give me an hour." He said stilling her hands.

"Why what did I do wrong? I thought everything was fine after the way things went Friday evening." She asked confused.

Jed rubbed her upper arms. "Um, we had a little help."

"What about yesterday morning in the shower?" She countered.

"Guess it worked longer than expected." He answered with a shrug.

Removing herself from his lap, she allowed the past to fuel her emotions with bitterness. "So it was a blue pill that had you interested, you didn't really want me."

"Wait a minute!" He jumped up from the chair to reach out to her. "I chose pharmaceutical intervention because I want you so much it aches when I can't be with you."

His admission stopped her in her tracks. Or was this merely a ruse?

As if he felt her warring thoughts, he gently turned her to face him. "I want you! It just takes an hour for my parts to get with the program."

She squirmed feeling uncomfortable at being so forward.

"I shouldn't have come in here." She commented as she walked towards the door.

He let her leave the room. From the bedroom, she heard him banging drawers loudly.

A couple minutes later he slammed into the hall. "Lucy! Put on some shoes and grab your federal I.D. We're going out!"

Drying her eyes, she protested. "But I look awful."

Standing in the doorway holding a pistol case, he remarked. "Not that you'll believe this, but you always look beautiful to me. Now move your ass!"

She obeyed. On the way to the garage, he handed her a ball cap. He put one on his head too.

In the rover, she asked. "Where are we going that I need my I.D.?"

"Wait and find out." He stated in his no nonsense tone.

Fifteen minutes later, he turned into a fenced parking lot outside the city limits. There were definitely enough federal signs posted. None of which identified what they'd be doing here. Stepping from the vehicle, she heard what sounded like gunfire. It had to be a firing range for him to have brought his small duffel. They slid their cards through the reader. The light went green for both. He led her to the sign in area.

The soldier behind the counter greeted them. "Sir. Ma'am."

Jed nodded. Lucy smiled from below the brim of the cap. The soldier handed Jed the number of the lane they were assigned. She followed him. In their lane, he opened the bag. He handed her shooting glasses and ear plugs. Donning the same, he pulled out the pistol case.

Unzipping it, he said to her "Happy Anniversary!"

"What are you talking about Jed?" She asked.

"I've had this for you for awhile, but didn't have an occasion to give it to you. Our three month anniversary was Friday." Oddly his voice sounded unsure.

"You didn't need a special occasion to give me a present." Her reasoning faculties had been regained from earlier. "But now I feel bad. If I'd have known we were celebrating it, I'd have done something special too."

"Trust me Babe, you did." He smirked at whatever he was thinking.

Looking at the gun, she gushed hopping up and down. "It's a PPK! How did you know this was the exact gun I wanted?"

He hugged her. "I talked to your dad when we first got back. He mentioned he had something he'd been holding onto till the time was right."

She examined the handgun further.

"Oh my God! It's my grandfather's." She slid her fingers along it thinking of his soft iridescent white hair that contrasted starkly with his swarthy skin.

"Yes. Your dad said it seemed appropriate it be yours now." He remarked. "So are you ready?"

She nodded enthusiastically. Flipping his hat backwards on his head, he presented to her how to use the handgun properly. She fired it a few times on her own, but her aim was way off.

Jed teased from where he was standing. "Woman, how did you kill two terrorists if your aim sucks?"

"They were less than five feet from me. Not like I could miss." She retorted.

"Here let me show you." He said stepping behind her.

He placed one foot on either side of her. Molding his body to hers, he paralleled his arms with hers. Holding her hands with his, he aimed, and then fired. They did that for the ammunition remaining in the clip. She found it incredibly difficult to concentrate on the paper target at the far end. He backed away for her to change the clip to try it on her own. Her aim improved, but he wasn't happy. Again, he showed her what to do. And again, she fired on her own.

Finally he said. "You aren't holding your arms out straight enough to get a good aim."

Looking up at him fluttering her eyelashes, she said sweetly. "In case you hadn't noticed, there are two things in my way."

He didn't understand to what she referred.

Leaning in close because she didn't want to shout, she said "my boobs."

A shade of pink tinged his face as he smiled sheepishly.

Recovering quickly, he commanded. "Take your stance. Let's see if we can make necessary corrections."

She obeyed. This time he kept his arms with hers rather than making hers conform to his. It took the whole clip till they managed how to compensate. This time when she fired without assistance, she hit the center of the target. She jumped up and down with a feeling of accomplishment. He hugged her. The rigid bump of his badge pressed against her. She'd have to remind him to keep it closer to his hip than the center of his belt. Tem minutes later, he packed the bag for them to leave. On the way out, Jed kept steering her in front of him. Back in the rover, Lucy noticed Jed's badge clipped to his firearm. The firearm had remained in the console.

On the drive home, Lucy asked a question about handguns which had Jed reciting all of his knowledge of firearms. He was still talking when he parked in the garage. In the house, Lucy washed her hands and face while Jed put the gun in the study. Surprisingly, he stepped into the bathroom to wash off too instead of cleaning the gun. She met him in the hallway with a cold beer. Standing there he took a long swallow from it. Lucy tried to pass. Jed put his arm across to block her. Trading her lips for the bottle, he returned the kiss she'd given him in the study earlier. Lucy fervently kissed him in return.

Jed spoke first. "Do you still need me?"

"Yes!" She answered breathlessly.

He pulled her into the bedroom. The bottle plunked onto the dresser with force causing it to foam. They both stripped hastily. When Jed grabbed her into a kiss, Lucy realized it hadn't been his badge she'd felt earlier.

Devouring every inch of skin from her ears to her chest, Jed asked. "How do you want it?"

She answered shyly. "Like at the shooting range."

Peering up from where he had buried his face between her breasts, he said. "Really?"

She nodded.

In response, he slid his hand between her legs. He seemed pleasantly shocked she was ready. She turned around in his arms, taunting him by pressing her butt against him. He didn't need to be told twice. Positioning their legs, he eased into her carefully. His hands played with her boobs as he moved inside her. Taking one of his hands, she moved it down her front to where they were joined. They gasped together at the sensual feel of it. The way the sensations were building inside her, she reached forward to grab the metal curves of the footboard. It caused her butt to push out. He grunted his increased pleasure shifting him into high gear. When they climaxed, he said her name as if it had been ripped out of him. Then his knees buckled taking them both to the floor. He held onto her so tightly she couldn't turn to look at him.

Concerned she asked. "Are you okay? Did we hurt your back?"

He took longer to answer than she liked. "If we did, it was worth it."

"Jed! Don't joke about this." She warned.

Kissing her neck, he replied. "I'm not. I was coming when it popped, but I don't know if it was a good or bad pop."

"How could it be good if you dropped to the floor?" Her concern growing that he hadn't tried moving.

"Babe, you couldn't stay standing either." He stated pointedly.

"Point taken." She concurred. "But I am worried we messed up your back."

To test his back, he rolled away from her. She crawled to him on her hands and knees. Flexing his legs didn't cause him to cringe.

He smiled into her worried face. "So far so good."

Reaching to grab one of her swaying breasts, he teased. "I'm completely defenseless if you'd like to have your way with me."

"Jed!" She exclaimed. "When I know your back is okay, then you better be prepared for a full frontal attack."

He chuckled as he maneuvered to stand. Using the footboard as support, he pulled himself into a standing position. Standing upright he tested a few easy bends and twists.

Not finding anything, he stated. "Guess it was a good pop."

"Oh thank goodness". She sighed with relief as she wrapped her arms around him.

Snagging his discarded boxers, he put them on. "I need to fill up on calories to have the energy to satisfy my lusty wife's future attacks."

"I am ravenous." She giggled.

"Let's sate one hunger at a time." He held the robe for her to slip into before going to the kitchen.

With no leftovers to raid, they made grilled cheese sandwiches.

When those were eaten, Lucy asked. "Ready for dessert?"

"What did you have in mind?" He asked suspiciously.

She retrieved a canister of whip cream from the refrigerator.

"Bring it on Babe!" He urged.

She sprayed designs on his chest and stomach. After licking those areas clean, she moved lower. Aggressively snatching down his boxers she covered his tip with the sweet fluffy cream. Then she sucked it off.

Jed held onto the edge of the counter. "Oh Babe!"

Feeling cheered on, she continued what she was doing; the whip cream set aside.

He shuddered with pleasure from her ministrations.

Well into it, he touched her face. "Lucy I can't stand anymore."

She stopped for him to lie down on the floor. But as he did he pulled her on top of him. He undid the robe to knead her breasts. Straddling him, she sat up straight for him to go deep inside her. Which he apparently really enjoyed by the way he grasped her hips as she began to find a tempo. They were rocking and moaning to the peak of their mounting ecstasy.

"Hey guys I . . ." Leo entered the kitchen.

Lucy involuntarily screeched at the unexpected interruption. She grabbed for the robe that had fallen off from their movements.

"Oh my God! I'm so sorry!" Leo stammered with embarrassment.

Jed growled. "Naples get the fuck out of this kitchen so my wife can finish fucking me!"

"I'm really sorry." Leo repeated as he retreated.

Neither of them moved again until footsteps resonated on the stairs. Then it was Jed rubbing her bum to ease her into a rhythm.

"Come on Babe. We were really close." He coaxed her back into the moment.

As she swayed slowly, he continued guiding her. "Oh yeah that's it. Find the pace that feels good for you."

She tried for a while, but he must've felt she couldn't relax enough to get into it the way she had prior to the interruption.

He suggested, "Would you prefer if we went into the bedroom?"

She bobbed her head up and down vigorously. He held her hand while she climbed off him. He stood with a painful groan.

When she turned to check, he explained. "I'm okay. We need to avoid cold hard floors in the future."

His comment squeezed her heart. When they were in the bedroom with the door firmly shut, she enthusiastically tackled him. They fondled there way to where they had been before coitus interruptus.

He couldn't wait any longer. "Lucy please tell me you're ready? My dick is so hard it hurts."

"Semper fi." She gave him the go ahead.

He groaned "Hoorah!" as he entered her powerfully.

She couldn't believe how large he'd gotten. The feel of it overwhelmed her initially. She could see on his face, he was holding himself from coming until she did. As he moved inside her, she felt the waves of sensation increase with every thrust. Their rocking this time made the bed bang to the beat of their rhythm. Neither of them cared if Leo heard.

On the verge of climaxing, she clutched his buttocks pulling him in deeper to trigger the final myriad of sensations. "Jed!"

That's what he needed for his release to join her in the same ecstasy. Afterwards, they cuddled and chatted.

"Are you okay with Leo staying here after Friday night and just now in the kitchen?" He asked.

She made eye contact with him. "The embarrassment will pass. Wonder what he was told today."

"He sent a text while we were at the shooting range." Jed clued her in. "They found other structural integrity issues with the building. The building has to be demolished and rebuilt which will take till November."

She asked him the same question. "How do you feel about Leo staying with us for the next few months?"

He started calmly which built to irritation. "I don't mind you two having your girlie moments. But sometimes I feel invisible. And I don't want him seeing you naked ever again. Or interrupting us while we're . . . busy. Even the intimate moments we've had outside on the bench, he disrupts. This house needs to be a hell of a lot bigger and more doors with locks!"

She couldn't conceal her glee at what he'd shared. "Oh Jed thank you! I want to help him too, but it's like we can't find privacy for the two of us."

"Short of tossing him out on his ass what can we do?" The man did not have a plan.

"What if we found a house for us and rented this to him? And if he doesn't want to stay after November, there should be plenty of families from the base who'd be interested." She took the opening she needed.

"I'm not big into change. Let me think about it." He replied non-committal.

It was then she realized the flaw in her thinking. She had allowed herself to believe they both wanted a future together. Her future included a house with a big yard for a dog. When he'd referenced the future, it was about sex. One was permanent, the other fleeting. Either way, she'd be alright. If he didn't want to stay with her, she had a house to move into. If he wanted to look for a bigger house, she had one waiting for him. Oddly, she wasn't worried he might not like it.

"There's something else I've been putting off telling you." He started another topic.

The words filled her with trepidation.

He was getting good at reading her face. "Nothing serious, I have to take a trip to button down a few questions remaining from the investigation McCallister did for us. I'd been hoping I wouldn't need to, but my source here isn't cooperating. It should only be a couple of days. And Leo will be here with you."

"You're taking Myra with you?" She wondered why when Leo had been briefed on what McCallister found.

"No, I'm going alone. Guess with everything else, I forgot to tell you about her too." He hesitated.

They both had to get used to sharing information. "Myra is leaving us. Her significant other has gotten a really good job offer in Reno, Nevada. It took a while, but Myra finally got a position there working for Reno's CSI. Her last day is Wednesday."

"Good for Myra, no more worrying about 'don't ask, don't tell.'" She remarked.

He seemed astounded. "You knew!"

"Well yeah. Did you have a problem with it?" She gave him attitude.

"No. I keep forgetting how open minded you are about things like that." He kissed her.

She wondered, "You mean it didn't bother my macho marine either?"

"Not at all, she's a fine agent and great person." He said with sincerity.

Smiling that he felt the same as her on that subject, she pursued something else in relation to Myra. "Wednesday? You probably won't be back. Did you get her a card and present?"

"No. Did I need to?" He asked in all his male cluelessness.

"You are her boss. And you've worked with her and Leo for the last couple years on and off, right?" She verified the details.

He nodded. "That's correct, but she's leaving us. We provided the outstanding letters of recommendation."

Putting her hand on his cheek, she eased his mind. "I will take care of it."

The smile that formed on his face erased the age lines. "You are such a good wife."

Those words made her tense.

He noticed. "You don't like me saying that?"

She swallowed hard before answering. "I heard that exact phrase too many times in the past."

He shifted his position to get her to look at him. "Is there anything else you want to share in regards to that situation?"

"It depends on what you want to know." Her guard wavered.

He took her offer. "From the little you've mentioned, I've deduced he smacked you around and treated you like a second class citizen. Am I correct?"

"Yes. Physically smacking, pinching and grabbing intentionally to inflict pain. Emotionally he, um, he called me things like fat, ugly, stupid, whore." Saying it aloud to him made her choke.

As if knowing intuitively not to push her further on the subject, he hugged her close. "Hold onto me, we'll work through it."

She did just that till they drifted to sleep.

Like clockwork, another rendition of the nightmare played in her mind. When she jerked awake, Jed wasn't there. Putting on her robe, she went to find him. He was in the study packing his suitcase. Hearing her bare feet on the wood floor, he glanced up with a smile. Seeing her distraught face made his smile fade.

He opened his arms for her. "You've only been asleep an hour; your nightmare was early."

Snuggling her face in his chest hairs, she inhaled deeply. He sat in his chair tugging her onto his lap. She curled into the fetal position leaning against him. Sitting like that, Jed flipped through a file on his desk.

"I'm sorry I should let you finish packing." She slid off his lap.

He grabbed hold of the robe to stop her from scurrying away. "It's a good thing I don't need my robe for this trip."

Doing an about face, she responded. "This is the robe they gave me on the ship."

"Who do you think donated it?" He explained as he put his hands on her waist. "I didn't want any of those sailors seeing any of what I saw the last time we'd met."

"Did you really knock on the wrong door that day?" She had him.

With a sheepish grin he answered. "No, I knew it was your quarters. But I had no clue you were in the shower!"

"Why didn't you tell me who you were then?" Her face twisted in confusion.

"The timing didn't feel right. I tried to do things to impress you. The more I tried, the less you acknowledged my presence." The strong marine appeared hurt by this.

Placing her hands on his cheeks she laughed. "Silly man, we were there to do a job. And why in my right mind would I have thought a marine of your stature would want me enough to take the risk of having a dalliance on board?"

"I had to keep reminding myself of that. It also didn't help I was still wearing that damn girdle for my back." He kissed the palm of her hand. "When you called me a peacock, I didn't know what to think."

"Why did you allow the nickname to stick?" She slid her hands to his biceps.

Clearing his throat, he answered. "You had saved us once. Having you there for the Donny Do Right mission, which went without a hitch, made you a good luck charm. On future missions, because my code name was from you, it felt like you were somehow there watching over us."

Jed's story filled Lucy with the cherished feeling for which she'd longed. She gave him a warm affectionate kiss on the lips. Jed responded in a like manner, not asking for more. His body on the other hand reacted to the intimacy of it.

He backed away. "I'm sorry. I took half the dosage, but the blue pill is still working."

"You're going to be gone for a few days. Would you like to make use of that?" She said suggestively.

To tempt him further, she brazenly parted the front of the robe and her thighs as she sat on the edge of his desk.

Making a guttural sound in his throat, he slipped inside her with ease. Draping her legs on his buttocks, she arched to meet his thrusts. The items on the desk scattered onto the floor. They paid no heed to the noise it made. In the full throes of passion, the momentary appearance of Leo in the hallway with his sidearm drawn didn't stop them.

Shortly thereafter when they were catching their breath, Jed said. "Find us another house as soon as possible."

"Really?" She asked trying to contain her excitement.

"It's either that or he's going to tape us to sell on a porno site." His tone was dry.

"Jed we haven't done anything that risqué." She teased. "As for the show Leo just got; he should've realized from the noise we were at the point of no return."

"What Naples has witnessed is better than the average skin flicks." A huge grin transformed his face as he replayed it in his mind.

She laughed. "We weren't that good."

"Lucy you are an incredibly passionate woman who gives and receives without reserve." He stated seriously. "When we come together, we are better than good."

Her skin infused with a pink glow.

"No offense but I'll be ready to fall asleep in ten minutes and I have to finish packing." He gave her a kiss on a top cheek and a swat on a bottom cheek.

Obeying, Lucy exited the room to get a bottle of water to take into the bedroom with her. Ten minutes later, Jed snuggled against her. His head hitting the pillow put him immediately to sleep. Lucy relished the serene moment; hoping it would lull her into a happy dream state. The happy dreams eventually morphed into the unpleasantness from the past. Thankfully her alarm woke her before the worst of it. Jed didn't stir until she kissed him goodbye. But his words were incoherent with him face first into her pillow.

She gave him another soft kiss to whisper into his ear, "Be safe Peacock one."

This time when Jed mumbled it wasn't into the pillow and it sounded like "I love you Lucy" followed by a snore.

The words stunned her.

Chapter Sixteen

Throughout the day, Lucy would hear Jed's words in her head. Not having anything to do that evening, Lucy stayed at work reviewing a few things. With the director on forced vacation, she didn't have him to run things by. However, she did have use of his office. Jack hovered nearby, but didn't engage in anything more than small talk with her. She took an extended lunch to search jewelry stores for a man's silver wedding band. She didn't go home until after seven. A large glass of chocolate milk served as dinner. Hearing floor boards creaking upstairs, she went into the bedroom to avoid Leo. She changed clothes to climb into bed. Jed's pillow smelled like him. This comforted her as she lay there alone. Her cell phone played "Unchained Melody" indicating it was Jed. Her heart skipped a beat.

"Hello Jed", she answered.

"Hi Babe, I hope you had a good day." He said.

"I kept myself busy." She replied. "How's your trip so far?"

"Nothing substantial yet, just some background. Tomorrow should be more fruitful." He stated.

"That would be good." She missed him already. "The sooner you find answers, the sooner you come home."

"That's my plan Babe." He agreed. "You get some peaceful sleep. If you have a nightmare and need to talk, call me."

She protested. "I'm not going to wake you."

"Promise you will call if you need me?" He pressed.

She didn't want to argue. "If you say so."

"Lucy promise?" He demanded.

"I promise Jed." She gave in easily. "Good night."

"Good night Babe." He disconnected.

Drifting in and out of sleep prevented any dreaming. It also made for the lack of feeling rested.

The next day, the South Carolina realtor called to schedule the appointment to sign the closing papers. They agreed to meet at the house Friday afternoon. Lucy remained late at work again.

This time when Jed called, she brought up the house. "Do you know anything about the property that backs up against yours?"

"Ours" he corrected her. "Harry and Debbie Ringler own it. I looked at it a few years ago when Harry died. It needed work, but I really liked it. Debbie chose not to sell. Why?"

"Well her daughter-in-law and I met the other day through the gate. She mentioned they are moving Mrs. Ringler to South Carolina to live with them. The house was going to be put up for sale." Lucy gave him the bare minimum.

"Do you want to find who's listing it to get a viewing?" He suggested.

"Actually the daughter-in-law is a realtor. She let me have a look already." She held her breath.

"And . . . ?" He prompted.

She gushed. "I fell in love with it. The backyard is a great size for, um, having close friends over for cook-outs. The inside has been re-done with modern appliances. It has a claw foot tub to soak in . . ."

His chuckle interrupted her. "Okay, okay I get the picture. See if you can get an appointment for us to see it Friday afternoon."

"Will do." She agreed.

His tone changed. "How did you sleep last night? Any nightmares?"

She answered. "Like crap! Asleep, awake, asleep, awake, so I never got to dream state."

"No me so no nightmare." He misinterpreted.

"No! No you no sleep at all." She corrected.

"Oh!" He sounded happy.

"I admit I can't sleep without you and 'oh' is all you have to say?" She playfully harassed him.

He spoke quietly as if someone might overhear him. "I miss you too. The spare pillow doesn't have your curves."

"I like pillow talk, but that's not quite what I had in mind." She continued to tease.

He laughed. "I'll make it up to you when I get home."

"Promise?" she wondered.

He swore. "I promise Babe."

They disconnected their call.

Another lousy night of sleep affected Lucy's ability to concentrate at work on Wednesday. She met Myra for a coffee and to deliver a going away present. As anticipated, Myra was touched by the gesture. And promised she'd keep in contact. Getting home early, Lucy decided to make dinner for the two of them. The relocation company had called to discuss the closing costs for Friday. While they talked, she went into the study to write the pertinent information down. When Leo got home, she heard him walk straight back the hall to the kitchen. As soon as she hung up with the relocation representative, she called the mortgage company.

Leo pushed the study door open cautiously. "How long till we eat?"

"Twenty minutes" she answered absently waiting to be taken off hold.

He went upstairs to change his clothing. She was still on the phone in the study at Leo's return. Finally, having all of the information she needed, she went into the kitchen. Even though she was processing figures in her head, she noticed Leo had set the table. He handed her a beer after removing the cap.

She mumbled "thanks".

He sounded hurt as he asked, "Are you angry at me?"

"No" she kept her answer short.

"It's been days since you've talked or looked at me. What's going on?" He asked pointedly.

Lifting her gaze, she saw the worry lines on his young face.

To ease his discomfort she responded wryly. "Let's see you saw my naked chest, naked ass, and my husband and I going at it on his desk. It brings a whole new definition to embarrassment."

"How do you think I feel? There's an incredible sex goddess in the house and she prefers the old man to me." He replied with a smile tugging at the corners of his mouth.

Serving them, Lucy smiled back. "Goodness it must be eating you up inside. Some of my lasagna should fix it."

After dinner, Leo popped a movie into the DVD player.

During the sappy love store, Lucy broached a subject with Leo. "Do you mind if I ask your opinion on something personal?"

"Sure what?" he asked.

She tried to sound nonchalant. "Why does Jed, um, want me?"

Leo grabbed the remote to hit mute. "Say that again. I don't think I heard you right."

"Nevermind" she couldn't believe how ridiculous it sounded.

"You can't be serious. Why do you think he's obsessed with protecting you and acting like a mad dog to find answers?" He suggested.

"Because it's in his nature. It's what made him a good marine. And why he's a terrific agent." Lucy countered evenly.

Leo thought a few moments before speaking again. "You've never seen his face when he's waking you up from one of your nightmares or when I've interrupted an intimate moment."

"What are you talking about?" She didn't understand.

He examined her expression. "You really don't do you?"

Shaking her head and raising her eyebrows in inquiry, she prompted for enlightenment.

However, he chose to un-mute the movie.

"Leo?" She tossed a throw pillow at him.

He played innocent. "I know nothing."

"Leo" she growled through gritted teeth.

He chose a different approach. "You two got married. Doesn't that say it all?"

She realized if she took the conversation further, she'd have to explain how Jed and she had become husband and wife in the first place.

She forced herself to sound silly. "Yeah, I'm being stupid. I just miss him."

They finished watching the movie. When Lucy went to bed, Leo went upstairs after nightly patrol. Jed's nightly call was short.

"Hi Babe, called to say good night." He shouted to be heard above the background noise.

Concerned she asked. "Where are you?"

"Followed someone to a bar." Jed answered loudly. "He's on the move, gotta go."

"Bye" Lucy responded to a dead connection.

Shoving her face into Jed's pillow, she inhaled deeply. Sleep came. And so did the nightmare. Leo rushed into the bedroom as she woke.

"It's alright Leo. Go back to bed." She said.

He complied. After hearing no more footsteps, she put on her robe. She went into the kitchen. Perusing the refrigerator, she chose to heat a piece of lasagna. While the microwave whirred, Lucy called Jed.

"Mm yeah, Warloc" he spoke into the phone.

"Hi Jed it's me, Lucy." She stated quietly.

"Hey Babe, what time is it?" He asked making a rustling sound in the background.

"It's a little before three." She answered.

He sighed with frustration. "I'm sorry I'm not there to hold you. Was it the same as usual?"

"More or less" she replied. "Did you get what you needed tonight?"

"Yes, we still have to check one more thing before heading home." He responded.

She was taken aback. "We? Jed what do you mean we?"

"Babe, it's not what you think!" He said hurriedly.

"You lied to me?" She couldn't keep the upset from her voice.

"No. I didn't know Edison was joining me until right before I left." He explained.

She felt relieved, but needed more information. "Why didn't you tell me since?"

He replied. "Because when I call, I want to discuss you not him."

"Oh" for lack of any other response.

"We probably won't be in until late tomorrow night. Are you going to be alright?" his voice sounded caring.

"Well yeah, nothing earth shattering. You insisted I call." She replied.

"See you then Babe" he closed.

The microwave dinged. When Lucy had emptied the plate, she got ready for work. Going in that early would give her time to run to the credit union and the jeweler's in the afternoon. After getting home, she walked to the house to meet the younger Mrs. Ringler. There were a few minor things the contractor had to finish which needed Lucy's final approval. She and Leo had another dinner and movie night. A feeling of melancholy settled over her. The silver wedding ring sat in its box waiting for Jed to find it. She was anxious to see his reaction. Good fortune struck at finding a gift card with a peacock on it.

On the inside she'd written: "A love token to take on every mission to keep you safe. Love, Your Lucy".

The underside of the ring was engraved with "Your Lucy".

However, Jed hadn't arrived home prior to her crawling into bed. This time she woke pissed from her nightmare. She threw the blankets off with force as she leaped out of bed. Storming to the kitchen, she slammed things around.

"Lucy are . . ." hands landed on her shoulders.

She shrieked at being startled. She also swung around with fists balled striking a blow in the middle of Jed's chest.

"Oomph" expelled from him at the force of it.

"Jed! When did you get home?" She exclaimed.

He answered. "About two hours ago. And before you grouse at me for not waking you, I was exhausted."

Her eyes were momentarily transfixed on the silver wedding band on his ring finger as he rubbed at the sore spot she'd made on his chest.

Placing her hand next to his, she stated quietly. "And then I disturbed you with my temper tantrum."

"Yeah, what was that all about?" He asked putting an arm across her shoulders.

Her hand balled into a fist again. "That damn nightmare needs to stop. I'm fed up with it!"

Using a quiet soothing tone, he prompted. "Maybe if you'd tell me about it . . ."

"No. Let's go back to bed, you do look exhausted." She responded with a quick kiss on his lips.

He followed not saying anything more. The feel of him holding her made her smile. It didn't take long for the low rumble of his snores. In the morning, she didn't want to go to work. She looked forward to their afternoon appointment for Jed to see the house. Wouldn't he be in for a surprise if he wanted it, too?

Shortly after noon, she arrived home hoping to have lunch with her husband. He was nowhere to be found, but the range rover was in the garage. She called Leo. He said Jed had stayed home. Calling Edison didn't help either. Giving up searching, she dialed the man directly. No answer; she left a message. Making a sandwich in the kitchen, she thought she heard the heavy iron gate. She opened the screen door to see the back of the yard clearer.

Striding across the yard, Jed did a lousy Ricki Ricardo impersonation. "Luuucy, you got some 'xplainin' to do!"

She put on a face of doe-eyed innocence. "What?"

With a serious face and strict tone, he answered. "I walked over to check the exterior of the house and bumped into the realtor. She was quite informative as we walked through it."

"Did you like it?" She asked trying to keep him from getting angry.

"You, Babe, are incredibly lucky I really like what they've done." He stated wrapping his strong arms around her. "However, I would have preferred having a say in the price and the inspections."

"It's okay, I have it covered. My profit from the house in Denver and cashing in some of my Lorning stock paid for half, relocation is paying closing costs, and an extremely low interest 15-year mortgage will be easy to pay early." She tied it into a neat little package for him.

He dropped his arms from around her. "Maybe that's what the problem is."

She gave him a quizzical look. He didn't make a verbal response. Instead, he maneuvered around her to stride into the house. Grabbing a beer from the refrigerator, he also took a large bite of the sandwich she'd made. She followed him. It was his turn to give her a questioning look when she took a bite of the sandwich still in his hand. Whatever was churning in his brain, he chose to save it for another time. He handed the beer to her for a swig.

"So are we going to move this weekend?" He asked in a level tone.

She smiled. "That would be great! But we need more muscle than you and Leo."

Again, he gave her a strange expression. "I'll make a few calls and see what I can do."

Before he could, Leo called. He had to go into work. Good thing he'd only had two swallows of the beer. On his way out, he kissed her. It wasn't his usual quick kiss. His hand caringly caressed her cheek and down along her neck while his lips lingered on hers.

Lucy handled the scheduled closing on her own. After the realtor departed, Lucy wandered from room to room making crude drawings of where furniture should be placed.

Concentrating on the drawing for the bedroom, she heard Jed's voice. "Babe?"

"I'm back here." She called.

"We bought Chinese take-out for dinner." He stated stepping into the room with her.

"Great! Let's go." She replied taping the drawing to the door.

He looked at the picture as he spoke. "We brought it here."

Impulsively she hugged him with enthusiasm. "So you're happy with this?"

Placing his hands on her upper arms, he said seriously. "If it makes you happy . . ."

His answer seemed strange, but she didn't let it deflate the joy of the occasion. In the kitchen, Leo had opened beers for them. They clinked bottles.

"Do you mind if I have a look around?" Leo asked as he slurped lo mien noodles.

"If you drop any food, you better clean it up." Lucy warned.

"Yes missus." He replied walking towards the garage.

Jed leaned against the center island using chopsticks to eat from the take-out carton. They continued to eat in relative silence. It didn't take long for Leo to pass by them to view the master suite.

On his way by to the stairs, he grinned. "Love that tub!"

Jed said dryly. "Why do you think she wanted the house?"

"Care to tell me why you are suddenly cranky?" She asked pointedly.

"Just wait a few minutes." He replied.

Leo soon came down the stairs. "Wow, my room is spacious with a great view."

Raising one eyebrow and pursing her lips, she said to Jed. "You didn't talk to him?"

"Nope, we were working the case." He stated.

"I'm standing right here." Leo interrupted their sidebar.

Jed responded. "Leo you aren't moving with us."

"You're throwing me out?" The young man interjected.

Jed continued. "I'm not selling my house."

"You're getting a divorce?" Leo's voice hit a higher pitch.

Jed hesitated a moment before replying. "We are moving in here; you are staying at my place. But we expect you to cover the utilities."

Leo remarked. "You guys would do that for me?"

"We're doing it for us." Jed stated a bit harshly.

"O-o-oh" Leo said slowly as it registered.

Jed addressed Lucy. "We have to work tomorrow. But it may not be a total loss. Let's decide what stays for Leo. There are a few things I would prefer getting new for this house and leaving the old with him."

Taking a moment to consider this, she agreed. "Good idea."

Leo re-packed the take-out bag for the trip to the smaller house. On the way out the back, Lucy handed each of them a key.

As Leo tucked it into his pocket, Jed remarked. "That key is only to be used for emergencies."

The young man nodded.

By the time Jed and Lucy completed their circuit around the house, they had quite a list of things to buy.

He told her. "Put it all on one of your cards, when the bill comes give it to me to pay."

Normally she would have argued that she was more than capable of paying. However, yesterday she had doled out enough cash to cover half the price of the house—with a value triple his. That alone had probably done enough to threaten his own worth in his ability to take care of her. She wanted to do or say something to let him know it was unfounded doubt. This is where she had no idea what to do.

She attempted to broach the subject. "Jed is everything okay with us?"

He didn't answer right away.

When he did answer, it was apparent he chose his words carefully. "It's a lot to take in—buying the house, keeping secrets, moving."

She noticed he hadn't given a direct answer.

Then he said. "I didn't sleep as late as I wanted and with needing to go into work tomorrow, I'm going to bed."

There was no invitation to join him.

"Good night Jed" she said as he left the room.

No response and no goodnight kiss—these were not good signs. She turned on the television to distract her thoughts. It helped enough to keep her tears to sniffling. Hours later, she jerked awake. The DVD player clock displayed 2:37. She pulled the throw from the back of the sofa onto her for warmth. Flipping through channels, she had success with the dependable Turner Classic Movie channel. "Planet of the Apes" had started at 2:30. She only dozed between the scene with the discovery of the talking doll and the Statue of Liberty. She gave up trying. After starting a pot of coffee, she began packing boxes. When Jed stirred, Lucy went into the kitchen to make them breakfast.

Leo entered the kitchen first. "Good morning Lucy. That smells great."

"Morning Leo, help your self. Don't worry about clean-up. I'll do that after you boys are gone." She stated leaving the room.

Since Jed had finished with the bathroom, Lucy went in to take her shower. The next time she stepped into the kitchen the two men were filling their travel cups with coffee. Jed hung back when Leo headed for the front door. He didn't say anything; merely gave her a slow, lingering kiss like he had yesterday. After they were gone, she wondered what it meant. As soon as she finished cleaning the kitchen, she grabbed her purse and list. Her first stop was Home Depot. From there, she went to a furniture store followed by the mall. The rover was jam packed till she drove home late in the afternoon. The empty house echoed as she opened the front door. After unloading the items from the rover, Lucy drove to the smaller house. Jed called. They wouldn't be home for dinner. It also meant they wouldn't need to work Sunday. They'd be available to move stuff to the other house. Alone and exhausted from not sleeping, she took a whole sleeping pill. She left a note for Jed informing him in case he tried to wake her. When she woke 12 hours later, he was snoring next to her. She had breakfast keeping warm in the oven for them whenever they were ready. In the meantime, she carried boxes and smaller items. Plus, it kept her out their way. At 10 o'clock the two men finally appeared at the big house. Since it was only the two of them moving furniture today, they began with the study and the living room. By late afternoon, they were all ready to call it quits for the day. Jed promised he'd have two marines sent to take care of the bedroom on Tuesday afternoon. It worked perfectly; the same day she'd scheduled delivery for the new pieces of furniture. Jed had taken medication for his back at breakfast as a preventive measure. By the time they were done, he could take another dose. After a light dinner, he stretched across the bed. Lucy went upstairs to watch a movie with Leo. Later, she joined Jed for the night. For the first time in weeks, she slept peacefully through the night without taking a pill. Monday evening, Jed packed his woodshop. She organized the kitchen. Another night of easy slumber met her until Jed's phone rang.

"Warloc" he answered.

After a few minutes of silence, he replied. "Yes sir on our way."

He rolled out of bed. She read the clock by the bed: 04:23.

At the bottom of the stairs, he bellowed. "Naples, get your ass up! Be ready in ten minutes!"

He went into the bathroom. She made coffee for them. Both showers ran four minutes each. Leo came down the steps buttoning and tucking within Jed's ten minutes. She met him with the two travel cups of coffee. The young agent deeply inhaled the aroma to invigorate his senses.

Jed snatched one of the cups. "Thanks Babe."

He dropped a quick kiss on her cheek, then they were on their way. Lucy didn't bother crawling back into bed. Instead, she got ready and went to work too.

Chapter Seventeen

A bit past nine o'clock her cell rang. It was Director Edison.

Flipping the phone open, she stated "Good morning Wiley."

"Good morning Lucy. I need you to meet your husband at NCIS." He directed.

Warily she asked. "Why? Is something wrong? Is he okay?"

"He's fine. You may have a needed perspective on the case they were called out for at the crack of dawn." The director explained. "Now stop asking questions and go."

"Yes director." She obeyed.

Twelve minutes later, she walked to Leo's desk. "I was directed to report to my husband, but I don't see him."

Standing, he commented. "I'm supposed to take you to him in interrogation."

Leo led her into the room on the hidden side of the mirror.

Jed greeted her. "Babe, I need your help."

"With what?" Feelings of trepidation gnawed at her stomach.

"Captain Kelly Bayser called her commanding officer this morning to tell him she'd killed her husband. He involved us. Our problem is she won't tell us why. From the marks the doctor who examined her found, we have an idea. We need her to tell us. I'm guessing she'll only share that with an empathetic female." He explained showing her the medical report.

"But I don't know the rules of interrogation." She said unsure.

"Just talk to her; go with your intuition." He recommended.

Lucy went into the hall to enter the other room. "Hello Captain Bayser. My name is Lucy. What brings you under the scrutiny of NCIS?"

The comely female naval officer in her early thirties answered evenly. "I stabbed and killed my husband of six years."

Lucy asked the obvious. "Why?"

"You wouldn't understand." The captain replied.

Noticing fresh bruising on the woman's face, Lucy could guess why Jed wanted her help. "How'd you get the shiner?"

The other woman responded without looking at Lucy. "It happens."

Asking questions seemed to be keeping the female officer on the defensive.

Lucy went with her feelings. "You know Kelly, I used to get bruises like the ones you have, too. And not just on the face. I had a husband who appeared to be Mr. Wonderful. It was nothing but a facade. Everyone liked him. I had no one to go to who would believe me."

"Did you kill your husband too?" A glimmer of hope could be seen in the other woman's eyes.

"No, but it's not that I didn't want to. There were times the cruelty was so intolerable that I would've done anything to make him stop." Lucy forgot they had an audience.

The captain nodded with their unique understanding of each other.

Lucy continued walking her along their common path. "It's hard enough taking the belittling and derogatory comments, the hitting and grabbing. But it's like that control wasn't enough. What should have been the beautiful and fantastically exciting joining of two people; was turned into experiences of fear, pain and torture."

Tears welled in Lucy's eyes. Each time she blinked, one wet droplet would escape to roll slowly down her cheek.

Kelly's voice was shaky as she began relaying what happened. "I'd only been at sea for two weeks. We came into port shortly after midnight. As soon as I could leave, I rushed home. Tom had been so sweet each time we'd been able to talk on the phone. I thought maybe the time away had been enough for him to be nicer. But, but, . . ."

Lucy extended her hand to rest empathetically on Kelly's. "It's okay. Do you need a glass of water?"

Swallowing her pride, the naval officer revealed the rest of her story. "I need to say this. When I got home, I got into bed with Tom, my husband. He rolled over calling me 'Shana'. He kissed and caressed me so lovingly I thought maybe he was being funny. And then his eyes opened. First, he slapped me, I guess for not being her."

The captain choked back the tears. "Then he ripped my nightshirt and underwear while swearing at me. I fought back thinking this time he'd stop. When he rammed inside me like he had all of those other times, I . . . , I don't know. It was as if I had been in a darkened room and someone flung all of the shutters open at once. I managed to get him off me to run for the door. He threatened as he chased. He caught up with me in the kitchen. When he grabbed my arm, he punched me in the face. I reached for anything hard to hit him with. Six years of rage at being raped by my own husband must have gone into that blow. He slumped to the floor immediately. I stood there for a while staring at his shadow. I'm not sure for how long. Something snapped me out of it. My hands felt wet. When I looked at them, they were covered with blood. I rolled Tom over to see he had a knife in him. That's when I called 911. Then I called my commander, Commander Rowen. He must've requested NCIS."

The abused wife sobbed uncontrollably as the years of holding it in released. Lucy quickly circled the table to comfort her. Jed came into the room with a box of tissues and bottles of water. They made eye contact. In that instance, she knew. He had discovered her abuse had included being raped regularly, too. He exited as quietly as he'd entered. When Captain Bayser regained her composure, Lucy took a seat. Opening a bottle of water, Lucy offered it to Kelly. She accepted it. Lucy opened a bottle for herself.

Lucy noticed something interesting about her narration. "Captain, where did the knife come from?"

Clearing her throat, she answered. "I'm not sure. We hang our keys on the key rack in the kitchen by the door to the garage. So I went that way. But I don't know how the knife was on the counter. Knives are kept in the drawer on the other side of the center island. If Tom found a knife on the counter or anything else misplaced he'd go off. Even if I was preparing a meal, he'd remind me that I'd better clean up as soon as I was done. The very few times he'd made himself a sandwich, he'd have that knife in the dishwasher the second he didn't need it anymore."

"Would it be okay if Special Agent Warloc or Naples came in to ask you some questions?" Lucy knew Jed probably needed other details.

The female naval officer nodded.

As Lucy opened the door, Kelly said "thank you."

"You're welcome Captain. If you need someone to talk to after this is done, either special agent can give you my number." Lucy smiled sympathetically.

Lucy met the two men in the hall. Jed took hold of her hand. Leo reached for the door knob.

She stopped him. "Leo, I don't think they were alone. The Captain's explanation of why the knife should not have been there isn't a story. Six years of being badgered about how certain things have to be, it becomes an unconscious action. It'll take months or even years of forced effort for her to be able leave her kitchen less than spotless in any manner. Her subconscious expected to pick something else up to hit him with."

"We were discussing the knife too. We need to find Shana?" Leo stated.

After Leo closed the door behind him, Lucy and Jed were alone in the hallway. Jed pulled her into a fierce embrace.

Lucy spoke before he could. "When did you know I was raped too?"

His voice cracked with raw emotion. "I've suspected for some time. My trip last week was to find answers. I had already reviewed the medical and psychological records from the doctors you had at the time. But we located your ex-husband to have chat. Actually, Edison talked to him. I had to listen from the humvee or I'd have ripped him apart."

"How did you know the captain had a similar situation?" She asked.

"I noticed a faraway look on her face that you get sometimes. Then Leo remarked that she had the same haunted eyes as yours." Jed explained.

Lucy had a follow-up question. "Is that why you've been different since you're back?"

Jed confirmed through gritted teeth. "After hearing you ex-husband, I'm having a hard time with it."

The painful emotions his admission antagonized inside Lucy prevented her from speaking.

Jed gave her a gruff order. "Go home and take a hot bath in the claw foot tub. Edison doesn't expect you back at NRO for the rest of the day. And I can't get my game face on with you here for this situation."

Lucy agreed as he released her.

Avoiding his penetrating blue eyes, she left. The drive home was difficult through tears. She drove to the big house rather than the little one. A long hot soak sounded like the perfect treatment. Lucy had finally felt that Jed would be willing to work with her on whatever came their way. But she needed a little more time feeling secure to share her only secret. When she'd separated from her husband, she'd divulged everything to security. It had been a smart thing since Trevor began stalking her. The specifics of her abuse had been placed in a sealed envelope in her security file; only to be opened for the utmost emergency. What that entailed, was at their discretion. Evidently recent events hadn't been sufficient, otherwise Jed and Edison wouldn't have gone searching for answers. Then again knowing both men, they probably wanted those answers straight from the horse's mouth.

One of her stops on Saturday had included purchasing a crate of wine. Two of the bottles were chilling in the refrigerator. While the tub filled, she opened one. Not bothering with a wine glass, she poured it into a pilsner. Drinking half the glass in one swallow, she refilled it before putting the open bottle into the refrigerator. She selected CDs for the multi-Disc player. Leo had given it to them as a combined house warming and thank you gift. He'd casually moved it in with the other living room items. It wasn't till he'd been setting it up in conjunction with the television that Jed noticed. Leo had convinced her husband they needed speakers strategically situated for surround sound. Then Leo presented the small speakers. He had even calculated where they would work best without being obtrusive. Fiddling with the volume, she had to agree; Leo had done a good job. The heavenly hint of honeysuckle hung in the air on the walk to the bedroom. Stripping to step into the tub, she wished with all her heart that Jed would understand she'd overcome a lot the last few years. His scars could be seen; hers could only be felt. She didn't perceive his as marking him damaged goods. But could he do the same for her? Lucy sank into the suds to allow the hot water and aroma to permeate her senses. Forty minutes later she emptied the tub of the cooled water. The wine and soak were wonderfully relaxing. The muzzy side-effect made for languidness. After dressing, she stumbled to the kitchen to refill her glass. Standing there debating on whether or not to eat, the doorbell rang.

Two marines stood at attention on the front step. "Good afternoon missus Sergeant Major Warloc. We were sent to move some furniture."

"At ease boys, Jed is at the office." She remarked.

The two soldiers did as they were told.

"Follow me, then I'll leave it to you to decide how to handle it." She wiggled her finger.

They trailed behind her out the back, through the gate, into Jed's house. In the bedroom, she showed them what would need to be dismantled. Thankfully, Jed had remembered last night to put the tools needed on the kitchen table. Lucy stripped off the bedding to take with her. Struggling with carrying it all, she wrapped the blanket around her like a serape. In her house, she dumped the load in the washing machine. Still wearing the blanket, she took one of the pillows and her pilsner of wine to the gazebo. A while later the marines grunted by carrying one of the dressers. On their way to get another piece, she flagged one of them down.

"Are you alright missus?" The young soldier asked concerned.

With slightly slurred speech, Lucy answered. "Fine, just a rough day. In case I don't hear the bell, a delivery truck is coming. The bookcases go upstairs and a table in the kitchen."

"We'll take care of it missus." He stated.

She smiled gratefully. "Thank you."

"You're welcome missus." The strapping young soldier said politely.

He did an about face to resume his task.

Lucy laid across a bench listening to the birds sing. An odd sensation roused her only slightly. She was flying. No floating. Opening her eyes, her senses acknowledged she was being carried.

Jed's chest rumbled as he spoke. "It's Jed not Trevor."

As her muscles relaxed, she realized she must've unconsciously tensed at waking. "I'm sorry."

"Don't apologize." He grumped.

"Then why are you cranky?" She asked.

"I came home and couldn't find you." He stated. "I've been going crazy; especially after what happened with Captain Bayser."

In the house, he took her to the bedroom to set her gently on the bed. The blanket she had wrapped about her earlier fell to bunch at her feet.

"What happened with the captain?" Her stomach felt queasy.

He sat down next to her. "You were right. There was evidence another woman was in the house with them. Also, the angle the knife went into the victim lacked consistency for a woman of the captain's height. We felt she needed to be kept in protective custody. We took her home to get a few things. She seemed to be taking a long time in the bathroom. Till we broke the door open, she'd taken every pill in the medicine cabinet. We rushed her to the hospital to get her stomach pumped. When we left, they were transferring her to the psychiatric ward at Bethesda."

"Will I be able to visit her?" She asked.

He took a few minutes to answer. "I respect that you want to help her, but is that wise? I mean, won't it dredge it all up?"

"Already there with the nightmares." She quipped.

"What happened to . . . ?" He stopped talking suddenly.

He grabbed for her. "Lucy?"

She bolted towards the bathroom. Thankfully Jed used the toilet last and forgot to put the seat down. By the time Lucy finished retching, nothing remained in her stomach.

Jed knelt next to her to wipe her face with a wet cloth. "Other than the wine, did you eat anything?"

"No" she answered wishing the room would stop swaying.

He helped her stand. The room tilted, then flipped. And so did her stomach which initiated a bout of dry heaves. Afterwards, she sat propped against the vanity. He said something. It sounded like gibberish. She tried to tell him, but her words were equally as incoherent. When he leaned close to her, his face scrambled like a Picasso. He rushed out of the bathroom.

What felt like seconds, he returned with Leo in tow. She protested feebly when Jed lifted her. He slid into the backseat of the rover with her on his lap. The movement of the car made things worse. When she began to hiccup, he handed her a large Ziploc baggie. As expected, nothing came up. On the drive, Jed called someone. Leo pulled next to the emergency room entrance of the hospital. Jed carried her through the automatic doors. Inside, he spoke to the nurse that met them. After that everything blurred.

Lucy felt like she'd been hit by a bus. Opening her eyes, she glanced around the dimly lit room. An IV stuck out of the back of her hand. Turning her head to the side caused things to sway slightly. Swallowing to keep the nausea down, she noticed how raw her throat felt. Opening her eyes again, she searched in futility for the call button. A man in scrubs entered.

He spoke softly. "Hello I'm Nurse Dorn. How are you feeling Mrs. Warloc?"

"Like hell" she said barely audible.

Nurse Dorn took Lucy's vitals. "That's understandable. Inner ear infections usually hit without warning and make you feel like you've been body slammed by a gorilla."

"May I have some water please?" She hoped he heard her request.

"First, let's sit you up." The male nurse put his arms around her torso to pull her forward while placing pillows behind her.

Handing her a cup with a straw, he stated. "Sip slowly."

The water hurt going down. Her stomach gurgled in protest. The nurse traded the cup for a bed pan. But she didn't need to use it.

"The doctor will be in shortly." Nurse Dorn commented upon exiting.

A few minutes later, the door opened. Much to her relief, it was Jed. He looked like she felt.

Taking her hand, he spoke quietly. "Hey Babe."

She mustered a hint of a smile for him.

The doctor entered. He read her chart, then examined her.

Speaking to Jed, he requested "Mr. Warloc could I see you in the hall please?"

Smoothing her bangs back, he kissed her forehead before following. Soon Leo appeared.

"Hey Lady, you gave us quite a scare." He said cheerily kissing her cheek.

She gave him a quizzical look.

"After the day we had with the lieutenant, your husband began blaming himself for sending you over the edge too. He insisted they run a tox screen." He clued her in.

Rolling her eyes at the absurdity of it initiated another wave of nausea. She'd have to remember not to do that.

Leo shared his opinion. "Come on Lucy, you know he's just a mush of emotion under that rough-n-tough marine exterior."

"Am I really Naples?" The sarcasm dripped from Jed's voice as he remarked from the doorway.

It was Leo's turn to roll his eyes. "I was sharing with your wife how worried you were."

Jed moved to the bedside. "Babe, the doctor wants to keep you here overnight."

She pulled at his shirt.

He leaned in close. "What is it?"

She talked as loud as she could. "I want to go home."

He peered into her eyes for a few moments.

"Please!" She squeaked.

"Leo, get the rover. We'll meet you outside." Jed ordered his subordinate.

"Yes sir." Leo exited to follow orders.

Addressing her, Jed said. "I'll be right back."

It didn't take long for her to hear a commotion on the other side of the door. Jed returned with Nurse Dorn. The male nurse handed her clothing to Jed.

The nurse stated "this will sting a little" as he removed her IV.

"She's all yours. I'll have the form to sign and prescriptions waiting at the desk." Then the nurse left them alone.

Jed looked away while she pulled on her t-shirt. She needed his help with the jeans. As he helped her stand, the room whirled. She gripped his arms to stay upright while fighting hard not to gag. Jed got her jeans securely in place. Walking was almost impossible. She leaned heavily against Jed as he propelled her forward. At the front desk, she signed where he placed the pen.

Nurse Dorn handed Jed a bag. "This should be enough meds to hold her till you can get to a pharmacy to fill the prescriptions."

Jed replied sincerely. "Thank you."

"Hope you feel better soon Mrs. Warloc." The nurse said.

She managed to smile in appreciation. Outside Leo drove up to the curb. In case she needed it on the drive home, Jed handed her the unused baggie from earlier. She kept the bile in check till they got home. Leo barely had the rover stopped and she opened the back door to intentionally fall out onto her knees. To keep from staining the driveway, she used the baggie.

Jed knelt next to her. "We've done this before."

"Yeah, I could use some of that tea." She replied.

Helping her stand, he stated. "The ingredients are illegal in the states."

Walking into the house, she teased. "Did you drug me in the desert?"

"Yep" he said smiling. "Otherwise everything would have been a debate."

Their banter had eased the tension from his face.

In the bedroom, she stated "bathroom".

He maneuvered her to the sink. Leaving her there, he went back into the bedroom. The cool water on her face felt refreshing. Brushing her teeth got rid of the taste of vomit in her dry mouth. She managed to get to the bedroom. At her dresser, she selected a nightshirt. Sitting on the edge of the bed, she changed clothing. The dirty clothing piled on the floor. Jed entered the room stirring a small amount of cloudy water in a glass.

"This is for your stomach." He handed it to her. "Drink all of it."

She obeyed. It didn't taste like the tea. It resembled something from her childhood.

Taking the glass from her, he placed it on the nightstand. Then he tucked her into bed.

Placing a second pillow under her head, he kissed her cheek. "I love you."

He left the room without closing the door. Lucy's head spun for a different reason than the inner ear infection. His words resounded in her head as the medication took full affect.

During the night, she felt parched. Sitting to get out of bed, the room tilted. Waiting a moment to regain her equilibrium, she slid from under the covers. An instant chill made her shiver. Holding onto furniture along the way, she made it to the sink in the bathroom. The room barely lit from a glow light. It took a number of cups of water for her tongue to not feel like sand paper. Still standing at the sink, she felt out of phase with everything. As if the world was speeding around her. Suddenly Jed appeared in the mirror. She decided to take control of this dream before it turned into a nightmare.

She spoke to his image. "Why did you need to find answers about the abuse?"

He answered hesitantly. "Your nightmares were getting worse. I thought if I knew what they were about, I could help."

Still addressing the mirror, she retorted evenly. "If it was disturbing you that much, I could've slept somewhere else."

"That was the problem. I wanted you with me, not somewhere else." He stated.

"Why?" She needed answers.

His hand felt cool as he placed it tenderly on the back of her neck. Then he slid it to her cheek. The expression in the mirror displayed worry.

He remarked. "You're running a fever. Let's get you back to bed."

She didn't budge.

She chose to confront her fear. "Do you love me?"

She stared into the reflection of his face; waiting for it to morph into Trevor's.

Turning her to gaze into her eyes, Jed stated slowly and distinctly. "Yes, I love you."

She leaned forward resting her flushed cheek on his chest as she sighed. "I love you, too."

In his excitement, he seized her to peer intently into her face. "You do?"

Her eyes attempted to refocus too quickly. Everything whirled, then went black.

Feeling the rising of bile, she crawled to the white porcelain toilet. Thankfully it was once and done. However, it sapped all of her strength. Jed squatted next to her on the tile floor. He had a cool washcloth to gently wipe her face.

"That feels nice" she mumbled.

"Babe, you should be in bed." He stated with worry.

"It might be better if you bring my pillow and blanket in here." She felt the figment fading fast.

". . . Lucy?" Jed's face and voice drifted away in a haze.

And so the rest of the night continued in a macabre delusional state.

Chapter Eighteen

Lucy woke up with no more dizziness or queasiness. Her legs were wobbly on the way to the bathroom. Reaching for her toothbrush, she noticed how awful she looked. Also the nightshirt didn't match the one she donned last night. Her own smell disgusted her. Taking her time, she stepped into the shower stall. Jed's manly soap eradicated the stink causing germs. After the shower, Lucy wrapped the robe around her. She wanted to lie down again, but the sheets had the same sick smell. Wandering slowly out the hall, she found no one in the living room or kitchen. In the kitchen, she got a cup to fill with water. Sipping at it, she thought she heard metal bang outside followed by swearing. Soon Jed came storming inside.

Seeing her, he came to an immediate halt. "Babe?"

She smiled. "Peacock one."

He hastened to her and gave her a hug. "How do you feel?"

"Like a rag doll, but so far no dizziness." She rested against him.

"Good, are you ready to try soup or anything?" He asked.

Yawning she answered. "No, just thirsty."

"Come on, back to bed." He insisted.

"The sheets need changing." She explained.

"I suspected as much." He remarked. "Mm you smell like my soap."

"Do you mind me using it?" she asked.

He kissed the top of her damp head. "Not at all."

In the bedroom, Lucy watched as he stripped and remade the bed.

"What were you working on outside?" She queried.

He didn't answer right away. "Just a project, I'll show you when it's done."

"Okay" she could wait.

When he'd finished with the sheets, he helped her to lie down again. "I'll be right back."

He disappeared out the hall. A couple minutes later, he returned carrying a glass of cloudy water and the blanket that she remembered on the bed last night.

Seeing her face, Jed asked. "What's wrong?"

"The blanket, my pajamas aren't the same." Her eyebrows furrowed with confusion.

After flipping the blanket across her, he sat with her.

Caressing her face, he spoke quietly. "The last 12 hours have been rough. Your fever kept spiking where you'd have everything soaked. Then you added sleep walking to your quirks."

"I'm sorry I haven't done that since I was little." The snuggly warmth enveloped her.

"It's okay. We made it through together." He stated sincerely.

"Sleepy . . ." she mumbled.

Jed kissed her lightly.

Thursday morning Lucy woke with Jed's arms around her.

"Good morning Babe." His low voice rumbled.

"Good morning." She replied as her stomach growled.

Chuckling he remarked. "Evidently I better get up and make you breakfast."

Stretching she said "I am actually hungry."

"Tea and toast coming up!" He said rolling out of bed.

"Do we have any chai?" She asked.

"I'll check." He hurried to the kitchen.

She got out of bed realizing she'd slept in the robe. Securing it tightly, she joined him in the kitchen.

"What are you doing? I was going to bring it to you." He groused teasingly.

"I needed a change of scenery." She answered.

"Alright, but let's keep you warm." He ushered her to the sofa where he tucked a blanket around her legs.

Picking up the remote, she flipped through the channels. It didn't take long for him to bring her the cup of chai soon followed with the toast. Holding his coffee, he sat down with her. A Doris Day film marathon was playing on American Movie Classic channel. "That Touch of Mink" had just started. For the next 90 minutes, the two of them enjoyed the movie together. He kept both their cups filled. When he scrambled eggs for his own breakfast, he shared a few bites with her. She couldn't help thrilling in this effortless sharing. At the end of the movie, she went to shower. As she was rinsing the conditioner from her hair, he joined her.

She remarked "I was finishing up."

"Not a problem, just wanted to see my wife naked." An easy grin exhibited on his face.

Her own smile formed self-consciously. He noticed.

"After everything, how can you still be embarrassed by that?" He shook his head in amazement.

She stepped out of the stall without answering.

He called to her. "Lucy?"

Hurriedly drying, she wanted to be dressed by the time he finished. She almost made it. He walked into the bedroom with the towel draped across his hips before she'd made it to the door.

He snatched her into an embrace. "Why are you running away?"

"If I stayed, I won't know what to do or say." She answered truthfully.

Gazing into her eyes, he probed. "If you stay, you don't have to say or do anything. Why not just enjoy the view?"

She looked down. He countered with tugging the towel off to toss onto the foot of the bed frame. There was no mistaking she had an affect on him. She raised her focus to his chest.

"Lucy?" His hand under her chin gently coaxed her to make eye contact again.

In a small voice she said. "Things are different now that you know. And I don't know how to fix it."

"Did I miss something?" He seemed perplexed.

"Outside the interrogation room you said it bothered you. So all I can think is that you're having second thoughts about us. Then you had to take care of me for two days because I got sick." Her words rambled with her thoughts. "Somewhere along the way I thought you'd actually be okay with it, I was waiting for the right time. But I guess I was fooling myself into thinking it was possible."

The expression on his face indicated a dawning realization filled with sadness. Then his jaw tightened as it quickly changed to anger. Roughly he turned her to face the other direction. She tensed with dread at what he'd do next. From the mirror, she could see him dressing. He threw on similar clothes to hers—sweatshirt and jeans. On his way out of the room, he grasped her hand. She followed with trepidation.

He sat on the sofa pulling her down next to him. "First, if I had second thoughts, I wouldn't have bothered putting on the wedding band you had waiting for me when I got home after finding out. Second, I didn't have to bring you home from the hospital. I chose to. And thirdly, I . . ."

The doorbell rang interrupting his tirade. He answered it.

A familiar female voice chirped. "Hi, where should Danny park the van?"

"LuLu you guys are early." He stated shocked. "Come in, I'll go help Danny."

He headed outside in his bare feet.

"LuLu?" Lucy stood surprised at seeing her best friend.

LuLu rushed across the living room to hug Lucy. They hugged and cried tears of joy.

"When Jed called us yesterday to say you had an inner ear infection, we debated whether to wait until next weekend to visit. But Danny said I seemed so disappointed that we'd come anyway. And that he was sure when you saw me you'd feel better." LuLu chattered.

"This is a wonderful surprise. But the guest bedroom doesn't have a bed yet." Lucy replied.

"Really? When Danny called Jed last night to double check the directions, he said everything was ready for us." The older friend responded.

Lucy suggested, "Let's go upstairs and find out."

Opening the door to the guest bedroom revealed it contained a bed.

LuLu commented "Guess the medication knocked you out cold."

Lucy quipped. "Being out cold was better than the hallucinations from the fever."

"Inner ear infections tend to cause high fevers. How was your stomach?" LuLu cringed.

"I puked enough for this lifetime. With the dizziness gone, I don't think it will be a problem anymore." She expounded.

They went downstairs. Lucy showed LuLu the rest of the house.

From the window in the laundry room door, a pluming tail came into view.

Lucy said with excitement. "You brought the dogs?!"

LuLu nodded. "But of course."

Her old canvas boat shoes were kept in the laundry room. Slipping into them, she also grabbed Jed's grubby pair. Outside the three dogs surrounded her wooing in enthusiastic greeting. She knelt down to hug them all. Then she went to hug Jed.

He chuckled. "Happy?"

"Yes!" She gave him a big kiss.

"Oh here are your shoes." She said pulling away to give them to him.

"Thanks, the ground is still cold." He said appreciatively.

Lucy noticed a 12x12 kennel set up on the far end of the patio. It had an igloo attached to a side opening, a tarp on top and big water containers. That must have been Jed's project. It would definitely keep Brando and Luna out of trouble. The old girl, Daisy, would be fine in the yard without supervision.

"I'm going to help Danny with their bags." He said with a quick kiss.

LuLu gave her a look. Lucy walked her to the gazebo. They watched the dogs investigate the yard. The stone fence fascinated them. Brando tested occasionally to see if it could be scaled. Thankfully his attempts failed. Daisy lay at their feet.

"Lucy the house is beautiful. It suits you. And so does your husband." Her dearest friend gushed. "I take it things worked themselves out since Tuesday when you left your message?"

"Actually we were finally starting to discuss it when you rang the doorbell." She stated.

"Oh dear, our timing couldn't have been worse. We got on the road earlier than we expected and hit no traffic." She sounded contrite.

Lucy sighed. "Don't give it another thought. It's our problem to work out. I just hope he wants to."

LuLu looked at her with disbelief. "Lucy he's still here. Didn't you say his house is on the other side of the fence? He's got an easy walk if he wanted to leave."

"He did bring me home from the hospital when I asked rather than heeding doctor recommendation to stay overnight." Lucy admitted.

"See!" LuLu hugged her. "And you know I tell Danny everything. When I told him about Jed's willingness to take Viagra, he was impressed. And the desk sex made him jealous."

The women giggled together.

"So do I need to ask how good the sex is?" LuLu teased.

Lucy turned red. "Jed swears Leo is going to tape us for a porno film."

LuLu clapped her hands. "Well now that says something doesn't it!"

Soon the men joined them in the gazebo. They brought hot drinks for their wives.

Danny stated. "It was Jed's idea."

Jed parried. "My wife's sick."

"Lucy, I think you're faking it." Danny teased.

"Swing me around once and find out." She volleyed.

They enjoyed the camaraderie. When Lucy and LuLu's stomach began growling, Jed recommended they go inside for lunch. LuLu took care of kenneling Luna and Brando while Daisy trotted into the house. Jed ladled homemade chicken soup into their new bowls. He made sure Lucy's had mostly broth. Everyone else's contained chunks of chicken, carrots and celery.

"You made this yourself?" Danny asked.

"Yes sir. I made it yesterday so it could go in the slow cooker today." Jed answered.

"Very good, I think I have some competition." LuLu's husband stated.

"Not likely. I only know how to make a few basic meals that will last for days or freeze well." He responded modestly.

Lucy piped up. "He makes a mean burger on the grill, too."

LuLu chimed in. "But can he bake?"

"No ma'am, I leave that to my talented wife." Jed squeezed Lucy's hand.

Danny and LuLu both nodded in agreement. "Yes, we've had her cheesecake."

Jed released her hand abruptly. "You make cheesecake? You've been holding out on me woman!"

It took a moment for Lucy to realize he was merely jesting.

She sassed back. "When over the last few weeks would I have had occasion to make one? Let alone try to hide it from Mr. I See Everything, and I mean everything, Naples."

LuLu burst out laughing and poor Danny almost choked on his food. Jed couldn't hold back his chuckles either. At the end of the meal, Lucy helped Jed with the dishes. Danny and LuLu went upstairs to unpack. With the kitchen clean, Jed took advantage of the moment alone. Pulling her into an embrace, he kissed her playfully.

"What was that for?" She asked perplexed.

"That Mr. I See Everything remark was priceless." He gave her a good squeeze as the other couple came down the stairs.

"Naples is at work, we can show you the other house." Lucy suggested.

They all went for a walk, leaving Daisy in the big yard. As they toured the smaller house Lucy discovered from where the furniture in the guest bedroom had been taken.

Jed explained. "Before you defend our prodigal son, he received his insurance check for his ruined furniture. We're going to do some painting and refinishing floors before he gets new stuff."

"That makes sense." She stated matter-of-fact.

Both LuLu and Danny liked the house, but they could definitely see how it wasn't big enough for three adults. LuLu agreed with Lucy, the separate tub and shower in the big house is a necessity. The men smiled indulgently at their wives. Back at the main house, the men went into the workshop while the women chatted in the master bedroom. Lucy sent Leo a text message asking him to pick up a few groceries for her. Late in the afternoon, Jed and Danny went on an errand. Lucy couldn't believe Jed willingly went during peak traffic hours. Some time later, the women heard a call for help from the yard. Rushing out the back door, they giggled at seeing Daisy happily wooing at a frightened Leo.

Seeing the women, he yelled. "Help! I'm being attacked by a wolf!"

LuLu called Daisy, but it did no good with her going deaf from old age. Lucy tried not to laugh.

"Leo, Daisy wouldn't hurt a flea." She told him.

He began walking quickly towards the house. When the other two dogs howled from the kennel, he ran the last few steps.

LuLu commented as they followed him. "All this time I thought you were exaggerating."

Inside, Leo hugged Lucy. "I'm glad you're better. That night you came home you were a handful. I kept saying we should take you back to the hospital, but the ole' man wouldn't do it."

"I'm sorry I worried you." She said rubbing his back like one would an upset child.

"After all that you told us in your feverish state. I can understand why the boss man was so upset when we rushed you to the hospital earlier. Especially with the incident we'd had with the lieutenant right before we found you that way." The young man said compassionately.

"What all did I tell you that night?" Lucy asked agitated.

"The kind of things that made us want to apologize for the whole male species. And why your nightmares were so horrific." He hugged tighter.

"Can't breathe!" She gasped.

"Oh hi, I'm special agent Leo Naples. I work for Jed and rent a house from the Warloc's." Leo said extending his hand at noticing LuLu.

"Leo, this is my best friend LuLu from New York. Jed invited her and her husband Danny down for the weekend."

LuLu shook the young man's hand. "I'd say you know Lucy and Jed far more intimately than your introduction infers."

He got wide eyed with embarrassment.

Lucy punched his chest ineffectively. "Snap out of it Leo. We are all family."

"Am I going to get a dinner invite while Aunt LuLu and Uncle Danny are in town?" He asked sheepishly.

"That would be up to Papa Peacock." Lucy responded.

"Alright, I'll go back to the house where all the rooms echo with loneliness." He hung his head in dejection. "Nice to meet you Aunt LuLu."

He went for the door only to jump away from it. Daisy sat there waiting; her tail wagging in anticipation. LuLu opened the door for Daisy to enter and Leo to exit. The old dog examined the house with her sniffer running full throttle. LuLu assisted Lucy by mixing the cheesecake filling while Lucy made the crust. It made it into the oven a few minutes prior to the men arriving home. The running dishwasher hid the incriminating mixing bowls. The men had two bags of groceries and a case of beer. Jed and Danny prepared dinner—steaks and baked potatoes on the grill. Lucy had two small bites from Jed's steak and half a baked potato. Since the men made dinner, Lucy and LuLu took care of the kitchen. The cheesecake had cooled sufficiently to hide in the refrigerator. LuLu kept an eye on the men while Lucy wrapped it. She placed it as far back on the bottom shelf as possible. The dogs had been run and fed for the night. Daisy stretched on the floor between the kitchen and living room. The men had rented a couple of first run movies to watch. When everyone retired for the night, Daisy chose not to attempt the wood stairs. Since Jed and Lucy slept with the door open, Daisy slept on the floor by Lucy's side of the bed.

At dawn, Daisy roused Lucy. She released the other two from the kennel for their morning exercise. She also got the coffee going. LuLu and Danny planned to spend the day at the Smithsonian and on the mall. Jed decided to go into the office for the day. After everyone had departed, Lucy filled the tub for a luxurious bath. Dinner would be tequila lime chicken with roasted peppers with the cheesecake for dessert. The majority of the day she spent on the sofa with Daisy watching old movies and napping. Late morning she made a call to Edison to update him.

Edison answered his cell. "Lucy Babe, how are you feeling?"

"Hello Wiley. Much better, I wanted to let you know I should be in on Monday." She replied to her boss ignoring his use of Jed's endearment.

"I figured as much after speaking to your husband yesterday." He stated. "Today is my first day after they lifted my forced vacation. Things are hectic."

"Okay, have a good weekend." She ended their call.

"Guess they don't need to bother with me." She quipped rubbing Daisy's ears. "That's okay, cuz you love me!"

The old dog covered Lucy's face with kisses. She sighed at how much she missed having fuzzy faces full of unconditional love.

"What do you think Miss Daisy?" She said rubbing her face with the big dog.

Daisy's tail thumped happily against the sofa. Jed called to say he and Leo had to run to the airport, but he should be home around six. Oddly, LuLu sent a text stating the same time. Even stranger, the van followed the rover into the driveway shortly after six.

Lucy greeted them at the door. "What are the chances you'd pull in at the same time?"

Danny answered. "We were looking for a gas station and forgot where to turn. I called your husband for directions."

Jed broke in "I gave them directions to the other house by accident. So I met them there, then they followed me home."

As the other couple headed upstairs, Lucy asked "Dinner in a half hour good with everyone?"

They agreed. Jed disappeared back the hall for a few minutes. When he reappeared he'd changed his clothes.

He hugged and kissed his wife. "How was your day?"

"Wonderfully relaxing." She answered, then gave him a lingering kiss.

He took full advantage of her receptiveness. He kissed her with longing. It was a kiss she didn't want to end. It took effort for them to separate.

"I'll go get Leo for dinner." He stated in a raspy voice.

"Okaym but he's afraid of the dogs. Please kennel Brando and Luna. Daisy can stay in here." She suggested as he strode to the door.

He acknowledged with "got it".

Having momentarily forgotten the vegetables were on final broil, she quickly checked to make sure they weren't burning. She did it just in time. Turning the oven off completely, the vegetables were moved to the rack below the chicken. The couple came downstairs. Danny opened the bottle of wine Lucy selected. Suddenly Daisy started hopping up and down excitedly. Lucy figured she saw Leo.

When Lucy grabbed the hot pads to pull the food out of the oven, LuLu stopped her. "Not yet."

Lucy didn't argue. Leo entered the house in front of Jed. Daisy wooed loudly. A squeaky kind of yip came from somewhere. Leo stepped aside to reveal Jed holding something in his arms. A black and white fur ball burrowed into his chest. Jed grinned from ear to ear as Lucy hurried towards him.

He remarked, "I know it's not a bouquet of daisies, but this will last longer."

Lucy gladly accepted the Alaskan malamute puppy he offered.

"Oh Jed he's adorable!" As she appreciatively kissed Jed, the puppy buried his face in her cleavage.

Noticing the puppy's freshly shampooed smell and damp fur, Lucy put the puzzle together. "Wait, is this why you had to go to the airport? And why you two followed him home from the other house."

They all smirked at their earlier subterfuge.

LuLu explained. "He's a Ruby puppy. When you told me about the house and yard, I told Kayla to let me know if one of the boys needed a home. At first they were all spoken for. Then one of the prospective buyers changed their mind. Kayla called me since she didn't have your new cell number. I called Jed to see if he wanted to surprise you."

Jed continued the story. "Not once did she let slip about the other house. When the flight arrangements had been made, we turned it into them visiting too."

"I expected he'd pee on himself on the flight. We planned to meet at the other house to give him a bath. Then you could love him up when you saw him." LuLu added the final details.

Lucy giggled. "It worked. You surprised me in the most wonderful way."

They all went outside to let the puppy investigate the yard. Initially he was timid from the trauma. Grandma Daisy's coddling got him to putter in the yard with her. Luna wooed at him playfully coaxing him to the kennel. However, once he got too close, Brando erupted in alpha male manner. The puppy scurried to hide behind Grandma Daisy. The group went inside. The men disappeared into the garage. When they reappeared, they had the old metal crate Lucy had stowed in the shed. It had been disinfected and new flooring added. The puppy went into it willingly. It had a towel to lie on, toys to play with and a bucket of water to drink. The blanket draped on it didn't quite make it to the floor. This allowed enough space for Daisy's muzzle.

Everyone sat at the table while Lucy fetched the hot food from the oven. Jed had to open another two bottles of wine. They volleyed suggestions for the puppy's name. Danny and LuLu talked about their day sightseeing. After dinner, Lucy put on a pot of coffee to go with dessert. The puppy slept peacefully in his crate. It took an hour till the men began to question the serving of the next course. When Lucy presented the cheesecake, they fought for who got the first piece. Afterwards, Jed collected the empty plates to place in the dishwasher. The puppy stirred. Lucy took him outside. Jed followed. A clear night at almost full moon gave plenty of illumination without the patio light. Mid-yard he caught her in an embrace. A breathtakingly sensual kiss ensued.

He murmured as he nibbled her ear. "Would it be rude to make love to my wife while we have house guests?"

"Why do you think I made the guest bedroom the room over the garage?" She remarked.

His lips descended to the space between her ample bosoms. "Just one of the many reasons I love you."

She wasn't sure if he was referring to what she'd said or where his face was. Loving her for her most prominent physical attribute linked directly to her ex-husband. She froze. He did, too, ceasing his seduction. His muscles tensed for a few minutes with his own warring emotions.

"What happened? Why did you go cold?" He asked barely keeping his anger in check.

"If I tell you, you'll think it's ridiculous and get mad." She said uncomfortably.

Gritting his teeth, he stated. "I'm already angry at what I can only guess Trevor interrupted! Now talk!"

She answered hesitantly with tears forming. "What you just said about 'one of the many reasons I love you' and where your face was . . ."

A few moments passed as he processed her cryptic statement. His muscles relaxed. His hands methodically rubbed her upper back.

"After hearing Trevor talk I think I understand." He spoke in a much calmer tone. "We need to finish the conversation we were having yesterday and maybe we can avoid similar situations in the future."

She asked hesitantly. "Are you upset with me?"

"With the situation and trying to understand, but not with you" he answered kissing her on the forehead.

The puppy jumped on their legs to get their attention.

Jed bent down to pick up the fur ball. "Let's go inside. We have to postpone this conversation."

She couldn't believe how one minute they couldn't get enough of each other to the next, feeling horrible dejection. Worse yet, it was her fault.

As if Jed read her mind, he put an arm around her shoulders. "Don't dwell on this. We will work it out together."

The puppy accentuated his words by licking the tears off her face. They met Leo on his way across the yard. The young man thanked them for dinner on his walk home. Once inside, Jed placed the puppy on the floor to check his new home. An hour of play tuckered out the black and white fur ball. The people were yawning, too. Daisy laid next to the crated puppy as the people went to their rooms.

In the bedroom, Lucy shut the door. Jed eyed her suspiciously in the mirror.

"Can we talk for a little bit now?" She asked hesitantly.

"If you want to." He replied.

They both remained standing; the expanse of the room between them.

She dove into it. "If you and LuLu have been burning cell phone minutes for the last three weeks, why didn't you ask her about my ex-husband instead of seeking him out?"

The question didn't seem to bother Jed.

"I did ask LuLu what happened between you and your ex. She refused to answer. When I asked her questions like: 'do you consider him a controlling asshole?' and 'did he force himself on you?' she would confirm." He answered without hesitation. "I needed to meet him and hear what he had to say. The first night we found him at a restaurant having dinner with two other men. We played it straight. Edison was on the radio. I introduced myself as a federal investigator who had a few questions about his ex-wife."

While Jed spoke, they completed their nightly routine.

"He had nothing pleasant to say about you, but no specifics. I wanted to beat him within an inch of his life. Edison told me to cut it short. He had an idea. His idea was the indirect approach. To talk in general about women and let Trevor hang himself. It worked. He said things that made it difficult even for Edison to continue playing along. When Edison paid his tab at the bar, he bought a bottle of scotch. In the hotel room, we emptied the bottle." He ended his narrative walking into the bathroom to brush his teeth. Lucy had just finished brushing her teeth.

She perched on the edge of the tub. "I'm sorry I ruined things outside earlier. I know you and Trevor are nowhere alike. But then a familiar comment or action from the past drags me into those insecurities."

When she stopped talking, she looked up at him. He was brushing his teeth while watching her in the mirror. After spitting and rinsing, he joined her on the edge of the tub.

"You said it yourself the other day. Years of a conditioned response can take years to eradicate. But it only holds true if they are actively tested and questioned. The ones we're encountering you haven't come face to face with till now." He said with soft wisdom.

"So you pay for what he did to me!" Her bitter sarcasm fueled from the emotions of the past.

Moving his fingers to make contact with hers, he responded. "I happen to think you're worth it."

"Why?" the question was a knee jerk reaction.

He stood to pace into the bedroom; she followed him to the bed. He chose not to answer that query.

Instead he went after one he'd been asking for weeks. "Tell me what was in your nightmares."

"You know already. Leo said I talked about them when I was sick." She protested.

Squatting in front of her, he stated. "But you were delirious. Until you face it on a conscious level, it can't heal."

"Been doing your research special agent Warloc?" she asked wondering how he'd suddenly become knowledgeable on the topic.

"With the case involving Captain Baynes, it gave me the opportunity to talk to psychologist who specializes in abuse." He expounded.

He had gone to great lengths to understand her. And what could be done to help her move away from that terror. He deserved to know everything.

"It starts pleasantly with you and me. As things get intimate, you morph into Trevor. I argue with him that we've been divorced for years. No matter how much I fight, he still rapes me. The moment he, um, uh, succeeds is the moment I wake up screaming." By the time Lucy finished, her body was shaking.

He sat on the bed to embrace her. "Thank you."

In a soothing voice, he said. "Everything that freaks or freezes you links directly to that scenario."

"Oh my God!" the words exploded from her. "That's exactly what I was afraid of in the yard. You said 'one of the reasons', but I didn't know if you were referencing the placement of the guest room or my chest. I reacted to the latter."

He responded solemnly. "If you share what's going on in your head, we can do this . . . together."

She faced him, wrapping her legs and arms around him. She kissed him with gusto at knowing he felt she was worth the effort.

"Do I need to tell you what's going on in my head or can you figure this one out?" She teased playfully.

He responded by pushing her back onto the bed so their bodies made full contact. Their kiss filled with the same passion as earlier fed their instinctively erotic body motions.

With undeniable desire he requested. "I don't want to rush you, but I don't know how long it will last."

"You mean . . . ?" she asked breathlessly.

"It's all you Babe." His declaration was full of fervor.

They tore at each other's clothing. Once naked, they joined. Their need for each other urged them to climax quickly. Afterwards, they drifted into a serene slumber.

During the middle of the night, Daisy scratched at the bedroom door. Lucy slipped into her robe to let the old dog and the puppy outside. Meandering about the yard to keep the puppy moving, she'd stop occasionally to gaze at the stars like diamonds in the sky. One of the times she paused, the puppy bumped into her. She bent to pick him up. The black and white fur ball licked her face with exuberance.

"What are we going to call you my little cutie tootie?" She asked the puppy.

"Just don't call me Leo." Unexpectedly Jed said in a cartoon-like voice.

She shrieked as she whirled around. This caused a dizzy spell. He grabbed her and the puppy.

"You okay?" He asked worried.

"Yeah, guess the dogs like you or they'd have warned me you were out here too." She laughed at her own reaction to being startled.

The puppy licked and nipped at their faces. Jed took him out of her arms to set on the ground. Taking her hand, they walked towards the house. The puppy and Daisy followed.

Chapter Nineteen

Sunday morning, at 7 o'clock the two couples said goodbye. They all had a wonderful weekend. The fuzzy-wuzzy puppy had a name—Panda. This came from his great-uncle Panda. Panda's owner, Annie, and Lucy had worked together for a few years. Last Lucy heard about Annie was that she'd quit the business to move to the backwoods of Vermont. LuLu had recently bumped into Annie and her husband at a dog show in northern New Jersey.

Puppy Panda experienced distress at finding himself alone in the big backyard. Lucy and Jed sat on the garden bench to relieve this anxiety. Mid-morning Leo opened the back gate, sending Panda bounding with exuberance to greet him.

Leo yelled. "Good morning!"

The couple waved in response.

Jed asked in a low voice. "Did you invite him?"

"No, but get used to it. He loves us." She answered.

Jed snorted with displeasure. She hid her giggle by sipping at the warm brew in her cup.

Leo neared, "I don't have any coffee. May I have some please?"

"Sure thing" Lucy said standing to go inside for it.

Leo remained outside with Jed.

At the door, she paused at hearing Leo ask. "How are her nightmares?"

Jed responded with "None since that night she ran fever."

"That's progress." Leo said enthusiastically.

Jed's tone belied his emotions. "I wonder if it's enough."

Disbelief plainly noted with Leo's counter comment. "Ole' man if you can't see how much she loves you, then you're as messed up as she is."

"I know she does, but is she willing to admit it to herself let alone me?" Her husband shared with the younger man.

The breath caught in her throat. The scene in the bathroom had been real.

Not wanting to eavesdrop anymore, Lucy spoke as she pushed the door open. "Leo, you ran to the store for me the other night, why didn't you get coffee?"

Leo smiled sheepishly. "Because it wasn't on the list you gave me."

She rolled her eyes. "What are we going to do about you boy?"

"Pa usually threatens to fire me." The young man kidded.

Jed growled. "Yeah well, if I have to see you again before tomorrow morning in the office, I just might this time."

"Thanks for the coffee Lucy." The young man took his leave.

Panda chased after him to the gate.

Lucy remarked. "Why'd you have to say that to him? You don't really mind him over here do you?"

"It's not him. It's that I want us to have time together alone for the rest of the day." He stated.

He stood to go inside. Panda raced from the far end of the yard to join them. She held the door open for him to scurry through. While he poured himself another cup of coffee, she pulled the leftover cheesecake out of the refrigerator.

His eyes got wide. "I thought we had eaten it all."

She smiled sweetly. "I saved us a piece to share today."

Without warning, he pulled her into his arms for a passionate kiss. His hands caressed her curves seductively. Kisses traversed down her neck to her chest. Her not wearing a bra gave him easy access to her nipples.

"You like my cheesecake that much?" She teased breathlessly.

Moving his lips back to hers, he murmured. "It tastes like you. Sweet, creamy and the best I've ever had."

Reciprocating his passion play Lucy moaned. "Compliments like that will get you anything you want."

"What I want is for you to love me, like I love you." His voice cracked with emotion.

She knew it was now or never. "Jed, if you love me as much as I love you . . ."

He stilled his actions. She took a deep breath to let the possibility sink in. Staring into his eyes, she felt a spark ignite deep inside her which she'd never experienced.

"You really do." She stated with awe.

She kissed him with abandon. He responded unable to hold his own emotions in check.

Breaking for a moment, she avowed with intensity. "I can't imagine loving anyone as much as I love you."

Squeezing her tightly, he stated. "Marry me the right way, with our families and friends watching."

"You want to hold court?" She asked shocked.

"According to Edison, we are his royal couple." He used the director's words.

"And Leo is the court jester?" She replied.

The couple laughed together.

Then soberly Lucy answered. "Yes Jed, I will marry you for real."

Jed kissed her with the promise of a love to last forever.

End